CW00324281

THE RIVER KING

BY THE SAME AUTHOR

Property Of

The Drowning Season

Angel Landing

Fortune's Daughter

Illumination Night

At Risk

Seventh Heaven

Turtle Moon

Second Nature

Practical Magic

Here on Earth

Local Girls

ALICE HOFFMAN

THE RIVER KING

Chatto & Windus
LONDON

Published by Chatto & Windus 2000

First published in the United States in 2000
by G.P. Putnam's Sons, Penguin Putnam Inc.

2 4 6 8 10 9 7 5 3 1

Copyright © 2000 by Alice Hoffman

Alice Hoffman has asserted her right under the Copyright, Designs
and Patents Act 1988 to be identified as the author of this work

This book is sold subject to the condition that it shall not,
by way of trade or otherwise, be lent, resold, hired out,
or otherwise circulated without the publisher's prior
consent in any form of binding or cover other than that
in which it is published and without a similar condition
including this condition being imposed on the
subsequent purchaser

First published in Great Britain in 2000 by Chatto & Windus
Random House, 20 Vauxhall Bridge Road, London SW1V 2SA

Random House Australia (Pty) Limited
20 Alfred Street, Milsons Point, Sydney, New South Wales 2061, Australia

Random House New Zealand Limited
18 Poland Road, Glenfield, Auckland 10, New Zealand

Random House (Pty) Limited
Endulini, 5A Jubilee Road, Parktown 2193, South Africa

The Random House Group Limited Reg. No. 954009
www.randomhouse.co.uk

A CIP catalogue record for this book is available from the British Library

ISBN 0 7011 6798 X

Papers used by Random House are natural, recyclable products made
from wood grown in sustainable forrests; the manufacturing processes
conform to the environmental regulations of the country of origin

Printed and bound in Great Britain by Mackays of Chatham, PLC, Chatham, Kent

TO PHYLLIS GRANN

THE RIVER KING

THE IRON BOX

THE HADDAN SCHOOL WAS BUILT in 1858 on the sloping banks of the Haddan River, a muddy and precarious location that had proven disastrous from the start. That very first year, when the whole town smelled of cedar shavings, there was a storm of enormous proportions, with winds so strong that dozens of fish were drawn up from the reedy shallows, then lifted above the village in a shining cloud of scales. Torrents of water fell from the sky, and by morning the river had overflowed, leaving the school's freshly painted white clapboard buildings adrift in a murky sea of duckweed and algae.

For weeks, students were ferried to classes in rowboats; catfish swam through flooded perennial gardens, observing the disaster with cool, glassy eyes. Every evening, at twilight, the school cook balanced on a second-story window ledge, then cast out his rod to catch dozens of silver trout, a species found only in the currents of the Haddan River, a sweet, fleshy variety that was especially delectable when fried with shallots and oil. After the flood subsided, two inches of thick, black silt covered the carpets in the dormitories; at the headmaster's house, mosquitoes began to hatch in sinks and commodes. The delightful watery vistas of the site, a landscape abundant with willows and water lotus, had seduced the foolish trustees into building much too close to the river, an architectural mistake that has never been rectified. To this day, frogs can be found in the plumbing; linens and clothes stored in closets have a distinctly weedy odor, as if each article had been washed in river water and never thoroughly dried.

After the flood, houses in town had to be refloored and re-roofed; public buildings were torn down, then refashioned from cellar to ceiling. Whole chimneys floated down Main Street, with some of them still issuing forth smoke. Main Street itself had become a river, with waters more than six feet deep. Iron fences were loosened and ripped from the earth, leaving metal posts in the shape of arrows adrift. Horses drowned; mules floated for miles and when rescued, refused to eat anything but wild celery and duckweed. Poison sumac was uprooted and deposited in vegetable bins, only to be mistakenly cooked along with the carrots and cabbages, a recipe that led to several untimely deaths. Bobcats showed up on back porches, mewing and desperate for milk; several were found beside babies in their cradles, sucking from bottles and purring as though they were house cats let in through front doors.

At that time, the rich fields circling the town of Haddan were owned by prosperous farmers who cultivated asparagus and onions and a peculiar type of yellow cabbage known for its large size and delicate fragrance. These farmers put aside their plows and watched as boys arrived from every corner of the Commonwealth and beyond to take up residence at the school, but even the wealthiest among them were unable to afford tuition for their own sons. Local boys had to make do with the dusty stacks at the library on Main Street and whatever fundamentals they might learn in their very own parlors and fields. To this day, people in Haddan retain a rustic knowledge of which they are proud. Even the children can foretell the weather; they can point to and name every constellation in the sky.

A dozen years after the Haddan School was built, a public high school was erected in the neighboring town of Hamilton, which meant a five-mile trek to classes on days when the snow was knee-deep and the weather so cold even the badgers kept to their dens. Each time a Haddan boy walked through a storm to the public school his animosity toward the Haddan School grew, a small bump on the skin of ill will ready to rupture at the slightest contact. In this way a hard bitterness was forged, and the spiteful sentiment increased every year, until there might as well have been a fence dividing those who came from the school and the residents of the village. Before long, anyone who dared to cross that line was judged to be either a martyr or a fool.

There was a time when it seemed possible for the separate worlds to be united, when Dr. George Howe, the esteemed headmaster, considered to be the finest in the Haddan School history, decided to marry Annie Jordan, the most beautiful girl in the village. Annie's father was a well-respected man who owned a parcel of farmland out where Route 17 now runs into the interstate, and he approved of the marriage, but soon after the wedding it became apparent that Haddan would remain divided. Dr. Howe was jealous and vindictive; he turned local people away from his door. Even Annie's family was quickly dispatched. Her father and brothers, good, simple men with mud on their boots, were struck mute the few times they came to call, as if the bone china and leather-bound books had robbed them of their tongues. Before long people in town came to resent Annie, as if she'd somehow betrayed them. If she thought she was so high and mighty, in that fine house by the river, then the girls she grew up with felt they had reason to retaliate, and on the streets they passed her by without a word. Even her own dog, a lazy hound named Sugar, ran away yelping on those rare occasions when Annie came to visit her father's farm.

It quickly became clear that the marriage had been a horrid mistake; anyone more worldly than Annie would have known this from the start. At his very own wedding, Dr. Howe had forgotten his hat, always the sign of a man who's bound to stray. He was the sort of person who wished to own his wife, without belonging to her in return. There were days when he spoke barely a sentence in his own home, and nights when he didn't come in until dawn. It was loneliness that led Annie to begin her work in the gardens at Haddan, which until her arrival were neglected, ruined patches filled with ivy and nightshade, dark vines that choked out any wildflowers that might have grown in the thin soil. As it turned out, Annie's loneliness was the school's good fortune, for it was she who designed the brick walkways that form an hourglass and who, with the help of six strong boys, saw to the planting of the weeping beeches beneath whose branches many girls still receive their first kiss. Annie brought the original pair of swans to reside at the bend in the river behind the headmaster's house, ill-tempered, wretched specimens rescued from a farmer in Hamilton whose wife plucked their bloody feathers for soft, plump quilts. Each evening, before supper, when the light above the river washed the air with a green haze, Annie went out with an apronful of old bread. She held the firm belief that scattering bread crumbs brought happiness, a condition she herself had not known since her wedding day.

There are those who vow that swans are unlucky, and fishermen in particular despise them, but Annie loved her pets; she could call them to her with a single cry. At the sound of her sweet voice the birds lined up as politely as gentlemen; they ate from her hands without ever once drawing blood, favoring crusts of rye bread and whole-wheat crackers. As a special treat, Annie often brought whole pies, leftovers from the dining room. In a wicker basket, she piled up apple cobbler and wild raspberry tart, which the swans gobbled down nearly whole, so that their beaks were stained crimson and their bellies took on the shapes of medicine balls.

Even those who were certain Dr. Howe had made a serious error in judgment in choosing his bride had to admire Annie's gardens. In no time the perennial borders were thick with rosy-pink foxglove and cream-colored lilies, each of which hung like a pendant, collecting dew on its satiny petals. But it was with her roses that Annie had the best luck of all, and among the more jealous members of the Haddan garden club, founded that very year in an attempt to beautify the town, there was speculation that such good fortune was unnatural. Some people went so far as to suggest that Annie Howe sprinkled the pulverized bones of cats around the roots of her ramblers, or perhaps it was her own blood she cast about the shrubs. How else could her garden bloom in February, when all other yards were nothing more than stonewort and bare dirt? Massachusetts was known for a short growing season and its early killing frosts. Nowhere could a gardener find more unpredictable weather, be it droughts or floods or infestations of beetles, which had been known to devour entire neighborhoods full of greenery. None of these plagues ever affected Annie Howe. Under her care, even the most delicate hybrids lasted past the first frost so that in November there were still roses blooming at Haddan, although by then, the edge of each petal was often encased in a layer of ice.

Much of Annie Howe's handiwork was destroyed the year she died, yet a few samples of the hardiest varieties remain. A visitor to campus can find sweet, aromatic Prosperity, as well as Climbing Ophelia and those delicious Egyptian Roses, which give off the scent of cloves on rainy days, ensuring that a gardener's hands will smell sweet for hours after pruning the canes. Among all of these roses, Mrs. Howe's prized white Polars were surely her finest. Cascades of white flowers lay dormant for a decade, to bloom and envelop the metal trellis beside the girls' dormitory only once every ten years, as if all that time was needed to restore the roses their strength. Each September, when the new students arrived, Annie Howe's roses had an odd effect on certain girls, the sensitive ones who had never been away from home before and were easily influenced. When such girls walked past the brittle canes in the gardens behind St. Anne's, they felt something cold at the base of their spines, a bad case of pins and needles, as though someone were issuing a warning: Be careful who you choose to love and who loves you in return.

Most newcomers are apprised of Annie's fate as soon as they

come to Haddan. Before suitcases are unpacked and classes are chosen, they know that although the huge wedding cake of a house that serves as the girls' dormitory is officially called Hastings House—in honor of some fellow, long forgotten, whose dull-witted daughter's admission opened the door for female students on the strength of a huge donation—the dormitory is never referred to by that name. Among students, the house is called St. Anne's, in honor of Annie Howe, who hanged herself from the rafters one mild evening in March, only hours before wild iris began to appear in the woods. There will always be girls who refuse to go up to the attic at St. Anne's after hearing this story, and others, whether in search of spiritual renewal or quick thrills, who are bound to ask if they can take up residence in the room where Annie ended her life. On days when rosewater preserves are served at breakfast, with Annie's recipe carefully followed by the kitchen staff, even the most fearless girls can become lightheaded; after spooning this concoction onto their toast they need to sit with their heads between their knees and breathe deeply until their metabolisms grow steady again.

At the start of the term, when members of the faculty return to school, they are reminded not to grade on a curve and not to repeat Annie's story. It is exactly such nonsense that gives rise to inflated grade averages and nervous breakdowns, neither of which are approved of by the Haddan School. Nevertheless, the story always slips out, and there's nothing the administration can do to stop it. The particulars of Annie's life are simply common knowledge among the students, as much an established part of Haddan life as the route of the warblers who always begin their migration at this time of year, lighting on shrubbery and treetops, calling to one another across the open sky.

Often, the weather is unseasonably warm at the start of the term, one last triumph of summer come to call. Roses bloom more abundantly, crickets chirp wildly, flies doze on windowsills, drowsy with sunlight and heat. Even the most serious-minded educators are known to fall asleep when Dr. Jones gives his welcoming speech. This year, many in attendance drifted off in the overheated library during this oration and several teachers secretly wished that the students would never arrive. Outside, the September air was enticingly fragrant, yellow with pollen and rich, lemony sunlight. Along the river, near the canoe shed, weeping willows rustled and dropped catkins on the muddy ground. The clear sound of slow-moving water could be heard even here in the library, perhaps because the building itself had been fashioned out of river rock, gray slabs flecked with mica that had been hauled from the banks by local boys hired for a dollar a day, laborers whose hands bled from their efforts and who cursed the Haddan School forever after, even in their sleep.

As usual, people were far more curious about those who'd been recently hired than those old, reliable colleagues they already knew. In every small community, the unknown is always most intriguing, and Haddan was no exception to this rule. Most people had been to dinner with Bob Thomas, the massive dean of students, and his pretty wife, Meg, more times than they could count; they had sat at the bar at the Haddan Inn with Duck Johnson, who coached crew and soccer and always became tearful after his third beer. The on-again, off-again romance between Lynn Vining, who taught painting, and Jack Short, the married chemistry teacher, had already been discussed and dissected. Their relationship was completely predictable, as were many of the love affairs begun at Haddan—fumbling in the teachers' lounge, furtive embraces in idling cars, kisses exchanged in the library, breakups at the end of the term. Feuds were far more interesting, as in the case of Eric Herman—ancient history—and Helen Davis—American history and chair of the department, a woman who'd been teaching at Haddan for more than fifty years and was said to grow meaner with each passing day, as if she were a pitcher of milk set out to curdle in the noonday sun.

Despite the heat and Dr. Jones's dull lecture, the same speech he trotted out every year, despite the droning of bees beyond the open windows, where a hedge of twiggy China roses still grew, people took notice of the new photography instructor, Betsy Chase. It was possible to tell at a glance that Betsy would be the subject of even more gossip than any ongoing feud. It wasn't only Betsy's fevered expression that drew stares, or her high cheekbones and dark, unpredictable hair. People couldn't quite believe how inappropriate her attire was. There she was, a good-looking woman who apparently had no common sense, wearing old black slacks and a faded black T-shirt, the sort of grungy outfit barely tolerated on Haddan students, let alone on members of the faculty. On her feet were plastic flip-flops of the dime-store variety, cheap little items that announced every step with a slap. She actually had a wad of gum in her mouth, and soon enough blew a bubble when she thought no one was looking; even those in the last row of the library could hear the sugary pop. Dennis Hardy, geometry, who sat directly behind her, told people afterward that Betsy gave off the scent of vanilla, a tincture she used to dispel the odor of darkroom chemicals from her skin, a concoction so reminiscent of baked goods that people who met her often had an urge for oatmeal cookies or angel food cake.

It had been only eight months since Betsy had been hired to take the yearbook photos. She had disliked the school at first sight, and had written it off as too prissy, too picture perfect. When Eric Herman asked her out she'd been surprised by the offer, and wary as well. She'd already had more than her share of botched relationships, yet she'd agreed to have dinner with Eric, ever hopeful despite the statistics that promised her an abject and lonely old age. Eric was so much sturdier than the men she was used to, all those brooders and artists who couldn't be depended upon to show up at the door on time let alone have the foresight to plan a retirement fund. Before Betsy knew what had happened she was accepting an offer of marriage and applying for a job in the art department. The Willow Room at the Haddan Inn was already reserved for their reception in June, and Bob Thomas, the dean of students, had guaranteed them one of the coveted faculty cottages as soon as they were wed. Until that time, Betsy would be a houseparent at St. Anne's and Eric would continue on as senior proctor at Chalk House, a boys' dormitory set so close to the river that the dreadful Haddan swans often nested on the back porch, nipping at passersby's pant legs until chased away with a broom.

For the past month, Betsy had been simultaneously planning both her classes at Haddan and her wedding. Perfectly rational activities, and yet she often felt certain she had blundered into an alternate universe, one to which she clearly did not belong. Today, for instance, the other women present in the auditorium were all in dresses, the men in summer suits and ties, and there was Betsy in her T-shirt and slacks, making what was sure to be

the first of an endless series of social miscalculations. She had
bad judgment, there was no way around it; from childhood on,
she had jumped into things headfirst, without looking to see if
there was a net to break her fall. Of course, no one had bothered
to inform her that Dr. Jones's addresses were such formal events;
everyone said he was ancient and ailing and that Bob Thomas
was the real man in charge. Hoping to erase her fashion blunder,
Betsy now searched through her backpack for some lipstick and
a pair of earrings, for all the good they would do.

Taking up residence in a small town had indeed left Betsy disoriented. She was used to city living, to potholes and purse
snatchers, parking tickets and double locks. Whether it be morning, noon, or night, she simply couldn't get her bearings here in
Haddan. She'd set out for the pharmacy on Main Street or to Selena's Sandwich Shoppe on the corner of Pine and arrive at the
town cemetery in the field behind town hall. She'd start for the
market, in search of a loaf of bread or some muffins, only to find
that she'd strayed onto the twisting back roads leading to Sixth
Commandment Pond, a deep pool at a bend in the river where
horsetails and wild celery grew. Once she'd wandered off, it
would often be hours before she managed to find her way back to
St. Anne's. People in town had already become accustomed to a
pretty, dark woman wandering about, asking for directions from
schoolchildren and crossing guards, and yet still managing to
take one wrong turn after another.

Although Betsy Chase was confused, the town of Haddan
hadn't changed much in the last fifty years. The village itself was
three blocks long, and, for some residents, contained the whole
world. Along with Selena's Sandwich Shoppe, which served
breakfast all day, there was a pharmacy at whose soda fountain

the best raspberry lime rickeys in the Commonwealth could be had, as well as a hardware store that offered everything from nails to velveteen. One could also find a shoe store, the 5&10 Cent Bank, and the Lucky Day Florist, known for its scented garlands and wreaths. There was St. Agatha's, with its granite facade, and the public library, with its stained-glass windows, the first to be built in the county. Town hall, which had burned down twice, had finally been rebuilt with mortar and stone, and was said to be indestructible, although the statue of the eagle out front was tipped from its pedestal by local boys year after year.

All along Main Street, there were large white houses, set back from the road, whose wide lawns were ringed with black iron fences punctuated by little spikes on top; pretty, architectural warnings that made it quite clear the grass and rhododendrons within were private property. On the approach to town, the white houses grew larger, as though a set of stacking toys had been fashioned from clapboards and brick. On the far side of town was the train station, and opposite stood a gas station and mini-mart, along with the dry cleaner's and a new supermarket. In fact, the town was sliced in two, separated by Main into an east and a west side. Those who lived on the east side resided in the white houses; those who worked at the counter at Selena's or ran the ticket booth at the train station lived in the western part of town.

Beyond Main Street the village became sparser, fanning out into new housing developments and then into farmland. On Evergreen Avenue was the elementary school, and if a person followed Evergreen due east, in the direction of Route 17, he'd come to the police station. Farther north, at the town line that separated Haddan from Hamilton, deposited in a no-man's-land neither village cared to claim, was a bar called the Millstone, which offered live bands on Friday nights along with five brands of beer on tap and heated arguments in the parking lot on humid summer nights. There had probably been half a dozen divorces that had reached a fevered pitch in that very parking lot and so many alcohol-induced fights had taken place in those confines that if anyone bothered to search through the laurel bordering the asphalt he'd surely find handfuls of teeth that were said to give the laurel its odd milky color, ivory with a pale pink edge, with each blossom forming the shape of a bitter man's mouth.

Beyond town, there were still acres of fields and a crisscross of dirt roads where Betsy had gotten lost one afternoon before the start of the term, late in the day, when the sky was cobalt and the air was sweet with the scent of hay. She'd been searching for a vegetable stand Lynn Vining in the art department had told her sold the best cabbages and potatoes, when she happened upon a huge meadow, all blue with everlasting and tansy. Betsy had gotten out of the car with tears in her eyes. She was only three miles from Route 17, but she might as well have been on the moon. She was lost and she knew it, with no sense whatsoever of how she had managed to wind up in Haddan, engaged to a man she barely knew.

She might have been lost to this day if she hadn't thought to follow a newspaper delivery truck into the neighboring town of Hamilton, a true metropolis compared to Haddan, with a hospital and a high school and even a multiplex cinema. From Hamilton, Betsy drove south to the highway, then circled back to the village via Route 17. Still, for some time afterward, she'd been unable to forget how lost she'd become. Even when she was beside Eric in bed all she had to do was close her eyes and she'd continue to see those wildflowers in the meadow, each and every one the exact color of the sky.

When all was said and done, what was so wrong with Haddan? It was a lovely town, featured in several guidebooks, cited for both its excellent trout fishing and the exceptional show of fall colors that graced the landscape every October. If Betsy continually lost her way on the streets of such a neat, orderly village, perhaps it was the pale green light rising from the river each evening that led her astray. Betsy had taken to carrying a map and a flashlight in her pocket, hopefully ready for any emergency. She made certain to keep to the well-worn paths, where the old roses grew, but even the rosebushes were disturbing when they were encountered in the dark. The twisted black vines were concealed in the black night, thorns hidden deep within the dried canes until a passerby had already come close enough to cut herself unwittingly.

In spite of the police log in the *Tribune,* which reported crimes no more heinous than jaywalking across Main Street or trash bags of leaves set out on the curb on Tuesdays when yard waste would not be collected until the second Friday of the month, Betsy did not feel safe in Haddan. It seemed entirely possible that in a town such as this, a person might walk along the riverbank one bright afternoon and simply disappear, swallowed up in a tangle of chokeberry and woodbine. Beyond the river there were acres thick with maple and pine, and the woods loomed darkly at night, flecked with the last of the season's fireflies.

Even as a girl, Betsy had hated the countryside. She'd been a difficult child; she had whined and stomped her feet, refusing to accompany her parents on a picnic, and because of her ill-tempered ways, she'd been spared. That day, there were seven separate fatalities due to lightning. Ball lightning had ignited fence posts and oak trees, before chasing people across meadows and fields. There had been several sightings of rocket lightning, which burst from cloud to ground in seconds flat with a display not unlike fireworks exploding in a deadly white flash. Instead of taking her place in the meadow with her parents, lying beside them in the burning grass, Betsy had been sprawled upon the couch, leafing through a magazine and sipping a tall glass of pink lemonade. She'd often imagined how the course of events might have altered if only she'd accompanied her hapless parents. They might have run for their lives instead of being caught unawares, too puzzled and stupefied to move. They might have followed Betsy's lead and been wise enough to crouch behind a flinty stone wall, which would have turned so burning hot when it took the strike intended for them that for months afterward it would have been possible to fry eggs on the hottest of the stones. Ever since, Betsy had possessed a survivor's guilt and was often in search of punishment. She raced red lights and drove with the gas gauge on empty. She walked city streets after midnight and gravitated outside on stormy days without the benefit of a rain-coat or an umbrella, long ago deciding to ignore any Samaritans who warned that such foolhardy behavior would only ensure that sooner or later she'd wind up electrified, ignited from her fingers to her toes.

Before meeting Eric, Betsy had been careening through her life with nothing much to show other than sheaves of photo-graphs, a black-and-white diary of landscapes and portraits stuffed into files and folios. A good photographer was meant to be an observer, a silent party there to record, but somewhere along the line Betsy had become a bystander to her own existence. *Just ignore me,* she would say to her subjects. *Pretend I'm not here and go about your normal routine.* All the while she'd been doing this, her own life had somehow escaped her; she herself had no routine, normal or otherwise. When she'd come to Haddan, she'd been at a low point. Too many men had disappointed her, friends weren't there for her, apartments had been broken into while she was asleep. She certainly hadn't expected any changes in her life on the day she came to take the yearbook photos at Haddan, and perhaps there wouldn't have been any if she hadn't overheard one student ask another, *Why did the chicken leave the Haddan School?* Curious, she'd eavesdropped, and when she'd heard the answer—*Because he had an aversion to bullshit*—Betsy laughed so loudly that the swans on the river startled and took flight, skimming over the water and raising clouds of mayflies.

Eric Herman had turned to see her just at the moment when her grin was its widest. He watched her arrange the soccer team in size order and then, in what he assured her afterward was the first impulsive action of his life, he had walked right up to her and asked her to dinner, not the next night or the one after that, but right then, so that neither one had time to reconsider.

Eric was the sort of attractive, confident man who drew people to him without trying, and Betsy wondered if perhaps she had simply happened to be in sight at the very moment he decided it was high time for him to marry. She still couldn't fathom what he could possibly want with someone such as herself, a woman who would spill the entire contents of her backpack on the floor of a quiet auditorium just as she was attempting to stealthily extract a comb. There wasn't a member of the Haddan faculty who didn't hear the coins and ballpoint pens rolling down the aisle and who then felt completely validated in his or her initial opinion of Betsy. Long after Dr. Jones had completed his lecture, people were still collecting Betsy's personal belongings from beneath their chairs, holding items up to the filtered light as though studying foreign and mysterious artifacts, when in fact all they'd gotten hold of was a notepad or a vial of sleeping pills or a tube of hand cream.

"Don't worry," Eric whispered to her. "Act naturally," he advised, although acting naturally was exactly what always got her into trouble in the first place. If Betsy had trusted her instincts, as Eric suggested, she would surely have turned tail and run the first time she walked through the door of the girls' dormitory where she was to be the junior houseparent. A chill had passed across her back as she stepped over the threshold, the cold hand of anxiety that often accompanies a bad decision. Betsy's cramped set of rooms at the foot of the stairs was nothing less than awful. There was only one closet and the bathroom was so small it was impossible to exit the shower without jamming one's knees into the sink. Paint was peeling from ceilings and the panes of old, bumpy glass in the windows allowed in drafts but not sunlight, turning even the palest rays a foggy green. In this setting, Betsy's furniture looked mournful and out of place: the couch was too wide to fit through the narrow doorway, the easy chair appeared threadbare, the bureau would not stand on the sloping pine floors, and instead lurched like a drunkard each time a door was banged shut.

In her first week at Haddan, Betsy spent most of her nights at Eric's apartment in Chalk House. It made sense to take the opportunity to do so now, for when the students arrived, they'd have to monitor their own behavior as well as that of their charges.

And there was another reason Betsy had avoided sleeping at St. Anne's. Each time she spent the night in her own quarters, she was wrenched from her slumber in a panic, with the sheets twisted around her and her thoughts so muddled it was as if she'd woken in the wrong bed and was now fated to lead someone else's life. On the night before school was to begin, for instance, Betsy had slept at St. Anne's only to dream she'd been lost in the fields outside Haddan. No matter how she might circle, she went no farther than the same parcels of uncultivated land. When she wrested herself from this dream, Betsy staggered out of bed, disoriented and smelling of hay. For an instant, she felt as though she were a girl again, left in someone's strange, overheated apartment to fend for herself, which was exactly what had happened when friends of the family took her in after her parents' accident.

Quickly, Betsy switched on the lights to discover that it was only a little after ten. There was a thumping coming from the direction of the stairs and the radiators were banging away, gushing out a steady stream of heat, even though the evening was unusually warm. No wonder Betsy couldn't sleep; it was ninety degrees in her bedroom and the temperature was still rising. The orchid she had bought that afternoon at the Lucky Day Florist, a bloom accustomed to tropical climates, had already lost most of its petals; the slim, green stem had been warped by the heat and was now unable to hold up even the most delicate flower.

Betsy washed her face, found a stick of gum to ease her dry mouth, then pulled on her bathrobe and went to call on the senior houseparent. She assumed people at Haddan exaggerated when they called Helen Davis a selfish old witch, the fitting owner of an ugly black tomcat who was said to eat songbirds and roses. Clearly judgments were harsh at this school, for weren't many people already calling Betsy a kook after the fiasco at the welcoming lecture? Wasn't Eric referred to as Mr. Perfect by those who failed to measure up to his standards of excellence and forever after resented him? For her part, Betsy was the last to accept anyone else's opinion, but when she knocked at Miss Davis's door no one answered, even though there was clearly someone on the other side. Betsy could practically feel Miss Davis's displeasure at being disturbed as the older woman peered through the peephole. Betsy knocked again, more forcefully now.

"Hello! Can you help me out? I just need some advice about my radiator."

Helen Davis was tall and extremely imposing, even when answering the door in her nightgown and slippers. She carried herself in the manner women who were once beautiful often do; she was standoffish and confident in equal measure and she certainly did not feel the need to be civil when an unwanted visitor came calling at such a late hour.

"My radiators," Betsy explained. Having come directly from bed, Betsy's choppy hair was sticking straight up and her eyes were ringed with mascara. "They simply won't turn off."

"Do I look like a plumber?" Helen Davis's smirk, as many of her students might confirm, was not a pleasant sight. Her disapproval could turn a person's blood cold, and there had been several occasions when a tender freshman had fainted on the floor of her classroom when asked the simplest of questions. Miss Davis had never tolerated smart alecks nor the practice of chewing gum, nor did she invite guests into her private quarters.

The administration had failed to mention to Betsy that none of her predecessors had lasted more than a year. So she dove right in, asking for assistance when anyone else would have slunk away. "You must have experience in dealing with the heating system," Betsy said. "Surely, it can't be classified information."

Miss Davis glared. "Are you chewing gum?" she asked sharply.

"Me?" Betsy immediately swallowed, but the gum clogged in her trachea. As she was doing her best not to choke, a horrible squalling creature ran by. Instinctively, Betsy drew herself against the wall to let it pass.

"Afraid of cats?" Miss Davis asked. Several junior houseparents who'd left claimed to be allergic to her pet. Although Betsy herself was not a fan of any sort of wildlife, cats included, she could tell that life at St. Anne's would be bearable only if she won Helen Davis over to her side. Eric had often made fun of Miss Davis's habit of quoting Ben Franklin whenever she wished to prove a point, and now Betsy used this information to her advantage.

"Wasn't it Ben Franklin who said the best dog of all is a cat?"

"Ben Franklin said nothing of the sort." Still, Miss Davis knew when she was being flattered, and no one ever said flattery was a crime. "Wait in the hall and I'll get you what you need," she directed.

Standing in the dark, Betsy felt an odd elation, as though she'd just aced an exam or been named teacher's pet. When Helen Davis returned, Betsy could see a slice of the apartment behind her; these quarters had remained constant for the past fifty years and included a collection of clutter that had surely taken that long to amass. In spite of the high-backed velvet love seat and a good rug from Afghanistan, the place was in serious disorder. Books were everywhere, along with half-filled teacups and forgotten crusts of sandwiches. There was the foul odor of old newspapers and cats. Helen swung the door closed behind her. She reached out and deposited a quarter in Betsy's open hand.

"The secret is to bleed the radiators. Turn the screw at the rear with this quarter and be sure to keep a pan underneath to catch the drips. After the steam's released, the radiator will cool down."

Betsy thanked the senior houseparent, then with her typical ungainliness, she dropped the quarter and was forced to retrieve it. Seeing her from this angle, crawling about on hands and knees, Helen Davis at last realized that her caller was the same individual who had made a scene in the auditorium during Dr. Jones's speech.

"You're Eric Herman's girlfriend," Helen declared. "That's who you are!"

"Hardly a girl." Betsy laughed.

"Yes, hardly. Far too old to be taken in by him."

"Oh, really?" Betsy stood, quarter in hand. Perhaps people were right about how nasty Helen Davis was. It was said she graded on a negative curve, deliberately failing as many students as possible, and that she had never once changed a grade, not even when self-mutilation or nervous breakdowns were threatened. The last houseparent to share duties with her at St. Anne's had quit midterm to go to law school, reporting back that torts and constitutional law were a breeze after dealing with Helen Davis.

"Eric Herman is the most dishonest man I know. Just take a look at his ears. A man with small ears is always dishonorable and stingy. All the great men had large ears. Lincoln was said to move his at will, much like a rabbit."

"Well, I like a man with small ears." Regardless, Betsy made a mental note to take a closer look at Eric's physiognomy.

"He's after my job," Helen Davis informed Betsy. "You might as well know right now, he's a whiner and a complainer. A man like that will never be satisfied."

"Oh, he's satisfied, all right," Betsy said, although she had already been privy to Eric's many complaints about the history department. Helen Davis, he liked to joke, ought to be fired first, then guillotined, with her head displayed on one of the posts of those iron fences on Main Street. At least then the old woman would finally serve a purpose as she scared away crows rather than students. "He's happy as a clam," Betsy reported.

Miss Davis chortled at that. "Look at his ears, my dear, they tell the whole story."

Betsy peered down the hallway; again there'd been a noise on the stairs. "What is that awful thudding sound?"

"It's nothing." Helen's tone, which had been warming as she critiqued Eric, now turned sharp. "The hour's a little late for these shenanigans, I might add."

When Miss Davis closed her door, Betsy heard the lock click shut. At least Helen Davis had bestowed a quarter; no one else at Haddan had offered Betsy so much as a helping hand since she'd arrived. Even Eric had been so busy preparing for his classes that he'd been, it was true, stingy with his time. Still, he was a good man, and Betsy could hardly fault him for being as focused as he was dependable. Tonight was hardly the time to reassess her own opinions in light of Miss Davis's observations, which were surely self-serving at best. It was most likely the emptiness of the dormitory that now set Betsy's doubts to work, but there'd soon be a cure for that. By tomorrow, the hallways would be filled with girls and it would be Betsy's job to soothe the homesick and shore up the meek and manage the wild as best she could. It would be her responsibility to make certain each and every one slept tight beneath this roof.

As Betsy returned to her apartment, she became aware of the scent of roses drifting down the stairway, richly fragrant in the overheated corridor. She found the odor in her own rooms, fainter yes, but disturbing enough so that she hurried to bleed the radiators, scalding her hands in the process. When she went back to bed she expected to toss and turn, but for once she slept deeply. In fact, she overslept, and needed to gulp down a quick cup of coffee in order to be ready for the first arrivals. It was then Betsy noticed the green vine outside her window. A few of Annie Howe's prized white roses were still blooming; they were as big as cabbages, as white as snow. In the early morning sunlight, their innermost petals appeared to be a pale, pearly green. Betsy laughed at herself then; what a fool she'd been to be nervous last night. For every odd occurrence there was a rational explanation, or so she had always believed. She tidied up, then went to get dressed, comforted by the sight of the roses. But if she'd only paused long enough to open her window she would have discovered that Polar roses have no scent whatsoever. Even the bees avoid these creamy buds, preferring thistles and goldenrod instead. Take a scissors to the stems of these roses and they'll fall apart at the touch. Try to pick one barehanded, and every thorn will draw blood.

THE TRAIN TO HADDAN WAS ALWAYS LATE, AND this day was no exception. It was a spectacular afternoon, the fields rife with late-blooming asters and milkweed, the sky as wide and as clear as heaven. In the pine trees along the railroad tracks, hawks perched in the tallest branches; red-winged blackbirds swooped across the distance. Stands of oak and hawthorn made for pockets of dark woods where there were still plenty of deer, as well as an occasional moose that had wandered down from New Hampshire or Maine. As the train passed slowly through the neighboring town of Hamilton, several boys ran alongside the cars; some waved cheerfully to the passengers on board, while others rudely stuck out their tongues and pulled their faces into freckled smirks, the grimaces of wild angels unafraid of the gravel and dust that was always stirred up as the train rolled by.

Today, there were more than a dozen Haddan students on board, ready for the start of the term. Girls with long, shiny hair and boys in freshly pressed clothes that would soon be torn and stained in soccer games congregated in the club car. Their good-natured rowdiness drifted through the train when the conductor opened the doors, but the racket didn't reach as far as the last car. There, in the farthest seat, a girl named Carlin Leander, who had never before left home, gazed out at the countryside, appreciating every haystack and fence that came briefly into sight as the train rolled on. Carlin had been planning to get out of Florida all her life. It had made no difference that she was the most beautiful girl in the county where she'd been born, with pale ashy hair and the same green eyes that had gotten her mother into trouble at the age of seventeen, pregnant and stranded in a town where a traveling carnival was considered a cultural event and any girl with a mind of her own was thought to be an aberration of nature's plan.

Carlin Leander was nothing like her mother, and for that she was grateful. Not that Sue Leander wasn't pleasant and warm, she certainly was. But to be agreeable and kindhearted was not Carlin's goal. Whereas her mother was pliant and sweet, Carlin was obstinate and opinionated, the sort of girl who went barefoot in spite of all warnings to watch out for snakes. She never paid the least bit of attention to the boys who followed her home from school, many of them so moony and stupefied by her beauty that they rode their bikes into ditches and trees. Carlin was not about to get trapped, not in a locality where the heat continued to rise after midnight and the mosquitoes were a year-round annoyance and most folks chose to celebrate a girl's weakness and ignore her strengths.

Some people were simply born in the wrong place. The first thing such individuals searched for was a map and the second was a ticket out. Carlin Leander had been ready to leave Florida since she could walk, and she'd finally managed her escape with a swimming scholarship to the Haddan School. Although her mother had been reluctant to let her go all the way to Massachusetts, where people were bound to be dishonest and depraved, in the end Carlin won the battle, using a plan of attack that included equal amounts of pleading, promises, and tears.

On this beautiful blue day, Carlin had a single battered suitcase thrown beneath the seat and a backpack crammed with sneakers and bathing suits. She had very few other belongings left at home, only some threadbare stuffed animals on her bed and an awful coat her mother had bought as a going-away present at Lucille's Fine Fashions, a fuzzy acrylic monstrosity Carlin had hidden in the utility shed, behind some retreaded tires. Carlin planned to keep her plane ticket as a souvenir, forever and ever, if it didn't dissolve first. She'd handled the ticket so many times that the print had worn off on her skin; she'd washed and she'd scrubbed, but there remained little gray flecks on her fingertips even now, the marks of her own ambition.

All the while she was on the jet traveling north, and then again as the train sped through Boston's endless construction sites, Carlin had felt little knobs of doubt rising beneath her skin. Who was she to think she could forge such a completely different life for herself? Here she was, dressed in a cheap pair of jeans and a T-shirt she'd purchased at a secondhand store, her blond hair pinned up haphazardly with metal clips that were rusty from the Florida humidity. Anyone could see she didn't fit in with the other well-dressed passengers. She didn't own a decent pair of boots, and had never had her hair cut by a professional, always snipping the ends herself when too much chlorine took its toll. She had swamp dust on her feet and nicotine stains on her fingers, and came from a universe of hash and eggs and broken promises, a place where a woman quickly learned there was no point crying over spilled milk or bruises left by some man who claimed to love a little too hard or too much.

But in spite of her history, and all she believed she was lacking, Carlin felt hopeful once they were out of the city. They passed acres of goldenrod and fields where cows were grazing. It was the season of the warbler migrations and huge gatherings skimmed over the meadows, wheeling back and forth as if of one body and mind. Carlin struggled to open the sooty window in order to savor the September air, and was caught off guard when a tall kid toting a huge duffel bag approached to help raise the jammed window. The boy was far too skinny, with a shock of unruly hair that made him seem elongated, even storklike. He wore a long, black coat that hung like a sackcloth on his spindly frame and his work boots were unlaced, leaving his feet to slop around as if they were fish. An unlighted cigarette dangled from his wide mouth. Even with the fresh air streaming in through the open window there was no way to disguise the fact that he stank.

"Mind if I sit down?" Not bothering to wait for an answer, the boy took the seat directly across from Carlin, setting his duffel bag in the aisle, unconcerned that it might cause a navigational problem for anyone wishing to pass by. He had the sort of luminous skin that can only be achieved by spending hours in a dark room while recovering from a migraine or a hangover. "God, those idiots in the next car from the Haddan School were driving me crazy. I had to escape."

Carlin noticed that he was nervous in her presence, she could tell from the flutter of a pulse beneath his eye. A very good sign, for a boy's apprehension always set Carlin at ease. She repinned a stray lock of loose hair with one of the silver clips. "That's where I'm going," she informed her fellow traveler. "The Haddan School."

"But you're not an idiot. That's the difference." The ungainly boy searched through his gear until he found a Zippo lighter. When Carlin pointed to a no-smoking sign, he shrugged his bony shoulders and lit up anyway. Carlin smiled, entertained for the first time since she'd set off from home. She leaned back in her seat, waiting for this oddity to try to impress her again.

He introduced himself as August Pierce from New York City, sent to Haddan by his overburdened father who hadn't had a moment's peace since the day Gus was born, shouldering the burden of raising his son after the death of his wife. The old man was a professor of biology with high expectations for his one and only boy; there were those who insisted upon rooting for loved ones long after they'd been thoroughly disappointed, and such was the case with Gus Pierce's father. Having failed again and again, Gus believed he owed his father one last try. Not that he himself anticipated the least bit of success. Why should Haddan be any different from the other schools he'd attended? Why should anything good ever happen to him? He had been born on the seventh day of the seventh month and he'd always had bad luck. He could cross his fingers, he could knock on wood, and he'd still hit his head upon every ladder; he'd take every wrong turn possible. While everyone else progressed on the flat, straight road toward the future, Gus fell into manholes and gutters face first, with no visible means of escape.

He viewed his own life as a prison sentence and experienced his existence much as a condemned man might have. If anything, the beauty of the world confounded him and made him more despondent. It therefore came as a pleasant surprise that a simple encounter could fill him with such optimism. He'd thrown himself into the seat across from Carlin in a fit of jitters, half expecting her to call for the conductor and have him bodily removed, and now here she was, talking to him. A sparrow flying out of his mouth would have been more anticipated than a beautiful girl such as this offering him a piece of gum. Girls like Carlin usually looked right through him; he existed in a sub-universe, a world of losers, a world of pain, located in the basement of reality, several levels beneath the realm of pretty faces and possibilities. If Carlin was leaning forward, listening to his falsified life story without laughing in his face, anything might happen: Blackbirds might turn into ginger cakes. Willow trees might burst into flame.

"Choose a number between one and twenty," August Pierce

now suggested to his newfound companion. "Don't tell me what it is." He had picked up several tricks with which to amaze, and this seemed as good a time as any to put his talents to use.

Carlin did as she was told, although her expression had hardened into a disbeliever's stare.

Gus closed his eyes and made a show of his prestidigitation, at last plucking a number from the air. "Seven," he said, triumphantly, or at least he hoped for triumph as he was attempting a ruse any beginning conjurer who knew the first thing about logic could neatly manage.

Yet for all the trick's success, Carlin was not pleased. She hated to be transparent and she certainly didn't wish to be revealed in any way. Even now, she was in the process of perfecting a story that would alter her background and create a new identity. She intended to tell people that her parents worked for the government, and although they had never settled down they had always encouraged her swimming, transporting her to races and events no matter where they might be living. A far better tale to tell than one that included a mother who worked the cash register at the Value Mart, a father she'd never seen, and the dozens of times she'd had to hitchhike to swim meets. With deception as her plan, a boy who could read her mind was a definite liability, for seven was indeed her chosen number.

"It's simple probability," Gus explained when he realized Carlin hadn't appreciated the trick. "Most people will choose either three or seven."

Carlin glared at him, scornful. Her eyes were a shade of green that could turn gray in an instant, like shallow water that mirrored any change in the weather. "I'm not most people," she told him.

"No," Gus Pierce agreed. Even a nitwit such as himself could make that distinction. "You're definitely not."

The train had begun to lurch into Haddan Station; the whistle blew long and low, rattling windows in houses closest to the train tracks, frightening crows from treetops and telephone lines. Carlin grabbed for her backpack. She had a hundred and fifty dollars in her wallet, which she planned to use toward a return ticket home in June, and no assurances of anything in between. She probably would have deserted Gus even if he hadn't pulled his stupid mind-reading stunt, and it came as no surprise to him when she hurried to get to the door before the train came to a standstill, dragging her suitcase out from beneath the seat. When Gus offered to help, Carlin appraised him carefully. Experience had taught her it was best to inform someone when she knew she'd never be attracted to him. It saved so much bother and confusion in the end.

"We might as well get this over with," she said. "I'm not interested."

Gus nodded his agreement. "Why would you be?"

He was so baffled by the notion that he might ever stand a chance with her, and so sincere, Carlin couldn't help but grin before she headed for the exit. Watching her walk away, Gus realized that her hair was the color of stars, those pale distant galaxies that are too far away ever to be charted or named. He fell in love with her in the very instant he was disclaiming his interest. When he and Carlin met next she would probably walk right past him, as though he were a piece of litter or trash. But perhaps not; strange things had been happening ever since Gus had set off for Haddan. On the shuttle from New York, for instance, the flight attendant had given him a complimentary mini-bottle of Chivas, no questions asked. In the club car, he'd requested a bag of potato chips only to have the cashier throw in a tuna sandwich on the house. Most unexpectedly and most wonderfully, a beautiful girl had not only spoken to him, she'd smiled at him. In all honesty, this was the best run of luck August Pierce had ever possessed.

As he stepped off the train, his good fortune appeared to continue. Two seniors from Haddan—Seth Harding and Robbie Shaw, good-looking, serious boys of the sort who would never associate with Gus under any circumstances—were holding up a sign with his name. When he approached, they grabbed his duffel bag and clapped him on his back as though he were a long-lost brother. Out in the sweet country air, with all that blue sky above him and the warblers chattering in every bush, Gus felt dizzy with confusion and with something that, had he been anyone else, would have been easily recognizable as joy.

"Are you sure you've got the right guy?" Gus asked as his cohorts loaded his gear into a BMW idling at the curb.

"Perfect score on your aptitude tests? Editor of the school newspaper in eighth grade at the Henley School in New York? You're the one," Seth and Robbie insisted.

Gus squeezed his long legs into the back of Seth's car even though the information they'd gathered was clearly sketchy at best, stray pieces of his autobiography garnered from his Haddan application, a portrait that carefully omitted his tendency toward depression and rebellion and the fact that he'd been suspended from the Henley School for laziness and insubordination. But what the hell, at worst he had a free lift to school, and when they passed Carlin hauling her heavy suitcase down a brick-paved sidewalk, he turned to gaze at her mournfully, wishing she'd see him accompanied by his unlikely comrades.

On the short ride to the school, Gus was informed that he'd been granted the honor of residing at Chalk House, although for his part, he could not figure out why he'd been chosen for this distinction nor could he understand what was so desirable about the dilapidated old house at which they arrived. On the outside, Chalk was no different than any other dorm on campus. A squat, boxy place, it was covered with white clapboards; there was a wide front porch, littered with Rollerblades and hockey sticks, and around back, a latticework entranceway where garbage cans were stored alongside expensive mountain bikes. On the first floor were several gracious rooms that boasted mahogany woodwork and working fireplaces, but these were always bequeathed to upperclassmen, who had already paid their dues; freshmen were relegated up to the attic. At the rear of the house, two private apartments had been tacked on. In one lived the coach, Duck Johnson, whose snoring had been known to rattle windowpanes; in the other lived Eric Herman, who spent more time in his office at the humanities building than he did in his own quarters.

Because of its proximity to the river, Chalk House was by far the dampest building on campus. A film of mold coated any item left in the showers overnight, and in the evenings, snails left slippery trails along hallways and walls. Each term brought boys who couldn't resist climbing onto the roof, where they aimed their piss directly into the Haddan River from atop their perilous roost. None of these boys had ever been successful and, thankfully, none had fallen in such an attempt, but even the alumni association, never the champion of change, had agreed that the building was structurally unsound. Last spring a railing had finally been built along the roof. Still, the house was in miserable condition, with a dreadful electrical system that blinked on and off during storms and ancient plumbing that grumbled and clogged. In the rafters, on the far side of the damp plaster walls, there lived generation after generation of ill-tempered raccoons who squabbled and paced at night, so that bickering and snarling drifted into the dreams of the freshmen in the attic, and not a single one of these boys ever had a good night's sleep until their first term was over and done.

Yet no one would dare to suggest that this venerable house be torn down, and most people envied its residents. There were rumors that students could buy their way in, and suggestions that the odds of being chosen for Chalk were greatly increased if one's father or cousin had been a boarder. Indeed, there were distinct advantages for Chalk House residents. At all other houses, students had to vacuum floors and clean bathrooms, but at Chalk a maid was employed by a group of alumni; she came in every Wednesday to sort laundry and on Thursdays she made up the beds with fresh linens. Chalk boys were the first to register for courses and because the house had its own parking area, seniors were allowed to have cars on campus. Such entitlement had clearly paid off. For more than a hundred years, boys at Chalk had graduated at the top of the class, guided into a world of privilege with the help of those who had gone before them. There were Chalk alumni on most college admission committees and out in the world more alumni were eager to hire a brother who'd lived in the old house beside the river, that falling-down pile of wood and bricks where the wind rattled down the chimney and the swans always put up a good fight when chased off the porch.

The students who had not been chosen for Chalk, those boys who lived in Otto House or Sharpe Hall, felt a sort of bitterness from their very first day on campus, as if already, before anyone had seen their faces or knew their names, they had been judged lacking, fated to belong to a lower echelon where they would always be second best, chosen last for teams, never dating the prettiest girls from St. Anne's or daring to hope for a kiss under the weeping beeches. But these petty jealousies arose later on in the term; during the first weeks of school there was a sense of good fellowship as everyone settled in. The trees were still green and evenings were warm; the last of the crickets called in the meadows, a constant song most people found comforting, for it reminded them that there was still a world beyond the confines of Haddan.

Some people fit in easily at the school, but each year there were bound to be those unable to accommodate or conform, whether they were sullen or frightened or shy. In a place where teamwork and good cheer were highly regarded, loners were easily identified, and Carlin Leander was clearly among them. Although she was pretty and had quickly proven herself a worthy member of the swim team, she was moody and spent too much time on her own to be one of the crowd. As soon as practice ended, she took off by herself, like one of those bobcats people said roamed the woods, a breed too high-strung and suspicious to be among its own kind.

Such was the case with most unhappy students; they avoided even one another, so intent on their own unhappiness they failed to notice the other lost souls around them. These students often found their way to the pharmacy on Main Street. They cut classes and sat at the counter in the afternoons, ordering cups of coffee, trying to work up the nerve to buy cigarettes. They clearly had no idea that Pete Byers, the pharmacist, had never sold tobacco to a minor in his life. Anyone looking for that sort of thing would have far better luck at the mini-mart, where Teddy Humphrey would sell just about anything to a kid from Haddan; damn them but not their money as far as he was concerned. Have a good fake ID in hand and it was not Teddy's job to wonder why, but simply to sell a six-pack of Samuel Adams beer or Pete's Wicked Ale to any customer who waited in line.

Most people in town paid no attention to the Haddan students. There were new ones each year, and although every freshman class brought an aura of high hopes and even higher energy, they'd be gone in four years, the blink of an eye really, when sorted into the history of a town like Haddan. In this village most people stayed put; the farthest a resident might move was to a house around the corner when they married or, eventually and sadly, perhaps down to the rest home over on Riverview Avenue.

Every September, when the new students settled in, they came to buy boots at Hingram's Shoe Shop, then went about setting up a bank account at 5&10 Cent Bank where pretty Kelly Avon, who was always so helpful, had learned to keep a straight face whenever some fourteen-year-old wanted to deposit a check for several thousand dollars. Nikki Humphrey, who'd stayed married to Teddy from the mini-mart for far too long, never took it personally when groups of Haddan girls come sashaying into Selena's, ordering lattes and blueberry scones, expecting quick service, as if Nikki were nothing more than an automaton or a household servant. Before long these girls would be gone and

Nikki would still be in Haddan, putting all the money spent on lattes and scones to good use by remodeling the kitchen of the cute little house she'd bought on Bridal Wreath Lane after her divorce.

Some local people actually looked forward to September; they enjoyed witnessing all that youth spilling onto their sidewalks and into their stores. Lois Jeremy, from the garden club, often sat out on her gabled porch facing Main Street on Friday afternoons just to watch for those Haddan School boys and girls. It brought tears to her eyes to think of the expectations she'd had for her own son, AJ, and for a moment or two she ignored her perennial border, which she always covered with marsh grass rather than store-bought mulch to protect the bulbs from early frosts.

"Aren't they adorable?" Lois would call to her best friend, Charlotte Evans, who lived right next door and who'd had quite a year herself, what with Japanese beetles destroying half her garden and her youngest daughter going through that nasty divorce from that nice psychologist, Phil Endicott, who no one would have ever expected to be the sort of individual to have a girlfriend on the side.

"They couldn't be cuter." Charlotte had been deadheading her lilies and pulling damp leaves from between the twisted canes. She leaned on her rake to take a closer look at the Haddan boys in their khaki pants as they headed into town, and all those lovely, young girls trailing after them. The girls reminded her of her own daughter Melissa, the one who was crying all the time and taking Prozac and every other antidepressant she could get her hands on.

"I'd guess they're having the time of their lives." Lois Jeremy's

lips trembled as she watched. Two girls had begun to skip, showing off for the boys; their long hair swung out behind them and
they giggled, but their childish gait could hardly belie their wom-
anly legs.

"Oh, I'd say so," Charlotte agreed, feeling slightly dizzy herself, perhaps from all the raking she'd done or from thinking too
much about Melissa's divorce. "Isn't it lovely to see people who
are happy?"

Of course Mrs. Jeremy and Mrs. Evans could not be expected
to guess how many girls at St. Anne's cried themselves to sleep.
Unhappiness seemed to double when trapped beneath one roof.
Mood swings were common; behavior marked by half-truths and
secrets. One tall, dark girl named Peggy Anthony refused all solid
food, choosing instead to drink only milk, supplemented by the
candy bars she hid in a suitcase stored under her bed. There was
a senior named Heidi Lansing who was so nervous about college
applications she had pulled out half the hair on her head before
she'd even begun to write her essays, and a sophomore named
Maureen Brown who lit black candles on her windowsill before
bed and so alarmed her roommates with the wicked conversations she held in her sleep that these anxious girls had taken to
spending nights in the bathroom, unrolling sleeping bags on the
tile floor, so that anyone wanting to take a shower or use the toilet was forced to step over their slumbering forms.

Carlin Leander did not cry herself to sleep or starve herself,
yet unhappiness coursed through her, even when she plunged
into the cold water of the pool. In fact, she hadn't much to complain about; she'd been granted a large airy room on the third
floor and roommates who were perfectly pleasant. It was not
these girls' fault that they had more than Carlin: more money,

more clothes, more experience. Both Amy Elliot and Pie Hobson had filled their closets with boots and wool jackets and dresses so expensive a single one cost more than Carlin had spent on her yearly wardrobe, most of it bought at secondhand stores and at the Sunshine Flea Market, where it was possible to buy five T-shirts for a dollar, never mind the fraying seams or the moth holes.

Lest her roommates take her up as a charity case, Carlin elaborated on the story she'd come up with on the train: the only offspring of a father and mother who traveled the world, she'd far more important things to worry about than clothes. Unlike her roommates, she hadn't the chance to covet or hoard. She and her family weren't the sort of people who'd had time to gather personal effects or put down roots. They were better than that, her story implied, superior in some deep and moral way. So far, no one had challenged her story, and why should they doubt her? Truth had very little to do with a girl's image at St. Anne's; here, an individual was whoever she claimed to be. Those who had never been kissed professed to be sexually wild, and those who'd been through more boys than they cared to remember insisted they would remain virgins until their wedding day. Identity was a mutable thing, a cloak taken on and off, depending on circumstance or phases of the moon.

Carlin's only bad moments had come with the swim team, and that was because she'd been foolish enough to let down her guard. If she'd been thinking straight she would never have trusted Christine Percy, the senior who had informed her that all girls on the team were required to shave their private parts. Afterward, they had all teased Carlin, along with Ivy Cooper, the other new girl, for being so gullible. There were jokes about how chilly Carlin and Ivy would now be. Everyone had been through the same hazing; losing a little hair and a little pride was believed to strengthen team bonds. After this initiation, a girl was welcomed as a true teammate, at a celebration with some contraband wine, bought at the mini-mart with Christine's fake ID. Carlin, however, became even more withdrawn; it didn't take long before the other girls learned to leave her alone.

Each night, Carlin waited for the hour when she could flee from St. Anne's. After curfew, she lay unmoving in her bed, until at last her roommates' breathing shifted into deep, even rhythms; only then was she ready to make her escape out her window, in spite of the thorny vines that coiled up the fire ladder and left traces of blood on her fingers as she climbed to the ground. In an instant she felt free, let loose into the sweet, inky Massachusetts night, away from the steam heat and close quarters of St. Anne's. At first, she only stayed out long enough to have a quick cigarette beside the old rosebushes, damning the spiked vines as she pricked herself accidentally, then sucked the blood from her fingers. But after a while she dared to go farther, walking down to the river. One night, when there was no moon and the sky was perfectly black, the need to stray took hold. A ribbon of mist had settled onto the horizon, then flattened out to wind through the shrubbery. In the smooth still air, the edges of things melted, disappearing into the deep night, so that an elm tree might suddenly appear in the path; a wood duck might unexpectedly arise from the lawn. Although Carlin's shoes sank into the mud, she was careful to stay in the shadows to ensure that no one would catch her out after curfew.

The air was surprisingly chilly, at least to someone with thin Florida blood, and although Carlin was wearing a fleecy jacket, on permanent loan from her roommate Pie, she still shivered. In the dark, she couldn't tell east from west, and once she reached the edge of campus, she thought it best to follow the river. The evening had been leaden, with gray skies and the threat of rain, but now, as Carlin crossed a playing field and found her way into a meadow, the clouds began to clear, allowing a few pale stars to shine in the sky. She passed beneath an old orchard, where deer often congregated at this time of year. Burrs hidden in the tall grass clung to her clothes; field mice, always so bold in the hallways of St. Anne's after midnight, scurried away at her approach. For more than a hundred years, Haddan students had been following this same route, venturing beyond the riverbanks and the meadows in search of a place where rules could be broken. A passageway leading to the old cemetery had been cut through the brambles and witch hazel. Rabbits had often used this trail as well, and the impression of their tracks—two small paw prints close together, then the larger back feet swung out to land in front—had beaten down a clear path in the grass.

The first citizens to be buried in the Haddan School cemetery were four boys who gave their lives in the Civil War, and every war since has added to their number. Faculty members who preferred this spot to the churchyard in town could also be interred within these gates, although no one had asked for this privilege for more than twenty years, not since Dr. Howe had passed on at the age of ninety-seven, too stubborn to give in to death until he'd neared the century mark. This cloistered location offered the sort of privacy Carlin had been searching for; if given a choice, she preferred keeping company with the dead rather than having to put up with the girls of St. Anne's. At least those who'd passed on did not gossip and judge, nor did they wish to exclude anyone from their ranks.

Carlin unhooked the lock on the wrought-iron gate and slipped inside. She didn't realize she wasn't alone until the flare of a match illuminated not only the enormous elm in the center of the cemetery, but the figure beneath it as well. For a moment, Carlin felt her heart heave against her chest, then she saw it was only August Pierce, that silly boy from the train, sprawled out upon a flat, black slab of marble.

"Well, well. Look who's here." Gus was delighted to see her. Although he'd been coming to the cemetery since his first night at Haddan, he was nervous in the dark. There was some dreadful bird in the big elm tree that snickered and called and every time there was a rustling in the bushes Gus felt the urge to run. He had been ever alert, fearing he might have to defend himself against a rabid opossum or a starving raccoon willing to do battle for the Snickers candy bar Gus had stored in his inner coat pocket. With his luck, it was most likely a skunk lying in wait, ready to douse him in a vile cloud of scent. Expecting all of these dreadful things and finding Carlin Leander instead was more than a relief. It was bliss.

"Automatic suspension if we're caught smoking," he informed her as they inhaled on their cigarettes.

"I don't get caught." Carlin had come to perch on the marker of Hosteous Moore, the second headmaster of the Haddan School, who had insisted on swimming in the river every single morning, despite rain, sleet, or snow, only to die of pneumonia in his forty-fourth year. He had been a smoker, too, preferring a pipe, which he took daily, right before his swim.

Gus grinned, impressed by Carlin's bravado. He hadn't the least bit of courage, but it was a trait he greatly admired in others. He stubbed his cigarette out in the dirt beneath a hedge of Celestial roses. Immediately, he lit another. "Chain-smoker," he confessed. "Bad habit."

Carlin pulled her pale hair away from her face as she studied him. In the starlight, she looked silvery and so beautiful, Gus had to force himself to look away.

"I'll bet it's not the only bad habit you've got," Carlin guessed.

Gus laughed and stretched out on the black marble slab. *Eternus Lux* was engraved beneath Dr. Howe's name. Eternal light. "How right you are." He paused to blow a perfect smoke ring. "But unlike you, I always get caught."

Carlin would have suspected as much. He was so vulnerable, with his wide, foolish smile, the sort of boy who would chop off his foot in order to escape from a steel trap, too intent on his own agony to notice that the key had been there beside him all along. He was doing his best to appear casual about their chance meeting, but Carlin could practically see his heart beating beneath his heavy black coat. He was such a nervous wreck it was actually quite sweet. Dear Gus Pierce, ever cursed and denied, would make a true and faithful friend, that much was evident, and Carlin could use an ally. However strange, however unlikely, Gus was the first person she'd truly felt comfortable with since her arrival in Massachusetts. For his part, by the time they walked back along the river, August Pierce would have died for Carlin had he been asked to do so. Indeed, she had read him correctly: in return for a single act of kindness, he would remain forever loyal.

Carlin's roommates and the rest of the girls in St. Anne's

could not fathom the friendship, nor understand why Carlin soon spent so much time in Gus's room at Chalk House, where she lounged on his bed, head resting in the crook of his back, as she read from her Ancient Civilizations text for her class with Mr. Herman or made sketches for Beginning Drawing with Miss Vining. The other girls shook their heads and wondered if Carlin had any sense at all. The boys they wanted were the ones they couldn't have, the seniors at Chalk, for instance, such as Harry McKenna, who was so good-looking and smooth he could cause someone to grow weak in the knees by bestowing one of his famous smiles on a sweet, unsuspecting girl, or Robbie Shaw, who'd gone through so many coeds during his first year at Haddan he was nicknamed Robo-Robbie, for his inhuman stamina and lack of emotion.

That the girls at St. Anne's had no understanding of what should be valued and what was best cast away did not surprise Carlin in the least. She could well imagine what they might do if they ever got hold of the true details of her life before Haddan. Wouldn't they love to know that her supper often consisted of sandwiches made of white bread and butter? Wouldn't they be amused to discover she used liquid detergent to wash her hair because it was cheaper than shampoo, and that her lipsticks had all been swiped from the makeup counter at Kmart? The girls at St. Anne's would have gleefully gossiped for days had they known, so why should Carlin be influenced by their remarks? She chose to ignore Amy's nasty comments when Gus left notes in their shared locker or sent e-mails; she did not flinch when the house phone rang and Peggy Anthony or Chris Percy shouted up to tell her that her devoted slave was calling, yet again, and could she please tell him not to tie up the phone.

Carlin particularly looked forward to the messages Gus managed to sneak to her during swim practice. How he got past the matron was simply a mystery, but somehow he achieved what most boys at Haddan only dreamed about: total access to the girls' gym. He knew any number of worthwhile tricks and had inscribed a nasty message with rubbing alcohol on Amy's mirror that appeared one day when the air was especially damp. He could unlock the door to the cafeteria after midnight with a skeleton key and, once inside, manage to pry open the freezer and treat himself and Carlin to free Popsicles and ice cream bars. He could pay Teddy Humphrey at the mini-mart for a pack of cigarettes, yet walk out the door with the coins still in the palm of his hand. But the most amazing and astounding feat of all was that Gus Pierce could make Carlin laugh.

"I don't get it," Amy Elliot had said when Gus's rude remarks surfaced on her mirror. "Does he think this is the way to get people to like him?"

"My roommates don't get you," Carlin told Gus as they walked along the river on their way to the cemetery, wondering if he'd have a reaction and not surprised to find he didn't care.

"Few do," Gus admitted.

This was especially true in regard to the residents of Chalk House. Chalk was said to be a brotherhood, but as is the case in some blood families, Gus's brothers did not appreciate him. After a week they were eager to be rid of him. Ten days more and they downright despised him. As often happens in such close quarters, Gus's peers did not hold back their distaste; before long, the attic began to stink with their sentiments as they left gifts that announced their disdain: old egg salad sandwiches, decaying fruit, piles of unwashed socks.

This year there were three freshmen in the attic: David Linden, whose great-grandfather had been governor of the Commonwealth, Nathaniel Gibb from Ohio, the winner of a tristate science fair, and Gus, mistake of mistakes, whose presence testified to the fact that although an individual's statistics might look fine on paper, in the flesh they could spell disaster. As for Gus, he had come to Haddan with no appreciation for the human race and no expectations of his fellow man. He was fully ready to confront contempt; he'd been beleaguered and insulted often enough to have learned to ignore anything with a heartbeat.

Still, every once in a while he made an exception, as he did with Carlin Leander. He appreciated everything about Carlin and lived for the hour when they left their books and sneaked off to the graveyard. Not even the crow nesting in the elm tree could dissuade him from his mission, for when he was beside Carlin, Gus acquired a strange optimism; in the light of her radiance the rest of the world began to shine. For a brief time, bad faith and human weakness could be forgotten or, at the very least, temporarily ignored. When it came time to go back to their rooms, Gus followed on the path, holding on to each moment, trying his best to stretch out time. Standing in the shadows of the rose arbor in order to watch Carlin climb back up the fire escape at St. Anne's, his heart ached. He could tell he was going to be devastated, and yet he was already powerless. Carlin always turned and waved before she stepped through her window and Gus Pierce always waved back, like a common fool, an idiot of a boy who would have done anything to please her.

From the day he'd arrived in the attic, unpacking at breakneck speed, if that's what anyone could call tossing belongings haphazardly into a pile in the closet, Gus had known his arrival at Haddan was a mistake. One afternoon, Harry McKenna had knocked on his door to announce there was to be a house meeting that evening, coolly suggesting that Gus had better be there on time. Gus, who didn't appreciate the superior tone of the older boy any more than he was inspired to take orders, instantly resolved to dodge what was bound to be a boring evening, one he'd just as soon avoid.

Instead, he had met Carlin in the cemetery and together they watched Orion rise into the eastern sky, high above a line of poplars and maples. It was a beautiful night, and poor Gus sensed something that felt like hope rise within him, not that the euphoria had lasted long. Gus hadn't understood that what he'd been offered by Harry McKenna was not an invitation, but a mandate. This he realized only upon his return to his room. He'd gotten through the front door of Chalk House unnoticed, nearly two hours past curfew, and had safely made his way up the stairs, but as soon as he reached the attic he knew something was amiss. The door to his room was ajar, and even if he hadn't remembered closing it when he left, the house was much too quiet, even for such a late hour. Someone wanted to ensure that he learn his lesson and the lesson was extremely simple: Certain invitations best not be ignored.

In his room, bedding and clothes had been heaped together, then urinated upon. Lightbulbs had been removed from his lamp to be broken and sprinkled on his window ledge, where the glass glittered prettily, like a handful of diamonds displayed on the peeling wood sash. Gus stretched himself out on his mattress with a bitter taste rising in his throat and lit a cigarette in spite of the no-smoking ordinance, and watched the smoke spiral upward, toward the cracks in the ceiling. In his experience, this was what happened; an individual paid dearly for all that was sweet. Spend the evening with a beautiful girl, walk through the woods on a cool, pleasant night, lie peacefully on another man's grave to watch the three brilliant stars of Orion, and soon enough a message would arrive to remind you of what you were up against.

Gus rolled onto his stomach and stubbed his cigarette out on the floor beneath his bed. Red sparks rose up in a stream that made his eyes tear, but he didn't care; fire was the least of his problems. He was so thin that his bones pressed into the springs of his mattress. Although he was tired, he knew he wouldn't be able to sleep, not tonight and probably not on any other night. If someone were to weigh the beauty of moonlight against the depth of human cruelty, which would win? Moonlight could not be held in the palm of one's hand, but cruelty could cut deep. Who could begin to describe the color of moonlight once it had been replaced by the clear light of day? Who could say it had even existed, if it had ever been anything more than a dream?

After Gus had swept up the broken glass and washed his laundry in the bathtub, he went to check himself into the infirmary. His headache and nausea were real, as was his elevated temperature. Frankly, there weren't many at Haddan who missed him. His teachers were relieved by his absence; he was a difficult student, disruptive and challenging one moment, bored and withdrawn the next. Carlin was the only one who worried about him, and she looked for him in vain, searching the cemetery and the dining hall. When she finally tracked him down, the school nurse, Dorothy Jackson, informed her there were no visiting hours at the infirmary. And so, Carlin did not see Gus for eight days, not until he was up in his own bed, his coat wrapped around him like a blanket. In the dim light he stared at the ceiling. He had just punched a hole through the old horsehair plaster, the act of someone with no recourse other than shortsighted destruction. There were bits of plaster dusting the floor and the mattress. When she found him, Carlin threw herself down beside him on the bed to examine the results of his anger. It was possible to view the clouds through the hole in the eaves; a square of blue sky peeked at them from between the rotted shingles.

"You're insane," Carlin told Gus.

But in fact, his actions had just cause. Upon his return, he'd stumbled over the gift his brothers had left for him while he'd been in the infirmary. A bloody rabbit's foot, so fresh it was warm to the touch, had been deposited on his desk. Gus had picked it up gingerly, wrapped it in tissue, and placed this dreadful talisman into the garbage. And that was how he'd become a desperate individual, a boy who punched holes through plaster, brought low by injustice and shame.

"Did you think I was normal?" he asked Carlin. During his stay at the infirmary, he hadn't once changed his clothes. His T-shirt was filthy and his hair was uncombed. He'd often locked himself in the infirmary bathroom, where he smoked so many cigarettes there was still a film of nicotine on his skin and the whites of his eyes had a yellow cast.

"I didn't mean insane in a negative way," Carlin recanted.

"I see." Gus's mouth curled into a smile despite his despair. Carlin could do that to him, cheer him even in the depths of his misery. "You meant insane in a positive way."

Carlin propped her feet up against the wall, her long body stretched out against Gus's even longer one. She held her hand up to the sunshine streaming in through the ceiling, completely unaware that her complexion had turned golden in the light.

"What will you do when it snows?" she asked.

Gus turned his head to the wall. Impossible, impossible; he was about to cry.

Carlin leaned up on one elbow to study him. She gave off the scent of chlorine and jasmine soap. "Did I say something wrong?"

Gus shook his head; there was a catch in his throat and the sound he emitted resembled the call of that dreadful crow in the cemetery; a wail so dispirited and broken it could barely begin to rise. Carlin lay flat on the bed, the beat of her heart quickening as she waited for him to stop crying.

"I'll be gone by the time it snows," Gus said.

"No you won't be. Don't be ridiculous, you big baby." Carlin wrapped her arms around him and rocked him back and forth, then tickled him, knowing it would make him laugh. "What would I do without you?"

This was exactly why Carlin had never wanted to be close to anyone. When she was younger, she'd never even asked for a dog, and was temperamentally unfit to own a pet. It was so easy to be drawn in, to care and to comfort; before you knew it, you'd find yourself responsible for some defenseless creature.

"Was somebody mean to you?" Carlin threw herself on top of Gus. "Tell me everything and I'll make them pay. I'll defend you."

Gus rolled over to hide his face. There was a limit to how much humiliation even he could take.

Carlin sat up, her back shoved against the wall, her shoulder blades in the shape of an angel's wings. "I'm right. Somebody is being mean to you."

Down in the cellar, where tadpoles hatched in the trickle of groundwater that always seeped through the concrete no matter how often repairs were made, Harry McKenna and Robbie Shaw had drawn two orange crates close to the air vent. Both boys were good-looking, fair and rawboned, but Harry McKenna possessed a truly extraordinary face. His straw-colored hair had been clipped close to his skull, a style that showed off his outstanding features. Girls swooned when they saw him, and it was said that no one could deny him once he turned on the charm. Sitting in the basement of Chalk House, however, he was not at all pleased, and his irritation showed. His beautiful mouth was twisted into a scowl and he snapped his fingers repeatedly, as if that simple action could erase what he heard through the vent, a flattened piece of metal that ran from the rear of the closets in the attic rooms down to this cellar. Through the vent it was possible to hear nearly every word that was said up above. Even whispers resonated through the tube; a cough or a kiss could be caught and sliced apart for purposes of examination or entertainment. The older Chalk boys always listened in on the new residents, and for this practice they made no apologies. How better to know exactly who was to be relied upon and who needed to be taught a lesson still?

Pierce was proving himself to be a washout at this very moment, pouring out his heart to some girl, bellyaching like a loser. Harry and Robbie had been eavesdropping for quite some time, hunched over until Harry's long legs were riddled with cramps. Now he stood to stretch his back. Usually, he liked the benefits of his height, both with girls and on the playing field. He liked any advantage he could get and this was to be the year of his advantage. He was the senior in charge of Chalk House, and as such retained the honor of residing in what was once Dr. Howe's office, before the new administration building was built. The room's focal point was its handsome oak fireplace; tiny serrations had been carved into the side of the mantel, marks that were said to represent every woman Dr. Howe had slept with, and if the fireplace notches were to be believed, there had been quite a crowd.

Harry appreciated Dr. Howe's room, just as he valued all his many privileges. He was a boy who was grateful and greedy in equal measure. Certainly, he wasn't about to have some nitwit like August Pierce come in and ruin things. It was a cruel, cold world, wasn't it? A universe spinning through the dark, without any pledges or guarantees. A person had to take what he wanted or be left behind, flattened by circumstance. Nowhere was this more true than in the gentle Massachusetts countryside, where the weather continually proved that most circumstances couldn't be controlled. Chalk boys were certainly well aware of the wreckage that could be made of a life, an unfortunate observation made in the very first year, for these were the boys who had suffered the worst loss in the flood so many years ago. In the mayhem of the rising waters, the grades of every boy from Chalk House had evaporated from the dean's marking book. It was a thoughtful fellow from Cambridge who discovered this calamity while mopping up the dean's waterlogged office, and he ran back to tell the others what he had learned before any teachers found out.

All of their hard-earned A's in biology, their B's in Latin and Greek were gone, the letters washed away in blue pools of ink that had stained the floorboards a terrible cobalt that refused to come clean no matter how often the mop was applied. The Chalk boys wondered if the river had singled them out for torment. Why had this happened to them rather than the others? Why should their lives and careers be sacrificed? In the face of this disaster, a suggestion was proposed, a possibility voiced so humbly no one was ever quite sure whose idea it had been. *Twist fate*, that was the notion, one that was taken up immediately, by each and every boy. *Turn calamity into compensation. Take what has been denied you.*

It was a spring night, the thirteenth of May, when the boys at Chalk House changed their grades. The peepers were calling in a rush of damp music from every flooded corner of the campus; the moon floated above the library in a soot-black sky. The boys let themselves into the dean's office, where they substituted their names for those of the students from Otto House and Sharpe Hall, claiming grades they hadn't earned. The task was easily done, an elementary act of delinquency handily accomplished with a pick from the locksmith and some India ink, a simple bit of conjuring, but one so effective they decided to call themselves magicians, even though they had no true skills but one.

At the close of the term, the boys from the other houses who had once been assured an acceptance to Harvard or Yale roamed the campus, as despondent as they were confused. These students wondered what had happened to all their hours of study, for their grades had disappeared entirely, and from that day forward the term fair play was erased from their vocabularies. For those boys at Chalk who had thrown their lot in with the Magicians' Club, all that was demanded was full loyalty. If any among them did not have the temperament for cheating, no time was wasted. The others dragged boys who might be the least bit unreliable out to the meadow where the rabbits made their homes and they beat such individuals senseless. In protecting themselves and their brothers, the boys learned an important lesson about unity. Rules bound people close, true enough, but breaking rules bound them closer still.

This philosophy had been explained to Dave Linden and Nathaniel Gibb, and then to Gus when he grudgingly attended the first official meeting of the term. A circle was formed in a clearing beyond the river, although it was true that the weather had always been more foe than friend to the members of the Magicians' Club. The thirteenth of any month could be depended upon to be foul, with high snows or thunder or drenching rains. On this September meeting date, the fields were damp and the sky had turned the shade of gunmetal, with fog blanketing the fields. There were only bits of color: some green holly in the woods, a few strands of mulberry on the vine, a startled wild turkey that raced out from the underbrush in a flash of gold and red when disturbed by the intrusion. There was a chill in the air and the purple blooms of the flowering joe-pye weed had begun to turn indigo, always a sign of a cold and miserable winter to come. The boys sat around in a jumble of a ring, some lounging on the grass, others sitting on an old log that was often used to conceal contraband whiskey and beer. Those who knew what was to come and had been through it themselves were good-humored, even boisterous. But of course they'd already completed their hazing; they'd experienced the anxiety that Dave Linden and Nathaniel Gibb and even that idiot Gus Pierce, who was lying prone on his back, surely must be feeling as their induction approached.

To join, the rule was simple. An act of mayhem must be committed. Be it lawless or illicit, immoral or illegal, there was to be one hateful exploit: the single red thread that cross-stitched an individual's fate, binding him to his brothers. When told what they must now accomplish, Nathaniel Gibb and Dave Linden averted their faces and stared at the ground. Everyone knew they were hiding their tears, not that this show of emotion would be held against them. If anything, this meant they took the initiation seriously. What was far more disturbing was the lazy manner in which Gus Pierce blew smoke rings and gazed through the dark, leafy branches overhead.

There was only one way to avoid initiation and still retain membership with full privileges, and that was to perfect the trick Dr. Howe insisted his wife execute in exchange for her freedom. Who could blame Annie Howe for wanting to dissolve their union, considering those notches on the fireplace and the cruel way she'd been cut off from family and friends? But Dr. Howe was no fool; the only way he would agree to her demands was to set forth a single impossible task. She could leave anytime she wished to, all she need do was take one of her favorite flowers, those icy white roses that grew beside the girls' dormitory, and there before her husband's eyes, she must turn the bloom red.

"She killed herself instead," the older boys told whoever was not already informed of Annie's fate. "So we don't advise you to try it."

Instead, it was suggested to the new boys that they look for one of the rabbits found in the meadows and the woods. These small, shy creatures were easily caught with some patience and fishing net. All that was needed was a strong piece of wire to wrap around the front foot, and a bloody little souvenir would allow admittance to the club. The best inductees, however, were considerably more creative than this, forsaking rabbit hunts and playing a game of one-upmanship of who could execute the most original or most illegal act. Who would go down in Chalk history as the most daring was still a title ready to be claimed. One year a joker from Baltimore had used a handsaw on the dean's chair in the dining room, so that when Bob Thomas sat down to his dinner, he collapsed in a heap of splinters and beef. The previous autumn, Jonathan Walters, a quiet boy from Buffalo, had dipped into the school's computer files, searching out any college recommendations that weren't positive and altering critical passages to ensure that each letter afforded a wholehearted endorsement. There had been a wide range of induction activities, from thievery to high jinks; all that was necessary was that the deed performed would get a fellow in serious hot water if it was ever found out. That was the thread that bound them together: they were all guilty of something.

Some boys, it was true, used the initiation to serve their own twisted purposes. Three years ago Robbie Shaw climbed up the fire escape that led to the room where Carlin now slept; it was a holiday weekend and many of the students were gone, a situation Robbie was well aware of, since he'd planned his mission carefully. He told the fourteen-year-old girl he had targeted if she ever said a word about what he'd done, he'd come back and slit her throat. But as it turned out, there was no need for further coercion; the girl in question transferred to a school in Rhode Island the very next week. Robbie was criticized for going too far with his initiation, but privately his daring and his ability to choose his victim so well were applauded, for although the girl in question knew who her attacker was, she never did tell a soul.

Unfortunately, the decision to select August Pierce had not been as wise. Throughout the meeting, Gus kept quiet; it was impossible to gauge what he was feeling as he lay sprawled upon the damp grass. Afterward, he walked away without a word, and the other boys watched him carefully. There were those who would not have been surprised had Gus Pierce gone directly to the dean to report them, and still others who would have predicted that he'd hightail it to the police station in town, or maybe he'd simply phone home and beg his daddy to come and retrieve him. But in fact, Gus did none of these things. Perhaps another person with his convictions would have left that very night, simply packed his bags and hitchhiked down Route 17, but Gus was obstinate and he always had been. And perhaps he was prideful, too, because he thought he might just win at this game.

Gus had lied to Carlin about his father; the elder Pierce was not a professor, but rather a high school teacher, who on weekends performed at children's birthday parties. In spite of himself, Gus had learned quite a lot on those Sunday afternoons when he sullenly ate cake in honor of some stranger's birthday. He knew that a coin digested one moment cannot reappear in the palm of your hand seconds later. A bird pierced with an arrow cannot shake itself and then fly away. And yet, he was well aware that certain knots could be slipped open with a single touch and that doves fit quite nicely into jars with false bottoms. He had sat at the kitchen table with his father for hours, watching the same trick repeated, time and again, until what had once been a clumsy attempt was transmuted into seamless ability. Throughout his life, Gus had been taught that for every illusion there was a practical explanation, and such an education can prove worthwhile. After an upbringing such as this, Gus was aware of possibilities someone else might have overlooked, or taken for granted, or simply ignored. This much he knew for certain: for every locked trunk, there was sure to be a key.

NEEDLES AND THREAD

IN THE MONTH OF OCTOBER, when the elms lost their leaves and the oaks became yellow all at once, the mice in the tall grass beyond the river came searching for shelter. Girls at St. Anne's would often find them curled up in dresser drawers, or nesting in shoes left beneath the bed. Wasps, too, went looking for warmth, and passersby would hear them buzzing in tree stumps and fence posts. The woods were laced with an undergrowth of brambles that had previously been hidden by green leaves; rain, when it came, fell in buckets. It was the time of year when people found themselves in foul moods, plagued by headaches and bad fortune. On damp mornings, electrical appliances tended to mutiny. Cars wouldn't start, vacuum cleaners spit up dirt, coffeepots sputtered and then shut down. In the very first week of the month, there were so many people lined up at Selena's for coffees-to-go in the early, chilly A.M., and nerves were so frayed, it wasn't unusual for a fight to break out between some ordinary resident waiting on line and some obnoxious hothead, like Teddy Humphrey, whose own wife, Nikki, had been smart enough never to talk to him before he'd had his morning coffee back when they were still married, especially in the dark days of October.

One cold evening, when the swans on the river were paddling quickly to prevent ice from forming beneath them, Betsy went to dinner with Eric at the Haddan Inn. The evening was meant to be a special occasion; at last, some time alone. They'd ordered lamb and mashed potatoes, but halfway through the meal Betsy found she simply couldn't eat; she excused herself and stepped outside for a bit of fresh air. Alone on the porch of the inn, she gazed at Main Street, the white houses turning lavender in the fading light. The evening was perfect; a mockingbird perched on a fence post and sang the most beautiful song, invented or stolen, it really didn't matter, the melody was exquisite. Standing there, Betsy couldn't help but wonder if that long-ago lightning storm that had chased people over meadows and field had managed to strike her even though she'd been safe at home. Certain emotions had been burned right out of her and she'd never even missed them. Surely she had all the ingredients for happiness. What more could she want than a man she could depend on, a steady job, a future that was assured? Why was it she felt so reluctant, as though she'd been backed into this life she'd begun to lead by fear, not desire?

Thankfully, by the time Betsy returned to the table to order a raspberry trifle and cappuccino, her head had cleared. This inn was the place where she would marry next June; these were the dishes on which her wedding dinner would be served, the glasses with which they would toast their happiness.

"I'm glad we're having the reception here," she told Eric as they were leaving, but she didn't sound as convinced as she might have.

"Not too stuffy?"

"It's very Haddan," Betsy had said, and they'd both had a laugh over that, for the very word exuded a sense of order and predictability. Despite its traditional style, the inn was the nicest place in town. Rooms had already been booked for out-of-town guests, and Eric's mother, a finicky woman prey to a bad back, had asked for an extremely firm mattress. Betsy had visited the inn only days earlier to test the beds, finding the perfect model in a second-floor room, a mattress so hard that an egg dropped upon it would surely break in two.

"I wish we could stay here tonight," Eric told Betsy as they began the walk back to the school.

"Then let's. We can sneak out at midnight and check in. No one will know." Betsy ran a stick along the metal railings of Mrs. Jeremy's fence until the porch light suddenly switched on. She threw the stick away when Mrs. Jeremy peeked out her bay window, an annoyed expression on her thin face. "The kids sneak out all the time. Why shouldn't we?" By now, Betsy had come to understand why rooms at St. Anne's with fire escapes were so coveted; that pale girl, Carlin, was particularly adept at navigating the metal rungs after curfew without the slightest bit of noise.

"We're supposed to set an example," Eric reminded Betsy.

Betsy looked closely to see if he was mocking her, but no, his handsome, serious face showed only concern. He was not a man who took his responsibilities lightly, and in fact it was a good thing that Betsy returned that night. She came in from dinner to find twenty girls huddled in the dark parlor, uncertain what to do next. At St. Anne's, fuses continually blew, and no one, save for Maureen Brown with her supply of candles, had known what to do. Upon her arrival, Betsy marched over to Helen Davis's quarters, where she discovered that rather than coming to anyone's aid, the senior houseparent was sipping tea in a room illuminated by a heavy-duty flashlight, as if the well-being of their girls was the farthest thing from her mind.

A few days later there was another incident Helen Davis chose to ignore. Carlin Leander's roommate Amy Elliot was bitten by a wren that had managed to get into the house, flying above the girls' beds, crashing into ceilings and walls. Terrible luck was said to afflict anyone who suffered such a bite, with worse luck to come if the stricken party should kill the offending bird, which was exactly what Amy did. She smashed her Ancient History text atop the wren, instantly crushing its skull and spine. Within minutes, Amy's leg swelled up and turned black. Her parents in New Jersey had to be phoned, painkillers were dispensed, ice packs procured. And where had Helen Davis been while Betsy ran around like a lunatic, chauffeuring Amy over to the emergency room in Hamilton and ferrying her back ever so carefully over the rutted Haddan roads? Helen had gone back to her reading, and if she heard the wren's mate tapping against her window, she ignored it, and the sound disappeared completely as soon as she let her cat out for the night.

"Aren't we supposed to be in charge? Aren't we supposed to help them?" Betsy complained to Helen that very night. "Isn't that our job?"

It had been a trial to care for Amy, who had howled all the way to the hospital, terrified that the bird bite might cause her to lose her leg, although in the end all that was needed was antibiotics and bed rest. The evening had taken the worst toll on Betsy, for upon her return to St. Anne's she'd had to dig a grave for the battered little wren, now buried beneath some junipers. When she came to knock on Helen's door, her hands were muddy and her complexion had turned blue with the cold. Perhaps Helen Davis took pity on the younger woman because of her wretched appearance.

"They're big girls, dear. Time for them to learn a thing or two, wouldn't you say? Our job is to help them grow up, not baby them. You've been subjected to teenagers for too long." In spite of Helen's determination never to be agreeable, she found she had taken a liking to Betsy. "Schools like Haddan will drain you dry if you let them, and teenagers will do the very same thing."

There did appear to be something in the air at Haddan that caused good judgment to dissolve. Betsy had noticed that several of the girls in her care had been growing progressively wilder. More girls climbed out their windows at night than stayed in their beds, and some were so blatant in their disregard for rules that Betsy had insisted they clean the common rooms as a punishment for their late hours and careless ways. In fact, there was a reason for such bad behavior: girls at St. Anne's most often fell in love in October. Every year there was a rush of romance from the first day of the month to the last, a tumbling falling in love at first sight that occurred with such intensity anyone would have guessed no one on earth had ever fallen in love before. Love like this was contagious; it spread in the manner of measles or flu. Couples stayed out until morning, only to be discovered at the canoe shed, wound in each other's arms, Girls stopped eating and sleeping; they kissed their boyfriends until their lips were bruised, then dozed through their classes, daydreaming as they failed quizzes and exams.

Girls in love often had odd appetites, for cucumber pickles or pumpkin pie, and some of these girls were convinced that any rash acts were acceptable, if done in the name of love. Maureen Brown, for instance, did not seem embarrassed in the least when Betsy found a boy from Chalk House hiding beneath her unmade bed. There would always be girls with such unstoppable cravings they turned their backs on all reason and good intentions, forsaking everything but romance. Why, even Helen Davis herself had once been easy prey for love. Nowadays, people at school insisted that Miss Davis was so cold a single touch from her hand could freeze water in a glass, but this wasn't always the case. During her first year at Haddan, when she was twenty-four and the month of October was especially fine, Helen paced the hallways every night, until a path in the carpet had been worn from her tread. She fell in love with Dr. Howe in a single afternoon, long before he'd ever called her by name. That October the moon was orange, it shimmered with light, and perhaps its shine was blinding, for Helen chose to ignore the fact that Dr. Howe was already married. She should have known better, she should have held back, but before the month was done, she had agreed to meet him in his office late at night, without the wisdom to guess she was neither the first nor the last woman to do so.

Shy Helen, who had always been so serious and reserved, was now consumed by her own longings. Within this grid of passion, Dr. Howe's wife was nothing more than a woman with red hair who worked in the gardens, only a stumbling block in the path of

Helen's own resolve to win the man she loved. All through the winter, Helen ignored Annie Howe; she did not raise her eyes when they passed each other on the paths, and this was the reason Helen was among the last to know Annie was expecting a child in the spring, not that such a situation could stop Dr. Howe from straying.

Helen paid Annie no mind at all until the day in March when the roses were all cut down. She happened to be coming from the library that afternoon, carrying half a dozen books, when she noticed Mrs. Howe crouched on the ground, a pair of shears from the groundskeeper's shed in her hands. Annie had already been through most of the campus; vines and branches were everywhere, as though a storm had passed through, leaving only thorns and twisted black bark. Annie was a tall woman and in pregnancy she was even more beautiful. Her hair was the color of fire, her skin like satin, luminous and pale. But with the shears in hand, she appeared dangerous; Helen stopped, frozen in place, as Annie tore through the bare canes of the cinnamon ramblers that grew alongside the library. Helen was only a young and foolish girl, witnessing something she had neither the capability nor the experience to understand, but even she could tell that she had come face-to-face with real sorrow. Standing beside the weeping beeches, frightened for her life, Helen gleaned, for the very first time, that she might actually be the guilty party.

But for her part, Annie had no interest in Helen. Far too intent on her mission, she saw no one at all. There was no wind that day, and the aroma of cloves was powerful when Annie moved on to the scented snowbird roses that grew beside the dining hall, destroying each vine so thoroughly it would never flower again. She didn't seem to notice that her hands were lacerated and torn as she moved across the quad, in the direction of the girls' dormitory. There was the arbor Annie had commissioned the grounds crew to build, and the Polar roses she had nurtured for ten years, with no success until now. For on this raw March day a dozen white roses had bloomed months ahead of schedule, each one shivering with cool silver light. Annie began to chop at the vines, but she was careless, and before she realized what she'd done, she had clipped off the top of her ring finger. Immediately, blood began to flow. Although Helen startled, Annie herself did not even cry out; instead, she reached for one of the cut roses. Despite the thorns she held it close, letting her blood fall onto the petals. If Helen wasn't mistaken, Annie smiled as she held the one bloom that had begun to turn red.

When the swans spied their mistress there on the lawn, they came rushing to her, clucking with distress, pulling out their feathers. Their racket seemed to wake Annie from her reverie, and she gazed at the damage she'd done as though she were a sleepwalker with no idea of how she'd managed to wander so far. Her finger still bled, the blood coursing more and more thickly. Already the rose was so saturated it had begun to dissolve in her hands and she carefully put it back together again, petal by crimson petal. By then, Annie's rampage was common knowledge in Haddan. The authorities were called in by one of the faculty wives, who had run all the way to the police station, in fear for her life. Two of the three men on the Haddan force were nearing retirement, and so it fell to Wright Grey, the young lieutenant, to hurry on down to the school.

Annie had known Wright all her life. As children they'd been to school together, walking the distance to Hamilton; they'd gone swimming at Sixth Commandment Pond on hot, hazy days. Now when Wright politely asked her to accompany him to the hospital in Hamilton, Annie did as he asked. All these years later, Helen Davis can still remember how carefully Wright helped Annie from the grass; she noticed his blue eyes and his look of concern as Annie insisted he wrap his handkerchief not around her wounded hand, as he clearly would have liked to, but around the stained white rose.

In less than a week's time, Annie returned from the hospital, but she didn't look the same. Now she wore her hair in a single braid, the way women in mourning often do. She was heavier and she moved more slowly; if spoken to, she appeared puzzled, as if she had lost the ability to understand even the simplest command. Perhaps this was because she had truly believed her husband would let her go if she turned a single rose red, but he'd laughed when she unwrapped the linen handkerchief she'd borrowed from her old school friend. In time what was crimson turns black, and the petals of dried roses fade to ashes. Annie Howe might as well have given her husband a handful of soot as deliver the rose she had stained with her blood.

As for Helen, she could no longer pretend that Dr. Howe was hers, nor ignore the fact that he was a father-to-be. Now when he kissed her, it was Annie's red hair Helen thought of. When he unbuttoned her dress, she heard the swans' cry. She went out of her way to avoid him until one morning, when the sky was still dark and the girls in the dormitory were safely asleep in their beds. It was then Helen heard a tread upon the stairs. She pulled on her robe and went to the door, guessing that one of her charges needed help, but instead, she found Dr. Howe in the hall.

"Go back to sleep," he told Helen.

Helen blinked as she stood on the threshold. Was it possible for him to be standing there? Perhaps she had conjured him out of thin air and might just as easily conjure him away. But no, Dr. Howe was flesh and blood; Helen knew this because of the weight of his hand on her arm.

"Close your door," Dr. Howe said, and because of the seriousness of his tone and the lateness of the hour, Helen did exactly that, leaving herself to wonder, forever after, what would have happened if she'd disobeyed him. At the very least, she might have learned the truth.

Several hours later, two fourteen-year-old girls found Annie Howe in the attic. Their screams woke everyone in the house and so frightened the rabbits in the thickets that they were overtaken by an instinct to flee, dashing madly across the green in broad daylight, only to be scooped up by the red-tailed hawks that perched in the beech trees in anticipation of exactly such moments of panic. Annie had hanged herself with the sash from Helen's coat, left on a hook in the corridor near her back door. The coat, recently bought at Lord & Taylor, had been considerably more expensive than Helen could afford, but that didn't dissuade her from depositing it in a trash barrel behind the library that very afternoon.

Because Annie Howe had taken her own life, there was no service and no burial in either the Haddan School cemetery or the churchyard behind town hall. For weeks afterward, the house where she'd died smelled of roses, even though the weather was dismal and no flowers bloomed. The scent was in the stairwells and in the cellar and in the corners of every room. Some girls began to have migraines brought on by this odor, some became sick to their stomachs, still others burst into tears at the slightest provocation, whether it be an insult or a dashed hope. Even when the windows were closed and the doors were shut, the scent remained, as if roses had grown through the floorboards of the overheated hallways. Up in the attic, the fragrance was especially overpowering, and when several girls crept up to see the scene of the crime, they fainted dead away, then had to be carried downstairs and put to bed for a week before they regained their senses.

Only Helen Davis was resistant to the scent. When she walked through the dorm, there was only the tang of soap, the sharpness of shoe polish, the cloying fragrance of violet cologne. Helen buried her face in curtains and carpets; she went to the attic and breathed in deeply, desperate for the scent of roses, but she never did find it, not in that house and not anywhere else. Even now, when Helen approached an ordinary rosebush in the village, say a Velvet Fragrance, whose dark crimson buds emitted such a powerful perfume every bee in the county had been called forth, Helen couldn't smell a thing. She could stroll past Lois Jeremy's famed damasks, known for their lemony fragrance, and breathe in nothing but cut grass and clean country air.

In memory of the Howes' unborn child, a little stone lamb was erected in the Haddan School cemetery, and there were some women in town who still draped garlands around the statue's neck, hoping to ward off illnesses and protect their own daughters and sons. And why shouldn't such charms be possible? To this day, the scent of roses in seasons when no flowers grew continued to occur at St. Anne's, affecting only the girls who were the most sensitive and high-strung. Amy Elliot, for one, who was allergic to roses, had to be sent to a specialist in Hamilton after moving into St. Anne's and was prescribed an inhaler along with shots of cortisone. Several girls in the attic, including Maureen Brown and Peggy Anthony, went searching for the cause of the red rose-hive bumps that marked their arms. They cleaned out bureaus and rooted through closets, but in the end they found nothing but stray bits of twine and crumbs of toast left behind by the mice.

Old houses always have their flaws—radiators that bang, unexplainable odors—but they have their pluses as well. St. Anne's, for instance, was surprisingly private, the thick horsehair plaster walls serving to keep sound to a minimum. Students could throw a party on the first floor and the girls in the attic wouldn't hear a thing, thanks to the insulation and the heavy oak doors. Only a few people knew that Carlin Leander often sneaked out at night, with fewer still having any idea that Peggy Anthony rooted around in her suitcase for chocolate bars to gorge upon, and even fewer aware that Maureen Brown had a series of boyfriends who secretly spent the night. It was this level of privacy that had enabled Helen Davis to keep her illness to herself for the past two years. She suffered from congestive heart failure, and although her doctors in Boston had done their best with surgery scheduled over summer vacation and then with the prescribed course of medication, Helen's condition had grown progressively worse. Her heart, weakened by a bout of rheumatic fever in childhood, was not pumping enough blood; already, her lungs were overworked, and she coughed through the night.

At last, Helen's doctors had admitted there was nothing more to be done. In light of the finality of this diagnosis, her life had unwound, as if she herself were nothing more than a spool of thread, body and spirit combined. In all of Haddan, the only one who knew of her situation was Pete Byers, the pharmacist, and

they had never once discussed the status of her health. Pete simply filled Helen's prescriptions and talked about the weather, all
the time wearing the thoughtful expression he always had, no
matter if a customer's ailment was cancer or a simple sunburn.
Although he never said a word, Pete had taken notice of how frail
Helen had become. The last time she'd come to pick up her
medication, she'd been so exhausted Pete had closed up shop
and driven her back to school.

Lately it had become an effort for Helen to slip on shoes or
button a blouse; it was too much work to fill the bird feeder or set
down a bowl of cream for the cat. Last week the most humiliating situation yet had occurred: Helen discovered she could not
lift her book bag after class, she simply could not manage its
weight. She'd remained at her desk, watching mournfully as the
room began to clear, cursing the wreckage of her weak heart. She
watched with envy as boys and girls hauled heavy backpacks over
their shoulders, as though toting nothing more than feathers or
straw. How could they ever imagine what it might be like to have
every object suddenly turn to stone? Put a stone in the palm of a
boy's hand and he'd merely toss it across the river. Give a girl a
stone and she'd crush it beneath the heel of her shoe, then string
the shards to wear around her neck, as though she possessed diamonds or pearls. But to Helen stone was that and nothing more;
every book on her desk, every pencil and pen, the clouds, the sky,
her very own bones, all of it turned to stone.

Betsy Chase might have been among those who had never
guessed anything was wrong if Helen hadn't invited her in for a
cup of tea. It was an invitation offered on impulse, a misguided
attempt at civility that was bound to backfire, as it soon was to
do. Waiting in the living room, Betsy heard the kettle whistling

unattended and, when Miss Davis failed to respond, she grew concerned. She went to the kitchen, where she discovered Helen at the table, unable to rise from her chair. The room itself was a disaster, with stacks of newspapers on the floor and un-washed dishes in the sink. In spite of the daily presence of Miss Davis's cat, the mice had all but taken over; they ran through cupboards and pantries alike, as fearless as wolves. The refriger-ator was all but empty; for quite some time Miss Davis had been eating nothing more than bread and butter. In point of fact, after she'd invited Betsy in and put up the water, she had realized she was out of tea as well. It served her right for being so foolish as to think she might have a guest; company, as anyone with sense could tell you, always caused trouble.

"There's nothing wrong," Helen said when she saw the worry on Betsy's face. It was pity that showed there, absolutely the last thing Helen needed.

Betsy went to turn off the kettle, and as she did she thought of Carlin Leander, the pretty scholarship girl who wore the same clothes nearly every day and never went out on weekends with the rest of the crowd. "I think you need some help around here and I know someone who'd be perfect. She needs the money, you need a strong pair of hands."

"There's nothing I want less than help." Helen felt dizzy, but with effort she managed to sound almost as ill-tempered as usual. This time around, however, she certainly wasn't scaring Betsy, who had begun to search the cupboards, at last finding something worthwhile, a jar of freeze-dried coffee.

Although the coffee Betsy fixed was awful, Helen did feel somewhat revitalized after a taste. If asked, she could probably walk to the history department and back right now. She could lift her damned book bag right over her head, couldn't she? In fact, she was feeling so much better she didn't notice Betsy sniffing around the pantry.

"Where are the roses?" Betsy asked. "They're definitely here somewhere."

"There are no roses." As usual, the scent had eluded her. Helen no longer imagined she would ever be able to experience that which had always passed her by, any more than she expected to be granted forgiveness for her youthful mistakes. "It's nothing. Some air freshener. An old sachet."

As she spoke, Helen remembered that Annie Howe had been known for a particular recipe, rose angel cake, baked only on special occasions, Easter, for instance, or to celebrate a student's birthday. Fresh vanilla beans and rose petals were added just before the tins went into the oven, and maybe that was why students all over campus were drawn to Annie's kitchen, with the more forward among them knocking at her back door to beg for a taste. These days, nobody baked anymore, let alone added roses and vanilla to the batter. People were perfectly satisfied with store-bought desserts and quick divorces and watery instant coffee. Perhaps Helen had lived too long; certainly there were days when it felt that way. So much had changed, she wasn't the same person anymore as the girl who'd come to Haddan, that foolish child who thought she knew so much. She used to work all night long; she used to wait up for the sunrise. Now she was lucky if she was able to walk from her kitchen to her bedroom without her legs giving out. She was too weak to go to the market, and could no longer carry her groceries home. Lately there had been nights when she found herself wishing for company or a hand to hold.

"Fine, if you insist," Helen Davis said. "Send the girl."

HARRY McKENNA DECIDED HE WANTED CARLIN as soon as he spied her in the doorway to the library one rainy afternoon. In the low branches of a weeping beech, there sat a pair of phoebes, birds who mate for life and sing an uncommonly tender song. Most birds hide in the rain, but not these phoebes, and the girl with the green eyes was pointing them out to Gus Pierce, who had somehow managed to be lucky enough to be there beside her at the moment when Harry first saw her.

Carlin was laughing, unaware of the rain; her hair was damp and silvery. Harry knew right then that he had to have her, never doubting for a moment that like everything else he had ever wanted, she'd be his before long. He began to attend swim meets, watching from the bleachers, applauding her efforts with such vigor that before long everyone on the team was whispering about Carlin's not-so-secret admirer. In the dining hall, he watched from a nearby table, his interest so apparent and scorching that girls all around him wilted from the heat.

"You'd better watch out," Gus Pierce said to Carlin when he observed Harry McKenna. "He's a monster."

But of course, as soon as she heard that remark, Carlin did what any sensible girl might have done and looked for herself. She expected to find some leering creature, but instead she caught sight of the most beautiful boy she'd ever seen. Yes, she'd been aware that someone had been rooting for her at swim meets, and she'd known that someone had been following her, and she'd surely heard Amy and Pie gossiping about her Harry, how gorgeous he was, how unattainable. But Carlin had had her share of admirers and she hadn't paid the slightest bit of attention to this one, until now. She smiled at Harry McKenna for an instant, but that one look was enough to assure him that with the right amount of patience and fortitude he would get what he wanted.

Harry had always been well versed in seduction; he had a gift for such things, as though he'd been born with compliments tumbling from his mouth. Already, he'd been through the prettiest of the senior and junior girls. There were girls whose lives he had ruined, and those who persisted in calling him long after his disinterest was evident, and still others who waited steadfastly for him to return and be true. He was bored by such girls and primed for a challenge, and it amused him to wait for Carlin outside the gym. When she came out with her teammates, there he'd be, so obvious in his intentions that the other girls would elbow one another and trade jealous remarks. Before long, Carlin had begun to walk back to St. Anne's with him. They held hands before they looked into each other's eyes; they kissed before they spoke. It should not have brought Carlin pleasure to know how the other girls at St. Anne's envied her, and yet it did exactly that. Her skin flushed prettily whenever she felt their resentful eyes upon her. If anything, she had become even more beautiful. In the dark she was luminous, as though she'd been ignited by the other girls' spite and lust.

Of course, she told Harry nothing of her real background; he had no idea that she hadn't the money for a cup of coffee at Selena's, had barely enough for books, and that her wardrobe was sorely lacking. She had no decent socks, no winter clothes, no boots. She'd been forced to take Miss Chase's suggestion and had begun to work for Miss Helen Davis, twenty hours a week of shopping, cleaning, and running errands. As for Miss Davis, she found that having Carlin around was not as dreadful as she'd imagined it might be. This particular girl was quiet and quick. Unlike most of the spoiled students at Haddan, she knew how to use a mop and a broom. Carlin had begun to fix Miss Davis's supper, nothing fancy, a broiled chicken breast perhaps, prepared with lemon and parsley, served with a baked potato. There was a cache of old cookbooks in the cabinets, never used, and she began to experiment with desserts, preparing grape-nut pudding one night, cranberry-prune compote the next, graham cracker chocolate cheesecake on Fridays.

These supper were by far the most delicious meals that had been set upon Miss Davis's table for some time. She'd spent the past fifteen years eating canned soup and crackers in the evenings rather than face the ruckus in the dining hall. "I hope you don't think I'll raise your grade because of this," she said every time she sat down to her supper.

Carlin no longer bothered to remind her employer that she was not in Miss Davis's freshman class, having had the bad fortune to be scheduled into Mr. Herman's Ancient Civilizations seminar, which she found a complete bore. Still, she never replied to Miss Davis's remarks. Instead, Carlin remained at the sink washing dishes, her posture straight, her hair ashen in the dim light. She rarely spoke. She only stirred the pot of soup on the rear burner of the stove, nearly ready for the next day's lunch, and dreamed of a pair of boots she'd noticed in the window of Hingram's Shoe Shop, black leather with silver buckles. She thought about the way she'd lied to Harry McKenna, not only about her family's background, but about her own experience in matters of love. In truth, she had never even been kissed before. She'd been running from love, exactly as her mother had raced straight toward it, headlong and without any doubts. Now, her involvement with Harry had knocked the wind out of her. She had set out on a path she neither understood nor recognized, and because she was accustomed to being in control, the whole world seemed to be spinning past her.

"What's the matter with you anyway?" Helen asked one evening. Carlin had worked for her for several weeks and hadn't said more than a mouthful of words. "Cat got your tongue?"

Helen's own cantankerous cat, Midnight, was sitting on her lap, waiting for bits of chicken. The cat was ancient, and although wounded in many battles, it insisted upon going out every evening. It leapt down and scratched at the door until Carlin went to let it out. Twilight was coming earlier, and the low clouds turned scarlet at dusk.

"I'll bet you're in love." Helen was quite smug about her ability to tell which girls had been stricken each October.

"Did you want custard?" Carlin returned to the stove. "It's butterscotch."

Rather than admit she was desperate for money, Carlin told people she was helping Miss Davis in return for a community service credit. She had planned to tell this to Gus also, if she ever got the chance to talk to him, for it seemed he had begun to avoid her. If he noticed her heading toward him, he'd manage to disappear behind a hedge or a tree, skittering down a path or a lane before Carlin could catch up. He disapproved of Harry, that was the problem, and lately it seemed as if he disapproved of Carlin as well. In fact, it was a single image that kept him at bay. One afternoon, Carlin had leaned over the gate outside

St. Anne's to kiss Harry good-bye, even though she should have known better than to share a kiss over a gate, an action that it is said to cause a rift between a girl and her beloved before the day is through. When she looked up, Carlin saw that Gus was watching. Before she could call out to him, he had vanished, like those foolhardy assistants in magic shows who crawl into trunks to be dismembered and put back together again. Unlike those individuals, however, Gus had not reappeared.

People said he was taking his meals in his room, and that he no longer changed his clothes, and there were those who reported he would not respond even when called by name. Indeed, he had been cutting classes, preferring to spend his time wandering through town. He had gotten to know Haddan's topography, particularly the deserted areas beside the river, where the marbled salamanders lay eggs in the green waters of Sixth Commandment Pond. He walked the lanes, watching as large congregations of blackbirds flew overhead. Plenty of Haddan residents were enjoying the outdoors at this time of year. It was the height of the fall colors, and meadows and woods offered dizzying displays of yellow and damson and scarlet. The fields were thick with blooming redtop and ripe wild grapes; on porches and in backyards all over town there were pots of chrysanthemums and asters in shades of crimson and gold.

In spite of his rambles, August Pierce was not especially drawn to the landscape; rather, his nature walks served only to help him avoid the Haddan School. By the time other students were in morning classes, Gus was already at his regular seat at the pharmacy lunch counter, ordering black coffee. He hunched over the counter as he worked on a crossword, often staying right on through noon. Ordinarily, Pete Byers didn't care for students hanging around during class time, but he had come to appreciate Gus and he sympathized with the boy's trials at school. Pete had been privy to more personal matters than anyone else in town; he knew people's appetites and their downfalls far better than their own husbands and wives ever did, and he was quite familiar with the private lives of Haddan students as well.

People who were well acquainted with Pete knew he didn't gossip and he didn't judge. He was as pleasant to Carlin when she came looking for earplugs to prevent swimmer's ear as he was to old Rex Hailey, who'd been frequenting the drugstore all his life and who liked to chat for an hour or so whenever he came to pick up the Coumadin that would hopefully prevent another stroke. When Mary Beth Tosh's father was going through colon cancer and the insurance money wasn't on time, Pete gave Mary Beth whatever medicine was needed without any charge, happy to wait for the correct payments. In his long career, Pete Byers had seen too many people sick and dying, far more, he would wager, than those young doctors over at the health center in Hamilton ever had. These days, people never seemed to have appointments with the same doctor twice, with HMOs shuffling their patients around as if they had no more weight and importance than playing cards. Dr. Stephens, who had kept an office on Main Street for forty-five years, was a great old man, but he'd closed up his practice and moved to Florida, and even before the doctor had retired, it was Pete people came to when they wanted to talk, and as a matter of fact, they still do.

Pete had never discussed any of the information he'd been told, not even with his wife, Eileen. He wouldn't think of telling her which member of the garden club had bunions or who was trying out Zoloft for her nervous condition. Once, years ago, Pete hired a clerk from Hamilton, a fellow named Jimmy Quinn, but as soon as Pete discovered that his new assistant had taken to perusing customers' medical histories while eating his lunch, Quinn was fired, let go that very same day. Ever since, Pete has kept his ledgers under lock and key. Not even his nephew, Sean, sent up from Boston in the hopes he'd finally fly right and manage to finish out his senior year at Hamilton High, had access to the files. Not that Sean Byers was the type to be trusted. He was a dark, handsome kid of seventeen who had managed to mess up his life fairly well, at least well enough to convince his mother, Pete's favorite sister, Jeannette, to step in and take action when Jeannette had always been the easygoing type, preferring to leave well enough alone. Sean had stolen two cars and been caught with one of them. Because of this, he had been placed under his uncle's watchful eye, away from the evil influence of the city, stuck in the middle of nowhere. When Sean reported to work after a day in Hamilton High School he was always grateful for Gus's company. At least there was one other individual in Haddan who hated the town as much as he did.

"Maybe we should trade places," Sean suggested to Gus one day. It was late afternoon and Sean had his eye on a table of girls from the Haddan School, none of whom would have given him the time of day, despite his good looks. His job in the drugstore spelled instant invisibility to girls like these. "You go to the public high school and come here to wash dishes, and I'll sit in your classes and stare at all the pretty girls."

Gus's hands were shaking from his high level of caffeine and nicotine consumption. Since his arrival at Haddan, he had lost ten pounds from his already scrawny frame.

"Trust me," he assured Sean Byers. "I'd get the better part of the deal. The Haddan School would do you in. You'd be jumping out a window in no time. You'd be begging for mercy."

"Why should I trust you?" Sean laughed. He was a boy who always needed proof, particularly when it came to issues of faith. He had lived the sort of life that had soon revealed that any man who asks for undying loyalty is the man most likely to get you killed.

Gus decided to take Sean's challenge and prove his worthiness. He had ordered one of the hot rolls that had just come out of the oven, exactly what he needed for his next trick. "Give me your watch," he demanded, and although Sean wasn't so quick to hand it over, he was interested. Sean had been through a lot, yet in some ways he was an innocent, which made him the perfect mark.

"Don't you want to find out if you can trust me?" Gus asked.

The watch had been a gift from Sean's mother on the day he left for Haddan. It was the one thing of any worth that he owned, but he unhooked the band and deposited the watch on the counter. Gus made the prerequisite movements to distract his reluctant audience, and before Sean could tell what had been done, the watch was gone. Even the Haddan School girls had begun to pay attention.

"I'll bet he swallowed it," one of the girls declared.

"If you put an ear to his belly button you can probably hear him ticking," another girl added.

Gus ignored them and concentrated on his trick. "Do you think I lost your watch?" he goaded Sean. "Maybe I stole it. Maybe you made a big mistake trusting me."

Sean was now as interested in the manner of the watch's reappearance as he was in the watch itself. All his life he'd thought he knew the score. *Get the other guy before he gets you; live fast and fierce.* But now he realized he'd never thought of any

other possibilities. Maybe the world was not as simple as he'd always believed. He placed both hands on the cool countertop and
he didn't care which customer called for a check or who demanded a coffee-to-go. His attention was riveted. "Come on," he
said to Gus. "Make your move."

Gus took a knife from the counter and cut open the roll on his
plate. There, amidst the dough, lay the watch, steaming hot.

"Man." Sean was impressed. "You're amazing. How'd you do
that?"

But Gus merely shrugged and went to pick up a prescription
Pete had filled for him. Gus wasn't about to tell Sean the details
of the trick. You had to be careful what you divulged, but now
and then even the most wary had to take the leap and put his
trust in someone. Like so many before him, the person Gus had
chosen to confide in was Pete.

"What about my other problem?" he asked the pharmacist as
he signed the insurance form for his medication. It was the thirteenth of the month and Gus had been hoping Pete might help
with his problem at Chalk House.

"I'm working on it," Pete assured him. "I've got a few ideas.
You know if you went to school instead of sitting here all day
you'd show the other fellows how smart you are, and you'd win
out. That's what I've been telling Sean."

"Have you been telling him about the tooth fairy, too? About
truth and justice and how the meek shall inherit the earth?"

Gus was already convinced that the meek were not about to
inherit anything in Haddan, which is why he packed a bag that
evening and went down to the train station. He had no intention
of participating in the barbarous rituals of the Magicians' Club.
At the hour when Nathaniel Gibb was unwrapping a bloody rab-

bit's foot from the cotton handkerchief his grandmother had given him at Christmas, Gus was keeping an eye out for the eight-fifteen into Boston. It was a chilly evening, with frost soon to come. Waiting for the train, Gus thought about his father and the high hopes the elder Pierce still had. He thought about how many hours it took to get to New York, and how many times he'd transferred to new schools, and what a disappointment he must be. And then, before he could stop himself, he thought about Carlin Leander's silver hair and the way she smelled like soap and swimming pools. At a little before eight a police car drove by, and one of the cops leaned his head out the window to ask Gus what he was waiting for. Gus hadn't the slightest idea, and so he took his suitcase and walked back to the school, the long way, through the village. He went past Lois Jeremy's perennial garden, with its mums the size of pie plates; past Selena's, where Nikki Humphrey was closing up for the night. At last, he turned onto the path that would lead him past the weeping beeches Annie Howe had planted long ago. He did so grudgingly, returning to the place he feared most, his own room, for on this dark, blue night when the weather was about to turn, August Pierce had nowhere else to go.

IN THE MIDDLE OF THE AFTERNOON, MAUREEN Brown noticed a patch of bloodied grass in the far meadow. Intent upon searching for specimens for her biology lab, most especially the shy leopard frog, she went farther, making her way past birches and pines, at last inching along beneath thistles and thorns to the place where she found the carcass of a rabbit with one foot cut off. It was the time of year when the leaves on the wild blueberry bushes had become flame red and woody stalks of goldenrod could be found everywhere, in the fields and gardens and lanes. Deeply shaken, Maureen took to her bed after her dreadful discovery. She had to be carried up to her room on the third floor of St. Anne's, and afterward she refused to return to classes until she was allowed to drop biology. Although it was halfway through the term, Maureen was allowed to enroll in Photography 1, bringing with her a hurt expression and absolutely no talent. Due to the circumstances, however, Betsy hadn't the heart to turn her down. Eric couldn't understand her pity.

"Imagine finding something like that," Betsy said to Eric as they walked down to the pharmacy for a late breakfast on Sunday morning. "What a shock."

"It was only a rabbit," Eric told her. "When you think about it, they have rabbit on the menu over at the inn. They boil them and sauté them every afternoon and no one says boo, but find one in the woods and it's a huge event."

"You're probably right," Betsy said, even though she was far from convinced.

"Of course I'm right," he assured her. "The death of a rabbit, however sad, is hardly a federal case."

In the past few weeks, Eric and Betsy had been so overwhelmed by their duties they'd hardly seen each other. In all honesty, they both had been too busy for intimacy and it didn't seem possible to find any privacy at the school. If they were in Eric's rooms, there was always the fear that a student might knock at the door and interrupt. The few times they'd managed to get the least bit romantic, they'd been awkward with each other, like strangers who'd gone too far on a blind date. Perhaps

their estrangement was unavoidable; what little energy they had
was given over to students, such as Maureen, whose traumatic
experience in the woods had taken up most of Betsy's week.

"Did it ever occur to you," Eric said now, "that girl of yours
might be a spoiled brat?"

For a man with a doctorate in ancient history to be embroiled
in the social lives of adolescents who couldn't handle the slightest mishap on their own was ridiculous, Betsy had to agree. Oh,
how Eric wished he were teaching at a university, where students
took care of their own petty problems and the quest for knowledge was the issue at hand. This year the most bothersome member of Eric's class was that boy August Pierce, who was clearly no
student. Gus had been hanging around Eric's door for several
days, obviously wanting something. At last Eric asked if there
was a problem, knowing full well that with students such as Gus,
there was always a problem, and that most of these difficulties
were best left alone.

When Gus skipped the meeting on the thirteenth of October,
there'd been quite a price to pay. When they got hold of him,
they dragged him into the lounge and locked the door. Harry
McKenna had held a lit cigarette to his arm, a brand to remind
him that rules were rules. For days afterward, Gus couldn't get
the odor of his own singed flesh out of his head; he felt as though
he were still on fire, even now, beneath his sweater, beneath his
coat. He had been shoring up the courage to speak to a houseparent for days. "Could I come in for a minute?" he asked Mr.
Herman. "Can I talk to you privately?"

Of course the answer was no. Inviting students into one's
home bred both familiarity and contempt, not at all in keeping
with Haddan's code of etiquette. Gus Pierce, therefore, had

been forced to trot alongside as Eric hurried to the library. The boy coughed and sputtered and began to spin some far-fetched story about his mistreatment. He hated to come to Eric like a tattletale on a playground, and Eric had no choice but to listen as the details spilled out. The sunlight was weak, yet Eric had felt a line of sweat on his forehead. No one on the faculty liked talk such as this; it was anti-Haddan, the sort of inflammatory non-sense that fueled lawsuits and ruined careers.

In point of fact, the kid claiming to be victimized was over six feet tall, not exactly the size and shape of a victim. When Gus pulled up his shirt Eric did note bruises on his back and ribs and a fresh burn Gus claimed had been recently inflicted, but what did any of this prove? Soccer could easily be the cause of such in-juries, as could a wild game of football. More likely, such wounds were self-inflicted, the actions of a student whom many at school had already judged to be unstable. August Pierce was failing sev-eral of his classes; only last week there'd been a meeting wherein his teachers and the dean had discussed his wretched perfor-mance in class. Frankly, the odds were not in his favor, and sev-eral of his teachers did not believe Gus would survive the semester.

"Maybe you need to take responsibility for your own actions," Eric said. "If someone's bothering you, stand up for yourself, man."

Eric could tell the boy wasn't listening.

"I'm trying to help you here, Gus," Eric said.

"Great." The boy nodded. "Thanks a million."

Watching Gus lurch away, Eric felt satisfied that his respon-sibility toward the boy had been met. Certainly, he did not wish to take up Gus's case, even if the other fellows were giving him a hard time. In all probability, he deserved whatever bitter ration was dished out to him. He was annoying and exasperating. What had he expected? That his roommates would admire him, that they'd be delighted to have him among them? Eric knew a hierarchy existed at Chalk House, exactly as it had when he himself was in high school, and again when he'd joined a fraternity at college. Well, boys would be boys, wasn't that the saying? Some were bound to be evil and others bound to be good and the rest would fall somewhere in between, bending one way or another given certain circumstances or friends who led the way.

Pressure, too, was bound to affect people differently. Dave Linden, for instance, never complained about cleaning the seniors' rooms or cheating on their behalf, but he'd begun to stutter. Nathaniel Gibb, on the other hand, found himself suffering from nightmares; one night, he'd awakened to find himself standing at his window, facing the darkened quad below, as if someone with his promise might actually consider leaping from the ledge. Gus's method of dealing with the Chalk boys' offensive was to offer passive resistance. Whether they burned him or berated him, he thought only of empty space, how it went on forever and ever, how every human being was nothing more than a speck of dust. He was not in the least surprised to find that Eric Herman wouldn't help him; rather, he was ashamed of himself to have looked for help in the first place.

And so he let himself be beaten without a struggle; frankly, he did not believe a struggle would succeed. He began to avoid the Haddan campus even more than he had before, spending nearly all his time in town, going so far as to unroll a sleeping bag for the night in the alley behind the pharmacy and the Lucky Day Florist. Sean Byers often met him there in the evenings, for the boys had formed an alliance based on their mutual disdain for their surroundings. They smoked marijuana in the alleyway, breathing in the rank stench of the Dumpster along with the sweet aroma of hemp. Gus was so relieved to be away from Chalk House he didn't even mind the rats that lived in the alley, silent shadowy creatures that searched the garbage for scraps. From this vantage point, he could see Orion rise out of the east at midnight, making everything in town deliriously bright. The great square of Pegasus hung in the sky, a lantern above him as he huddled in the alley. Whenever Gus smoked pot beneath that awesome horizon, he felt shimmery and free, but this was only an illusion, and he knew it. He had grown convinced that his only method of escape was to perfect the trick no one had ever managed before. If he tried, it might be possible to succeed where Annie Howe had failed and at last turn the roses red.

IT WAS CUSTOMARY FOR THOSE WHO LIVED IN the big white houses to place lighted jack-o'-lanterns on their front porches on Halloween night as an invitation to children who might otherwise not be allowed past the front gate. The youngest trick-or-treaters set out in the late afternoon, dressed as pirates and princesses, demanding sweets at one house before rushing on through piles of crumbly leaves to the next. The stores in town had bins of free candy inside their doorways, and Selena's was known to give out free mocha lattes. At the inn, complimentary pumpkin pie was served at dinner, and over at the Millstone, those customers who dressed in plastic masks and clown noses to celebrate the holiday were always the ones who drank so much they needed to be escorted home at the end of the evening.

In the village of Haddan, Halloween was a night that often spelled trouble. Extra police were on duty, with the usual force of eight officers supplemented by a few local men hired for the evening at an hourly rate. Often the sight of a patrol car parked on the corner of Lovewell and Main was enough of a threat to minimize high jinks and misdemeanors. Still some people were bound to go wild on this night of the year, no matter what the consequences. There were always those who wrapped toilet paper around trees, particularly upsetting to Lois Jeremy, whose Chinese cherry trees were exceedingly fragile, and others who insisted upon egging front doors and passing cars. One year, the front window of Selena's was smashed in and another year the back door to the florist's was chopped down with an ax. Pranks such as these could cause more trouble than intended: A shop owner might turn out to have a gun behind his counter, even in Haddan. A car full of teenagers might speed away, taking the turn onto Forest or Pine too quickly, with its occupants winding up in the hospital and the cartons of eggs they'd brought along forgotten and broken to bits.

There are those who will use any excuse to throw caution to the wind, especially on dark nights when goblins roamed Main Street, their hands sticky with chocolate and sugar. This year there was an east wind, always a bad omen, the fishermen say, and it went to work shaking the last of the leaves from the trees. The night was murky, with a threatening mackerel sky, but that didn't deter the boys from Chalk House, who had a party in the woods every Halloween. It was an invitation-only affair, with two kegs of beer Teddy Humphrey had agreed to supply for a surcharge of a hundred bucks, with another fifty thrown in for carting the heavy kegs into the woods.

Carlin Leander had of course been invited. She had become the girl of the moment, the beautiful girl everyone wanted to be near. True, she was maintaining an A average and was thought to be the most talented swimmer on her team, but the most important factor in her sudden rise at the Haddan School was based upon a single fact: She had Harry McKenna. She'd come out of nowhere and won him without trying, infuriating several girls who had been after him for years. Amy Elliot was so envious that she sat at the foot of Carlin's bed, begging for bits of information. Did Harry close his eyes when he kissed her? Did he whisper at such moments? Did he sigh?

Amy wasn't the only girl at St. Anne's who wished she were in Carlin's place, and there were those who had taken to copying Carlin, buying the same boots at Hingram's that she had purchased, quick to forsake their own calfskin boots purchased for three times the price. Maureen Brown had begun swimming laps on weekends and Peggy Anthony now pinned up her hair with silver clips. Only days earlier, Carlin noticed Amy wearing a black T-shirt exactly like one of her own. When the shirt in question was tossed in the laundry basket, Carlin realized it was indeed her own, and that Amy had stolen it from her bureau drawer, a turnabout that gave Carlin the greatest of pleasure, for the coveted item had cost exactly two dollars and ninety-nine cents and was probably the cheapest bit of cloth Amy had ever worn.

And yet there were times when Carlin wondered if she'd outsmarted herself. Harry was her very first love, but, every now and then, she didn't recognize him. She would spy him across the quad and blink. He might have been any one of the senior boys, waving and calling her name. Carlin was reminded of how lonely her mother often seemed, in spite of a series of boyfriends.

Much to her chagrin, Carlin understood that brand of loneliness now, for it was Gus Pierce she missed. His absence pained her; she felt it the way someone might feel a laceration or a broken bone. But what was she to do? Harry had persuaded her it was impossible to befriend Gus. Pierce was doing himself in with his bad attitude. Not a single student would sit next to Gus on those rare instances when he came to class; he stank and muttered to himself, his behavior growing more bizarre by the day. He was best avoided, for who knew where his odd ways would lead him?

On Harry's advice, Carlin hadn't mentioned the Halloween party to Gus, but being at this festive occasion without him felt wrong. She was all dressed up in an outfit she'd borrowed from Miss Davis, having a horrible time, as bored as she was guilt-ridden. A fifth of rum had been added to the punch and one of the kegs had already run dry. Maureen Brown, plastered after two cups of beer, was showing off her orange silk Halloween panties to anyone who wished to partake of the view. As far as Carlin was concerned, the whole lot were nothing more than tiresome drunks, many of them in costume, with plastic vampire teeth and black wigs and white pancake makeup, items that were always on sale at the pharmacy at this time of year.

A bonfire had been lit, and the sound of crackling wood echoed through the glen. Every shadow belonged to someone Carlin wished to avoid—that awful Christine Percy from the swim team, for one, and that horrible Robbie Shaw, who couldn't keep his hands to himself. From where Carlin stood, on the dark edges of the party, she could spy Harry, preoccupied with keeping the bonfire alight, hooting with his friends each time a spray of cinders shot into the sky. Harry, too, was drunk and Carlin guessed he wouldn't miss her if she slipped off for a while. She rid herself of her plastic cup of beer, which was warm anyway, and before anyone noticed, she took off in the direction of the graveyard and what she was sure would be far better company.

The vintage black dress Carlin had borrowed from Miss Davis was made of old-fashioned chiffon, and the skirt collected burrs that tore into the fabric as she made her way across the meadow. Even here, she could hear the raucous party behind her; the bonfire threw thousands of sparks into the sky. By their foul, smoky light, Carlin could see that Gus was exactly where she expected to find him, stretched out on Dr. Howe's marker. He gazed up as she approached.

"Have fun at the orgy?" he called. Aside from the sparks lighting up the sky, the night was pitch dark and Carlin couldn't make out either his expression or his intent.

"It's not exactly an orgy, just a keg of beer and some idiots dancing around a fire." The air had a bitter scent, like woodbine or damp weeds. It was late; carloads of local teenagers had already cruised down Lovewell Lane, spraying shaving cream on poplar trees and boxwood hedges.

"Are you sure you're supposed to be talking to me?" Honesty was painful, and Gus wasn't much in favor of it, but he'd been seriously hurt. True enough, Carlin had told him from the start that she'd never be his, but the fact she'd chosen Harry cut him deeply. It was as though he were bleeding anew each time he saw them together. "Maybe you'd better run along and play."

Carlin went to sit on Hosteous Moore's grave. "What is wrong with you? I came here to see you and you're attacking me."

"Aren't you afraid your boyfriend will see us together?" Gus rubbed out his cigarette and embers skittered across Dr. Howe's headstone into the tall grass, where a hedge of ballerina roses still bloomed weakly. "Bad girl," Gus chided. "I'm sure you'll be punished for not doing as you were told."

In was then, in the midst of this argument, that Betsy happened to come up the path. She had left the faculty party for a bit of air. It had been a silly event; even the costumes had been disappointing. Dr. Jones's toga had been fashioned from a bath towel worn over his suit, and Bob Thomas and his wife had come as bride and groom, decked out in their old wedding clothes, outfits that had caused everyone to point to Betsy, calling out *You're next*, as if it were the guillotine that awaited her in June rather than a lovely reception in the Willow Room. Betsy had stepped outside on the porch for only a moment, but as soon as she had, the wind seemed to be pushing her forward. She walked briskly, the sound of her breathing filling her head; she was doing her best not to be disappointed in Eric. True, he had made certain she was introduced to everyone, and he'd fetched her a drink, but when it came down to it, he'd seemed a good deal more interested in talking to Dr. Jones than to her. It was the bonfire Betsy spied first, and she thought that perhaps the woods had been set alight. Soon enough, the music and laughter assured her that it was only a party. Probably she should have gone over to break up the fun, but instead she went through the meadow and along the path, not realizing that anyone was there in the cemetery until she was almost upon them. Betsy recognized the boy as a tall, gawky freshman she'd occasionally noticed wandering through town during school hours. The angry girl who was smoking a cigarette was Carlin Leander. So many rules were being broken tonight, Betsy would have had just cause to order that both of these students be suspended immediately, had she been so inclined.

"I thought you were smarter, Carlin," she heard the boy say. "But now I see you're just like all the rest."

His words must have stung, for there were tears in Carlin's eyes. "You're just jealous because no one wants you at their parties," Carlin fired back. "No one even wants to talk to you, Gus. They won't sit next to you because you're so disgusting."

"Is that how you feel, too?" Gus said. "Friend."

"Yes, that's how I feel! I wish I'd never met you!" Carlin cried. "I wish I'd told you to leave me alone when you first started bothering me on the train!"

Gus stood up, his long arms drooping by his sides. He seemed tipsy, as though he'd been struck with a fist or an arrow. Watching him, Betsy felt a wave of sorrow; so that's what love was like, she thought, that's what it did to you.

"I didn't mean that," Carlin quickly recanted. Her words had come in the white heat of pain, twisting themselves into sharp little barbs before she'd had time to be measured or true. "Gus, really, I didn't mean it."

"Oh, yes you did." From the look on his face it was clear he could not be convinced otherwise. "You meant every word."

The wind from the east was getting stronger, frightening deer mice and meadow voles into hiding, causing sparks from the bonfire to rise even higher into the black sky. Already, the trout in the river had found their way to the coldest pools in Sixth Commandment Pond, and had settled there for the night, in pockets so deep the wind passed right over them.

Carlin was shivering in her borrowed black dress; she felt frozen inside and out. Gus expected too much, from her and from everyone. "Maybe it would be better if we didn't talk to each other anymore," she told him. They had both been wounded now, hurt in the way only people who care can be. "For both our sakes. Maybe we should just take a break."

"Right," Gus said. "I deeply appreciate your concern."

He turned then and fled. Even though the gate had been left open, he went over the fence, in too much of a hurry to head for the path. Luckily for Betsy he went through the trees. There was nothing for anyone to do but watch him run, like a scarecrow fleeing his field, crisscrossing in and out of the shadows, his black coat flapping behind him. He carried so much suffering that it radiated out in waves. Sorrow is like that: whenever a person runs, it comes after him; it leaves an endless trail of pain. The night was dark and the woods thick with brambles, but Gus paid no mind. Some people were fated to win and some were meant to lose, and he knew exactly who he was. He was the boy who stumbled over his own big feet, the one whose heart slammed against his rib cage as he ran away into the woods, the one she would never love.

A miserable night, but it wasn't over yet, and even a loser such as himself might still win a few rounds. Gus walked with the wind at his back, destroyed and invigorated at the very same time. So Carlin no longer wished to associate with him—in a way, that decision freed him. Now he had nothing whatsoever to lose. The hour was late, and the village had emptied, with most trick-or-treaters already home in bed, dreaming of wicked tricks and of sweets. The bands of unruly teenagers had finished their holiday handiwork, hanging old sneakers on the branches of the elms along Main Street, threading ribbons of toilet paper through the spikes of Mrs. Jeremy's fence. Candy corn had spilled onto the sidewalks, and whatever the wind didn't blow away would be greedily devoured by squirrels and wrens before long. Shutters slammed and garbage cans rolled into the gutters. In front of town hall, the statue of the eagle looked more formidable than usual, having been painted black by a gang of local boys who'd then been forced to wash their telltale clothes in the frigid waters of Sixth Commandment Pond as they tried their best to get rid of the evidence, discovering for themselves that some things can never be washed away.

In the woods, damp piles of leaves whirled up with every cold gust, frightening rabbits and foxes alike. Gus Pierce whistled as he went along, a sparse melody that soon disappeared in the wind. He thought about smoking a little weed, just to take the edge off, then decided against it. He could see the bonfire through the trees; he could hear his fellow students enjoying themselves. Because of this, he avoided the clearing as he made his way along the riverbank. He could hear wood rats nearby, a scurrying and then a splashing as they paddled in the shallows, fleeing his footsteps. Those rats were smart enough to make a trek through Lois Jeremy's garden, then cross Main Street to search the Dumpsters for food; they were far too wary ever to be trapped by the boys from Chalk House the way those luckless rabbits were every year.

Gus thought about Carlin in her black dress and how he'd made her cry. He thought about all the times he'd failed. He paid no attention to the sinking feeling he had that this might be his last chance, nor did he consider the rattle of his own destiny. He was ready to prove himself, on this night above all other nights. Throughout his life, August Pierce had been on the run, but now, at this cold and brutal hour, he began to slow down, ready to stand his ground. For the secret he'd recently discovered was that he had far more courage than he'd ever imagined, and for that unexpected gift, he thanked his lucky stars.

THE RING
AND THE DOVE

THEY FOUND HIM ON THE FIRST
morning of November, half a mile down-
river, caught in a tangle of rushes and reeds
on a clear blue day when there wasn't a
cloud in the sky. Everything but his black
coat was submerged, so that at first it appeared as if something with wings had
fallen from above, an enormously large bat
or a crow without feathers, or perhaps an
angel who had faltered, then drowned, in
the tears of this poor tired world.

Two local boys playing hooky discovered
the body, and they never again cut school
after that day. All these boys had wanted
was to catch a trout or two, when they'd
come upon something drifting in the shallow water at the bend where there was an
old stand of willows. One of the boys

guessed what they spied was only a large plastic bag drifting downstream, but the second boy noticed an object so white it was easily mistaken for a water lily. Only after being prodded with a stick did this flower reveal itself to be a human hand.

When the boys realized what they'd discovered, they ran all the way home and pounded on their front doors, screaming for their mothers and vowing that from this day forward they'd always behave. Twenty minutes later, two members of the town police clambered through the chokeberry and the holly, down to the banks of the Haddan, where they waited uneasily for the forensics team from Hamilton to arrive. Both officers wished they hadn't gotten out of bed that morning, not that either one would ever admit that sentiment out loud. These were men of duty who kept their feelings in check, not an easy task on this day. In spite of the height of the body, it was only a boy who'd been mired in a blanket of duckweed, just a boy who should have been starting his life, walking under the clear blue sky on such a rare and beautiful November day as this.

The detectives who'd been called in made up exactly one fourth of the Haddan police force and had been best friends since second grade. Abel Grey and Joey Tosh had fished from this exact spot when they were eight years old; frankly, they'd cut school plenty in their day. They could easily find the best places to dig for bloodworms, and it would be hard to total the hours they'd spent waiting for a bite from one of the granddaddy trout that haunted the deep, green center of Sixth Commandment Pond. They knew this river better than most men know their own backyards, but today both Abe and Joey wished they were far from Haddan; they would have liked to be back in Canada, where they'd spent time this past July when Joey's wife, Mary

Beth, let him take off for two weeks with Abe. On the very last day of their trip, loons had led them to some of their best fishing. There, on a silvery slip of a lake in eastern Canada, a man could forget all his troubles. But some things are not so easily put aside, the heavy pull of the water, for instance, as they reached with two long sticks to turn the body over. The color of the drowned boy's cold, pale skin. The gasping sound as they hauled him closer to shore, as if it were possible for the dead to draw one last breath.

The morning had felt all wrong from the start; these two detectives shouldn't have been assigned the case, but they'd traded shifts so that Drew Nelson could go to an out-of-town wedding and that act of fellowship had made them the guardians of this dead boy. The notion that snapping turtles or catfish might soon set to work on the remains forced them to act quickly. Both men also knew that eels had a particular taste for human flesh, and it was a relief that none had already begun to feast on the softer areas on the body, the nose and fingertips being favorite places, along with the smooth base of the throat.

When they couldn't bring him in with sticks, Joey Tosh ran to the car to get a tire iron from the trunk, and they used it to dislodge the leg that had become wedged fast beneath a rock. The sun was strong this morning, but the water was frigid. By the time the body had been brought to shore, both officers were chilled to the bone; their clothes had been drenched, their shoes filled with silt. Abe had gashed his finger on a sharp rock and Joey had pulled out his shoulder, and now all they had to show for such backbreaking work was a tall, skinny boy whose milky eyes were so unnerving that Abe went back to the car for his rain slicker, which he placed over the corpse's face.

"What a way to start the day." Joey wiped some of the mud from his hands. He was thirty-eight and he had a great wife, three kids, with another one on the way, and a nice little house over on the west side of Haddan, on Belvedere Street, a block away from where he and Abe grew up. He also had a lot of bills coming in. Recently, he'd taken a weekend job as a security guard at the mall in Middletown for the extra cash. One thing he certainly didn't need was a dead body and all the paperwork it would generate. But as soon as he started to yammer about how much he had waiting for him on his desk, Abe cut in; he knew exactly where Joey was headed.

"You're not weaseling out of doing the report," Abe told him. "I'm keeping track. It's definitely your turn."

Abe had the habit of second-guessing his friend and getting to most places first, and today was no exception. Back when they were in high school over in Hamilton, Abe had been the one all the girls had wanted. He was tall, with dark hair and pale blue eyes and a silent demeanor that could easily convince a woman he was listening to her, when he wasn't really hearing a word she said. He was even better-looking now than he had been in school, so much so that several women in town, grown women with good marriages, had the habit of sitting in their parked cars to watch when Abe took over traffic duty from one of the uniformed officers during lunch hour at the elementary school. Some women in town tended to call the station at the slightest provocation—a raccoon on the front porch that was growling and acting peculiar, or keys accidentally locked in a car—all in the hope that Abe would be sent over and they could present him with a cup of coffee to show their gratitude after he'd chased off the raccoon or unlocked the car. If, after all he'd done for them, he happened to want more than coffee, that would be all right, too. That would be just dandy, as a matter of fact, although the truth was, it was extremely difficult to get Abel Grey's attention. A woman could stand there half naked, and Abe would simply go about his business, asking which window had been broken into or where the suspicious footsteps had last been heard.

In spite of Abel Grey's good looks and the way women threw themselves at him, Joey had wound up married and Abe was still alone. In Haddan, it was common knowledge that any woman looking for a relationship was bound to be disappointed in Abe. He was too unsettled to lose his heart to anyone; he was detached at worst and distant at best, even he admitted that. He'd never once disagreed when a woman accused him of being cut off from his feelings and unwilling to commit. But here, on the banks of the Haddan, keeping watch over the drowned boy, Abe felt a wave of emotion, and that wasn't like him. Certainly, he'd seen dead bodies before; not more than a month had passed since he'd had to extricate two men from a crash over on Main Street, only to find neither one had survived. In a small town such as Haddan, police officers were often called upon to check on older residents when a ringing phone or doorbell went unanswered. On more than one occasion Abe had been the one to discover an elderly neighbor sprawled out on the kitchen floor, the victim of a stroke or an aneurysm.

Up until now, the worst death Abe had seen in his duties as a police officer was the one he'd witnessed last spring, when he and Joey were called in to assist over in Hamilton. A fellow there had beaten his wife to death, then barricaded himself in his two-car garage, where he shot himself in the head before they could jimmy open the door. Afterward, there was so much blood they had to wash down the driveway with a fire hose. One of the forensics guys, Matt Farris, who'd grown up down the street from the murdered woman, went out in the field behind the house to vomit, while the rest of the men did their best to pretend to ignore him, along with all that blood and the smell of death in the mild April air.

That incident in Hamilton had particularly affected Abe. He'd gone out and gotten drunk and disappeared for three days, until Joey finally found him out at his grandfather's abandoned farm, sleeping on the floor in a pile of hay. Considering how people say nothing ever happens in small towns, Abe had seen plenty, but the only other corpse of a teenaged boy he'd seen before today was that of his own brother, Frank. They wouldn't let him look, but he saw Frank anyway, there on the floor of his bedroom, and then, forever after, he wished he hadn't. He wished that for once he'd listened to his father and waited outside, out in the yard where the cicadas were calling and the leaves of the hawthorns were folding in on themselves, in anticipation of rain.

This boy on the riverbank was only a few years younger than Abe's brother was in that horrible year, the one Abe and Joey still didn't discuss. People in the village remembered it as the time there were no trout; a man could fish for hours, all day, if he liked, and not catch sight of a single one. Several environmentalists came out from Boston to investigate, but no one ever determined the cause. That wonderful species of silver trout seemed destined to become extinct, and people in town were simply going to have to learn to accept the loss, but the following spring, the trout reappeared, just like that. Pete Byers from over at the pharmacy was the first to notice. Although he himself was too gentle a soul to go fishing, and was known to faint at the sight of a bloodworm cut in two, Pete loved the river and walked its banks every morning, two miles out of town and two miles back. One fine day, as he headed for home, the river looked silver, and sure enough, when he knelt down, there were so many trout he would have been able to catch one in his bare hands, had he been so inclined.

"I hate waiting around like this," Joey Tosh said now as the two officers stood guard. He was tossing pebbles into the river, frightening the minnows that darted beneath the reeds. "Emily has a dance recital this afternoon and if I don't pick up my mother-in-law by three and bring her over to the ballet school I'll never hear the end of it from Mary Beth."

This particular bend in the river was muddy, with the depth of a wading pool; it wasn't a place for drowning. Abe knelt to get a better look, knees in the muck. Even with the boy's face covered, Abe knew the deceased was a stranger. If there was one thing to be thankful for, it was that he and Joey wouldn't have to drive up to some friend's or neighbor's house, maybe one of the guys they'd fished with for years, and break the news about the loss of a son. "He's not from around here."

Abe and Joey knew nearly everyone born and raised in Haddan, although with so much new construction on the outskirts of town and so many families relocating from Boston, it was definitely getting more difficult to place faces and names. Not long ago, every resident in the village was well acquainted with every family's history, which could easily work against an individual who'd been in trouble. Abe and Joey, for instance, had been wild boys. As teenagers, they'd driven too fast, smoked as much marijuana as they could get ahold of, used fake IDs to buy liquor over in Hamilton, where nobody knew them by name. Perhaps because they were the sons of police officers, they seemed fated to get into as much trouble as possible. Certainly, no one had to talk them into bad behavior; they more than willingly obliged. Ernest Grey, Abe's father, was the police chief until eight years ago, when he retired to Florida, following in the footsteps of his own father, Wright, who had been the chief before him for thirty years, and something of a local hero besides. Not only was Wright the best fisherman in town, he was renowned for his rescue of three foolish kids from the Haddan School who'd skated onto thin ice one unseasonably warm January day, boys who would have surely died had Wright not arrived with a rope and his own obstinate refusal to let them drown.

Pell Tosh, Joey's dad, was a good man as well; he was killed by a drunk driver while parked in his cruiser on Christmas Day in that same horrible year, the one they still didn't discuss, even though they were now grown men, older than Pell had been when he died. They lost Frank Grey in August, Pell in December, and after that the boys were completely out of control. Who knows how long it might have gone on if they hadn't at last been caught robbing old Dr. Howe's house at the Haddan School? When their life of crime was revealed, people from the west side felt they'd been betrayed and those on the east side felt vali- dated. They'd never liked those boys anyway; they hadn't trusted them past the front door.

There had been a big to-do about the robbery, with resent- ments between townspeople and students at an all-time high. Before long, there were fights in the parking lot behind the inn, serious, bloody altercations between boys from town and Had- dan boys. One night, in the midst of a particularly heated con- frontation, the granite eagle outside town hall was tipped over, its left wing permanently chipped. Every time Abe drove past that eagle he was reminded of that year, and this was the reason he usually took the long way into town, down Station Avenue and right onto Elm Drive, thereby managing to avoid both the statue and his memories.

Other boys might have been sent to a juvenile detention facility, but Wright Grey spoke to Judge Aubrey, his fishing buddy, to ask for leniency. To make amends for their wrongdoings, Abe and Joey were forced to commit to a year of community service, sweeping floors at town hall and emptying trash cans at the library, which may well be another reason Abe stays away from both places. In spite of their punishment, Abe and Joey continued to rob houses the whole time they were completing their community service. It was like an addiction for them, an illegal balm that soothed their souls and kept their anger in check. Because neither one could deal with his grief, they did what seemed not only reasonable, but necessary at the time: they ignored their bereavement. They didn't say a word, and they kept on breaking the law. Abe in particular couldn't seem to stop. He wrecked cars and was suspended from Hamilton High three times in a single semester, a record that remains unmatched to this day. He and his father could not be in the same room without an argument breaking out, although both of them knew that every disagreement was based on a single shared perception that the wrong son had died.

In the end, Abe moved out to live with his grandfather, and he stayed at Wright's farm for nearly two years. Wright's house was tilted, with small twisting steps leading up to the second floor, built for a time when men were shorter and their needs less complicated. The place was far more rustic than the houses in town, with a toilet that had only recently been tacked onto the back hall, and a kitchen sink made out of soapstone that was wide enough to comfortably gut a trout or bathe a hound dog. Every spring, flocks of blackbirds roosted on the property, gorging on wild blueberries.

"How can you stand living out here?" Joey would say whenever he came to visit. He'd spend the longest time adjusting the TV antenna to try to pick up some reception on Wright's old set, never with any success.

Abe only shrugged when questioned, for the truth was he didn't like everything about his grandfather's house. He didn't like the mile and a half he had to walk to the school bus, or the canned food they ate six nights out of the week. What he did like, however, was the way dusk fell across the fields, in slats of shadow and light. He liked the sound of the blackbirds taking flight as he slammed through the back door, startling whole flocks into the sky. On mild evenings, Abe went to the meadow where a fence had been put up around a grassy area, unadorned except for some stones streaked with river mica. There was an unmarked grave inside the fence, the final resting place of someone his grandfather had known long ago, a woman who had always been searching for peace. It was peace that could be found here, both by the living and the dead, and Abe wished his brother had been buried out in the meadow as well. Their father, of course, would have never allowed that, for it would have been an admission that Frank had taken his own life. Abe's parents had insisted Frank's death was an accident.

If there were people in town who thought otherwise, then they knew well enough to keep their mouths shut. There was one bad moment at the funeral parlor when Charlie Hale, whose

family had been preparing residents of the village for the journey
beyond for more than a hundred years, implied that burial in hal-
lowed ground might be denied due to the circumstances of
death. It didn't take long for Ernest Grey to set Charlie straight.
Ernest took him outside, out of earshot of the boys' mother, and
he told Charlie precisely what he would do to any self-righteous
fool who interfered with his son's final resting place. After that,
the funeral went ahead as scheduled, with half the town paying
their respects. All the same, it would have brought Abe more
comfort to have Frank laid to rest in the meadow where the tall
grass smelled sweet and clean and wild dog roses climbed along
the fence. It was lonesome out in the grass, but one afternoon
Abe looked up to see his grandfather by the back door, watching.
It was a windy day and the laundry on the line was waving back
and forth with a snapping sound, as though something had broken apart in the sweet blue air.

All during this time, Joey never questioned Abe if he put his
fist through a plate-glass window or started a fight down at the
parking lot of the Millstone. He didn't need to ask why. And although twenty-two years had passed since that horrible year, Abe
and Joey continued to run their lives in the same guarded manner, with Abe especially firm in his belief that it was always best
to leave well enough alone. *Don't get involved* was not just his
motto, it was his creed, or at least it had been until now. Who
knows why sorrow strikes on one day rather than another. Who
can tell why certain circumstances rend a man's heart. There was
no reason for Abe to unbutton the dead boy's black coat, and yet
he did exactly that. He knew the body should be left untouched
until the forensics team arrived, but he folded back the heavy
waterlogged fabric of the coat, and then he uncovered the boy's

face, in spite of those wide-open eyes. As he did so, a breeze began to rise, not that there was anything unusual about cold weather at this time of year; anyone who'd grown up in Haddan knew that a chill on the first of November meant that bad weather would surely last until spring.

"What's your guess?" Joey knelt down beside Abe. "Haddan School kid?"

Joey tended to let Abe do the thinking. With all the pressure he had at home, he had enough on his mind without cluttering it up with suppositions and theories.

"I'd say so." Close up, the boy's skin looked blue. There was a purple bruise on the forehead, so dark it was almost black. Most probably, the skull had smashed into rocks as the current carried the body downstream. "Poor kid."

"Poor kid, my ass." The forensics guys were taking their time and when Joey glanced at his watch he knew he was going to miss Emily's dance recital; his mother-in-law would bitch and moan about how he never thought about anyone but himself and Mary Beth would try her best not to accuse him of not being there for the children, which would only make him feel worse. "No one at the Haddan School is poor."

Kneeling there on the riverbank, Abe felt the cold seep through his clothes. His dark hair was too long, and now it was damp, and perhaps that was why he was shivering. He had always prided himself on being hardheaded, but this situation had somehow undone him. The dead boy was almost Abe's height, but so thin his white shirt stuck to his ribs, as if he were already a skeleton. He couldn't have weighed more than a hundred and twenty pounds. Abe guessed that he was smart, too, like Frank, who'd been the valedictorian at Hamilton High and was scheduled to go off to Columbia in the fall. His whole life was ahead of him, that was the thing; it made no sense for a boy of seventeen to take his grandfather's shotgun and turn it on himself.

Joey stood up and placed one hand over his eyes; he strained to see the road through a grove of wild olive. Still no team from Hamilton. "I wish they'd take all those Haddan kids and launch them in a rocket back to Connecticut, or New York, or wherever the hell it is they come from."

Abe couldn't help but observe that in spite of Joey's resolute family values and the advice he dispensed on how much happier Abe would be if he settled down, the same old belligerent punk endured within. Joey was a scrapper and he always had been. One hot spring afternoon when they were kids, Joey had dived into Sixth Commandment Pond, naked as the day he was born, unaware that a band of Haddan School kids had hidden nearby, waiting for the opportunity to steal his clothes. Joey was shaking with cold by the time Abe found him, but he quickly heated things up that same night. They brought along Teddy Humphrey, who would fight anyone, anytime, anyplace. Before long they had ambushed a group of Haddan students on their way to the train station; they caught them unawares and beat the crap out of them, and it wasn't until much later that Abe wondered why he and Joey hadn't really cared whether or not this was the same troop that had been responsible for the theft at the pond.

"You're still wasting your time hating Haddan kids?" Abe was amazed by how single-minded his friend could be.

"Each and every one. A little less so if they're dead," Joey admitted.

Both men recalled the way old Dr. Howe had looked at them when their robbery case came to trial, as though they were insects, nothing more than specks in his universe. Dr. Howe was ancient by then, so weak he had to be carried into the courthouse, but he'd had the energy to stand up and call them thugs, and why shouldn't he? Wasn't that what they'd been? Yet somehow they were the ones who felt violated each time a Haddan student recognized them in town and crossed over to the other side of the street. Maybe this dead boy would have done the same had he been their contemporary; maybe they would have been mere specks to him as well.

"What's your best guess?" Joey was thinking suicide, but he surely wasn't about to say the word aloud in Abe's presence. Although such incidents were rumored to happen at Haddan—a first-year student breaking under the academic rigors or collapsing from the social pressure—these matters were kept quiet, as had been the case with Francis Grey, the son of the chief of police and the grandson of a local hero as well. There hadn't been an autopsy or a medical examiner's investigation, only a closed casket. No questions asked.

"I'd say accidental drowning." Why shouldn't that be Abe's first guess? Accidents happened, after all, they happened all the time. Look away and a person might trip, he could fall down the stairs, crack his skull upon a stone, pick up a gun he thought was unloaded. It was possible to aim and fire before there was time to think. Death by misadventure, it was called. Death by mistake.

"Yeah." Joey nodded, relieved. "You're probably right."

Abe and Joey would both much prefer a simple accident, rather than a complicated mess, like the death of Francis Grey. People in town who were a mile away at the time swore they could hear the shot. They still remember exactly where they were at that moment, out picking beans in their gardens or up in the bathroom, drawing a cool bath. It was the burning, white center of August, always an unmerciful month in Haddan, and the beech trees and raspberry bushes were dusty with heat. A storm had been predicted, and it was possible to smell rain in the air; neighbors stopped what they were doing, drawn to their windows and front porches. Many thought what they heard that afternoon was thunder. The echo rose above the village for a full minute, which to some people seemed an eternity, a reverberation they continue to hear whenever they close their eyes.

Long ago, in the villages of Massachusetts, stones were set atop the graves of those responsible for their own deaths; such desperate spirits were said to walk, unable to give up the world of the living, the very world they'd denied themselves. In the towns of Cambridge and Bedford, Brewster and Hull, a stake was driven through the heart of any man who had taken his own life, and burials were hastily accomplished in a piece of farmland that was sure to be barren from that day on. There are those who believe that an individual who truly means to go through with a plan to take his own life can never be stopped. Those who live beside rivers and lakes insist it's unlucky to save a drowning stranger, convinced that in the end such a man will surely turn on his rescuer. But some men can't abide standing idly by when a body lies prone on the shore, and Abe couldn't leave well enough alone and wait for forensics. He drew up the boy's sopping white shirt and found a series of thin bloody lines along the stomach and chest. Rocks in the Haddan were sharp, and currents fast, so it made sense that a body would be battered from traveling downstream. The odd thing was, the blood still appeared to be flowing, with trickles issuing from the boy's wounds.

"What's going on?" Joey fervently wished he was someplace else. He'd much prefer to have stayed in bed with Mary Beth, but if he couldn't have that, he'd rather be out directing traffic on Route 17 than standing here with Abe.

"He's not done bleeding," Abe said.

There was a splash in the water and both men turned as if shot. The noisy culprit turned out to be nothing more than a water shrew, searching for a meal, but the little beast had done a fair job of spooking them. The shrew wasn't the only thing that had rattled them. Both men knew that a corpse didn't bleed.

"I'll bet water got under the scrapes and cuts and mixed with blood and now it's all kind of leaking out. He's waterlogged," Joey said hopefully.

Abe had heard that the blood of a murdered man will always liquefy rather than dry, and when he looked more closely he saw that several dark, oily pools had already collected on the ground. It was the scent of blood that had most probably drawn the shrew.

"Tell me I'm right," Joey said.

There was silence except for the flow of the river and the call of a wood thrush. The hawthorns and oaks were almost bare, and although there were still a few stands of flowering witch hazel, the buds were so dry they disintegrated when the wind blew. The marshy riverbanks had already turned brown, and past the tangles of mulberry and bittersweet, the fields were browner still. It was possible to taste death out here, and the taste was not unlike swallowing stones.

"Okay," Joey said, "here's another possibility. We probably shook him up when we took him out of the water. That's why it seems like he's still bleeding." Joey was always nervous around a corpse, he had a sensitive stomach and a tendency toward queasiness. Once, when they'd been sent to retrieve the body of a newborn baby, neatly swaddled in a towel and deposited in a trash container behind the Haddan School, Joey had fainted. An autopsy concluded the infant was dead before birth, but the idea that someone would get rid of a newborn in such a callous way left the whole town disturbed. They never did find out who was responsible, and although Dr. Jones over at the school insisted that anyone in town could have had access to the Dumpster, the Haddan School Alumni Association bequeathed a recreation center to the village that same year.

Such donations always followed a delicate situation at the school. The addition to the town library had been built after some Haddan kids out joyriding rammed their car into Sam Arthur's station wagon when he was driving home from a town council meeting and Sam wound up in the hospital with two fractured ribs and a leg that had to be put back together again with metal pins. The new public tennis courts were the result of a drug bust that involved the son of a congressman. These gifts that had been presented to the town meant very little to Abe. He didn't use the library and one evening of Ping-Pong with Joey and his kids at the rec center was enough to give him a headache. No, Abe was far more interested in this purple bruise on the boy's forehead. He was interested in a wound that would not close.

By now, there was an odd sensation in the back of Abe's throat, as though something sharp had lodged there. It was a shard of someone's death, and it didn't belong to him but was there all the same. Already, Abe's pale eyes had taken on a vacant look, always the telltale sign that he was about to wreck another part of his life. He'd alienate the chief, Glen Tiles, by refusing to let old Judge Aubrey off with a warning when the judge was stopped on his way home from the Millstone, driving with an elevated blood alcohol level, or he'd issue a citation to the mayor for speeding when every cop in Haddan knew to let him go with nothing more than a cheerful warning. These foolhardy actions applied to Abe's personal life as well. He'd break up with some woman who was crazy about him, like that pretty Kelly Avon, who worked at the 5&10 Cent Bank, or he'd forget to pay his bills and not even notice that his electricity had been turned off until the milk in the refrigerator turned sour. If Joey hadn't covered for Abe occasionally, he would surely have been fired by now, in spite of his father's and grandfather's reputations. Today, as he had so many times before, Joey tried his best to cheer Abe out of one of his black moods. On to the next subject, and more hopeful matters.

"What happened last night?" Joey asked, knowing that Abe had taken out a new woman, someone he'd met at the scene of a traffic accident on Route 17. By now, Abe had been through most of the single women in Haddan and Hamilton alike, and they all knew he'd never commit. He had to look farther afield for women still willing to give him a chance.

"It didn't work out. We wanted different things. She wanted to talk."

"Maybe no one's told you, Abe, but talking to a woman doesn't mean you're asking her to set a wedding date. How can I live vicariously through you at this rate? I'm not getting any excitement out of your love life. Too much complaining, not enough sex. You might as well be married."

"What can I say? I'll try to have more meaningless one-night stands so I can report back to you."

They could hear sirens now, so Joey headed up toward the road in order to flag down their backup from Hamilton.

"You do that," Joey called cheerfully as he climbed the hillock.

Abe stayed beside the boy, even though he knew it was risky. His grandfather had warned him that anyone who remained with a dead body for too long ran the risk of taking on its burden. In fact, Abe did feel weighted down, as though the air was too heavy, and in spite of his old leather jacket, he continued to shiver with cold. On this first day of November, he realized just how much he wanted to be alive. He wanted to listen to the river and hear birdsongs and feel the pain in his bad knee, which always acted up in damp weather. He wanted to get drunk and kiss some woman he truly desired. This boy he stood guard over would never do any of these things. His chances had been washed away, into the deepest pools of the river, those places where the biggest trout hid, huge fish, or so people said, with brilliant fins that reflected the sunlight upward, blinding fishermen and allowing for a clean getaway each and every time.

Later in the morning, after the Haddan School had verified that one of their students was indeed missing, the drowned boy was wrapped in black plastic, then packed in ice to prepare him for the trip to Hamilton, since there weren't facilities to do a proper autopsy in Haddan. Abe left work early; he went out behind the station to watch as the ambulance was made ready. Wright's old police cruiser was parked beside the loading dock, kept mostly for sentimental reasons, although every so often Abe took it out for a spin. His grandfather liked to ride along the bumpy river road, and when Abe was growing up Wright often took his grandson along, although it wasn't always trout Abe's grandfather was searching for. He would leave Abe in the car and come back with bunches of blue flag, the native iris that grew along the banks. Those flowers had looked so small when held in Wright's huge hands, as if they were little purple stars plucked from the sky. It was almost possible for a child to believe that if these flowers were tossed aloft, as high as a man could throw, they might never come down again.

Some other big man pulling up wildflowers might have appeared to be a fool, but Wright Grey seemed like anything but. Riding back to the farm, Abe was always instructed to hold the flowers carefully and not to crush them. Every once in a while, on a hot spring day, a bee would accompany the irises into the car and they'd have to open all the windows. On several occasions the bee would stay along with them all the way home, buzzing like mad and flinging itself at the bouquet; that's how sweet those wild irises were. Wright never brought the flowers into the kitchen where Abe's grandmother, Florence, was fixing supper. Instead, he walked out behind the house, to the fields where the tall grass grew and that woman he'd known long ago had found peace. Maybe that's when Abe's suspicious nature got ahold of him. Even back then, there seemed to be a truth he couldn't quite get to, and now he wondered why he hadn't fought harder to find it out and ask the simplest and most difficult question of all: Why?

For the longest time, he had wished there was a way for him to speak to the dead. Not knowing was the thing that could haunt a man; it could follow him around for decades, year after year, until the accidental and the intentional had twisted into a single hanging rope of doubt. All Abe wanted was ten minutes with any boy who might have chosen to end his own life. *Did you mean to do it?* That's all he wanted to ask. *Did you cry out loud, your voice echoing upward through the treetops and clouds? Was it the blue sky you saw at the end or only a black curtain, falling down fast? Did your eyes stay open wide because you weren't yet done with your life and you knew how much more there was to see, years of it, decades of it, a thousand nights and days you would no longer have?*

As the drowned boy was taken to Hamilton, he would surely turn blue along the way, just as silver trout did after they'd been hooked and stowed in a tackle bag, along with empty beer bottles and unused bait. In all probability, there were no facts to go after and nothing to prove, but the boy's wounds nagged at him. Abe got into his grandfather's car, deciding to follow the ambulance, at least for a while. He did this even though he was absolutely certain his life would be a whole lot less complicated if he'd only turn back.

"Are we getting an escort?" the ambulance driver called through his open window when they stopped at the town line. Abe recognized the driver from back in high school, Chris Wyteck, who had played baseball and wrecked his arm senior year. It wasn't yet happy hour, but the dirt lot of the Millstone was already half full. If the truth be told, Abe's car was often parked among the Chevy vans and pickup trucks, a fact Joey Tosh tried to keep from Glen Tiles, as if it were possible to keep any secret in this town for long. But on this November afternoon, Abe didn't have the slightest urge to take his regular seat at the bar. Truth was funny that way; once a man decided to go after it, he had to keep right on going no matter where the facts might lead.

"You bet," Abe called to Chris. "I'm with you all the way."

As he drove, Abe recalled that his grandfather always told him that any man who took the time to listen would be amazed at all he could discover without even trying. A truly observant individual could lie down beside the river and hear where the fish were swimming; why, the trout would practically give directions to any man who was willing to study them. And because his grandfather was the best fisherman in town, and had always given out good advice, Abe started listening then and there. He thought about that dark mark on the boy's forehead, a bruise the color of wild iris, and he decided that for once in his life he'd pay attention. He'd take note of what this drowned boy had to say.

NEWS TRAVELED QUICKLY AT HADDAN, AND BY NOON most people knew there had been a death. After the initial course of hearsay and gossip, people overloaded on rumors and simply shut down. All across campus there was silence in unexpected places. In the kitchen, pots and pans didn't bang; in the common rooms, there were no conversations. Teachers canceled classes; soccer practice was called off for the first time in years. There were those who wanted nothing more than to go about their business, but most people could not so easily ignore this death. Many had encountered Gus at the school, and most had not been kind. Those who had been cruel knew who they were, and there were legions of them. Those who would not sit at his table in the cafeteria, those who would not lend him notes for the classes he missed, who talked behind his back, who laughed in his face, who despised him or ignored him or never bothered to learn his name. Girls who had thought themselves too supe-

rior to speak to him now took to their beds with headaches. Boys
who had thrown volleyballs at him during phys ed class paced
their rooms gloomily. Students who'd delighted in taking pot-
shots at an easy target now feared that their past iniquities had
already been charted in some heavenly book with a brand of
black ink that could never be erased.

Gus's peers were not the only ones to feel the sting of remorse; several faculty members were so sickened when they
heard of Pierce's death they couldn't bring themselves to eat
lunch, although chocolate bread pudding, always a big favorite,
was served for dessert. These teachers, who'd dispensed D's, and
decried the sloppy script and coffee stains that accompanied the
papers Gus had written, now found that beneath the slipshod
penmanship there had been a bright and original mind. Lynn
Vining, who'd been looking forward to failing Gus in retribution
for the series of black paintings he'd executed, removed the can-
vases from a utility closet and was startled to see luminous
threads of color she hadn't noticed before.

An all-school meeting had been called and in the late afternoon the entire community gathered in the auditorium to hear
Bob Thomas refer to Gus's death as an unfortunate mishap, but
word had already spread and everyone said it was suicide. Bereavement specialists were stationed at tables outside the library
and Dorothy Jackson, the school nurse, dispensed tranquilizers
along with ice packs and extra-strength Tylenol. There was particular concern for the residents of Chalk House, who had been
closest to the deceased, and Charlotte Evans's ex-son-in-law, the
psychologist, Phil Endicott, was brought in for an extra counsel-
ing session before supper. The meeting was held in the common
room at Chalk House, and clearly such an action was needed.

The freshmen who had shared the attic with Gus looked especially shaken, and Nathaniel Gibb, who was more softhearted than most, left halfway through the session when Phil Endicott had reviewed only two of the five stages of grief. At the end of the meeting, Duck Johnson advised his charges to go out and make every day count, but no one was listening to him. Because of the thin walls and ancient plumbing, they could all hear Nathaniel vomiting in a nearby bathroom; they could hear the toilet flush, again and again.

On the other side of the green, girls at St. Anne's who had never spoken to Gus now sobbed into their pillows and wished they could have altered the chain of events. Any boy who died in a mysterious fashion could easily become the stuff of dreams: a girl was free to wonder what might have happened if only she had been walking along the river on that last night in October. She might have called to him and saved him, or perhaps she herself might have drowned, pulled down in the midst of her selfless act.

Carlin Leander was disgusted by this sudden outpouring of false sympathy. She herself was boiling, a stew of fury and regret. She refused to attend the dean's assembly; instead, she locked herself in the bathroom, where she tore out her pale hair and raked at her skin with ragged, bitten-down nails. Let others think what they wanted, she knew quite well who was to blame for Gus's death. Her wretched actions on Halloween night had destroyed both Gus and their friendship and gone on to form something cold and mean in the place where Carlin's heart ought to be. To let out all that was vile within, she took a razor from a shelf in the medicine chest. A single strike and drops of blood began to form; another, and a crimson stream coursed down her arm.

All in all, Carlin cut herself six times. Her own flesh was a ledger upon which she measured all she'd done wrong. The first cut was for avarice, the second for greed, the next was for the petty delight she had taken in other girls' jealousies, then one for vanity, and for cowardice, and the last and deepest cut was for the betrayal of a friend.

On the night Gus died, Carlin had dreamed of broken eggs, always a portent of disaster. Rising from her bed in the early morning, she had gone to her window and the very first thing she saw was a dozen ruined eggs on the path below. It was only a silly prank, some local boys had egged St. Anne's, as they did every Halloween. But looking down on that path, Carlin had known that there were some things she could never put back together again, no matter how she might try. And yet once the announcement had been made she could not believe that Gus was really gone. She ran to Chalk House, half expecting to crash into him in the hall even though the place was deserted when Carlin arrived, with many of the boys wanting to avoid the confines of the house. No one stopped Carlin when she went up to the attic, or noticed when she entered Gus's room. She curled up on his neatly made bed. By then the fury and the heat had been drained away, leaving Carlin's tears icy and blue. Her cries were so pitiful they chased the sparrows from the willow trees; rabbits in the bramble bushes shuddered and dug down deeper in the cold, hard earth.

It was nearly the dinner hour when the two officers arrived. Neither man had ever been comfortable on campus and both flinched when their car doors slammed. Abe had already driven to Hamilton and back, Joey had filed their report. Now they were here to meet with Matt Farris from forensics and give the deceased's lodgings a quick once-over. Abel Grey noticed, as he had before, that tragedy tended to create an echo. Coming upon an accident on an icy road, for instance, he'd heard sounds he'd never been aware of before: leaves falling, the crunch of pebbles beneath his tires, the hiss of blood as it melted through snow. At Haddan, it was possible to hear the air moving in waves. There was the call of birds, the rustle of the branches of the beech trees, and just beyond that, someone was crying, a thin ribbon of anguish rising above rooftops and trees.

"Did you hear that?" Abe asked.

Joey nodded toward a boy racing by on a mountain bike that most likely cost a month of a workingman's salary. "The sound of money? Yeah, I hear it."

Abe laughed, but he had an uneasy feeling in his gut, the sort of apprehension he experienced late at night when he found himself looking out his window, waiting for his cat to return. He hadn't wanted the cat in the first place, it had simply arrived one night and made itself at home, and now Abe worried when it wasn't there on the porch when he got home from work. On several occasions he'd stayed up past midnight, until the damned cat had seen fit to appear at the door.

"Hey," Abe called to some kid walking by. Immediately, the boy froze. Boys of this age could always identify a cop, even the good kids with nothing to hide. "Which one is Chalk House?"

The kid directed them to a building so close to the river the branches of weeping willows trailed across the roof. When they reached the house, Abe stomped some of the mud off his boots, but Joey didn't bother. There were several more of those expensive bikes tossed down carelessly. Haddan wasn't the sort of town where bikes needed to be locked, nor front doors latched for that matter, except back when Abe and Joey were on the loose and people from the village went down to the hardware store in droves, asking for Yale locks and dead bolts.

Once the men had stepped inside the dim hallway of Chalk House, Abe's first thought was exactly the one he'd had all those years ago when they were breaking into houses: *Nobody's stopping us.* That's what had always surprised him. *Nobody's in charge.*

Matt Farris was waiting in the student lounge smoking a cig-arette and using a paper cup as an ashtray.

"What took you?" he asked, something of a joke since he and his partner, Kenny Cook, were usually the ones to be late. He stubbed out his cigarette and threw the whole mess into the garbage.

"You're just on time because Kenny's not with you," Joey joked.

"Trying to start a fire?" Abe asked of the smoldering waste-basket.

"Burn the place down? Not a bad idea." Matt was a local boy, with the local prejudice against the school, and it amused him to see bits of trash simmer before he doused it all with a cup of water.

"No photographs?" Abe asked now. Matt's partner, Kenny, was the man with the camera, but he had a second job, over at the Fo-tomat in Middletown, and wasn't readily available for emer-gencies.

"The word from Glen was don't bother," Matt said. "Don't take up too much time with any of this."

Abe managed a look at some of the rooms on their way past the second floor; all were predictably sloppy, ripe with the stink of unwashed clothes. The men went on, stooping as they made their way up the last flight of stairs, trying their best not to hit their heads on the low ceiling. There was even more need to crouch when they reached the rabbit warren of an attic, with paper-thin walls and eaves so pitched a man of Abel's height had to slouch at all times. Even Joey, who was barely five-eight, quickly began to feel claustrophobic. In all those years of imagining how the other half lived, they had never imagined this.

"What a frigging dump," Joey said. "Who would have thunk it."

They'd always believed Haddan students lived in luxury, with feather beds and fireplaces. Now it seemed what they'd envied had turned out to be nothing more than a cramped attic, with floorboards that shifted with every step and pipes that jutted out from the ceiling.

As they neared Gus's room, Abe heard the crying again. This time, Joey and Matt heard it, too.

"Just what we need. Some spoiled brat in hysterics." Joey had less than twenty minutes to get home, eat dinner, placate Mary Beth for all the household tasks he'd forgotten or would forget soon, and get to his job at the mall. "We could leave," he suggested. "Come back tomorrow."

"Yeah, right." Abe took some Rolaids out of his pocket and tossed a few into his mouth. "Let's get this over with."

The nagging feeling Abe had been having was turning sour. He never could stand to hear anyone cry, although by now he should be used to it. He'd witnessed grown men sobbing as they pleaded for another chance after he'd pulled them over for a DUI. He'd had women lean on his shoulder and weep over minor traffic accidents or lost dogs. In spite of his experience, Abe was never prepared for displays of emotion, and it only made matters worse when he opened Gus's door to discover that the person in question was only a girl, one not much older than Joey's daughter Emily.

For her part, Carlin Leander hadn't heard anyone approach, and when she saw Abe, she was immediately ready to run. Who could blame her? Abe was a big man, and he seemed especially huge in the tiny attic room. But in fact, Abe wasn't paying much attention to Carlin. He was far more concerned with a bit of visual information that surprised him far more than a crying girl: the room was spotless.

Carlin had risen to her feet; she judged Abe to be a police officer even before he'd introduced himself as such, and for one stupefying instant, she thought she was about to be arrested, perhaps even charged with murder. Instead, Abe went to the closet, where he found the shirts neatly placed on hangers, the shoes all in a row. "Was this the way Gus usually kept his room?"

"No. His clothes were usually spread all over the floor."

Joey was out in the hall along with Matt Farris. When he peered into the room, he didn't like what he saw. Another rich Haddan student, that was his estimation, a pampered girl likely to burst into tears every time she couldn't get what she wanted.

"Maybe we should bring her down to the station. Question her there." Joey had a way of saying the wrong thing at the right time, and this was no exception. Before Abe could assure Carlin they'd do nothing of the sort, she darted from the room. Down the hallway she went; down the stairs two at a time.

"Brilliant move." Abe turned to Joey. "She might have known something and you had to go and scare her off."

Joey came to look in the closet; he reached along the top shelf. "Bingo." He withdrew a plastic bag of marijuana, which he tossed to Abe. "If it's there, I'll find it," he said proudly.

Abe slipped the marijuana into his pocket; he might or might not turn it in. Either way, he couldn't quite figure how in a room so neat and tidy, a bag of weed could be carelessly left behind. While Matt Farris dusted for fingerprints, Abe went to the window to see the drowned boy's view; they were so high up it was possible to spy birds' nests in the willows, blackbirds soaring above the church steeple in town. From this vantage point, the woods on the far side of the river seemed endless, acres of hawthorn and holly, wild apple and pine. No dust on the window ledge, Abe noticed, and the panes of glass weren't smudged either.

"Two scenarios." Joey had approached to stand beside Abe. "Either the kid killed himself, or he got good and stoned and accidentally drowned."

"But you're not voting for the accident theory," Abe said.

"From what I've heard, the guy was a loser." Having realized what this implied, Joey quickly backtracked, in honor of Frank's memory. "Not that only losers kill themselves. That's not what I meant."

"I wish they'd sent Kenny along." Abe was not about to discuss Frank. Not here. Not now. "I'd still like some pictures of this room, and I know how to get them."

He had caught sight of the woman with the camera on the path below, and he nodded for Joey to take a look.

"Not bad," Joey said. "Great ass."

"It was the camera I wanted you to see, you moron."

"Yeah, I'm sure it was the camera that attracted you."

As she walked across the quad, Betsy Chase was wondering if she'd been among the last to see Gus Pierce alive. She could not get past the moment when he'd scaled the cemetery fence, devastated by his argument with Carlin. Was there anything Betsy herself might have done to save him? What if she had called out as he disappeared into the woods, or if she'd gone forward into the cemetery? Might she have changed what was about to happen? Could a single word have redirected that pitiful boy's fate, much the way a single star can guide a traveler through a storm?

Betsy's camera banged against her ribs in its usual, comforting way, but she felt spacy and light-headed, perhaps the effect of crossing from the dim, shaded path into the last of the day's sunlight. In the shadows a recent death cast, even the thinnest rays could be dizzying. Betsy leaned up against one of the weeping beeches to regain her balance. Unfortunately, the swans were nesting nearby. They were such territorial creatures that anybody with sense would have known to walk on, but Betsy brought her camera up to her eye and began to focus. She much preferred to look at the world through glass, but before she could continue, someone called out to her. Betsy placed one hand over her eyes. There was a man on the front porch of Chalk House and his gaze had settled onto her.

"Is that a camera?" he called.

Well, that much was obvious, but no more obvious than the fact that his eyes were a pale, transparent blue and that he had the sort of stare that could hold a person in place, unable or unwilling to move. Betsy felt akin to those rabbits she came upon when she went walking at dusk; although it was clear they should run, they stayed where they were, frozen, even when it was clear they were in the direct path of trouble.

Abe had begun walking toward her, and so it would be ridiculous to bolt. When he took out his ID, Betsy glanced at the picture. Such snapshots were usually laughable, a portrait from the gulag or the prison farm, but this man was good-looking even in his ID photo. Best not look for too long if Betsy knew what was good for her. He was the handsomest man she had seen in Haddan, and a handsome man could never be trusted to appreciate anything as much as the reflection he saw in his own mirror. Still, Betsy couldn't help but notice a few basic facts as she scanned his ID: his date of birth, along with his name, and the color of his eyes, which she already knew to be astoundingly blue.

Abe explained what he needed and led her toward Chalk House. As Betsy walked beside him, she kept a watch on the swans, expecting them to charge, hissing and snapping at coats and at shoes, but that didn't happen. One merely peered out from the nest, while the other followed along on the path, which encouraged Betsy to quicken her pace.

"I saw Gus Pierce last night," Betsy found herself telling the detective. "It was probably right before he wound up in the river."

Abe had often noted that people gave you more information than they were asked for; without the least bit of prodding, they'd answer the exact question that should have been posed, the important detail that hadn't yet come to mind.

"He was with another student." Betsy tossed some of the crusts in her pockets onto the path, but the swan ignored her offerings and hurried after them, feet slapping the concrete. Thankfully, though, they had reached the dormitory.

"A blond girl?" Abe asked.

Betsy nodded, surprised he would know. "They were arguing in the old cemetery."

"Bad enough for him to kill himself over?"

"That all depends." What was wrong with her? She couldn't

seem to shut up, as if silence might be even more dangerous in the presence of this man than speech. "It's hard to tell how people in love will react."

"Are you speaking from personal experience?"

Color rose at her throat and cheeks, and Abe felt oddly moved by her discomfort. He stepped closer, drawn by a most delicious scent, reminiscent of homemade cookies. Abe, a man who never cared much for desserts, now found he was ravenous. He had the urge to kiss this woman, right there on the path.

"Don't answer that question," he said.

"I didn't intend to," Betsy assured him.

In fact, she had absolutely no idea what people in love might do, other than make fools of themselves.

"You're a teacher here?" Abe asked.

"First year. What about you? Did you go to school here?"

"No one from town goes to the Haddan School. We don't even like to come onto the property."

They'd reached the door, which had locked behind Abe; he pressed his weight against the wood, then ran his gas credit card under the bolt, bypassing the coded entry lock.

"Pretty good," Betsy said.

"Practice," Abe told her.

Betsy felt such a ridiculously strong pull toward him, it was as if gravity were playing a nasty little trick. It was nonsense, really, the way she couldn't catch her breath. The attraction was on the same level as wondering what the postman's kisses might be like, or what the groundskeeper who tended the roses would look like without his shirt. She and Eric would surely laugh about it later, how she'd been roped into police work by a man with blue eyes. It was her civic duty, after all. To keep matters businesslike, she'd make certain to charge the police department for film and processing.

"I see you caught yourself a photographer." Matt Farris introduced both himself and Joey when Betsy was brought up to the attic. With so many people standing around, Gus's room seemed tinier still. Matt suggested they step into the hall and let Betsy work away. "Not bad," he commented to Abe once they had.

Joey craned his neck to get a good look while Betsy set up in Gus's room. "Far too smart and pretty for you," he told Abe, "so I'm not giving out any odds."

Local people liked to joke that ninety percent of the women in Massachusetts were attractive and the other ten percent taught at the Haddan School, but these people had never met Betsy Chase. She was more arresting than pretty, with her dark hair and the sharp arc of her cheekbones; her eyebrows had a peculiar rise, as though she'd been surprised in the past and was only now beginning to recover her equilibrium. The fading light through the attic window illuminated her in a way that made Abe wonder why he'd never noticed her in town. Perhaps that was just as well; there was no point in getting worked up over Betsy, who wasn't even close to his type, not that Abe had ever found his type before. A woman with zero expectations, that's what he'd always wanted in the past. Someone like Betsy would only make him miserable and reject him in the end. Besides, it was too late for him to start any emotional attachments now; he probably couldn't if he tried. There were nights he sat alone in his own kitchen, listening to the sound of the train headed toward Boston, when he'd stuck pins into the palm of his hand, just to get a reaction. He swore he didn't feel a thing.

"Maybe I can get her number for you," Joey said.

"I don't know, Joe," Abe ribbed him back. "You're the one who seems interested in her."

"I'm interested in everyone," Joey admitted. "But in a purely theoretical way."

They were all having a good laugh over that one when Betsy finished and came to join them in the hall. Abe suggested he take the roll of film off her hands, which suddenly made her feel cautious. Perhaps it was all that male laughter, which she rightly imagined might be at her own expense.

"I develop my own film," Betsy told Abe.

"A perfectionist." Abe shook his head. Definitely not his type.

"Fine." Betsy knew when she'd been insulted. "If you want to take the film, take it. That's fine."

"No, it's okay. Go ahead and develop the photos."

"Lovers' quarrel?" Joey asked sweetly as they cleared out of Chalk House.

"No," they both answered at the very same time. They stared at each other, more confused then either one would have cared to admit.

Joey grinned. "Aren't you two peas in a pod."

But in fact it was now time for them to go their separate ways. Matt Farris headed over to the lab in Hamilton, Joey went out to the porch to use his cell phone and check in with his wife, Betsy started back on the path she'd been on when Abe had first called to her.

"You can send the prints to the station." Abe hoped his tone was one of disinterest. He didn't have to go after every woman he met, as if he were some undisciplined hound. He waved cheerfully, the good policeman who wanted nothing but justice and truth. "Don't forget to include the bill."

After she'd gone, he stood there moodily, not noticing the swan's approach until it was nearly upon him. "Scat," Abe said, to no effect. "Go on," Abe told the creature.

But if anything, the swan came closer. The Haddan swans were known for their odd behavior, perhaps because they were trapped in Massachusetts all winter, searching for crumbs outside the dining hall door like beggars or thieves. Huge flocks of Canada geese passed over the village, pausing only to graze on the lawns, but the swans were forced to stay on, nesting in the roots of the willows or huddled beneath hedges of laurel, spitting at the ice or snow.

"Stop looking at me," Abe told the swan.

From the way the bird was eyeing him, Abe thought it meant to attack, but instead it veered off behind Chalk House. Abe watched for a while before he, too, went around to the rear of the dormitory. He didn't want to think about women and loneliness; far better to concentrate on the trail that led from Chalk House's back door to the river.

When Joey was through arguing with Mary Beth about whether or not he had to be in attendance when her parents came for dinner on Sunday, Abe signaled him over. "Something's not right here."

It was watery and dank in this hollow, and although it hadn't rained for days, puddles had collected in the grass.

"Yep," Joey agreed as he slipped his cell phone into his pocket. "It stinks."

"You don't see anything?"

That they could perceive things so differently always amazed Abe. Whereas Joey's attention focused on the clouds over Hamilton, Abe was only aware of the rain in Haddan. Joey spied a car crash, and all Abe noticed was a single drop of blood on the road.

"I see that damned swan watching us."

The swan had settled on the back porch, its feathers fanned out for warmth. It had black eyes the color of stones and the ability not to blink, not even when a jet broke the silence of the darkening sky up above.

"Anything else?" Abe asked.

Joey studied the porch, if only to appease his friend. "A broom. Is that supposed to mean something to me?"

Abe led him to the dirt path heading to the riverbank. It was neatly cared for; in fact, it appeared to have been swept. When they returned to the porch, Abe held the broom upside down; a line of mud edged the straw.

"So they're neatness freaks," Joey said. "They sweep the back porch. I've seen stranger."

"And the path? Because it looks like someone swept that, too."

Abe sat on the back steps and gazed through the trees. The river was wide here, and fast. There were no cattails, no duckweed or reeds, nothing to stop an object traveling downstream.

"Anybody ever tell you you've got a suspicious nature?" Joey said.

People had been telling Abe that all his life, and why shouldn't he? In his opinion, any man who wasn't cautious was a fool, and that was why he planned to think this situation through. He, who had always made certain not to get involved in anyone else's business, was already in way too deep. After he dropped Joey off at home he found himself thinking about boys who had died too soon and women who wanted too much, and before long he had grown confused on the streets he'd known all his life. He took a wrong turn on Main and another on Forest, mistakes any man who'd been distracted by a beautiful woman might make, and before he knew it he was driving down by the bridge where his grandfather used to park, the place where the wild iris grew. After so many years Abe could still find the spot, he could still pinpoint the exact location where the river ran slowly and deeply into Sixth Commandment Pond.

IT FELL TO ERIC HERMAN AND DUCK JOHNSON to meet the boy's father at the airport that evening, a duty no one would have chosen, least of all Duck, to whom talking itself seemed an unnatural act. They set out after supper and drove to Boston in silence. Walter Pierce was waiting for them outside the US Airways terminal, and although he looked nothing like his son, Eric and Duck knew him immediately; they could feel his sorrow before they approached to shake his hand.

They carried his suitcase back to Eric's car, an old Volvo that had seen far too many miles. As they drove, the men talked briefly about the inconstancy of the weather, perfect as they left Logan, but growing gray and windy as they progressed on I93; they then discussed the brevity of the flight from New York. It was the tail end of rush hour when they left the city, and by the time they turned onto Route 17, the road was empty and the sky was midnight blue. Mr. Pierce asked that they stop in Hamilton, at the lab where the autopsy had taken place, so that he might view the body.

Although Gus would be returned to Haddan in the morning,

where he'd be cremated at Hale Brothers Funeral Parlor, his remains readied to be taken back to New York, and although Eric and Duck were both exhausted and sick of the whole affair, of course they agreed to stop. Who could deny a grieving father one last look? But for his part, Eric wished that Betsy had come along. She'd had a bit of disaster in her own life, losing her parents at such a young age. She most likely would have gone along into the lab with the elder Pierce and would have offered some consoling words, the sort survivors yearn to hear. As it was, Walter Pierce went in alone to a building that was dimly lit and understaffed and where it took several tries before the body was located.

Waiting in the parking lot, Eric and Duck grumbled and ate the tinned peanuts Eric discovered in the glove compartment, then went on to share one of the energy bars Duck always kept handy. Proximity to bad fortune made certain people hungry, as if the act of filling their stomachs could protect them from harm. Both men were relieved that Mr. Pierce didn't hold them accountable, considering they'd been the adults responsible for his son. Although Eric and Duck had shared duties as houseparents at Chalk House for five years, they'd never been inspired to communicate much with each other. Now, there was absolutely nothing to say, especially when Mr. Pierce returned to the car. They could hear him crying as they traveled the road leading to Haddan, a band of asphalt that on this dark night seemed endless. From out of nowhere, Mr. Pierce suddenly asked why this had happened to his son. His voice was ragged and barely intelligible. Why now, when the boy's life was only just beginning? Why Gus and not some other man's son? But as neither Duck nor Eric knew the answer, they didn't say a word, and Mr. Pierce went on crying all the way to town.

They took him to the Haddan Inn, relieved to at last retrieve his suitcase from the trunk and say their good nights. After they'd safely deposited Mr. Pierce, Eric and Duck Johnson went directly to the Millstone. Most people from the school opted to frequent the inn, where a martini was expensive and the sherry was forty percent tap water. So be it, people born and bred in town always said, if top dollar and bad service was what the Haddan School folks wanted, but now it was whiskey and beer Eric and Duck were after and a quiet space where no one would bother them. They needed a tonic after an encounter such as the one they'd just experienced, but their usual haunt at the inn was definitely off-limits, as the elder Pierce might decide that he, too, needed a drink, so they found their way to the Millstone, an establishment they'd always looked down upon, although they quickly made themselves comfortable at the bar.

Haddan School people rarely were customers at the Millstone, with a few exceptions, such as Dorothy Jackson, the school nurse, who was thrifty and liked the happy hour when all drinks served were two for one. Some local people took fleeting notice of the newcomers, but no one approached them.

"Too bad Gus Pierce wasn't assigned to Otto House," Eric said to no one in particular. He neither cared about nor valued Duck Johnson's opinion and therefore felt free to say whatever he pleased in the other man's presence, particularly after he'd consumed his first drink, Johnnie Walker, neat, no water, no ice. "Then he would have been Dennis Hardy's problem," he said of the geometry instructor and Otto houseparent, a man no one particularly liked.

"Maybe we should have spent more time with Gus. We should have talked to him." Duck signaled for the bartender and

ordered another round. The coach was experiencing the uncomfortable feeling he sometimes had when he took a canoe out on
the river early in the morning before the sun rose, a time when
the birds were calling as if they owned the world. It was so
peaceful at that hour Duck could feel his aloneness, a huge dark
burden that wouldn't leave him be. A man by himself on the river
might begin to entertain thoughts he didn't want; he might go so
far as to examine his life. Whenever this happened to Duck, he'd
made sure to turn around and start back to shore.

"I did talk to him!" Eric had to laugh in recalling that the boy
had been as noncommunicative outside of class as he'd been in
Eric's freshman history seminar, although whether or not Gus
was truly in attendance depended upon one's point of view. The
kid kept his sunglasses on, and several times he'd had the nerve
to turn the volume of his Walkman up so high the entire class
had been subjected to the driving bass line resonating from the
headphones. Eric had been looking forward to failing Gus
Pierce, and to some extent he now felt cheated out of doing so.

But Eric's biggest concern was the faculty committee. He
worried that this Gus Pierce fiasco would leave its mark. Facts
were facts: Eric was the senior houseparent and a boy in his care
was dead. Not that there was anything to say that Eric, or anyone
else, for that matter, had been negligent. All freshmen had a
tough time, didn't they? They were homesick or overwhelmed by
the workload, and of course they were inaugurated into dorm
life, low men on the totem pole until they had proven themselves
worthy. Hadn't Eric told the boy exactly that? Hadn't he suggested Gus take some responsibility and pull his life together?

"The father's the one I really feel sorry for." Duck Johnson was
as morose as he'd ever been in his life. "The guy sends his kid

away to school, and before he turns around, the kid commits suicide."

That was what everyone was saying, and even Dorothy Jackson admitted that in retrospect there'd been warning signs during his stay in the infirmary: the depression, the headaches, the refusal to eat.

"Who wouldn't feel sorry for him?" Eric agreed, in part to appease Duck, for it seemed entirely possible that after one more drink, the coach would be in tears. Eric called for a last round, even though it meant he and Duck would be late for evening curfew check-in. Still, they might as well relax. Chalk House had already had its tragedy, hadn't it? Surely statistics would keep the place safe tonight without the men's presence.

Had Duck and Eric chosen to take their drinks at the inn on this night, they might have run into Carlin Leander and been forced to report her curfew violation to the dean. But fortunately for Carlin, they were on the other side of town. The village seemed especially quiet when she set out for the inn at a little after nine. The pharmacy and Selena's were already closed and there was very little traffic, only an occasional car passing by, headlights cutting through the dark before fading to black. The branches of the oak trees on Main Street shifted in the wind; leaves fell, then gathered in unruly piles beside fences and parked cars. The streetlamps, fashioned to resemble the old gas variety that preceded them, cast long shadows that angled across the streets in yellow bars of light. It was the sort of night when anyone out walking alone would naturally quicken her pace and arrive at her destination a bit shaken, even if her visit hadn't been fueled by torment and guilt.

The lobby of the inn was deserted, except for a woman posted at the desk who was so out of sorts that when Carlin asked if she might contact a guest, the clerk merely pointed to the courtesy phone. Carlin was wearing her one good dress, a stiff blue sateen her mother had bought on sale at Lucille's. The dress was ill-fitting and so summery that even if Carlin had worn a coat rather than the light black cardigan dotted with little pearl beads she had on, she would have been shivering.

As soon as she'd overheard Missy Green, the dean's secretary, mention that Gus's father had come to town, Carlin knew she had to see him. Now, her hands were sweating as she dialed the number to his room. Fleetingly, she considered hanging up, but before she could, Mr. Pierce answered and Carlin rushed head-long into asking if he would consider meeting her in the bar. The place was empty, aside from the bartender, who served Carlin a Diet Coke with lemon and let her perch on a stool, even though she clearly wasn't of legal age. At the inn, top-notch behavior was presumed; a person with other intentions would surely be better served at the Millstone, which had lost its liquor license twice in the past several years. Darts weren't played here at the inn, as they were at the Millstone; there were no noisy feats of strength, no fried fish and chips, no ex-wives chasing a man down for al-imony past due. Admittedly, the dark booths at the rear of the bar were sometimes frequented by people married to someone other than their evening's date, but tonight even these booths were empty; any affairs that were currently transpiring in Haddan were taking place elsewhere.

Mr. Pierce had been in bed when Carlin phoned, and it was fifteen minutes or more before he came downstairs. His face had the crumpled countenance of a man who'd been crying.

"I appreciate your meeting with me, since you don't know me

or anything." Carlin knew she sounded like some chatterbox idiot, but she was too nervous to stop until she looked into his eyes and saw the grief staring back at her. "You must be tired."

"No, I'm glad you contacted me." Mr. Pierce ordered a scotch and water. "I'm happy to meet a friend of Gus's. He always acted as if he didn't have any."

Carlin had finished her soda and was embarrassed to see there was a ring on the wooden bar. She guessed the management of the inn was used to dealing with such things; there was probably a polish that got rid of the circle so that no one would ever guess there'd been a water mark.

"I think you should know what happened was my fault," Carlin said, for it was this admission of guilt she had come to announce. In spite of her shivers, her face burned with shame.

"I see." Walter Pierce gave Carlin his full attention.

"We had a fight and I was horrible to him. The whole thing was stupid. We called each other names and I was so mad I let him walk away after we fought. I didn't even go after him."

"You can't possibly have been the cause of whatever happened that night." Mr. Pierce finished his scotch in a gulp. "It was all my fault. I should never have sent him here. I thought I knew best, and look what happened." Walter Pierce signaled to the bartender, and when he had his second drink in hand, he turned back to Carlin. "People are saying that it wasn't an accident."

"No." Carlin sounded sure of herself. "He left me notes all the time for no reason. If he'd meant to do it, he would have written to me." By now, Carlin was crying. "I think he must have fallen. He was running away from me, and he fell."

"Not from you," Mr. Pierce said. "He was running away from something. Maybe it was himself."

Because she couldn't seem to stop crying, Walter Pierce reached and took a silver dollar from behind Carlin's ear, an act that so surprised her she nearly fell off her stool. Still, the trick had the required effect; the tears were confounded from her eyes.

"It's an illusion. The coin is in the palm of my hand all the time." Gus's father looked particularly worn down in the dim tavern lighting. He would not sleep that night, and he probably wouldn't for several more. "It's my second profession," he told Carlin.

"Really?"

"He didn't tell you? I teach high school during the week, but on the weekends I entertain at children's parties."

"In New York City?"

"Smithtown. Long Island."

How absolutely like Gus to have concocted a false history, exactly as Carlin herself had. They'd been lying to each other all along, and this realization made Carlin miss Gus even more, as if every untruth they had told had tied them closer together with invisible twine.

Mr. Pierce suggested that Carlin take something that had belonged to Gus, a small keepsake by which to remember him. Although she hadn't planned to ask for anything, Carlin didn't hesitate. She wanted Gus's black coat.

"That horrible thing? He got it at a secondhand store and we had a big fight over it. Naturally, he won."

The Haddan Police Department had returned the clothes

Gus had been wearing when he was found, and these items were stored in Mr. Pierce's room. Carlin waited in the hallway for Mr. Pierce to bring out the coat, which had been folded and bound with rope.

"Are you sure you wouldn't rather have something else? A book? His wristwatch? This coat is still damp. It's junk. What do you need it for? It will probably fall apart."

Carlin assured him the coat was all she wanted. When they said their good-byes, Mr. Pierce hugged Carlin, which made her cry all over again. She cried all the way downstairs and through the lobby, making certain to avert her face as she passed the nasty woman at the front desk. It was a relief to tumble down the stairs of the overheated inn and be in the chilly air once more. Carlin walked the vacant streets in the village, her steps clattering on the concrete. She passed the shuttered stores, then cut behind one of the big white houses on Main Street, traipsing through Lois Jeremy's prize-winning perennial garden before she entered the woods.

The weather had turned, the way it often did in Haddan, the temperature falling a full ten degrees. By morning, the first frost would leave an icy veneer on front lawns and meadows, and Carlin found herself shivering in her thin clothes. It made sense to stop and slip on Gus's coat, even though Mr. Pierce had been right, the wool was still damp. It was also bulky and much too large, but Carlin pushed up the sleeves and pulled the fabric in close, so that it bunched around her waist. Instantly, she felt comforted. She made less noise as she stepped farther into the woods, as though she had donned a cloak of silence that allowed her to drift between hedges and trees.

It was past eleven, and should Carlin be discovered missing

from St. Anne's she would be marked late for curfew. Her penance would consist of cleaning tables in the cafeteria all weekend, nothing to look forward to, yet Carlin didn't bother to hurry. It felt good to be out alone, and she had never been particularly afraid of the dark. These woods might be dense, but they held none of the dangers of the swampy acres she was accustomed to in Florida. There were no alligators in Haddan, no snakes, no possibility of panthers. The most dangerous creature a person might meet up with was one of the porcupines that lived in the hollow logs. Coyotes were so shy of human contact they turned and ran at the scent, and those few bobcats who hadn't been hunted down were even more timid, hiding under ledges and in caves, rightfully terrified of guns and dogs and men.

Tonight, the only animal Carlin came upon was a little brown rabbit, a jittery thing so terrified by her presence it dared not move. Carlin got down on her knees and tried to shoo the rabbit away, and at last it ran off, fleeing with such speed anyone would have guessed it had narrowly escaped being skinned and thrown in a pot. As Carlin went on, she measured her steps; she would need to get used to the way the coat whirled around her legs, otherwise she'd trip and fall on her face. The sodden fabric must have floated out like a lily pad while Gus was in the water, heavy and still. As a swimmer, Carlin was well acquainted with the properties of water—a person moved through it quite differently than she did through the air. If she'd been the one who meant to drown herself, she would have taken off the coat first; she would have folded it neatly and left it behind.

She had already passed the wooden sign that announced Haddan School property and could hear the river nearby and smell the acrid scent of its muddy banks. She could hear a splashing in the water, some silver trout perhaps, disturbed by the sudden drop in the temperature. Out on the river, wood ducks huddled together for warmth and Carlin could hear them chattering in the chilly air. Mist rose, especially from those deep pockets where the largest of the fish could be found. The silver trout were so numerous that if every one had turned into a star, the river would have been shining with light; a man out on a skiff would then be able to find his way past Hamilton, all the way into Boston, guided by a shimmering band of water.

The Haddan River was surprisingly long. It did not stop until it branched in half—one section mixing with the dark waters of the Charles, to then flow into the brackish tides of Boston Harbor, the other end meandering through farmlands and meadows in a thousand nameless rivulets and streams. Even on windy nights, it was possible to hear the current almost anywhere in the village, and perhaps that was why most people in Haddan slept so deeply. Some men in town couldn't be roused even when an alarm bell rang right beside their heads, and babies often didn't wake until nine or ten in the morning. At the elementary school, attendance records were littered with tardies, and teachers were well aware that local children were a sleepy lot.

Of course there were bound to be insomniacs, even in Haddan, and Carlin had turned out to be one of these. Now that Gus was gone, the most she could hope for was to doze fitfully, waking at two and at three-fifteen and at four. How she envied her roommates, girls who managed to sleep so deeply, without a care in the world. As for Carlin, she preferred to be out in these woods at night, although the overgrowth made for difficult going; there were nearly impenetrable thickets of woody mountain laurel and black ash, and fallen trees blocking the way. Before Carlin could catch herself, she tripped over the hem of the black coat, a misstep that pitched her over the twisted roots of a willow. Although she quickly regained her balance, her ankle ached. Surely she would pay for this foray into the woods at swim practice the following day; her time would be thrown off and she'd probably have to visit the infirmary, where Dorothy Jackson was bound to recommend ice packs and Ace bandages.

Carlin bent to rub at the pain and loosen her muscles. It was then, crouching down, still cursing the spiral roots of the willow, that she happened to see the boys gathered in the woods. Peering through the dark, Carlin lost count after seven. In fact, there were more than a dozen boys seated in the grass or on fallen logs. There was a leaden quality to the sky now, as though a dome had been clamped down hard onto the face of the earth, and the cold was surprisingly harsh. Carlin had a funny feeling in her throat, the sort of sulfury taste that rises whenever a person comes upon something that is clearly meant to be hidden. Once, when she was only five, she'd wandered into her mother's bedroom to find Sue and a man she didn't recognize in a pile of heat and flesh. Carlin had backed out of the room and fled down the hallway. Although she never mentioned what she'd seen, for weeks afterward she didn't speak; she could have sworn that she'd burned her tongue.

She had that same feeling again, here in the woods. Her own breathing echoed inside her head and she crouched down lower, as though she were the one who needed to keep her actions shrouded. She might have gone unnoticed if she had cautiously risen to her feet, quietly and safely continuing on to the school before she saw any more. Instead, Carlin shifted her weight to ease the aching in her ankle and as she did, a twig broke beneath her heel.

In the silence, the popping sound of cracking wood was thunderous, reverberating as loudly as a shotgun's blast. The boys rose to their feet in a group, faces pale in the darkness. The meadow they occupied was particularly dismal, a spot where mayflies laid pearly eggs every spring and swamp cabbage grew in abundance. Something of this desolate place seemed to have settled onto the boys as well, for there was no expression in their eyes, no light whatsoever. For her part, Carlin should have been relieved to recognize them as boys from Chalk House, and even more thankful to spy Harry among them, for she might just as easily have come upon a nasty group of boys from town. But Carlin found little comfort in the fact that these were Haddan students; the way they were staring brought to mind the bands of wild dogs that roamed the woods in Florida. At home, when Carlin went out at night, she always carried a stick just in case she happened to meet up with one of these stray canines. She had the very same thought about these boys she went to school with as she did whenever she'd heard the dogs howling in the woods. *They could hurt me if they wanted to.*

To counter her fear, Carlin faced it, leaping up and waving. A few of the younger boys, including Dave Linden, with whom Carlin shared several classes, looked terrified. Even Harry appeared grim. He didn't seem to know Carlin, although he'd told her only nights before that she was the love of his life.

"Harry, it's me." Carlin's voice sounded reedy and thin as she called through the damp air. "It's only me."

She didn't understand how truly unnerved she'd been by those staring boys until at last Harry recognized her and waved back. He turned to the others and said something that clearly set them at ease, then he advanced through the woods, taking the shortest path, not seeming to care what he stepped on or what he might break. Bare wild blueberry and the last of the flowering witch hazel were crushed beneath his boot heels; horsetails and poison sumac were stomped upon. Harry's breath rose up in cold, foggy clouds.

"What are you doing out here?" He took Carlin's arm and drew her close. The jacket he wore was rough wool and his hand had clamped down tightly. "You scared the crap out of us."

Carlin laughed. She wasn't the sort of girl to admit she'd been equally frightened. Her pale hair curled in the damp, chilly air and her skin stung. In the underbrush, one of the frightened rabbits came nearer, drawn by the tenor of her sweet voice.

"Who did you think I was? A scary monster?" Carlin escaped from his grasp. "Boo," she cried.

"I'm serious. Two guys thought you were a bear. It's a good thing they didn't have guns."

Carlin hooted. "What brave hunters!"

"Don't laugh. There used to be bears in Haddan. When my grandfather was at school here, one came crashing into the dining hall. Grandpop swears it ate fifty-two apple pies and six gallons of vanilla ice cream before it was shot. There's still some blood on the floor where the salad bar is now."

"None of that is true." Carlin couldn't help but smile, charmed out of her misgivings about the gathering in the woods.

"Okay. Maybe not the salad bar part," Harry admitted. He'd ringed his arms around her, pulling her back to him. "Now, you tell the truth. What are you thinking, running around in the dark?"

"You and your boys are out here, too."

"We're having a house meeting."

"Right, and you're all the way out here because you're going to cut off puppy dogs' tails and eat snails or whatever it is you do."

"Actually, we're here to drink the case of beer Robbie managed to snag. I have to swear you to secrecy on this, you understand."

Carlin held a finger to her lips, an assurance that she never would tell. They laughed then at all the rules they had broken and how many consecutive suspensions could be levied against them. They had spent several nights in the boathouse, and such romantic evenings, although fairly commonplace among students, would land them in serious trouble if the houseparents ever found out.

Harry insisted on walking Carlin back to school. Although it was after midnight by the time they reached the campus, they paused to kiss in the shadows of the headmaster's statue, a bit of bad behavior they liked to engage in whenever they passed it by.

"Dr. Howe would be shocked if he could see us." Carlin reached over to pat the statue's foot, an act that some people said brought good fortune in matters of love.

"Dr. Howe shocked? You've obviously never heard the guy's history. He'd likely try to score himself and I'd have to fight him off." Harry kissed Carlin even more deeply. "I'd have to break his neck."

The leaves of the beech trees rattled like paper and the scent of the river was powerful, a rich mixture of wild celery and duckweed. When Harry kissed her, Carlin felt as though she herself were drowning, but when he stopped, she found herself thinking of Gus at the bottom of the river; she imagined how cold it must have been, there among the reeds, how the trout must have created currents as they rushed by on the way toward deeper water.

As if he knew, Harry's expression turned sour. He ran a hand through his hair, the way he always did when he was annoyed but trying his best to keep his emotions in check. "Is that Gus's coat you're wearing?"

They were standing on the hourglass path that Annie Howe had designed with lovers in mind, but now they no longer embraced. Red spots had appeared on Carlin's cheeks. She could feel the cold thing inside her chest that had formed when Gus died; it rattled and shook to remind her of the part she'd played in that loss.

"Is there a problem?" Carlin asked.

She had stepped away from him, and the chill she felt had sifted into her tone. Usually, the girls Harry went out with were so grateful to be with him they didn't talk back, and so Carlin's attitude was unexpected.

"Look, you really can't go around wearing Gus Pierce's coat." He spoke to her as he would to a child, tenderly, but with a degree of stern righteousness.

"Are you telling me what I can and cannot do?" She was especially beautiful, pale and colder than the night. Harry was more drawn to her than ever, precisely because she wasn't giving in to him.

"For one thing, the damned coat is wet," he told her. "Look for yourself."

Beads of water had formed on the heavy, black fabric and Harry's jacket had grown damp simply from holding her near. No matter; Carlin already held a fierce attachment to the coat and Harry could tell she wasn't about to back down. He also knew that the more sincere a fellow sounded in his apologies, the bigger the payoff.

"Look, I'm sorry. I have no right to tell you what to do."

Carlin's green eyes were still cloudy, impossible to read.

"I mean it," Harry went on. "I'm an idiot and I don't blame you for being pissed off. You'd be within your rights if you wanted to sue me for stupidity."

Carlin could feel the cold thing inside her beginning to dissolve. They embraced once again, kissing until their lips were bruised and deliciously hot. Carlin wondered if perhaps they would wind up in the boathouse again, but Harry broke their embrace.

"I'd better go back and check on my boys. I wouldn't want anyone to get suspended tonight. They're lost without me, you know."

Carlin watched Harry return the way they'd come, pausing to turn and grin before he stepped back into the woods. Harry had been right about one thing, the coat was sopping. A puddle had formed at Carlin's feet, there on the concrete path. The water that had collected was silvery, as if made out of mercury or tears. Something was moving within the puddle, and when Carlin bent down she was shocked to discover a pretty little minnow, the sort often found along the banks of the Haddan. When she reached for it, the fish flipped back and forth in the palm of her hand, cool as rain, blue as heaven, waiting to be saved. She really had no choice but to run all the way to the river, and even then, she had the sense that it was probably too late. She could race into the shallows wearing her good shoes, ignoring the mud and pickerelweed clinging to her dress, but the minnow might already be too far gone. One small silver fish brought her to tears as she stood there, her best clothes ruined, the water rushing around her. Try as she might, there would always be those it was possible to rescue and those whose destiny it was to sink like a stone.

WALKING ON FIRE

INDIAN SUMMER CAME TO HAD-
dan in the middle of the night when no one
was watching, when people were safely
asleep in their beds. Before dawn mist rose
in the meadows as the soft, languid air
drifted over fields and riverbanks. The sudden heat, so unexpected and so welcome at
this time of year, caused people to rise from
their beds and throw open their windows
and doors. Some residents went into their
own backyards sometime after midnight;
they brought out pillows and blankets and
slept beneath the stars, as disoriented as
they were delighted by the sudden change
in weather. By morning, the temperature
had climbed past eighty, and those few remaining crickets out in the fields called

hopefully, even though the grass was brown as sticks and there were no longer any leaves on the trees.

It was a gorgeous Saturday and time stretched out as it did on summer days. Unexpected weather often caused people to let down their defenses, and this was what had happened to Betsy Chase, who on this morning felt as though she were suddenly waking from a long, confusing dream. As she passed the old rambling roses on campus, some of which were still blooming on this mild November day, she thought of Abel Grey and the way he had looked at her. She thought about him even though she knew she shouldn't. She knew where such entanglements led. Love at first sight, perhaps; trouble, certainly. Betsy preferred the more sensible affinity she felt for Eric; she was not the kind of woman who fell hard and she planned to keep it that way. In her opinion, love that struck suddenly was too akin to tumbling down a well. She would surely hit her head if she took such a fall; she would regret it dearly.

And yet, try as she might, Betsy couldn't shake the attraction. It was as though he were still staring at her, even now, as if he had seen right through her. She tried to think of ordinary things, telephone numbers, for instance, and grocery lists. She recited the names of the girls at St. Anne's, a litany she always found difficult to recall, always confusing well-behaved Amy Elliot with uncooperative Maureen Brown, mixing up Ivy Cooper, who wept every time her grade fell below an A minus, with Christine Percy, who had yet to open a text. None of these tactics did the least bit of good. Try as she might, desire wasn't so easy to dodge, not on a day like this, when November was so very much like June anything seemed possible, even a notion as foolhardy as true love.

Work would help get rid of idle thoughts. It always did the

trick, managing to set Betsy back on track. Since her arrival at
Haddan, she had been so busy with students that she'd had little
time for her own photographs. The entire burden of St. Anne's
rested with Betsy, since Helen Davis was hopeless in that regard,
and Betsy was especially worried about Carlin Leander, who had
been closest to the dead boy. Although there was some debate
about whether or not Gus's death had been caused by his own
hand, despair could be contagious; suicide had been known to
spread through groups. There were always individuals who, already looking for a way out, came to believe they had found a
door leading through the darkness. When one person walked
through, the gate swung open, beckoning others to follow. This
was the reason Betsy made certain to check on Carlin, for she'd
heard the girl was refusing to eat and that she was skipping
classes, letting her grades fall dangerously low. Often, Betsy
found Carlin's bed empty at curfew, and although this was
against Haddan rules, Betsy never reported these transgressions.
She was well aware of the ways in which grief could affect those
left behind. Would it be so surprising if one of the girls in Betsy's
care took it into her head to eat a bottle of aspirin, or slit her
wrists, or climb onto her window ledge? Would Betsy then be expected to follow along after such a student, inching her way
along the roof, grabbing for any girl who might imagine she could
fly away from her sorrows and all her earthly cares?

In all honesty, Betsy herself had had such notions after her
parents' deaths. She'd been sent to live with friends of the family
in Boston, and one evening, at dusk, she'd climbed out to the
roof as storm clouds were gathering. Lightning had been predicted and residents were warned to stay inside, but there Betsy
was, without benefit of either coat or shoes, arms raised to the

sky. The rain was torrential, with winds so fierce that shingles were ripped from the rooftops, and before long gutters were overflowing. When lightning did strike, only blocks away, cleaving in two an old magnolia tree on Commonwealth Avenue that had always been appreciated for its huge, saucerlike flowers, Betsy had crawled back through the window. By then she was drenched and her heart was pounding. What had she wanted out there in the storm? To join her parents? To anesthetize her pain? To feel, for a few brief instants, the power of charting her own fate? And yet, in spite of how weary she was of this world, the very first sheet of lightning had sent her scrambling back to the safety of her room, so quick and so frantic she broke two fingers in the process, a sure sign of her attachment to the glorious world of the living.

Once again, on this oddly warm day, Betsy experienced the same charge she'd felt during that long-ago storm, as if she had not been completely alive and was slowly being shocked back, atom by atom. She unlocked the photo lab, glad to be rid of the burden of her girls if only for a few hours, in need of time alone. She had only one roll of film to develop, the one she'd taken in Gus Pierce's room, and even if the prints had not been commissioned by Abel Grey, she would have done her best. Betsy never rushed in the darkroom, knowing full well that images always profited when given extra care. Breath gave life to all that was human, but light was the force that animated a photograph. Betsy particularly wanted to illuminate this set of prints; she wanted each one to burn in Abel Grey's hand, the way his stare had burned through her. But somewhere along the developing process, something went wrong. At first Betsy thought her vision was failing; surely, it was only a matter of time until she saw straight. But soon enough she understood that her eyesight wasn't the problem. Betsy's vision was still twenty-twenty, just as it always had been, her one true gift, and perhaps this was the reason she'd always had the ability to see what others ignored. All the same, Betsy had never seen anything like this before. She remained in the photo lab for quite some time, but time wouldn't change anything. She could wait for hours or for days, but the same image would remain. There, seated on the edge of the bed, hands folded neatly in his lap, was a boy in a black coat, his wet hair streaming with water, his skin so pale it was possible to see through him, into thin air.

ABEL GREY, A MAN WHO USUALLY SLEPT LIKE a rock, unmovable until dawn, could not get to sleep when the weather changed. He felt as though he'd been set afire, and when at last he fell into an uneasy slumber, he dreamed of the river, as if perhaps its waters could cool him while he slept. His house was closer to the train tracks than it was to the Haddan, and the sound of the 5:45 A.M. to Boston often filtered through his dreams, but it was the river he heard on this night, when the weather was so warm mayflies swarmed the banks, although such insects were not usually seen until the mild, green days of spring.

In his dream, Abe was in a canoe with his grandfather, and all around them the water was silver. When Abe looked down, he saw his own image, but his face was blue, the shade it might have been had he drowned. His grandfather set aside his fly rod

and stood; the canoe rocked from side to side, but that didn't
bother Wright Grey. He was an old man, but he was tall and
straight and he had all his strength.

Here's the way to do it, he told Abe in the dream. *Jump in headfirst.*

Wright threw a rock as far as he could and the water before
them shattered. Now it was clear that this silver stuff wasn't water at all, but a mirrorlike substance that stretched on and on.
Wherever a man might look, he was bound to see himself, there
among the lilies and the reeds. When Abe woke, he had a serious
headache. He wasn't a man accustomed to dreams; he was too
levelheaded and suspicious in nature to put much stock in wispy
illusions or look for meaning where there was none. But today, his
grandfather's resonant voice stayed with him, as if they'd recently
been speaking and had been interrupted in midconversation. Abe
went into the kitchen, started some coffee, and gulped down
three Tylenol. It was early and the sky was perfectly blue. The big
tomcat who had adopted Abe was pacing back and forth, demanding breakfast. All in all, an extraordinary day, a morning
when other men might turn to thinking about fishing or love,
rather than the vagaries of an unexplained death.

"You don't have to get hysterical," Abe told the tom as he
opened a cabinet. "You won't starve."

As a rule, Abe had never liked cats, but this one was different.
It didn't fawn over a person, arching its back and begging for
scraps, and was so independent it didn't even have a name. *Hey,
you,* Abe called when he wanted to get the cat's attention. *Over
here, buddy,* he'd say when he reached for one of those cans of
overpriced cat food he used to say only an idiot would spend
good money on.

Surely, this cat had a history, for one of its eyes was missing. Whether this was the result of surgery or a badge of honor from some long-ago battle was impossible to tell. This injury was not the cat's only unattractive feature; its black fur was matted and its shrill meow brought to mind the call of a crow rather than the purr of its own kind. The one remaining eye was yellow and cloudy and could be extremely unsettling when it fixed upon someone. If the truth be told, Abe wasn't unhappy that the tom had taken up residence. There was only one troublesome sign: Abe had started to talk to the thing. Worse still, he had begun to value its opinion.

When Joey arrived to pick up Abe, as he had every day for the past fourteen years, Abe was showered and dressed, but he was still wrestling with his dream.

"What looks like water, but breaks like glass?" Abe asked his friend.

"Is this a frigging riddle at seven-thirty in the morning?" Joey poured himself a cup of coffee. When he looked in the fridge there was no milk, as usual. "It's so hot out there the sidewalks are steaming. I feel like Mary Beth is going to get after me to put the screens back in the windows."

"Take a guess." Abe got some powdered milk from the cabinet where the cat's food was stored and handed the box to Joey. "It's driving me crazy."

"Sorry, bud. No idea." Though the silverware was unwashed and the sugar only bare scrapings at the bottom of the bowl, Joey added a spoonful to his coffee and poured in the clumpy powdered milk. He quickly drank the potent mixture of caffeine and sucrose, then went to the sink to place his cup atop a pile of dirty dishes. Mary Beth would faint if she saw the way Abe kept his place, but Joey envied his friend's ability to live in a dump such as this. What he didn't understand was the addition of the cat, which now leapt onto the counter. Joey swiped at the animal with his newspaper, but it only stood its ground and mewed, if mewing was what the croaking sounds it emitted could be called. "Do you feel sorry for this disgusting animal? Is that why you have it?"

"I don't have it," Abe said of his pet, as he poured some powdered milk into a bowl, added tap water, then set the dish on the counter for the cat. "It has me." In spite of the tablets he'd taken, Abe's head was pounding. In his dream he had known exactly what his grandfather meant. Awake, nothing made sense.

"What's with you and the riddles today?" Joey asked as they went out to the car, the back door slamming shut behind them.

Joey had driven the black sedan through the car wash attached to the mini-mart on his way over and now sunlight was striking the beads of water on the roof, causing the black metal to resemble glass. Golden light streamed down Station Avenue and a bee drifted lazily over Abe's unkempt lawn, which hadn't been mowed since July. Up and down the street, people were out in their yards, marveling at the weather. Grown men had decided to play hooky from work. Women who had always been proponents of washer-dryers decided to hang their laundry out on the line.

"Will you look at this," Abe said beneath the deep and brilliant sky. "It's summer."

"It won't last." Joey got into the car, and Abe had no choice but to follow. "By tonight we'll all be shivering."

Joey started up the engine, and once they were on their way, he hung a U-turn and drove into town, making a right at the intersection of Main and Deacon Road, where the Haddan Inn stood. Nikki Humphrey's sister, Doreen Becker, who was the manager of the inn, had draped several carpets over the railing, taking advantage of the beautiful weather to beat the dust out of the rugs. She waved as they passed by, and Joey honked a greeting.

"What about Doreen?" Joey kept his eye on the rearview mirror as Doreen leaned over the railing to turn one of the carpets. "She might be the girl for you. She's got a great behind."

"That's the part you always notice, isn't it? I guess that's because they're always walking away from you."

"How did I get dragged into this? We were talking about you and Doreen."

"We went steady in sixth grade," Abe reminded him. "She broke up with me because I couldn't make a commitment. It was either her or Little League."

"You were a pretty good pitcher," Joey recalled.

Abe never took this route through town, preferring to cut across the west side on his way to work, thereby avoiding this part of the village entirely. The inn mostly served out-of-towners, Haddan School parents visiting for the weekend or tourists arriving to see the fall foliage. For Abe, the inn brought to mind the occasion of his brief and heedless involvement with a Haddan School girl. He'd been sixteen, smack in the middle of his bad behavior, in the year when Frank died. He was crazy back then, out at all hours, wandering through town in search of trouble, and as it turned out trouble was exactly what this girl from Haddan was after as well. She'd been the kind of student the school had been known for in those days, pretty and indulged, a girl who had no qualms about picking up a local boy and charging a deluxe room to her father's credit card.

Though he'd prefer to forget the incident entirely, and had never mentioned it to Joey, Abe remembered that the girl's name was Minna. He'd thought she'd said minnow at first, and she'd had a good laugh over that. Still, it had been quite some time since he thought about how he'd waited in the parking lot while Minna checked in. As they drove past the inn, he recalled how she had signaled to him from the window of the room she'd rented, confident that he'd follow her, anytime, anyplace.

"I didn't have time for breakfast," Joey said as they drove on. He reached past Abe for the glove compartment, where he kept a stash of Oreo cookies. He told people they were for his kids, but his kids were never in this car and Abe knew that Mary Beth didn't allow her children sugar. People did that all the time, and what was the crime? Most folks tossed out little white lies, as if truth were a simple enough dish to cook, like eggs over easy or apple pie.

"Let's say it wasn't suicide and it wasn't an accident, that only leaves one thing." Perhaps it was seeing the boy's open eyes that affected Abe so; you had to wonder what the synapses in the brain might have recorded, those last things the boy saw and felt and knew.

"Man, you are really into riddles this morning." It was early and the streets were empty, so Joey picked up speed; he still got a kick out of ignoring the town limit of twenty-five miles per hour. "See if you can figure out this one from Emily. What do you call a police officer with an ear of corn on his head?"

Abe shook his head. He was serious, and Joey refused to hear his concern. Hadn't that always been the way between them? *Don't ask, don't talk, don't feel anything.*

"Corn on the cop." Joey popped another cookie into his mouth. "You get it?"

"All I'm saying is that there is always the possibility of criminal intent, even in Haddan. Things aren't always what they seem."

A bee had managed to fly into the car through the open windows; it hit repeatedly against the windshield.

"Yeah, and sometimes they're exactly what they seem to be. At best, the kid had an accident, but I don't think that's what happened. I went through his files from school. He was in and out of the infirmary because of his migraines. He was taking Prozac and who knows what illegal drugs. Face it, Abe, he wasn't some innocent little kid."

"Half the people in this town are probably taking Prozac, that doesn't mean they jump in the river, or fall in, or whatever we're supposed to believe. And what about the bruise on his forehead? Did he hit himself on the head in order to drown himself?"

"That's like asking why does it rain in Hamilton and not in Haddan. Why does someone slip in the mud and crack his skull open while another man walks by untouched?" Joey grabbed the package of Oreos and smacked the bee against the glass. "Let it go," he told Abe as he tossed the crumpled bee out the window. "Move on."

When they arrived at the station, Abe continued to think about his dream. He usually did let things go; he was pleased to move on with no regrets, a trait to which most of the single women in Haddan could surely attest. But every now and then he got stuck, and that had happened now. Maybe it was the weather that was getting to him; he could hardly draw a breath.

The air-conditioning was officially turned off by town decree every year on the fifteenth of September, so the offices were sweltering. Abe loosened his tie and looked into the cup he'd gotten from the cooler in the hallway. *You can't see water, but you know it's there all the same.*

He was still mulling this over when Glen Tiles pulled up a chair to appraise next week's schedule, spread out in a heap on Abe's desk. Glen didn't like the look on Abe's face. There was trouble brewing; Glen had seen it all before. If Glen had had his way, Abe would never have been hired in the first place. For one, there was his past to consider, and second, he was clearly still unstable, in the good old here and now. He'd work overtime for weeks, then not show for the hours assigned on the schedule until Glen called him to remind him that he was a town employee, not a duke, not a prince, and not unemployed, at least not yet. You never could tell with Abe. He'd let Charlotte Evans off with a warning when she burned leaves—even though as a lifelong village resident she should have been well acquainted with the town bylaws—then he'd slap some newcomers out in one of those expensive homes off Route 17 with a huge fine for doing the very same thing. If Abe hadn't been Wright Grey's grandson Glen would already have fired him for his moody temperament alone. As it was, Glen still considered that option on a regular basis.

"I'm not so sure that boy from the Haddan School was a suicide," Abe was telling Glen, which was the last thing the chief wanted to hear on a beautiful morning such as this. Outside, those birds who hadn't migrated, the sparrows and the mourning doves and the wrens, were singing as though it were summer. "I'm just wondering if it isn't possible that someone had a hand in what happened?"

"Don't even think like that," Glen told him. "Don't start a problem where none exists."

Abe himself was a man who needed proof, and so he understood Glen's hesitancy. As soon as he wrapped up his paperwork, Abe went behind the station for the beat-up cruiser his grandfather used to drive, and headed to the river road. When he got out he could hear frogs calling from the sun-warmed ledges of rock. Trout splashed in the shallows, feeding on the last of the season's mosquitoes, wildly active in the unexpected burst of heat.

Abe liked the idea of all this life renewed on the banks just at the time when it usually faded away. Wrens fluttered past him, perching on the wavering branches of the Russian olives that grew here in profusion. In the coldest part of winter, the river froze solid, and it was possible to skate to Hamilton in under thirty minutes; a really good skater could make it to Boston in less than two hours. Of course, there was always the possibility of a sudden thaw, especially during the cold blue stretches of January and the fitful gloomy weeks of February. Disaster could strike any skater, as it had for those students from Haddan so many years ago. Abe had been only eight when it happened, and Frank had been nine. The roads were slick that day, but the air was oddly mild, as it was today; fog rose up from asphalt and ivy and from the cold, brittle front lawns. People could sense the world waiting beneath the ice; a taste of spring appeared in the form of the soft, yellowing branches of willows, in the scent of damp earth, and in the clouds of stupefied insects called back to life by the sunlight and warmth.

It was a fluke that Wright chose to ride along the river that day when the ice cracked. The old man kept his tackle box and several fly rods in the trunk, always anticipating good fishing weather, and when it came, he was ready. "Let's go looking for trout," he had told the boys, but instead what they'd found were three students from Haddan screaming for mercy and going down in the icy depths, the skates still strapped to their feet.

Abe and Frank stayed in the cruiser and didn't move a muscle, precisely as their grandfather had instructed. But after a while Abe couldn't sit still; he was the brother who could never behave, and so he climbed into the front seat to get a better look, pulling himself up to see over the steering wheel. There was the river, covered with ice. There were the boys who had fallen through, their arms waving like reeds.

He's going to be mad at you, Frank told Abe. Frank was such a good boy, he never had to be told anything twice. *You're not supposed to move.*

But in the front seat, Abe had a much better view of the proceedings. He could see that his grandfather had gotten a length of rope he kept beside the fishing rods in the trunk and was racing down the icy banks, shouting for the drowning boys to hold fast. Two Haddan students managed to drag themselves to shore, but the third was too panicked or too frozen to move, and Wright had to go in after him. Abe's grandfather took off his wool coat and threw his gun on the ground; he looked behind him before he dove in, thinking, perhaps, that this was his last view of the beautiful world. He spied Abe watching, and he nodded; in spite of Frank's warning, he didn't look mad at all. He appeared perfectly calm, as though he were about to go for a swim on a summer day when all that was waiting for him was a picnic lunch set out on the grass.

As soon as Wright dove into the water everything seemed to stop, even though the ice broke beneath him, shattering into thousands of shards, even though the drowning boy's friends shouted from the bank. Abe felt as though he himself were underwater; all he could hear was the sound of ice popping and the silence of the dark, still water, and then, with a whoosh, his grandfather was back, up through the hole in the ice, the boy right there in his arms. After that, everything was hugely loud, and there was a ringing in Abe's ears as his grandfather called for help.

Those Haddan School boys onshore were useless, too scared and cold to think, but luckily, Abe was a bright boy, or so his grandfather had always said. He had played in the cruiser often enough so that he knew how to place a call to the station asking for an ambulance and some backup. Afterward, Wright insisted that he would have turned blue on that riverbank with the foolish kid from Haddan dying in his arms, if his youngest grandson hadn't been sharp enough to call for an ambulance.

You didn't do anything so great, Frank whispered to his brother later on and Abe had to agree. It was their grandfather who was the hero of the day and for once the people at the school and the residents of the village had something on which they could agree. There was a big ceremony at town hall at which Wright was presented with an award from the trustees of the Haddan School. Old Dr. Howe himself, the headmaster emeritus, near eighty by then, sat on the podium. The family of the boy who'd fallen through the ice made a contribution to the town, funds used to build the new police station on Route 17 later named in Wright's honor. There in the crowd, Abe had applauded with the rest of the town, but for months afterward, he couldn't shake the image of his grandfather rising from the water with ice in his hair. *Didn't affect me in the least,* Wright always assured the boy, but from that day on, Wright's toes were blue, as though cold water flowed through his veins, and perhaps that was why he was the best fisherman in town, and, in Abe's opinion, the best man as well. Even now, if someone wanted to compliment Abe, all that needed to be said was that he took after his grandfather, not that Abe would ever accept such a statement as truth. He had the same blue eyes, it was true, and the height, and he chewed on his lip the way Wright always did when he listened to you, but never in his life could Abe be convinced he would be as good a man. Still, he wondered if he'd finally been given a chance at something with this boy they had found, a drowning of his own.

On this rare and beautiful day when men were leaving work early to go home and make love to their wives, and dogs were straying far into the fields, chasing after partridges and yapping with joy, Abe walked along the river. He wished that his grandfather still lived out on Route 17 and that he had the old man to guide him. He thought about the dream he'd had, and the silver river made of glass. He went over all the things it was possible to break: a lock, a window, a heart. He didn't come to it until he'd driven home, later in the day, when the sky had begun to darken in spite of the warm weather. He was parked in his own driveway, too tired and hungry and aggravated to think about riddles anymore when he finally understood his own dream. It was the truth that was always as clear as water until it had been broken; shatter it and all that's left is a lie.

PEOPLE IN THE VILLAGE OF HADDAN HAD LONG memories, but they usually forgave transgressions. Who among them hadn't made a mistake? Who had never run aground of good sense and simple reason? Rita Eamon, who ran the ballet school and was a well-thought-of parishioner at St. Agatha's, had been so drunk at the Millstone last New Year's Eve that she'd danced on the bar and flung off her blouse, but no one held it against her. Teddy Humphrey had been involved in a laundry list of mishaps, from accidentally targeting the gym teacher during archery practice back when he was in high school, to ramming his Jeep into his neighbor Russell Carter's Honda Accord after he discovered that Russell was dating his ex-wife.

Those who had called Joey and Abe hoodlums when they were young were pleased to note what upstanding citizens they'd become. Barely anyone could remember those times when the boys had ordered sodas and fries at the pharmacy with no money in their pockets, then had run for the door, half expecting Pete Byers to race after them with the hatchet he was said to keep by the register, in case of fire. Instead, Pete had merely waited for them to see the error of their ways. One morning, on the way to school, Abe had stopped by and paid off their debt. Several years later, Joey admitted he'd done the very same thing and the joke between them now was that Pete Byers was the one who'd wound up owing them money, with twenty or more years of interest tacked on.

On the second day of the heat wave, Abe was thinking about the grace with which Pete had handled that situation when he dropped by the drugstore, as he often did, for old times' sake and some lunch. There at a rear table, having tea and scones, were Lois Jeremy and Charlotte Evans from the garden club. Both women waved when they saw him. These two usually wanted something or other done for their precious club, which met every Friday at town hall, and Abe did his best to assist them. He felt particularly bad whenever he saw Mrs. Evans, from whose house he and Joey had once stolen three hundred dollars they'd found in a tin stored beneath the kitchen sink. The robbery had never been reported to the police or mentioned in the *Tribune,* and Abe later realized the money had been a secret kept from Mrs. Evans's husband, a well-known bully and bore. To this day, Abe will not write Charlotte Evans a parking ticket, not even on those occasions when her car blocked a fire hydrant or when she parked in a crosswalk. He'll go no farther than issuing a warning and telling Mrs. Evans to buckle her seat belt and have a nice day.

"Something is wrong with the safety precautions in this town," Lois Jeremy called from her table. "I see no reason whatsoever why we cannot have an officer posted outside the hall during our fund-raiser." She treated Abe as she did all civil servants, as though they were her own personal hired help. "Main Street will be a disaster if there's no one to direct traffic."

"I'll see what I can do," Abe assured her.

As a boy, Abe would take offense at the mildest slight, but he was no longer insulted when people from the east side talked down to him. For one thing, his line of work had allowed him to see behind the facade on Main Street. He knew, for instance, that Mrs. Jeremy's son, AJ, had moved into the apartment above her garage after his divorce because the police had been called in several times to quiet AJ down when he'd had too much to drink and was on a rant, scaring Mrs. Jeremy out of her wits.

Pete Byers, whose own wife, Eileen, was well known for her perennial garden, although she had yet to be invited to join the garden club, gave Abe a sympathetic look when Mrs. Jeremy was done with him.

"These ladies would be gardening if you set them down on the moon," Pete said as he placed a cup of milky coffee before Abe. "We'd look up at night and see daffodils instead of stars if they were the ones in charge."

Abe took note of the new boy working behind the counter, a dark, intense kid who had the hooded look of trouble Abe recognized.

"Do I know him?" he asked Pete Byers.

"Don't think so."

The boy was at the grill, but he must have felt the weight of Abe's gaze; he looked up quickly, then, even more quickly, he looked away. On his face was the polecat expression of a boy who knew his fate hung by a thread. He had a scar under one eye, which he rubbed like a talisman, as though to remind himself of something he'd lost long ago.

"He's my sister's boy from Boston," Pete said. "Sean. He's been living with us since the summer and now he's finishing up his senior year over at Hamilton." The boy had begun to scrape the grill, not a job anyone would envy. "He'll be all right."

Pete knew Abe was considering whether he needed to keep his eye on the boy should one of the ladies from the garden club have her car stolen or one of the houses on Main Street be broken into late one night. After he'd studied the specials board above the grill, which on this day included tuna salad on rye and clam chowder, the soup of the day for the past eight years, Abe observed the boy as he drank his coffee. The coffee tasted strange, so Abe signaled to Pete's nephew; here was reason enough to see what this kid was made of.

"What's this supposed to be?"

"It's a café au lait," the boy told him.

"Since when did the coffee here get so fancy?" Abe guessed Sean had gotten into trouble in Boston and that his worried relations had doled him out to his uncle in the country, where the air was fresh and the felonies less numerous. "What's next? Sushi?"

"I stole a car," Sean said. "That's how I wound up here." He had that edgy defiance Abe remembered so well. Anything said to him would be defined as a challenge; any answer would be a variation of a single thought: *I don't give a damn what you say or what you think. I'll live my life as I please and if I ruin it, that's my choice, too.*

"Is this an admission?" Abe stirred his milky coffee.

"I can tell from the way you're watching me, you want to know. So now you know. Actually, I stole two, but I only got caught with one."

"Okay," Abe said, impressed by the sudden integrity of such an answer.

People could be truly surprising. Just when you thought you knew what to expect from another individual, there'd be a complete turnaround; compassion would be offered when acrimony was expected, charity where before there had been only indifference and avarice. Betsy Chase had been equally surprised by the differing points of view that were held when it came to the subject of Abel Grey. Some people, like Teddy Humphrey over at the mini-mart where Betsy bought her yogurt and iced tea mix, said he was the life of the party, and that down at the Millstone there was a barstool that practically had his name carved into the wood. Zeke Harris, who ran the dry cleaner's where Betsy brought her sweaters and skirts, offered the opinion that Abe was a real gentleman, but Kelly Avon over at the 5&10 Cent Bank disagreed. *He looks great and all, but trust me,* Kelly had said, *I know from experience: he's emotionally dead.*

Betsy had not planned to refer to Abe as she ran errands in the village, but his name kept coming up, perhaps because she had him on her mind. She had been so disturbed by the photograph she'd developed, that she'd gone ahead and looked up Abe's number in the Haddan phone book. Twice she had dialed, then hung up before he could answer. After that, she couldn't seem to stop talking about him. She discussed him at the florist's, where she'd stopped to buy a pot of ivy for her windowsill, and had thereby discovered that Abe always bought a wreath at Christmastime rather than a tree. She had found out from Nikki Humphrey that he liked his coffee with milk but not sugar, and that as a kid he'd been crazy for the chocolate crullers that he nowadays eschewed in favor of a plain, buttered roll.

Although Betsy had fully expected to discover more details about him when she walked into the pharmacy to buy the *Tribune,* she hadn't expected to find the man himself there at the counter, drinking his second café au lait. It seemed to Betsy that she had summoned him by stitching together the facts of his life. By now, she knew as much about him as people who'd known him all his life did; she could even name the brand of socks he preferred, clued in by the clerk at Hingram's.

"There's no point in hiding," Abe called when he noticed her ducking behind the newspaper racks.

Betsy came to the counter and ordered a coffee, black; though she usually took sugar and cream she felt the undiluted caffeine might help her maintain some degree of prudence. Luckily, she had her backpack with her. "I've got the photos for you." She handed Abe the packet of perfectly ordinary prints she'd been carrying around.

Abe leafed through the photos, biting down on his lip, exactly as Wright used to whenever he was deliberating.

"I've got one other photograph that I took that day." Color had risen in Betsy's face. "You're going to probably think I'm crazy." She'd held the singular print back, afraid to present it, but now that she'd seen how thoughtful he was, she had reconsidered.

"Try me," Abe urged.

"I know it sounds crazy, but I think I've got a picture of Gus Pierce."

Abe nodded, waiting for the rest.

"After he was dead."

"Okay," Abe said reasonably. "Show me."

Betsy had studied the photograph, waiting for the image to disappear, but there he was still, all these days later, the boy in the black coat. At the top edges of the print, flashes of light had been recorded. These weren't errors in the developing process, which usually showed up in blotches of white, but a distinct illumination hovering below the ceiling of the room, as though a field of energy had been trapped inside. Betsy had always yearned to go beyond the obvious and reveal what others might not see. Now she had done exactly that, for what she believed she'd handed over was a portrait of a ghost.

"There was a mix-up with the film," Abe quickly decided. "Some old photograph already on the film was overlaid on top of the one you took in his room. That would explain it, wouldn't it?"

"You mean a double exposure?"

"That's what it is." She had him going for a minute there. He'd actually felt the cold hand that people say reaches out when the border between this world and the next splits apart. "It's just a mistake."

"There's only one problem with that theory. The water. He's drenched. How do you explain that?"

They both stared at the photograph. Streams of water ran down Gus's face, as if he'd risen from the river, as if he'd been held down too long and had already turned blue. There were the weeds threaded through his hair, and his clothes were so sopping that a puddle of water had collected on the floorboards at his feet.

"Do you mind if I keep this for a while?"

When Betsy agreed, Abe placed the photograph in his jacket pocket. It was his imagination, of course, but it was almost as though he could feel the damp outline of the image against his ribs. "That girl who was in Gus's room before you took the photographs, I thought I might talk to her."

"Carlin." Betsy nodded. "She's usually at the pool. I think she was Gus's only friend."

"Sometimes one is enough." Abe paid for their coffees. "If it's the right person."

They went out into the sunlight where a few bees rumbled around the white chrysanthemums Pete's wife, Eileen, had set in an earthenware pot in front of the store. Across the street was Rita Eamon's ballet school, where Joey's daughter Emily took lessons, as well as Zeke Harris's dry-cleaning shop, established more than forty years earlier. Abe knew every shop owner and every street corner, just as he knew that anyone born and raised in this village who was foolish enough to get involved with someone from the Haddan School deserved whatever consequences he received.

"We could have dinner sometime," Abe suggested. Immediately, he rethought the invitation, which sounded too serious and too formal. "No big deal," he amended. "Just some food on a plate."

Betsy laughed, but her expression was cloudy. "Actually, I don't think we should see each other again."

Well, he'd gone and done it, made a complete idiot of himself. He noticed that one of those damned swans from the school was traipsing along the sidewalk across the street, hissing at Nikki Humphrey, who had been on her way over to the 5&10 Cent Bank to make a deposit, but had become too alarmed to proceed.

"I'm getting married," Betsy went on to explain. She was smart enough to know that not everything a person might want was necessarily good for her. What if she were to sit down with a dozen chocolate bars and devour each one? What if she drank red wine until she swooned? "June seventeenth. The Willow Room at the inn."

Across the street, Nikki Humphrey was waving her hands around, trying her best to shoo away the swan. Abe should have gone over to help her out, but he remained in the doorway of the pharmacy. Plenty of people arranged weddings, but not every one went off exactly as planned.

"I'm not asking to be invited to the reception," he commented.

"Good." Betsy laughed. "You won't be."

She must be insane to be standing out here with him; she'd be better off anywhere else. But even on a beautiful day, it was impossible to predict behavior, human or otherwise. The swan across the street, for instance, provoked by the crowds and the heat, was going wild. It had scared Nikki Humphrey off the sidewalk and into the Lucky Day flower shop and was now crossing Main Street against the green light. Several cars screeched to a halt. People who couldn't see the swan leaned on their horns, wishing an official was present to direct traffic. Abe should have sorted out the mess himself—someone could get hurt with that swan flapping around in the middle of the street—yet he stayed where he was.

"You could invite me to something else," he said, as if he were a man who asked for rejection on a regular basis. "Anything other than a wedding, and I'll be there."

Betsy was unable to gauge whether or not he truly meant this declaration. She was staring at the swan, which had stopped in the middle of the road, plucking at its feathers and causing a tie-up of cars that reached all the way to Deacon Road.

"I'll think it over," she said, lightly. "I'll let you know."

"Do that," Abe said when she walked away. "Good to see you," he called, as if they were merely two people who had cordially exchanged recipes or household tips, suggesting vinegar for sunburn, perhaps, or olive oil for damaged woodwork.

Mike Randall, the president of the 5&10 Cent Bank, had come out to the street in his shirtsleeves, his suit jacket in hand. He went right up to the swan and shook his coat as though it were a matador's cape until at last the stubborn bird took flight, hissing as it rose into the air, and still sputtering angrily when it landed on the walkway in front of Mrs. Jeremy's house.

"Hey," Mike called to Abe when he caught sight of him, all moony and distracted in front of the pharmacy, standing in a square of sunlight and blinking his eyes like a lovesick boy. "What were you waiting for? A head-on collision?"

It was more like a train wreck, actually, the kind Abe had seen back when he was a kid and the train into Boston jumped the rails. For weeks afterward bits of clothing and shoes without soles could be found along the tracks. Abe had accompanied his grandfather to help search for personal items, such as wallets and keys. The accident was unavoidable and unstoppable; it had taken people unawares, so that they were tying their shoes or catching a catnap, completely unprepared for what was to come.

Late in the day, when the sky was turning inky and the last of the geese flew above Haddan traveling south, Abe drove over to the school and parked in the lot closest to the river. By then, the weather had begun to change, as everyone knew it would. Before long, all traces of the heat wave would be gone. Abe went around a mud puddle that would freeze solid by morning. He knew his way to the gym; local kids had always been envious of the basketball court and especially coveted the indoor pool. One night, when they were seniors in high school, Abe and Joey and Teddy Humphrey, along with half a dozen other guys they hung out with, spent an evening getting loaded, thinking of new ways to stir up trouble. Somehow, they'd chosen the Haddan pool as their target. They'd walked in during swim practice as though they owned the place, drunk on beer and fury, brimming with the sort of courage numbers can bring. They'd stripped off their clothes and dived right in, shouting and cursing, having a grand old time, naked as the day they were born.

The Haddan students who'd been swimming laps got out as fast as they could. Abe still recalled the look on one girl's face, the contempt in her glare. They were pigs to her, nothing more, morons who were easily amused by their own stupid stunts and would never amount to anything. One guy, Abe could no longer remember who, got up on the ladder and peed into the deep end, then

was wildly applauded for his efforts. It was then Abe found himself
agreeing with the girl who had considered them so disgusting.

He was the first to get out of the pool; he pulled his jeans and
T-shirt over his wet body, and it was lucky for them all that he
did, for someone had phoned the police and Abe was the one
who heard the sirens. He alerted his friends and they hightailed
it out of the gym before Ernest could walk in and blame Abe for
everything, the way he always did back then.

This evening, Abe was well within his rights as an officer to
come looking for Carlin at the pool, yet he felt the same trepida-
tion he had all those years ago. He went along the tiled corridor
until he reached the glass partition through which it was possible
to peer down at the swimmers. The girls on the team all wore
black bathing suits and caps, but he could pick Carlin out right
away. It was her attitude that distinguished her from the others.
She was a strong swimmer, clearly the best on the team; she had
talent, but most likely it was ambition that drove her, for when
other girls got out of the pool, Carlin kept on, exerting herself in
a way the others did not.

The rest of her teammates were already showered and
dressed by the time Carlin dragged herself out of the pool. She
sat on the ledge and pulled off her goggles; her black bathing cap
made her head look as sleek as a seal's. She swung her legs back
and forth in the water and closed her burning eyes; her heart was
pounding from exertion, her arms ached.

When she heard someone rap on the glass, Carlin looked up,
expecting to see Harry, but instead, she spied Abel Grey. Carlin
should have been upset to have a cop come looking for her, but
actually she was relieved. Being with Harry had been difficult
lately; whenever they were together, she had to hide a piece of

herself: all her sorrow, all her grief. She had stopped going to the dining hall at mealtimes, in part because she had no interest in food, but also as a way to avoid Harry. Unfortunately, he still expected Carlin to be exactly as she was when he first saw her on the library steps, but she wasn't that girl anymore. Now, she was the friend left behind, the one who couldn't stop wondering what it might be like to see light filtering deep underwater, to breathe in water lilies and stones rather than air.

"Harry was looking for you," Amy would inevitably say when Carlin came in at night from walking the paths Gus had taken, along the lanes and through the alleyways. "I don't know why you treat him the way you do."

Often, when Harry phoned or came calling, Carlin would have Amy tell him she was asleep or suffering from a migraine. "You're very peculiar," Amy marveled at such times. "Which is probably why he wants you. He grew up with girls like me."

It was too much work to be with Harry, to pretend life was made up of fun and games, when it was sorrow and river water Carlin was thinking of. At least she could be herself with this cop, as cold and as distant as she wished to be.

"What do you want?" she called to Abe, her voice echoing off the tiled walls.

Abe made a talking motion with his hand as though he were throwing a shadow puppet onto the tiles.

Carlin pointed to the door. "Meet me out front."

She went to the locker room, toweled dry, then dressed without bothering to shower. She found Abe outside, waiting beside Dr. Howe's statue. It was four-thirty but the sky was already darkening, except for the farthest horizon where there was still one delirious band of blue. The weather had returned to the usual chill of November, cold enough for ice crystals to form in Carlin's wet hair. It was foolish, she knew, but in the very back of her mind, she hoped this cop had searched her out to inform her that a mistake had been made and that Gus had been found. That's what Carlin wanted to hear: it was some other ill-fated boy who had fallen in the river and drowned.

Abe patted Dr. Howe's statue on the foot. Luck in love, he'd heard, came from doing so, although he'd never put much stock in such tales. "What a creep this guy was," Abe said of the illustrious headmaster. "A real fuddy-duddy."

"Supposedly, he screwed everything he could get his hands on." The cold center that had been growing inside Carlin ever since Gus's death was rattling around in her chest. "Didn't you know? He was a womanizer."

"Dr. Howe? I thought he was a bookworm."

"Bookworms have sex. It's just lousy." Or at least this was true for Harry, who had gotten more and more selfish, until it seemed he didn't really care who he was with, as long as she was a living, breathing girl who did as she was told.

Carlin took out her cigarettes, suggesting to Abe that they walk behind the gym, so she could smoke. As he followed her, Abe recognized her coat as the same one the dead boy had been wearing when they found him.

"Smoking will slow down your swimming." In spite of Carlin's bad temper, Abe pitied her. She looked so lost inside that big coat; you couldn't even see her hands.

"Gee whiz." Carlin lit up, that cold kernel throbbing right beside her heart. "No one ever told me that before."

"Fine. If that's the way you want it, go on. Don't give a shit. You've got my permission."

In spite of Gus's heavy black coat, Carlin was shivering. "Is that what you wanted to talk to me about? My smoking?"

She was shaky, either from the exertion of swimming or because she hadn't eaten since breakfast. She simply couldn't stop feeling bad no matter how hard she tried. Every now and then she sneaked into the bathroom and took the straight razor to her arm. This cold thing inside her had taken root and changed her into a foul little girl whose hair was turning green at the edges and who wanted to hurt someone, most of all herself.

"I came to talk to you because I'm trying to figure out what happened to your friend."

Carlin let out a short, harsh laugh, then quickly covered her mouth with her hand.

"Is that funny? Did I miss something?"

Carlin blinked back tears. "He's been contacting me. Gus or his spirit, or whatever. I know it sounds stupid. I don't even believe in any of it. It's crazy, right?"

She looked so desperate then, with her pale hair and her even paler face, that Abe couldn't bring himself to tell her about the photograph in his pocket for fear she'd be even more disturbed. He couldn't tell her how many times his own brother had spoken to him; night after night, he had heard his brother's voice, and what's more, he had wanted to. Even now there were times when he said Frank's name aloud in the dark, still hoping for an answer.

"He keeps leaving me things." Carlin punctuated her words with puffs of smoke. "Stones. Water lilies. Sand. I find fish all the time, little silver ones. And that's not all. I can hear him when it's quiet. It sounds like water, but I know it's him."

Abe waited politely as Carlin wiped her eyes with the back of her hands, then lit another cigarette from the one that had already burned down to ash. Watching her, Abe was grateful he was no longer young.

"Maybe he's leaving you things and maybe he isn't, but what I'm interested in is how he died," Abe told the girl when she'd composed herself. "I just have this need to be convinced, and when it comes to Gus, I'm not convinced of anything. Too many questions, not enough answers. So maybe you can answer something for me. Did he talk about suicide?"

"Never," Carlin said. "I already told Mr. Pierce, Gus would have left me a note. Even if it was just to make me feel worse, he would have written something down."

Of course, Abe knew that not everyone discussed such plans. You could live with someone in the very next room and have no idea what he might be capable of. As for Carlin, she appreciated the fact that Abe hadn't tried to comfort her the way most people would have. He was honest, and his doubts matched her own. He took a notepad from his pocket and jotted down his phone number.

"Call me if you hear anything about your friend. If he ate corned beef hash on the night when he died, I want to know. Any detail, no matter how unimportant it seems, I'd like to hear about it. These things can add up when you put them all together. You'd be surprised."

"Okay." Carlin had discovered that she didn't feel quite as vicious anymore. Her wet hair was freezing into disorderly strands and the black coat coiled around her legs as she walked with Abe across campus.

When St. Anne's came into view, Abe could see what was surely Betsy Chase's window. In all probability, Betsy had not thought to lock her windows, not here in Haddan, where the nights were so safe. For an instant, Abe thought he saw her, but it was only Miss Davis out on the porch, trying to fill her bird feeder with seed.

"I'd better go," Carlin said. "I work for her."

In the settling darkness, the thicket of quince beside Miss Davis's door trembled as the nesting finches fluttered with anticipation. Abe could tell that Helen Davis was ill; it wasn't her age that gave her away, but how carefully she lifted each handful of seed, as if such things were too heavy for flesh and blood to manage.

"Sorry I'm late," Carlin called. She would hardly have time to fix the cheese pudding and fruit salad she'd intended to serve; Miss Davis would have to make do with sliced cantaloupe and cottage cheese.

Helen peered through the darkness. "Of course you're late if you're spending all your time wandering around with strange men." She may have been speaking to Carlin, but it was Abe she was staring at.

"He's with the police," Carlin informed Helen Davis as she went inside to get supper on the table. "I was safe the whole time."

Right away, Abe noticed there were no locks on Miss Davis's windows. He went to appraise her door. Exactly as he thought, one of those useless hook and eyes any six-year-old could get past. "Your security is practically nonexistent."

"Are you always such a worrywart?" Helen Davis was intrigued. Ridiculous, but she was actually quite breathless in this man's presence.

"No, ma'am," Abe said. "I was the guy breaking in."

"Were you?" Helen tilted her head, the better to see him through the shadows. "You don't have to worry about me. No one would dare bother me. I've scared everyone off." Helen had finished with the bird feeder, she should have gone in and had her supper, but she could not remember when such a handsome man had appeared on her back porch.

Abe laughed at Miss Davis's remarks. He liked to be surprised by people and Helen Davis had surprised him. He'd expected some snooty sourpuss, but clearly he'd been wrong.

"If anyone broke in, they'd get nothing for their efforts," Helen assured Abe.

Beyond the thicket of quince, a motionless creature lay in wait below the bird feeder.

"What do you know." Abe whistled, then turned back to Helen. "There's my cat."

"That's Midnight," Helen corrected him. "My cat."

"It looks a hell of a lot like mine. Hey you," Abe called.

The cat turned to him disdainfully and glared. A nasty disposition and one yellow eye. No mistake about it.

"Yep," Abe said. "That's my cat."

"I can see how he recognizes you. He's practically jumping for joy. He is a he, for your information."

The cat had begun to wash its paws, exactly as it did every day upon arriving home. "He lives with me," Abe insisted. "Sheds all over my furniture."

"Highly doubtful. I've had him for twelve years. I think I know my own cat."

It had been a very long time since Helen had noticed how

blue a man's eyes were, but she noticed now. Talking to a stranger on her back porch went against her nature, but she had done all manner of strange things since she'd learned she was ill. Since that time, she had melted somehow. Things she had hitherto ignored she now felt hugely; time and again, she was engulfed in waves of emotion. When she walked onto her back porch, the scent of grass could make her weep. She could see a handsome man like Abel Grey and be overwhelmed by longing. The sting of cold air was delicious. The appearance of the first star in the eastern corner of the sky was just cause for celebration. Tonight, for instance, she had observed the three bright stars of Orion rising as daylight was fading. She'd never in her life noticed such occurrences before.

The heat wave was through, the temperature was dropping, and although Helen should have been concerned about her own poor constitution, it was Midnight she worried about on nights like this. Abel Grey was also eyeing her pet with concern, as though he had equal rights to worry and fuss.

"My cat," Helen reminded him. "And I've got the vet bills to prove it. When he lost that eye the doctor said he'd had a fight with another cat, but I think it was done with malice. Whenever he sees a teenaged boy he runs, so what does that tell you?"

"That he's highly intelligent?"

Helen laughed, delighted. "Malice. Believe you me."

"There is a lot of that in the world."

There was still a stretch of blue in the dark sky and the lights around the quad had switched on to form a circle of yellow globes, like fireflies in the dark.

"Think what you'd like," Helen said, as they said good night, "but he's not your cat."

"Fine," Abe conceded as he set out for his parked car. He waved as he crossed the green. "You tell him."

WHEN FRIDAY CAME AROUND AND THE WEEK-end stretched out ahead without plans or responsibilities, Abe was not among those who headed to the Millstone to get hammered in order to forget that Monday was only two days away. He wasn't fit company, that much was obvious, and even Russell Carter, the mildest among their group of friends, had noted Abe's bad temper when they'd gotten together to play basketball at the elementary school gym the previous night.

"I don't know." Russell had shaken his head. Abe was cursing every missed layup. "You're not yourself tonight, Abe."

"Yeah, well, who am I?"

"Maybe you're Teddy Humphrey, man of a thousand altercations. No offense," Russell had added.

Whoever he was, Abe had stopped off at the mini-mart attached to the gas station after work on Friday, where he bought a six-pack of Samuel Adams beer. His plan was to study the autopsy report on the Pierce kid, then go out and get some dinner. He was alive and well, happy enough to have a free evening with one beer started and five more waiting, but the more he looked over the report, the more the details troubled him. The contusions on the boy's forehead and along his back had been assessed as injuries incurred while traveling with the river's current. His health had been excellent, although his toxicology report had been positive for THC, noting that he had smoked marijuana within forty-eight hours of his death.

There was a sense of certainty to such official reports that irked Abe; facts always gave him pause, as so much depended on who the fact finder was and what his point of view happened to be. One detail in particular bothered him all the way through his second beer, so much so that he took the rest of the six-pack into the kitchen and telephoned his father down in Florida. Ernest Grey knew the Haddan River as well as anyone, he was the sort of man whose friends liked to joke would one day have to be surgically separated from his fly rod. In Florida he had bought himself a boat, much to Abe's mother's dismay, and had begun fishing for marlin. Still, there was no substitute for trout and Ernest continued to miss the Haddan River. One year, when he wasn't much more than a boy, Ernest had reeled in the biggest silver trout ever recorded in the county, a catch that had been mounted and was still displayed in town hall, right over the doorway that leads into traffic court.

Abe first spoke with his mother, Margaret, always the far easier task, for when his father took the receiver there was inevitably an uncomfortable silence between them. But the strained tenor of the conversation changed as soon as Abe mentioned that a boy from the Haddan School had drowned.

"That's a terrible situation," Ernest said.

"What bothers me most is that they found fecal matter in the lungs."

"Are you saying it's human waste?" Ernest was really interested now.

"Human as can be."

Abe started in on his third beer. He felt he was entitled to that at least; it was Friday and he was alone. Soon enough, the cat would arrive at the back door, clawing at the screen, happy as hell to be home, in spite of what Helen Davis believed.

"What that autopsy's telling you is impossible," Ernest said with complete certainty. "You won't find anything like that in the Haddan. We had an environmental study done back when the trout stopped running. That was when the town passed the strictest sewage laws in the Commonwealth." Neither man mentioned what else had happened that year, how their lives fell apart for reasons they still didn't understand, how the universe had exploded right under their roof. "A couple of folks over on Main Street had to install completely new septic systems," Ernest went on. "Cost a fortune and they weren't too happy about it. Paul Jeremy was on his last legs then and he raised holy hell, but we went ahead with it for the sake of the river and it's been running clean ever since. So don't tell me there's human shit in the Haddan, because there's not."

Abe thought this information over, then he called Joey, asking him to meet him at the pharmacy, pronto.

"This better be good," Joey said when he got there. He ordered coffee and two jelly doughnuts without bothering to take off his coat. He didn't have time to make himself comfortable; he wasn't staying. "Mary Beth and I were supposed to spend a little quality time together once the kids were in bed. She's so pissed at me for never being home that I'm not even allowed in the doghouse anymore."

The dog was a little terrier Joey hated, a present for Emily's last birthday, and it lived, not in the yard or in a doghouse, but on Joey's favorite chair.

"What if something was wrong with the autopsy report?" Abe said, his voice low.

"Such as?"

"What if he hadn't drowned in the Haddan River?"

"You just need one thing to convince me," Joey said. "Proof."

"I don't quite have that, yet."

"What do you have, buddy? Nothing?"

Abe placed the photograph of Gus on the counter.

"What's this supposed to be?" Joey asked.

"I don't know. A ghost?"

Joey laughed so hard they could hear him over in the notions aisle. "Yeah, right." He slid the photo back across the counter. "And I'm the reincarnation of John F. Kennedy." He bit into a jelly doughnut. "Junior."

"Okay. What do you think it is?"

"I think it's a damn bad photograph. I think you'd better hope that gal over at the school you've got your eye on is better in bed than she is with a camera."

"Maybe the image on that photograph is caused by a field of energy left behind by the deceased." Abe was refusing to let this go. He remembered old-timers down at the station insisting that murdered men could get stuck somewhere between this world and the next. They were probably just trying to scare Abe when they told him that whenever the wind came up it was one of these dead men, rattling at the doors, stranded here among the living.

"You're kidding, right?" Joey said. "Tell me you don't believe in this crap."

"You don't seem to have a better explanation."

"That's because there is none, Abe. You want to believe that someone who dies lives on in some way, I understand that—hell, I've lost people, too. But if you want to convince me of something, give me proof. Something I can see, touch, feel. Not ghosts."

Joey had had the very same reaction back in the old days when Abe told him he heard Frank's voice. As soon as he had seen the look on Joey's face, Abe had known he'd better shut up. He was feeling that same way now.

Joey still had time to stop at the mini-mart, pick up a bottle of wine, and try to get back in Mary Beth's good graces, so he said his good-byes, leaving Abe to get the tab. After he'd gone, Abe had another cup of coffee, while Pete Byers looked in the back room for one of the sterilized jars that customers used to bring urine samples to the health center in Hamilton. Abe had had too much to drink and now his head was aching. That pounding in his skull, however, didn't stop him from setting off once he had the glass jar from Pete. It was a blustery night, with fast-moving clouds illuminated by moonlight. On nights like this Frank could never sit still. People said he was restless, he had too much energy, but in recent years Abe had wondered if it might have been something more: a fear of the dark, and of himself, and whatever it was that was going on inside his head. When they were kids playing hide-and-seek, Frank had always carried a flashlight and he never ventured far into the woods. Once, Abe had come upon his brother in the backyard, looking up at the thousands of stars in the sky as though he were already lost among them, without any hope of finding his way back home. Never had Abe seen such loneliness, even though Frank was only steps from their own back door.

Thinking about such matters almost caused Abe to miss the first side street that would lead him to the river road. He parked on a sandy embankment, then walked along until he passed onto Haddan School property, even though he knew Glen and Joey never would have approved. He wanted a spot close to where

Gus might have first made contact with the river, and therefore made his way to the reedy area nearest Chalk House. Abe didn't feel like a trespasser; no sweaty hands, no butterflies in the gut. He had spent more time on this river than most men spent in their own living rooms, and could still recall a canoe trip with his father and grandfather at a time when he hadn't been more than three or four. There had been bowers of green leaves overhead and the slapping sound of water as they moved downstream. Whenever he had tried to speak, the men hushed him, warning that he'd scare the fish away. They were out on the river so long that day, Abe fell asleep in the bottom of the boat and awoke with dozens of mosquito bites. No one would believe him afterward when he swore he'd heard the fish swimming below them as he slept.

Abe had come to the old flat rock he and Joey used for diving in summers past, sneaking here whenever school wasn't in session and there was no one who might catch them on private property and call their parents to complain. There were more reeds than Abe recalled, and thickets of thorn bushes grabbed at his pant legs. Nonetheless, he went out onto the rock; his boots got wet and he knelt down and before long his jeans were soaked. He scooped water into the sterile jar, then closed it tightly, returning the jar to his jacket pocket.

By now, the night was so chilly Abe could see his breath in the air. Soon, a film of ice would form in the shallows, a layer so thin it might remain invisible unless stones were thrown. Since Abe had already come this far, he kept on, past the boathouse. Funny how people can keep things from themselves, but he truly didn't know where he was bound until he was standing outside St. Anne's. The hedges were rustling in the wind, and the thin, moonlit clouds raced by up above. He could see Betsy clearly through the window. She wore a cotton robe and her hair was wet from the shower; she sat in a frayed upholstered chair, her bare legs curled up beneath her, as she looked over her students' portfolios. A lamp inside the room cast a faint light so that looking inside was like peering into an Easter egg in which a scene had been designed, there for anyone to hold in his hand and view whenever he pleased.

Watching her this way, Abe felt completely reckless, exactly as he had all those years ago when he was robbing houses. Once more he was the victim of desire and circumstance. He could hear the sound of girls' voices from inside the dorm; he could smell the river, a pungent mixture of mold and decay. He moved a vine that blocked his vision. The difference between now and then was that now he was a grown man who made his own decisions, not a boy breaking into the headmaster's house. No one forced him to remain outside Betsy's window; there was no lock and key. A rational man would have turned and run, but this night had nothing to do with reason. Whenever Abe made an arrest he always tried to figure out the offender's motives. *What were you thinking, man?* he'd said time and time again as he waited for the ambulance with some teenaged boy who'd crashed his father's car, or as he drove to the jail in Hamilton with men who had slapped their wives around once too often or too hard. Most recently, he'd confronted a couple of kids who'd been caught stealing cartons of cigarettes from the mini-mart. *What were you thinking?* he'd asked as he peered into their backpacks. The boys had been terrified and they hadn't answered, but here at last was Abe's answer: they weren't thinking at all. One minute they were standing in the dark with no intention of doing anything out of the ordinary, and the next they were acting on instinct, barreling ahead with no thought in their heads other than *I want* or *I need* or *I've got to have it now.*

It was always possible to go back and consider the path not taken; in retrospect, bad decisions and mistakes leapt out so that even the most irrational individual would eventually see the failure of his ways. Later, Abe would wonder if he'd have been so irresponsible if he hadn't started in on that six-pack so early in the day, or if he hadn't stopped at the pharmacy, or if he'd held off going to the river to collect water. One alteration of his conduct might have prevented all the rest, a road strewn with poor choices that had led him to her window and kept him there now.

He thought about the boy who had died, gone so early he would never spy on a woman like this, all tied up in knots, caught up by his own appetites. Gazing into the yellow light, searching Betsy's beautiful, tired face, Abe could feel his own hunger; it was bitter and he hated himself for it, but it couldn't be denied. If he stayed any longer he might circle around to the rear of the building in order to watch her get ready for bed, and then who would he be? The sort of man he'd dealt with a hundred times before, whether it was at the scene of traffic accidents or in the parking lot of the Millstone, a man who was already out of control.

As he forced himself to turn away, Abe thought about all the times he hadn't cared; the girls in school he had kissed so thoughtlessly, the women he'd gone swimming with in the river on hot summer nights. There'd been far too many of them; why, there'd even been something with Mary Beth one New Year's Eve when they'd both had too much to drink, a heated, overwrought incident they both politely chose to forget. He had not cared about a single one of these women, an accomplishment for a man as wary as Abe, something of which he'd been proud, as if he'd won a point of honor by not loving anyone. And so it came as a great surprise to find he could want someone as much as he wanted Betsy. He had thought he could walk through life without any pain; he'd thought solitude would comfort him and keep him safe all the rest of his days, but he was wrong. His grandfather always told him that love never arrived politely, knocking on the front door like a kindhearted neighbor, asking to be let in. Instead, it ambushed a man when he least expected it, when his defenses were down, and even the most obstinate individual, no matter how bullheaded or faithless, had no choice but to surrender when love like this came to call.

THE VEILED WOMAN

AT THE END OF THE MONTH, A
cold rain began to fall at a steady pace, hour
after hour, until its rhythm was all anyone
could hear. This was no ordinary rain, for
the rainfall was black, a rain of algae, an
odd phenomenon some of the older residents in town recalled from the time when
they were children. Mrs. Evans and Mrs.
Jeremy, for instance, had played out in a
black rain when they were girls and were
rightfully punished by their mothers when
they flounced home in wet, sooty dresses.
Now, the two neighbors stood beneath the
shelter of their front porches and called to
each other, noting how lucky they were that
it wasn't spring, when their gardens would
be ruined by this strange substance, the

hollyhocks and delphiniums slick with black gunk, the leaves turned dark as coal.

People donned raincoats and hats and ran from their cars into houses or stores. Rugs were set out by back doors, but despite any precautions, black footprints were tracked across floorboards and carpets; dozens of umbrellas were ruined and had to be tossed out with the trash. At the Haddan School, the features of Dr. Howe's statue turned moody and dark, and those who approached him walked on quickly, their feet slap-dashing through puddles that seemed to be made out of ink. Betsy Chase may have been the only one in town who used the black rain to her advantage; she decided to send her students out to photograph the village in the midst of these strange circumstances. Although most of the prints that were later developed were nothing more than murky splotches, there were a few memorable images, including Pete Byers sweeping black rain off the sidewalk, Duck Johnson shirtless and grim as he hosed off canoes at the boathouse, and two black swans, hiding beneath a wooden bench.

When the rain finally stopped, the gutters flowed with algae and the town stank of mildew and fish. There was some flooding in the usual places: the hollow around town hall, the backyards of those who lived closest to the railroad tracks, the dank cellar of Chalk House. A hydraulic pump was brought in and while people fussed about how to best siphon out the muck that had collected in the basement at Chalk House and worried about what the next serious storm's effect would be on the structural integrity of the building, Betsy took the opportunity to go upstairs to the attic, to Gus Pierce's room, empty now, save for the desk and the bed. The windowpanes were splattered with black algae and only a faint, fish-colored light streaked through. Rain had seeped beneath the window, darkly staining the sash. In spite of the dim lighting, Betsy shot a roll of film, recording every angle of the room.

Once in the darkroom, Betsy was prepared for any oddities that might surface, but the film yielded only ceilings and doors, white walls and the single bed, unmade and unremarkable. That evening, when she met Eric for supper, Betsy was still wondering what she had done differently with that first roll of film. She found herself disappointed that another image had not appeared.

"Do you ever think about what comes after?" she asked Eric at dinner. Because of the season, the kitchen was serving turkey soup and potato-leek pie. The dining hall had been decorated with pilgrims' hats, which swung from the ceiling on strings.

"Chair of the department," Eric said without hesitation. "Eventually a university position."

"I meant after death." Betsy stirred her soup. Bits of carrot and rice rose to the surface of the cloudy broth.

"Luckily, we can both be buried in the Haddan School cemetery."

Betsy thought this over, then pushed her bowl away.

"How did you know I was the right person for you?" she asked suddenly. "What made you so sure?"

Before Eric could answer, Duck Johnson ambled over to join them, his tray loaded down. "Are you going to eat your fruit-cake?" he asked, always hungry for more.

"Guess who was invited to Bob Thomas's for Thanksgiving?" Eric announced as he passed on his portion of dessert.

"Congratulations." Duck nodded cheerfully. "Atta boy."

Only the chair of each department was invited to the dean's

dinner; this year, when Helen Davis declined, Eric had stepped up to take her place. This arrangement, however, was news to Betsy, who had been planning a trip to Maine over the long holiday weekend. It would be good to escape, not just from the school, but from any possibility of running into Abel Grey as she went about her errands in the village.

"We can go to Maine anytime," Eric assured her.

Betsy wished she wasn't reminded of Helen Davis's warning. Nonetheless, who didn't have doubts every now and then? Every couple needn't always agree or spend every moment in a delirium of happiness. Look at Carlin Leander, who should have been pleased that Harry McKenna was so enamored of her. The other girls at St. Anne's followed him across campus like a flock of trained birds, but Carlin had begun to avoid him. She could feel Gus's disapproval whenever she was with Harry and in time she began to notice the traits Gus had warned her about: the smile that could be turned on and off at will, the selfishness, the certainty that his own needs were at the very center of the universe. She pulled farther and farther away from Harry. If he brought her chocolates, she said she could not stomach sweets. If he came to call, she sent one of her roommates to inform him she was already in bed, far too tired or sick to see anyone at all.

Harry, always so accustomed to getting whatever he wanted, only wanted her more when she withdrew.

"He's worried about you," Amy Elliot told Carlin, for Harry had begun to confide in Amy, a good listener when it served her purposes. Amy had a little girl's voice that belied her determination to get what she wanted, which in this case was Harry. Since Carlin already had him, Amy had begun to take on her roommate's style, in the hopes that some of Carlin's luck would rub off. She wore a silver clip in her hair, and her brand-new black woolen coat echoed the lines of Gus's old coat. "What's wrong?" Amy asked. "Because if you don't want Harry anymore, believe me, there are plenty of us who do."

Girls like Amy believed they'd be granted whatever they wanted, if they only crossed their fingers or wished upon stars, but Carlin knew better. She carried her grief with her; she couldn't let it go. Betsy noticed this phenomenon when she photographed the swim team for the alumni newsletter. As she developed that particular photograph, Betsy began to wish Abel Grey were beside her, so he might see for himself what had begun to appear in the tray of developing fluid. If anything, love was like light, illuminating what no one would have ever guessed was there in the darkness. Carlin Leander was at the far end of a line of smiling girls, her grim expression separating her from the group. Her arms were crossed and a frown tilted her mouth downward, but even though she stood apart from the others, Carlin wasn't alone. He was right there beside her, leaning up against the cold, blue tiles, made out of equal parts liquid and air, a fish out of water, a boy with no earthly form, drowned both in this life and the next.

WHEN MATT FARRIS FAXED OVER THE REPORT from the lab the results were exactly as Abe's father had predicted. The water was clean and clear, with only trace amounts of fish eggs and algae, nothing more.

"Don't bother me," Joey said when Abe approached him with the report. "I'm writing up our monthly expenses."

Abe stood there, shirttail out, with an expression that might lead a person to believe he'd never heard of monthly expenses before. Ever since the night he'd looked through Betsy Chase's window, he had been preoccupied and more than a little confused. He'd forgotten to take out the trash so often it was piling up in his back hall; he hadn't once checked his mail, so that stray bills and circulars had begun to overflow from the delivery box beside his door. This morning, he had mistakenly taken one of his grandfather's old suits from the back of the closet. Once having settled the jacket onto his lanky frame, he was surprised to find that it fit. He hadn't thought he was as tall as his grandfather, but it turned out that he was, and because he was late, he'd worn the suit to work.

"Nice suit," Joey noted. "It's just not you."

Abe placed the lab report atop the set of figures Joey was working on. Joey looked at the printout, then sat back in his chair.

"So?"

"So there's human excrement in the kid's lungs, but none in the Haddan River."

"I repeat." Joey gulped down some cold coffee and shivered at the bitter taste. "So?"

"Does it make sense to you?"

"Not any more than the fact that I have to work as a security guard all weekend to bankroll a trip to Disney World. Nothing makes sense to me. Why should this? It doesn't mean a thing."

"You asked for proof. Here it is. He didn't drown in the Haddan."

Joey was looking at his old friend as though he were a crazy man, and maybe he was. Certainly, everything Abe had done in the past week would back up that assessment.

"You know why you think that? It's all because you haven't gotten laid in a really long time and you have nothing else to do with your mind other than come up with these preposterous scenarios based on nothing." Joey tossed the report back to him. "Let it go."

Abe wished he could simply file the lab report and stay out of affairs that weren't his business, but that wasn't the sort of man he was. At a little before noon, he went in to speak to Glen Tiles. It was bad timing on Abe's part. Glen had high blood pressure and his wife was starving him with his best interests at heart; set out on his desk were a container of cottage cheese and a lone apple. Abe should have known that mealtime wasn't the best hour to approach the chief, but he did so anyway. Glen surveyed the lab report, then gazed at Abe. "You want me to read about shit while I'm having lunch?"

"I want you to read about the lack of shit."

Abe sat across from Glen, watching him read. When he was done, Glen handed the report back and immediately started in on his cottage cheese.

"I don't think the kid drowned in the Haddan River," Abe said.

"Yeah, Abe, maybe he was an alien. Did you ever think of that?" Glen ate like a famished man. "Or maybe this is all a dream. Maybe it's my dream and you're not really here at all, you're just a participant in my dream. Which means I could make you do anything I want to. I could make you stand on your head right now and cluck like a chicken if that's what I wanted to do."

"He could have been killed somewhere else, then thrown into the river," Abe persisted. "I've talked this over with Ernest. You know he'd be the last person to agree with me, but even he thinks something's not right."

"That doesn't surprise me. Your father has grasped at straws before." There was an awkward silence, and in the end, Glen had no option but to apologize. "Sorry," he said. "That was out of line."

"This isn't about Frank, you know. This is Gus Pierce, dead with shit in his lungs in a river that has been clean for more than twenty years. It's probably the cleanest water in the whole damned Commonwealth."

"You may not be satisfied, Abe, but the Haddan School is very happy with our investigation. In fact, they sent a letter commending us, and what's more, the alumni fund made a donation to the benevolent association. They think we did a good job and I agree. The kid drowned in the river. End of story."

Abe folded the report in half, stowing it in his jacket pocket, alongside the photo of the dead boy. "You're wrong on this one. You're wrong all the way around."

"Is that Wright's suit you're wearing?" Glen called when Abe was leaving. "Because, man, it's way too big for you."

Abe went over to the mini-mart, where he picked up some lunch, then he kept on driving. He didn't have to think when he rode around Haddan, he knew it so well he might as well have dreamed the town. He could eat a sandwich, think about sex and murder, and navigate the streets all at the same time. He went out to Route 17 to consider his options, heading to his grandfather's house on instinct. Along with Wright's suit, he'd found a thin, black tie in the back of his closet, which he realized was choking him; he loosened it and undid the top button of his shirt, breathing a little easier at last.

This was the section of Haddan that had changed the most since Abe was a boy. Nowadays there were houses where there had only been fields, and a Stop & Shop market where Halley's farm stand once sold yellow beans and cabbages. The rutted dirt road where Abe used to catch the bus to the high school had been paved, but at least the fields outside his grandfather's farm were still the same. The deed was in Abe's name and he couldn't bring himself to sell the place to any of the developers who routinely put their feelers out, tracking him down and offering continuously escalating sums. Once he got to the property, Abe pulled over to finish his lunch and watch the songbirds that flew so low across the meadow their wings grazed the tall grass. On this day, Abe felt he was alone in the world. He had lived in the village all his life, had grown up with Joey and Mary Beth and Teddy Humphrey and all the rest, yet there wasn't a single one among them whose counsel he cared to seek. He wished he could talk to his grandfather, that was the problem. A man could confide in Wright Grey. What you told him stayed put—he didn't like people who aired their personal affairs in public or complained about their fate—and he certainly knew how to listen.

Abe got out of the car and walked toward the field. The meadow grass, although brown, smelled sweet. The whole world seemed like a mystery to Abe at that moment, and he thought about all he hadn't yet done. Wanting Betsy had unleashed a hundred other possibilities, and now he was a man at the mercy of his own longing. It was cold and Abe wasn't wearing a coat; the wind blew right through his grandfather's suit and Abe could feel it on his skin just as sure as if he'd been naked. There was a fence separating the road from the field, but Abe climbed to the other side. The grass reached his waist here, still he lay down in it, flat on his back. He looked up at the clouds and the sky above him. He could hear the north wind here, but he couldn't feel it; it passed right over him. Abe felt lucky somehow, for the first time in a very long while. Nobody in the world knew where he was, but he was here in the grass thinking about love and how he had blundered into it, kind of late in life, and how grateful he was, how completely and utterly surprised.

It wasn't the season for love; the days were dark and nothing grew save for a few renegade cabbages left from the days when Haddan was still mostly farmland. Hingram's Shoe Shop already had a display of winter boots in its front window, and all along Main Street the gardens were bare, with burlap hoods covering the most delicate plants, the rhododendrons and pink azaleas that were so susceptible to frost. With the long holiday weekend stretching out, the village grew quiet. Most Haddan School students had gone home for Thanksgiving and only a few remained, including Carlin Leander, who had decided against going to Connecticut with Harry in order to have dinner with Helen Davis. As for Harry, he didn't like this choice one bit; he begged and he pleaded, but Carlin would not change her mind, and in the end Harry brought Amy Elliot and Robbie Shaw home for the holiday.

By Thursday morning, there was no traffic on Main Street and the shops had all closed down, except for the mini-mart, which stayed open until midnight. Ever since his divorce, Teddy Humphrey no longer celebrated holidays. Instead, he was a guardian angel of sorts, ready and waiting should anyone run out of vanilla, or butter, or eggnog, all of which were readily available at twice the usual price.

Abe wore Wright's suit to Thanksgiving dinner at Joey and Mary Beth's, in spite of the fact that he always got down on the floor to play with five-year-old Jackson and three-year-old Lilly, and usually wound up with clay or chalk in his hair. Mary Beth's whole family was there, her parents and her two brothers and a cousin from New Jersey, a pretty blonde, recently divorced, who Mary Beth had thought would be a perfect match for Abe.

"I'm not interested," Abe told MB as he helped her load platters with turkey and the cranberry-apple stuffing that was her Thanksgiving specialty.

"Come on. You're always interested," Mary Beth joked as she finished carving the turkey. When Abe didn't laugh or kid her back, she held the knife in the air and studied him. MB was pregnant again, but she looked the same as she had when they were in high school, with her dark hair pulled back into a ponytail and her face fresh, without any makeup. "You've already got someone," she declared.

"You're wrong about that, Miss Mind Reader," Abe told her.

When dinner was over, the finale of pumpkin pie and vanilla ice cream was perfectly timed to coincide with the kickoff of the third televised football game of the day. While seconds of dessert were being served, Joey asked Abe if he wanted to get some fresh air. Abe assumed they were going for a walk and he hadn't expected Joey to head for MB's old station wagon. He got in amiably, scooping stray potato chips and raisins from the passenger seat. Joey put the car in gear and turned onto Belvedere Street.

"We're going to buy beer," Abe guessed, wishing he had thought to bring some along to dinner, but they passed the minimart without pause, not stopping until they reached the Haddan School. They parked in the lot between the dean's house and the headmaster's house, now inhabited by old Dr. Jones, who had inherited the place from Dr. Howe in a long line of illustrious educators reaching back to Hosteous Moore. "Don't tell me we're robbing the headmaster's house again."

"You could put it that way." Joey left the car running and got out, leaving Abe to think things over. Mary Beth's heater was on the fritz and before long Abe's breath had fogged up the windshield. He turned off the ignition, then climbed out to stretch his legs. The trees were bare and there was a coating of ice on the path Joey had taken to the dean's back door. This area was reserved for faculty housing, cottages set out in a row for married staff and their families. Bob Thomas's was the first and the largest of these, a two-story Victorian with a double chimney and a wide back porch where the dean and Joey stood talking.

Bob Thomas was a big man who enjoyed his dinner; he'd come to the porch without the benefit of a coat or a hat, while inside his house the festivities went on without him. Abe ambled closer, positioning himself beside a boxwood hedge where nuthatches were roosting, beating their wings to keep from freezing. He could see through the dining room window; quite a crowd had gathered. The meal had been cleared away, but guests were still enjoying the rum-enhanced eggnog and mulled wine.

Abe couldn't help but see Betsy; she and some man were there together. Abe figured this was the fiancé, for certainly, Betsy's companion looked as if he'd stepped out of an alumni bulletin. Crouching beside the boxwood in his grandfather's old suit, in need of both a haircut and a shave, Abe felt himself burn with shame. What had he been thinking? If he knocked on the kitchen door, they'd surely slam it in his face. To be honest, he wished Betsy and her perfect fiancé a miserable holiday. He hoped they choked on the petit fours Meg Thomas was now serving, sweet concoctions of chocolate and marzipan that could easily stick in a person's throat.

Abe waited in the fading light for Joey, his ill temper rivaling the disposition of those miserable Haddan swans. Just his luck, the pair nesting close by seemed interested in him; one had already begun to advance across the frozen grass.

"Don't come near me," Abe warned the swan. "I'll cook you," he threatened. "I will."

At last, Joey finished speaking with the dean. When he returned, he was as jolly as Abe had ever seen him. Abe, on the other hand, felt his evil mood taking a turn for the worse. The sun was setting and crimson clouds fanned out across the hazy sky. That swan was still eyeing him and Abe knew from experience that these birds weren't afraid to attack. He had been on duty on one such occasion, when a big male swan had wandered onto Mrs. Jeremy's property. Her son, AJ, had tried to chase it off only to wind up with a dozen or more stitches in his forehead.

"None too soon," Abe said as Joey reached him.

Joey's color was good; he'd been invigorated by the cold air and the business he'd completed. He had an envelope in hand that he smacked against his open palm. "This will cheer you up."

All over Haddan, people were finished with dinner; as for Abe, he wouldn't be able to eat another thing for twenty-four hours. It wasn't only Mary Beth's menu that had done him in, it was the queasiness he'd begun to feel when he spied the envelope in Joey's grasp.

"The town's gotten plenty from the school, why shouldn't we get something back?" Joey said. "Hell, they treat us like we're their personal security department, they can damn well pay us for our services."

Abe truly did feel ill. He wasn't used to rich food and even richer rewards. He liked things simple and plain and within the limits of the law. "Don't show me what's in that envelope. Put it away, man, otherwise I'm going to have to go to Glen on this."

"You think he doesn't know?" Joey laughed when he saw the look on Abe's face. "Wake up, friend. This has been going on for years. Since before your father retired. These services went on right under his nose, and he never knew the first thing about it."

"What exactly are our services?"

"We don't go digging around where we don't belong, and that means when some Haddan kid kills himself, we let it be."

Joey got into the car and started it up. The idling station wagon sputtered and exhaust spiraled into the air. When Abe didn't move, Joey rolled down his window.

"Come on. You're not going to be self-righteous like your old man always was, are you? That's why Glen kept you out of this in the first place."

Abe decided he didn't need a ride, not now. It was better to walk off a big meal; the exercise would do him good. When he started off, Joey shouted out for him and honked the raspy horn, but Abe continued on across the frozen grass. He left the campus, then turned onto Main Street. There were vines of woodbine and bittersweet twisted along the black wrought-iron fences and a glossy hedge of holly that was over six feet tall in Mrs. Jeremy's garden. If today's circumstances had been different, Abe would have stopped by to make certain that AJ was safely passed out in bed, but this was one holiday when Mrs. Jeremy would have to take care of her own family business.

It had been a long while since Abe had been through the east side on foot, and he was as uncomfortable as he'd been back when he was a boy. The rattle of a trash can, the bark of a dog in someone's yard, the slightest bit of noise and he was ready to run.

There had always been divisions in Haddan, lines drawn between the haves and have-nots, and maybe some payment was long overdue. Who was Abe to judge Joey, or anyone else for that matter? He himself hadn't always been on his best behavior, but even when he was the one breaking the law he'd known the difference between right and wrong. He thought of his grandfather, who'd truly believed a man's highest calling was to serve his fellow citizens. Wright had plunged into the frozen river when most men would have been too concerned for their own welfare ever to have left the shore.

As Abe walked home, he felt he, too, was stranded on that shore, unable to commit to a leap, as if the black Haddan mud were quicksand, pulling him down. The queasiness he'd begun to feel was growing worse, just as it had back when Frank died. It was the sense that he hadn't really known his brother and that they'd all been living a lie that had been most disconcerting. Abe had always admired his brother, but had he ever understood him? The smartest boy who'd ever attended Hamilton High, who faithfully washed their father's car on Saturdays and stayed up all night studying, was the same person who walked up the stairs and shot himself on that hot August day when Sixth Commandment Pond was perfect for swimming. How could he have given it all away, that dusty, torpid afternoon when they could have been fishing in one of the secret places their grandfather had shown them, the rocky ledges that overhung the deep cool pools where the biggest trout could be found.

It was Frank who came down for breakfast every morning and Frank again who kept the shotgun under his mattress in the hours before his death, one and the same, just as Joey was not only the man who accepted a bribe, but the boy who stood beside Abe at Frank's memorial service. It was Joey who'd walked all the way to Wright's farm on days when it was so cold ice formed inside his gloves and he needed to stand in front of the oven to defrost himself. Once again, Abe had taken for granted that he was privy to all there was to know about a person, just as he knew the village itself, but as it turned out, he'd been wrong yet again. It was as if someone had taken all the streets in town and thrown them sky high, letting them fall wherever they might, in a jumble that was unrecognizable.

Abe crossed the railroad tracks, taking Forest Street for a while before turning onto Station as dusk began to fall, like a curtain of soot. It was an especially dark sky on this holiday evening and people cherished the pleasures and warmth of their homes. Abe could see his neighbors through their front windows. He passed by Pete Byers's place and Mike Randall's neat cottage, far too small for his five children, but well kept up, with a new porch and fresh paint. He saw Billy and Marie Bishop at their big oak table, surrounded by half a dozen grandchildren. When he reached his own house, there was the cat, waiting, and he knelt to scratch its ears. Why, even this creature had a secret life, spending afternoons in the sunny window of the Lucky Day Florist, sharing lunch with Miss Davis.

"I hope you had your turkey someplace else," Abe told the cat.

Abe knew how easy it was to break into a house, and that was why he never bothered to lock his own door. He had nothing worth stealing, anyway; his TV was on the blink and the last time his VCR quit working he'd brought it to the appliance shop in Hamilton and never bothered to return for it. Even his doorbell was busted, which was why Betsy Chase had to pound on the door when she arrived.

It had been a day of surprises for Abe, but Betsy's appearance was the only pleasant one. He had been ready to have a few drinks and crawl into bed, defeated and disgusted by the day's events, but here was absolute proof that whenever a man thought he knew what his future would bring, something was bound to amaze him. He stood there looking at Betsy the way he had when they'd first met, causing the color to rise in her face. Every time she saw him she became flustered, as if she had no more sense than the girls from St. Anne's.

"I thought I saw you over at the school," Betsy said, but that was a lie; in fact, she was certain of it. She'd seen him through the dean's window, there beside the boxwood, wearing the same dark suit that still hung on his angular frame.

Abe swung the screen door open to allow Betsy into the hallway. She had left her coat in her car parked in his driveway, and was wearing an outfit that had seemed well suited to the occasion of a dinner at the dean's house, a black dress and a good pair of heels. Now, however, she felt awkward in these clothes, as if she were a stranger to herself. The hallway was so cramped they were forced close together. As if that weren't difficult enough, her shoes were killing her; she thought she might actually topple over. She was probably crazy to have come, subject to the green river light that always confused her at this hour.

"I brought over some photographs," she told Abe in a businesslike tone. She tapped on her camera bag, which was draped over one shoulder.

When they went into the kitchen, Abe realized what a mess

his place was, with dishes stacked in the sink and newspapers on the floor. A basket of laundry had been left on a chair, unwashed and forgotten; Abe removed it so that Betsy could sit at the table. As she did, she pointed to the countertop where the black cat was parading back and forth, mewing at the cabinet where the canned food was stored. "That's Helen Davis's cat."

"Nope." After getting two beers from the refrigerator, Abe took the chair across from Betsy's. "It's mine."

"I see it all the time on campus." Betsy started in on her beer, not that she wanted it, and she drank too fast, agitated in Abe's presence. His eyes were not unlike the ice that had recently formed in the shallows of the river, fluid and pale. Looking into them, Betsy had the sense that she could fall right through and keep on falling. She quickly took out her folder of prints. "I wanted to know what you thought of this."

Abe began to look them over, distracted at first, then more interested. After developing the prints of the swim team, Betsy had gone on to take a series of photographs. In each there was a shadow behind Carlin, the unmistakable shape of a tall boy.

"You're good." Abe fixed Betsy with those pale eyes of his. "These look real."

"They are real. It only happens when I use high-speed film. And when Carlin is around."

In one of the prints the shadow's features were particularly clear: a wide mouth, a broad forehead, the sorrowful expression of the denied and the lovelorn. Even in the haziest of the images, the shadowy figure appeared to be soaking wet; there were pools of water in every picture, on furniture and floors alike. Abe returned the photographs to the folder. "The girl told me he's leaving her things. Maybe he's got some need to communicate, so he's hanging around. Sort of the way you're hanging around me," he added.

"Oh, don't you wish." Betsy laughed and held up her hand, displaying her engagement ring to remind him of her situation.

"You keep showing me that ring, but here you are." Abe moved his chair closer to hers.

Instantly, Betsy stood and collected her photographs. "You're kind of an egomaniac, aren't you? I thought you were interested in Gus Pierce."

She had already started for the hallway and Abe followed along. "I am interested," he told her.

"In the photographs?"

"I'm more interested in you."

Betsy shifted her camera bag, so that it was directly between them, in self-defense, in self-denial. What was her situation, exactly? It was only days ago that she'd settled the dessert problem for her wedding with Doreen Becker at the inn. Doreen had been pushing the white ladyfinger variety, insisting that chocolate wedding cakes such as the one Betsy preferred always brought bad luck. It was said that several divorce lawyers in Hamilton ordered similar cakes delivered to churches and halls to ensure their continuing brisk business.

"Do you tell every woman you bring back here that you're interested?" she asked Abe now, realizing as she did that she didn't like the idea of other women being here with him.

"I don't bring anyone here," Abe said. "Let's not forget, you came here all by yourself. And I'm glad that you did."

And because she knew this to be true, it was Betsy who

kissed him first, there in the dark hallway. She meant for it to be just that once, but that's not what happened. Later, she would tell herself that she got swept up, she didn't know what she was doing; it was the beer she'd gulped down or her unpredictable reaction to holidays. No matter what the reason, she kissed him for a very long time, too long, even though she knew she was making a major mistake. She was reminded of lightning, the way it struck so suddenly a person never had time to get out of range until it was over and the damage had already been done.

Betsy told herself it would only be one night, just a few passionate hours, erasable, forgettable, surely not meant to hurt anyone. She didn't stop him when he pulled off the black dress she'd so carefully chosen for the holiday. It was thoughtless, and heedless, but she didn't care. What was desire anyway, when examined in the clear light of day? Was it the way a woman searched for her clothes in the morning, or the manner in which a man might watch her sit before the mirror and comb her hair? Was it a pale November dawn, when ice formed on windowpanes and crows called from the bare black trees? Or was it the way a person might yield to the night, setting forth on a path so unexpected that daylight would never again be completely clear?

AT THIS TIME OF YEAR, THE LUNCH COUNTER at the pharmacy offered its famous Christmas muffins, an item added to the specials board every year between Thanksgiving and New Year's, expertly baked by Pete Byers's wife, Eileen. This local treat, reminiscent of ginger cake, only richer and more dense, had become so desirable that several residents of the

largest houses on Main Street, well-dressed women who ordinarily wouldn't be caught at the lunch counter, arrived early in
the mornings to buy half a dozen or more at a time.

Although the lunch counter was crowded with Haddan
School students in the afternoon, the mornings belonged to local
residents. People discussed both old news and current events
over coffee for hours, and by noon everything from wedding an-
nouncements to nervous breakdowns had been hashed over. It
was here people began to wonder if something had happened to
Abel Grey. He was never at the Millstone anymore, where he'd
been a regular ever since he'd reached legal age, and several
women he occasionally dated—Kelly Avon, for instance, from
over at the 5&10 Cent Bank—hadn't heard from him in weeks.
Doug Lauder and Teddy Humphrey, with whom he often played
pool on Saturday nights over in Middletown, had started to
worry, and Russell Carter, who reported that Abe had stopped
showing up to play basketball, was so concerned he phoned
down to the station to make sure Abe was still alive.

As single men, these fellows had always depended on Abe's
availability to play cards or agree to a fishing trip on short notice;
now they couldn't get ahold of him anymore. They had no idea
that Abe could be found lying in the tall grass thinking about fate
or that he'd been so shaken up by love he had lost the ability to
tell time. He, who had always prided himself on being punctual,
was showing up not just at the wrong hour, but on the wrong day,
arriving to direct traffic outside town hall on Thursday mornings
when everyone knew the garden club didn't meet until Friday afternoon.

Abe's neighbors began to guess there was a woman involved
when they noticed him out on his porch late at night, gazing at

stars. They figured they had his number when he came into Selena's Sandwich Shoppe whistling love songs and completely forgetting what he planned to order, when he'd asked for a turkey on
rye for the last nine years. Some of the ladies from Main Street,
to whom Abe had always been so helpful, patted him on the back
when they saw him, pleased that at last he'd found love. Certainly, it was high time. Because of the lack of single men in Haddan—and no one counted Teddy Humphrey as such, since every
time he got good and drunk, he begged his ex-wife, Nikki, to take
him back—there were several women who were disappointed to
hear that Abe was no longer available. A few, like Kelly Avon and
Mary Beth's cousin, the one who'd been unsuccessfully set up
with him at Thanksgiving, tried to get the truth out of Joey Tosh,
who insisted that his lips were sealed, although when it came
right down to it, even Joey didn't know much.

Since their disagreement on Thanksgiving, Abe had avoided
his old friend. He drove himself to work in his grandfather's
cruiser and asked for assignments no one else wanted, traffic, for
instance, and domestic disputes, to ensure he'd be working
alone. When both men happened to be at the station at the same
time, Joey busied himself with paperwork or with the *Haddan
Tribune*. He had a shielded look that was impossible to read, the
same expression he'd had when Mary Beth was first pregnant
with Emily and they'd decided to get married without telling anyone.

Now and then, Abe caught Joey staring and one morning Joey
stopped at Abe's desk. "Man, you're the early bird these days."

Funny that Abe had never even noticed that when Joey was
upset he pulled at the right side of his face.

"You keep it up, you're going to make the rest of us look bad."

Abe sat back in his chair. "Is that what you're worried about, Joe? Looking bad?"

"That was my mistake on Thanksgiving. I shouldn't have brought you with me. I should have kept you out of it, like everyone said to."

"Yeah? I thought your mistake was taking the money."

"You're just pissed because I disagreed with you about the Pierce kid. You want me to say he was murdered? Fine, he was murdered. And maybe Frank was, too, while we're at it. Maybe somebody climbed up through his window and shot him. Is that what you want to hear?"

"If that's what you think I want, then you don't know me."

"Maybe I don't." Joey was looking his age and he seemed tired, even though Abe had heard he'd quit his second job at the mall. "Maybe I don't want to."

That was the way they left it, with the distance between them, as if they hadn't been best friends their whole lives long. Now when people asked Joey where his buddy was, and why Abe could no longer be found at the Millstone on Saturday nights, Joey just shrugged.

"I'm not his bodyguard," he'd say when asked. "Abe goes his way and I go mine."

Joey would never have known that Abe was involved with someone if Mary Beth hadn't informed him of the situation. She and Kelly Avon had sat down at Selena's with a list of every unmarried woman in the village, thereby determining that the person in question wasn't anyone they knew. People in town wouldn't have figured Abe to go and find himself someone from the Haddan School. That's the way things were in the village still, after all these years: it was fine for the people of Main Street to do as they pleased, and a few had gone so far as to send their sons and daughters to the Haddan School, but expectations were different for anyone from the west side. Though they owned the stores and supplied the other residents with their shoes and chrysanthemums and cheese, people were expected to stay on their own side of town when it came to personal matters. And if Joey might have predicted Abe would get involved with that teacher from Haddan, he would never have guessed how often Abe went to see her, always late at night, after curfew, when the girls at St. Anne's were asleep in their beds and the hallways were silent and dark.

Abe had become so familiar with this route that he no longer stumbled over the frayed carpet. He had learned to expect stray umbrellas and Rollerblades inside the doorway and was accustomed to the rushing sound of steam heat rising from the old metal radiators, as well as the scent of bath oil and musk, fragrances that might have caused a less experienced man to lose his bearings. Abe usually parked down by the river and walked the rest of the way, so that no one would notice his grandfather's car, not that anyone attended to who was going in and out of the dorm. There was absolutely no security in the building, all Abe had to do was jiggle the knob and push his weight against the door and he was in.

Each time they were together, Betsy promised it would be the last. But this was a pledge she made to herself after he'd gone, and it was a rather flimsy pact. While Abe was beside her, she wanted him far too much to let him go. It was Abe who usually realized he had to leave, quickly, before the bells rang and the girls at St. Anne's were awakened to find him in the hallway, shirttails out, boots in hand. How could Betsy let him go? Every time the wind tapped at her window glass, she wished that it might be him. She could hear him sometimes, out by the roses, watching her before he let himself in the front door, and the knowledge that he was there in the garden made her so light-headed she was willing to take risks she could not have imagined before. In time, she found that what happened between them at night was spilling into her daylight hours. While she taught her classes, while she showered, while she made coffee or kissed the man she was to marry, it was Abe she was thinking of.

It was nearly the end of December when Betsy realized how dangerous a game she was playing. She knew then she would have to end it immediately. It was a cold morning and they'd stayed in bed too long, sleeping past the bells; by the time they awoke it was after nine. Snow had begun to fall, and a silvery light coursed through the window; perhaps this pale sky was the reason they'd been so reckless, for the girls in Betsy's care were already dressed and on their way to classes. Betsy could hear the front door open and close as she lay there beside him. She recognized the sound of Maureen Brown giggling as the girl leaned over the porch railing to catch snowflakes on her tongue, and that awful Peggy Anthony's high-pitched wail as her leather boots skidded on the icy steps. How easy it would have been for Abe and Betsy to be caught on this morning. Say Peggy Anthony broke her leg on the icy stair. Say Amy Elliot had one of her allergic reactions and came pounding on the door. How long would it take for the news to drift to Chalk House? Fifteen seconds? Twenty? How long exactly, before Betsy ruined her life?

She had never told a lie in her life before this. She had never believed herself capable of such subterfuge, making up excuses not to see Eric, her deceit forming with such ease she surprised

herself. All that she'd wanted, the security of her life here in
Haddan, would be undone by her own hand, unless she stopped
now. She called a locksmith that same afternoon. After the new
electronic lock had been installed on the front door, Betsy insisted upon a house meeting. Her girls were told in no uncertain
terms not to give the code to either boyfriends or deliverymen.
Betsy then had a dead bolt placed on the door to her own quarters as well, one that the locksmith had assured her was impenetrable, except to the most experienced thieves, the sort who
would stop at nothing to get what they wanted.

Abe came back the next night, an inky blue night, as deep
and immeasurable as the farthest reaches of heaven. Betsy heard
him in the garden, but instead of going to the window to wave,
she drew the curtains. She imagined his confusion when he
found that the old lock had been replaced; it was an act not only
of self-preservation, but of cruelty, as well. Betsy knew this, but
she couldn't bring herself to face him. So she let him stand out
there on the porch until, at last, he went away. Afterward, she did
her best to avoid him. If a man even reminded her of Abel Grey,
if he was tall or had blue eyes, Betsy went the other way, ducking
behind hedges, fleeing the mini-mart before her purchases were
rung up. She wouldn't even go to the pharmacy for fear she might
run into him. She spent every night with Eric, as if he were the
remedy, the cure for a bothersome ailment, no different than a
fever or a cold.

Abe, however, was not so easy to dismiss. He had never envi-
sioned himself as a man in love, but that was what he had turned
out to be. He tried his best not to think about Betsy. He spent his
days immersed in his job, gathering as much information about
Gus Pierce as he could, telephoning the boy's father in New

York, going over his various school records, searching for a key to Gus's intent. Why people did the things they did, whether it be on impulse or a premeditated act, was always a puzzle. The boy in the water, the shotgun hidden in his brother's room, the locked door at St. Anne's. In the evenings Abe left his files and drove past the school, far more wounded than he'd ever imagined he'd be. When Kelly Avon suggested they meet down at the Millstone, he declined; he remained in his parked car, there on school property, where he didn't belong.

The holiday season was approaching and luminous silver stars had been affixed to the stoplights to celebrate the season. At the Haddan School, white lights decorated the porch balustrades. On the night when Abe finally decided to confront Betsy, he knew it was a bad decision. A light snow had begun to fall; it was just after supper and the campus was bustling. Abe was bound to be seen, not that he cared. He thought about all the times he'd been called in to settle altercations he hadn't understood: the heated fights of divorcing husbands and wives, the battles between brothers, the agony of thwarted lovers who had slit their exes' tires in the parking lot of the Millstone. All of them had been people whose love for each other had turned sour, deteriorating into a need for revenge or justice and a desire to hurt whoever had wronged them. Now Abe knew what those people were after; it was somebody's love they wanted, and they went after it the only way they knew how, exactly as he meant to do here tonight.

Two girls were sitting on the porch steps, letting the snow fall down on them. Abe had to lurch over them in order to get to the door.

"The combination is three, thirteen, thirty-three," one of the

girls on the porch told him, forgetting Betsy's demand for security and caution.

Abe punched in the code and let himself in. It was the free
hour between supper and study hall, when most students had
their radios blaring and the TV in the lounge was turned up. Abe
bumped into one girl who was toting a bag of laundry and almost
tripped over another who sat squarely in the hallway, nattering
away on the pay phone, unaware of anyone who passed by. St.
Anne's seemed a very different place from the dark, silent house
Abe was used to when he arrived in the middle of the night, not
that the crowded corridors stopped him from going on to Betsy's
quarters.

A dead bolt wasn't always as invincible as locksmiths would
have a buyer believe, not if a thief came prepared. Abe had
brought along a small screwdriver he most often used to tighten
the loose rearview mirror of his grandfather's cruiser; in no time
he had pried open the dead bolt, hoping that Betsy hadn't paid
much, since it was fairly worthless in warding off any serious
criminal intent. Going into her rooms uninvited, Abe had the
same itchy feeling he used to have as a kid. He was breathing
hard, not quite believing what he'd done, his hands were shaking, exactly as they had whenever he broke into a house. What he
needed was a cold beer and a friend to set him straight, but as he
had neither, he went on, into her bedroom. He ran his hand over
the lace runner on top of the bureau, then approached the night
table. Betsy had every right not to see him anymore. Hadn't he
done the exact same thing dozens of times, not bothering to call
some woman who'd made it clear she was interested, not even
having the decency to explain himself? He held the earrings
Betsy had left on the bureau, uncertain as to whether he wanted

to understand her or punish her. Either way, he was not really surprised when he heard the door open. With his run of bad luck, he'd expected as much.

Betsy could tell Abe was there right away; she knew it the way people say they know they are about to be hit by lightning, yet remain powerless to run, unable to avoid their fate. She panicked, as anyone might have when disparate parts of her life were about to crash into each other, certain to leave a path of anguish and debris. It was true that devotion could be lost as quickly as it was found, which was why some people insisted that love letters always be written in ink. How easy it was for even the sweetest words to evaporate, only to be rewritten as impulse and infatuation might dictate. How unfortunate that love could not be taught or trained, like a seal or a dog. Instead, it was a wolf on the prowl, with a mind of its own, and it made its own way, undeterred by the damage done. Love like this could turn honest people into liars and cheats, as it now did to Betsy. She told Eric she needed to change out of her clothes, but it wasn't the blue wool outfit she had worn to the dean's for dinner that made her feel faint in these overheated rooms.

"Can you open a few windows, too?" Betsy called as she went on to the bedroom, making sure to close the door behind her. She was burning hot and overwrought; she should not have had that drink at the dean's house after the dinner to which Eric had insisted they go. She was dressed in unfamiliar clothes, with the unfamiliar taste of whiskey in her mouth, so that it seemed as though she were the stranger here and Abe, there at the edge of her bed, was the one who belonged.

By now the snow outside was falling harder, but that didn't stop Betsy from going to raise her bedroom window. The falling snow began to drift onto the carpet, but Betsy didn't care. She had a prickly sensation up and down her spine. How well did she know this man in her room? How could she know what he might be capable of?

"If you don't change your clothes he'll wonder why you lied to him," Abe said.

The only illumination came from beyond the window, due to the streetlamp and the brilliance of the snow. In such light every-thing appeared distant; it was as if Abe and Betsy and whatever had been between them had already moved into the past. "He'll wonder what else you lied to him about."

"I haven't lied to him!" Betsy was grateful for the cold air com-ing in through the window. She was burning with shame, the penance of her own deception. Although she had been the one to refuse him, she still remembered what it was like to kiss him, how such a simple act could turn her inside out.

"I see. You just didn't tell him the truth." Abe would have laughed then, if he found such matters amusing. "Is that what you did when you were with me? You sidestepped the truth? Is that what happened between us?"

They could hear Eric in the kitchen, putting up the kettle, opening cabinets as he searched for sugar and cups.

"Nothing happened." Betsy's mouth burned. "There was noth-ing between us."

It was the one answer that could drive him away, and this was Betsy's intent. Abe went out through the window; he banged his bad knee against the window frame, collecting a bruise that would ache for days. The campus was already covered with two or three inches of new snow, and the falling flakes were large and swirly, the mark of a storm that would last. By morning, traffic would be a mess; a heavy snowfall in Haddan never went by without at least one bad accident, usually up by the interstate, and one local boy injuring himself on a makeshift sled or a borrowed snowmobile.

The snow was blinding as Abe walked away from St. Anne's; all the same, he was reminded of the hot afternoon when his brother died. He'd recognized the same thing then, how quickly the future could become the past, moments melting into each other before anyone could reach out and change them. He'd gone over how it all might have happened differently if he'd run up the stairs. If he'd knocked on the door, if he'd barged right in; how it might have changed had he denied his brother's request that morning and refused to go along to their grandfather's farm. It had been the sort of summer day that shone and glittered in the dusty sunlight like a miracle, all blue heat and endless white clouds, stifling hot, so quiet Abe could hear himself breathing when Frank hoisted him up so Abe could climb through the window to get the gun.

Afterward he'd had to do it again and again, compelled to repeat his thievery. At least these acts had stopped him from thinking, but now he was done with breaking into other people's houses. It had never done any good anyway, he'd carried his pain around inside him; it was still here on this snowy night. Maybe that was why he decided to leave his car where it was, parked by the river, and walk home. Once he started, he just kept going, past his house and halfway to Hamilton, not returning until sometime near dawn when he hitched a ride back with a plow Kelly Avon's little brother, Josh, was driving.

The next day he went walking again, even though he was supposed to show up for work, and Doug Lauder, a patrolman who grumbled under the best circumstances, was forced to take his shift, stuck directing traffic outside town hall until his toes turned blue. Before long, people in town noticed that Abe had quit stargazing. Why, he didn't even look up anymore as he walked through the village. He no longer whistled and his face was grim and he'd taken to being out at hours when decent people were all at home in bed. Several old-timers in town, Zeke Harris at the dry cleaner's, and George Nichols over at the Millstone, remembered that Wright Grey had done the very same thing for a while, walking so many miles he'd worn down his boots and then had to take them into Hamilton to be resoled.

Now it seemed that Abe had inherited this trait. Even when the weather took a turn for the worse, with ragged sleet and cold, blue ice, Abe kept at it. People would glance out their windows and there he'd be, on Main Street or on Elm, or over by Lovewell Lane, without even a dog as an excuse to slog through the slush. He had decided he would go on walking until he could figure things out. How was it, he wanted to know, that things could turn so quickly from love to locked doors? This was why he had resisted commitments for so long; he wasn't constitutionally fit for love. He had fallen into it headfirst, just like those fools he'd always made fun of, Teddy Humphrey, for instance, who was so driven he didn't care if he looked like an idiot; he'd park outside Nikki's house and blast his car radio, hoping all the songs of heartbreak he played would remind her that love that had been lost could also be found.

Abe pitied Teddy Humphrey, and now he pitied himself as well. Some days, he had a terrible feeling in the center of his chest that simply wouldn't go away. He'd even gone over to the clinic in Hamilton to have it checked out, knowing that Mrs. Jeremy's son, AJ, had been walloped with a heart attack two years earlier at the age of thirty-seven, but the nurses insisted nothing was wrong. *Get yourself an antacid,* they told him. *Stop drinking so much coffee. Stop walking in such bad weather, and make sure to wear gloves and a scarf.*

Abe went directly from the clinic to the pharmacy. "What's the difference between love and heartburn?" he asked Pete Byers, who was the one person in town who surely knew about such matters.

"Give me a minute." Pete, always a thoughtful man, assumed he'd need time to think it over. It seemed like a difficult riddle, but as it turned out, the answer didn't take long. "I've got it," he declared. "Nothing."

On that advice, Abe bought some Rolaids, which he swallowed right down, along with most of his pride. No wonder he hadn't trusted anyone before; you never could tell what people would do, one minute they'd be smiling at you and the next they'd be gone, without so much as an explanation or a civil good-bye. There wasn't a grown man on this planet who wound up with everything he wanted, so who was Abe to complain? He was still here, wasn't he? He woke every morning to see the sky, he drank his coffee, scraped the ice from his front steps, waved to his neighbors. He wasn't a boy who'd been cheated, who never got the chance to grow up and make his own decisions, right or wrong. The difference between tragedy and simple bad luck, after all, could be easily defined: it was possible to walk away from one, and that Abe would do, no matter how many miles it took or how many pairs of boots he wore through.

THE WATCH
AND THE LOAF

SNOW FELL ALL THROUGH DE-
cember, covering the Christmas tree in
front of town hall with a blanket of white
that would not melt until the tree was taken
down, as it was every year, on the Saturday
after New Year's. This was the season when
the north wind slammed around town, tossing garbage cans into the street, shaking
store awnings. The days were so short they
were finished by four, at which point the
sky turned black, and evenings were cold
enough to freeze a person's breath in the
crystal-clear air. There seemed to be handfuls of stars tossed right above the rooftops
in Haddan, keeping the town still alight at
midnight. Some people joked that it would
make sense to wear sunglasses after sun-
down, that's how bright the snow was; it

shone in the starlight, causing even the most serious people to put aside all caution and restraint and jump into the biggest of the drifts.

The boat shed at the Haddan School was unheated and drafty; it overlooked a bend in the frozen river, and although the building was closed until spring, that didn't mean it went un-used. On Friday nights kegs of beer were set up beside the tarp-covered kayaks and canoes, and several girls in the freshman class had already lost their innocence there beside the sculls. Al-though she was embarrassed to be like so many others, Carlin had spent a good deal of time in the boathouse with Harry, but by the end of the semester, all of that had changed. Now when-ever she was with Harry, she would discover a stone in the pocket of Gus's coat; some were black and some were white and others were a crystalline blue-gray, the color of the ice that formed in the shallows of the river. The floor of Carlin's closet was now covered by a collection of such stones; they rattled every time she reached for her boots, and soon she noticed the stones turned clearer as the hour grew later, so that by midnight they were transparent, nearly invisible to the naked eye.

When it came time for winter vacation, a group had arranged a week-long trip to Harry's family's place in Vermont. It was as-sumed that Carlin would be going with them, and she didn't let on that she was staying behind until the day before they were to leave.

"You're not serious." Harry was deeply annoyed. "We made all the plans and now you're not going?"

They were his plans actually; still Carlin did her best to ex-plain how difficult it would be for her to leave Haddan. Miss Davis could no longer rise from her chair and was often too tired for dinner, falling asleep at the table, her untouched plate before her. Miss Davis had been so grateful at Thanksgiving that Carlin didn't feel she could leave her employer alone for the holidays.

"I don't care," Harry said. "I'm selfish and I want you there with me."

But Carlin could not be convinced. At five the next morning she was in bed when she heard Amy leave. The van Harry had hired was idling in the parking lot, headlights cutting through the dark, and when Carlin listened carefully, she recognized the voices of the lucky few Harry had invited along on the ski trip. She kept her eyes closed until the van pulled out of the lot; the rattle of the engine drew farther and farther away as it turned onto Main Street, passing the fences decorated with white lights, and the brilliant tree outside town hall, and the graveyard behind St. Agatha's, where so many had already deposited wreaths to mark the season.

On the first day of vacation, St. Anne's was deserted, save for the mice. All of the girls had gone off with family or friends, and in the emptiness left behind there was a moment when Carlin felt lost. She went to the pay phone and called her mother, Sue, who cried and said it just wasn't Christmas without Carlin home to celebrate. As much as she loved her mother, by the time they were through talking, Carlin was glad enough to be in Haddan. Sue Leander had sent Carlin a present of white musk cologne, which Carlin rewrapped and presented to Miss Davis.

"You must think I'm trying to catch myself a man," Miss Davis said when she saw her gift, but she was persuaded to try out a dab or two on her wrists. "There," she proclaimed. "I'm a knockout."

Carlin laughed and set to work on the dressing for the goose, which she'd had delivered from the butcher in Hamilton. As it turned out, Carlin was a good cook. She, who'd been raised on frozen dinners and macaroni and cheese, could now julienne peppers and carrots in seconds flat; one afternoon she made a vegetable soup so delicious that when the aroma drifted through the dormitory several girls came down with a bad case of homesickness and they cried themselves to sleep, dreaming of their childhood homes.

"Pecans in the stuffing?" Miss Davis sniffed, as she peered over Carlin's shoulder. "Raisins?" Her voice was grave with mistrust.

Carlin held the goose up by the neck and asked if perhaps Miss Davis would like to take over. The goose looked rather naked and strange to Miss Davis's eyes and, truthfully, the notion that she might fix anything more complicated than a cheese sandwich was far-fetched at best, while the idea of her taking a dead goose in hand was nothing short of ludicrous. Quickly, she reconsidered. When all was said and done, pecan dressing would be fine.

Helen hadn't wanted to like this girl who worked for her; it was foolish to begin attachments now, when it was far too late for such things. She would never have admitted how glad she was that Carlin had stayed for the holiday. The girl was good company and had an exceptional talent for solving problems that seemed insurmountable to Helen, arranging, for instance, for a cab so that Helen could attend mass at St. Agatha's instead of going to the services led by Dr. Jones in the school chapel. Having been raised Catholic, Helen had always wished to go to St. Agatha's but she'd feared local parishioners would be unfriendly to an outsider, particularly a lost soul such as herself, who hadn't been to a proper mass for so long. As it turned out, the congregation had welcomed her warmly. Pete Byers helped her to her seat, and afterward some nice young man named Teddy had driven her back to St. Anne's. When she arrived home, she found that Carlin had set out a real Christmas dinner, which brought to mind the holiday meals Helen's own mother used to serve, with dishes of candied yams and brussels sprouts, and of course the goose with its lovely stuffing.

Halfway through dinner, Helen Davis gazed out the window and saw that handsome man again. Abel Grey was standing by the rosebushes, even though it was snowing. He was just about the best-looking man Helen had ever seen, and she thought now that she should have found herself a man like that back when she was young, rather than moping around after that worthless Dr. Howe.

"Look who's here," she said to Carlin, and she quickly sent the girl to fetch him. Carlin ran through the falling snow, the black coat flaring out over a white apron and her good blue dress.

"Hey," she called to Abe, who didn't seem happy to have been discovered. "Miss Davis wants you to have dinner with us. You might as well, since you're lurking around here anyway."

Carlin jumped up and down to keep warm, but at least the boots she'd bought at Hingram's were doing the job, and Gus's coat was a blessing in weather such as this. Those big snowflakes were still falling, and Abe's hair had turned white. He looked sheepish under all that snow, the way any man would be who'd just been caught peering through windows.

"I'm just out for a walk," he insisted. "I'm not lurking."

"Miss Chase went to a hotel in Maine with Mr. Herman. So you might as well have your dinner with us."

Abe had already had his Christmas lunch at the Millstone—
two drafts, a burger, and a large order of fries.

"Come on," Carlin urged. "I'll pretend I never saw you sneaking out St. Anne's at three in the morning and you can pretend
you're polite."

"What are you having for dinner?" Abe asked grudgingly.

"Goose with pecan stuffing and candied yams."

Abe was surprised. "You cooked all that?" When Carlin nodded, he threw up his hands. "I guess you talked me into it."

By now, the light had already begun to fade. Abe hadn't really
expected Betsy to be home, nor had he planned what he might
say should she be there. Would he have begged for her to reconsider? Was he that far gone?

As they approached St. Anne's, Helen Davis opened the back
door; when she saw Abe she waved.

"I think she's got a crush on you," Carlin confided.

"I'm sure she'll dump me before dinner's over." Abe waved
back. "Hey there, Helen," he called. "Merry Christmas!" The
black cat slipped out onto the frosty porch. "There's my buddy."
Abe clucked as if calling chickens, but the cat ignored him and
went instead to rub against Carlin's legs.

"Pretty boy." Carlin leaned down to pat the cat's ears.

"Again your cat has failed to recognize you," Helen noted as
they all traipsed into the kitchen, cat included. Helen had placed
a cover over the yams and she'd shoved a plate atop the bowl of
vegetables to keep them warm. A few small exertions and those
brief moments on the porch had left her exhausted. Standing
there at her own dinner table, holding on to the back of a chair,
Helen seemed likely to topple over, exactly like Millie Adams
over on Forest Street, who had been ill for years before she

passed on, so weak that Abe often stopped by on his way home
from work to make certain that Millie had made it through the
day. Now, Abe helped Miss Davis to her chair.

"How nice that you happened to be passing by," she said.
"Just in time for dinner."

Still wearing the black coat, Carlin hurried to the cupboard
for an extra plate. "He was lurking."

"Lurking," Miss Davis said, pleased.

"I was walking." Now that he saw the food before him, Abe
rubbed his hands together like a starving man.

Carlin was searching through the cutlery drawer for silverware with which to set another place when she felt something
move in her pocket.

"Take off that coat and sit down," Helen Davis instructed.
"We can't very well eat without you."

Carlin put down the silverware. She had a funny look on her
face. She had forgotten the cranberry relish, but she didn't move
to rectify that mistake. Midnight leapt onto Helen's lap and began to purr, low down in the back of its throat.

"What is it?" Helen said to the silent girl.

The worst part of caring about someone was that sooner or
later you were bound to worry, and to take notice of details that
wouldn't otherwise be apparent. Helen, for instance, now saw
that Carlin had grown pale, a wisp of a thing wrapped up in that
old black coat she insisted on wearing.

"What's wrong?" Helen demanded.

Carlin reached into her pocket and brought forth a small fish,
which she placed upon the table. Helen leaned forward for a better look. It was one of those silver minnows found in the Haddan
River, small and shimmering and gasping for breath. Helen Davis

might have dropped the little fish in a tumbler of water had Midnight not pounced on it and eaten it whole.

In spite of herself, Carlin laughed. "Did you see that? He ate it."

"You bad, bad boy," Helen scolded. "You rascal."

"I told you Gus left me things," Carlin said to Abe. "But you didn't believe me."

Abe leaned back in his chair, baffled, but Helen Davis was far less surprised. She had always believed that grief could manifest itself in a physical form. Right after Annie Howe's death, for instance, she had been covered by red bumps, which itched and burned into the night. The doctor in town told her that she was allergic to roses and must never again eat rosewater preserves or bathe in rose oil, but Helen knew better. She'd had nothing to do with roses. It was grief she was carrying around with her, grief that was rising up through the skin.

Recalling these times caused Helen immeasurable pain, or maybe it was her illness that was affecting her so. It was so awful that she doubled over and Carlin ran to get the tablets of morphine hidden in the spice cabinet.

"There's nothing wrong with me," Miss Davis insisted, but she gave them no further argument when they helped her to her room. Afterward, Carlin put up a plate for Miss Davis for tomorrow's lunch, then she ate her own dinner between bouts of cleaning up. Abe bolted his food, then checked to ensure that Miss Davis was sleeping. Thankfully, she was, but Abe was disturbed by how lifeless she appeared, pale as the deepest winter's ice.

When Carlin and Abe left Miss Davis's, the air was so cold it hurt a person's throat and lungs just to breathe; the sky was alight with constellations swirling through the dark. It was possible to see the Pleiades, those daughters of Atlas placed into the Milky Way for their own protection. How lovely it was with no people in sight and only the stars for company.

"How come you're so rarely lurking around anymore? Doesn't Miss Chase miss you?"

"She's got a fiancé." Abe had learned the constellations from his grandfather and as a child he'd gone to sleep counting not sheep but all the brilliant dogs and bears and fish that shone through the window.

"That didn't stop you before," Carlin reminded him.

"I guess the better man won." Abe tried to smile, but his face hurt in the cold.

"I'm in Mr. Herman's history seminar. Believe me, he's not even the second-best man."

The snow had stopped; it was the brilliant sort that made every step squeak.

"Christmas." Abe watched his own breath form little crystals. "What do you think Gus would have been doing right now?"

"He'd be in New York," Carlin said without hesitation. "And I'd be with him. We'd eat too much and see three movies in a row. And maybe we wouldn't come back."

"Gus couldn't have put that fish in your pocket. You know that, don't you?"

"Tell that to your friend." Carlin nodded to the cat, which had followed them from Miss Davis's. "He has fish breath."

Later that night, Carlin was still thinking of Gus as she went into the gym, using the key every member of the swim team was granted. She switched on the emergency lights in the entrance-way, then went to the locker room and changed into her suit, grabbing for her cap and goggles. Abel Gray didn't want to believe the fish at Miss Davis's dinner had come from Gus, but Carlin knew that some things never disappeared completely, they stayed with you for better and for worse.

Down at the pool, light reflected from the glassed walkway, and that was bright enough. The water looked bottle green, and when Carlin sat on the edge and swung her legs over, she was shocked by how chilly it was. Clearly, the heater had been turned off for the holidays. Carlin eased into the water, gasping at the cold. Her skin rose in goose bumps; her goggles steamed up the moment she slipped them on. She set about doing laps, using her strongest stroke, the butterfly, falling into her rhythm naturally. It brought relief to swim; Carlin felt as though she were out in the ocean, miles from land and all the petty concerns of humankind. She thought about the stars she had seen in the sky, and the snowflakes that had dusted the stone walkways, and the New England cold that could cut right through a person. By the time she was done, the action of her stroke had created a current; little waves slapped against the tiles. With her elbows resting on the edge of the pool, Carlin removed her goggles, then pulled off her bathing cap and shook out her hair. It was then she saw that she wasn't alone.

There was a greenish mist of chlorine rising from the surface, and for a moment Carlin thought she'd only imagined a figure approaching, but then the figure took a step closer. She pushed herself away from the edge; as long as she stayed in the center of the pool there was no way anyone could catch her, if catching her was what this individual was after. Whoever it was, he'd never be as fast as Carlin was in the water.

She narrowed her eyes, already burning with chlorine, and tried to make out his face. "Don't come any closer!" she commanded, and then was somewhat surprised when he did as he was told. He crouched down on his haunches and grinned, and that was when she saw who it was. Sean Byers from the pharmacy. Carlin could feel her heartbeat slow down, but the funny thing was, her pulse was still going crazy. "What do you think you're doing here?"

"I could say the same to you." Sean took off his watch and carefully placed it into the front pocket of his jeans. "I'm here two or three times a week, after closing. I'm a regular. Which is more than I can say of you."

"Oh, really? You swim?"

"Usually in Boston Harbor, but this does fine. No shopping carts or half-sunk boats to dodge."

Carlin continued to tread water; she watched as Sean took off his jacket and tossed it on the tiles. He pulled off his sweater and his T-shirt, then gave Carlin a look.

"You don't mind, do you?" he asked, one hand poised by his fly. "I wouldn't want to embarrass you or anything like that."

"Oh, no." Carlin tilted her head back, challenging him. "Go on. Be my guest."

Sean pulled off his jeans. Carlin couldn't help herself, she looked to make sure he was actually wearing a bathing suit and was amused to see that he was. Sean let out a holler as he jumped into the far end of the pool.

"You're a trespasser with no legal rights," Carlin said when he swam over. "I hope you know that." In the deep end, the water was so black it appeared bottomless.

Sean's face was pale in the dim light. "There's nothing to do in this town. I had to find some way to occupy myself. Especially with Gus gone. You're a good swimmer," he noted.

"I'm good at everything," Carlin told him.

Sean laughed. "And so modest."

"Well? Do you think you can keep up with me?"

"Definitely," he said. "If you slow down."

They swam laps together and Carlin didn't change her pace to suit him. To his credit, Sean managed to do fairly well; he hadn't been lying, he really was a swimmer, and although his stroke was awkward and wild, he was fast and competitive. It was lovely to be in the dark, alone, yet not alone. Carlin could have gone on this way forever, had she not noticed flashes of reflected light glittering before her. She stopped to tread water, thinking her vision would clear, but they were there, a stream of tiny minnows.

Sean came up beside her. His wet hair looked black and his eyes were black as well. He had a scar beneath his right eye, an unfortunate reminder of the car he'd stolen, the one that had wound up crashed on a side road in Chelsea and had landed him in juvenile court and then in Haddan. In spite of his injury, he had a beautiful face, the sort that had always brought him more fortune than he deserved. In Boston, he was known for his daring, but tonight, he felt uneasy. The pool was much colder than usual, but that wasn't the reason he'd begun to shiver. There was some movement grazing his skin, fin and gill, quick as a breath. A line of silver went past him, then circled and came back toward him.

"What are those?"

Sean had been wanting to get Carlin alone since the first time he saw her, but now he was far less sure of himself than he'd thought he'd be. Here in the water, nothing looked the same anymore. He would have sworn he saw fish darting through the pool, as ridiculous a notion as if stars had fallen from the sky to shine beneath them, giving off icy white light.

"They're only minnows." Carlin took Sean's hand in her own. His skin was cold, but underneath he was blistering. Carlin made him reach out along with her, so that the fish floated right through their fingers. "Don't worry," she said. "They won't hurt us."

PETE BYERS COULDN'T BEGIN TO COUNT THE times he'd hurried to his store during snowstorms, called there by frantic mothers whose babies were dehydrated and burning up with fever, or by old-timers who'd forgotten to pick up a much-needed medication without which they might not make it through the night. He opened when necessary and closed down when appropriate, locking his doors, for instance, to honor Abe Grey's grandfather when Wright was laid to rest. On that day, there was a funeral procession that reached from Main Street to the library; people stood on the sidewalks and wept, as if one of their own had passed on. Pete also came in after hours on the day Frank Grey shot himself, to fill a prescription for tranquilizers to ensure that Frank's mother, Margaret, would finally get some sleep.

Pete had told Ernest Grey it would be no bother for him to drop the prescription by the house, but Ernest must have needed to get out, as he insisted on coming down himself. It was late, and Ernest had forgotten his wallet; he went through his pockets, pulling out change, as if Pete wouldn't have trusted him to make good on whatever he owed. Then Ernest sat down at the counter and cried, and for the first time, Pete was grateful he and

Eileen had never had children. Perhaps what people said was true, that any man who lived long enough would eventually realize that the way in which he was cursed was also the blessing he'd received.

Since the town had changed so much in recent years, with so many new people moving in, it was difficult for Pete to know everyone by name, which meant service wasn't what it once was. But towns don't remain the same, they go forward, like it or not; there had even been talk about building a town high school, out near Wright's old farm, for there would soon be too many students to send to the Hamilton school district. It wasn't the way it used to be, that much was certain, back when a person would meet the same people at the Millstone on a Saturday night as he'd see at St. Agatha's on Sunday morning, knowing full well what there was to confess and what there was to be thankful for.

Lately, Pete had been puzzling over the issue of confidentiality, and it was this topic he was contemplating when Abe came in for lunch on the Saturday after Christmas. The few regular customers—Lois Jeremy and her cronies from the garden club, and Sam Arthur, a member of the town council for ten years running—all cried out a greeting to Abe.

"Happy holidays," he called back. "Don't forget to vote yes on the traffic light by the library. You'll save a life."

Anyone looking closely would be able to tell that Abe hadn't been sleeping well. Over this holiday break, he'd gone so far as to phone half a dozen hotels in Maine, like a common fool, searching for Betsy. At one hotel, a party named Herman had been registered, and although it turned out to be a couple from Maryland, Abe had been distressed ever since. Sean Byers, on

the other hand, looked just fine. He was whistling as he filled
Abe's order, which, like everyone else in town, he now knew by
heart—turkey on rye, mustard, no mayo.

"What are you so happy about?" Abe asked Sean, who was
practically radiating good cheer. It didn't take long for Abe to figure it out, for when Carlin Leander came into the pharmacy
Sean lit up like the Christmas tree outside town hall.

Carlin, on the other hand, was cold and bedraggled; she had
just been at the pool and the ends of her hair were a faint, watery
green.

"You went swimming without me?" Sean said when she approached the counter.

"I'll go again," Carlin assured him.

When Sean went to get Sam Arthur's bowl of chowder, Carlin sat beside Abe. It was because of a call from Carlin that Abe
was here today, and although she hadn't said what the reason
was, Abe grinned as he nodded toward Sean. Love was often the
explanation behind most emergencies.

"Who would have guessed."

"It's not what you think. We just go swimming. I know it
would never work out—you don't have to tell me not to get my
hopes up. I'm not that stupid."

"That's not what I was going to say." Abe pushed his plate
away and finished his coffee. "I was going to say good luck."

"I don't believe in luck." Carlin checked out the vinyl-covered
menu. For the first time in days the idea of food didn't make her
queasy. She was actually considering a mint chocolate chip ice
cream soda. Beneath Gus's old coat, she was wearing jeans and a
ratty black sweater, but as far as Sean was concerned, she could
not have looked more beautiful. He stared at her while he fixed a

raspberry lime rickey for Sam Arthur, who was there to pick up his insulin and would have been better served had he ordered a sugar-free cola.

"What's the other guy in your life going to think if you get involved with Sean Byers?" Abe asked.

"Harry?" Carlin had refused to think past vacation. Every night when she met Sean at the pool, it seemed as if they would have the school to themselves forever. Some other girl might have been frightened of staying on the deserted campus, but not Carlin. She liked the way her footsteps echoed, she liked the silence that greeted her in the hallways and on the stairs. All of the windows at St. Anne's were coated with blue ice and when the wind blew, icicles were shaken down from the roof with a sound that brought to mind broken bones, but Carlin didn't care. She was happy, but happiness can often be figured in minutes. First there were seven days before school began anew, then six, then five, then Carlin stopped counting.

"I can handle Harry," she said to Abe now.

"No," Abe said. "I meant the other guy. Gus."

Lois Jeremy stopped by on her way to pay her check; she wagged her finger at Abe. "You weren't posted outside town hall when we had our last meeting." She treated Abe, along with all the members of the Haddan police force, as though they were her own personal employees, but at least she was polite to the hired help.

"No, ma'am. But I'm hoping to be there next time."

"I can't believe her." Carlin was livid. "She treated you like a servant."

"That's because I'm at their service." Abe saluted as Mrs.

Jeremy and Charlotte Evans left, and the two women chuckled as they waved good-bye.

Carlin shook her head, amazed. "You've lived here so long you don't notice when someone's a snob."

"I notice, but if you care about what other people think, you're a goner. That's the lesson you learn in Haddan." Abe reached for his coat. "Thanks for calling me down here. I'm assuming you're paying my tab, especially now that you have this relationship with Sean. He'll probably give you a discount."

"I called you because I found something." Carlin opened the black coat to reveal an inside breast pocket, one she hadn't known existed before that morning. She took out a plastic bag of white powder.

Once again, Abe felt that his drowned boy wasn't at all like the Haddan student his grandfather had pulled from the river. This one kept on drowning, and any man foolish enough to get too close might be pulled down along with him.

"I wasn't going to show it to you, but then I realized Gus can't get into trouble. I don't even think it's his because I would have known if he was involved with this sort of drugs."

But Abe wasn't so sure. It was astounding how thoroughly someone you cared for could deceive you and just how wrong you could be. Back when Abe was a boy, he was the one who had liked gunplay a little too well. Whenever Wright had taken them to Mullstein's field for target practice, Frank sat on a bale of hay with his hands over his ears while Abe fired away; he'd shoot anything, even Wright's big, old twelve-gauge, the one they stole, a gun so powerful that after he pulled the trigger, Abe was often left flat on his back looking up at the clouds in the sky.

Abe opened the bag, but as he was about to test for the bitter edge of cocaine, Pete Byers stopped him.

"I wouldn't eat that stuff, son," Pete said. "It will burn right through your trachea."

Abe thought of all the things the powder might be: baking powder, arsenic, chalk dust, angel dust, cake mix, heroin. Sam Arthur was getting ready to leave, chatting with Sean about the lack of team spirit on the Celtics, mourning the days when Larry Bird could always be depended upon to pull a win out of a hat. The sky had been threatening snow all morning, but only a few flakes fell, just enough to cover the icy roads and make driving treacherous.

"If you know what this is, Pete, I need for you to tell me," Abe said.

People had a right to their own business, didn't they? Or so Pete had always believed. Take the case of Abe's own grandfather, who stopped taking his medications at the end of his life, simply refusing to come into town to pick up what the doctor ordered. One night Pete drove out to the farm; he knocked on the door with the nitroglycerin tablets that had been sitting on the counter in the pharmacy for days, but Wright hadn't invited Pete in with his usual hospitality. He'd merely looked through the screen door and said, *I've got a right to do this,* and Pete found he had to agree. Once a man began drawing the line, judging right and wrong, he'd need the stamina of an angel on earth, dispensing the sort of wisdom Pete Byers knew he didn't possess.

It had been difficult all these years, never divulging a confidence, lying beside Eileen in bed with a headful of information he could never discuss. When they went to the inn for the New Year's dance at the end of the week, he'd know which waitresses were using birth control pills, he'd be aware of how Doreen

Becker had tried nearly everything for that rash she had, just as he knew that Mrs. Jeremy's son, AJ, who always went to the inn to pick up platters of cheese and shrimp for his mother's yearly party, had begun to take Antabuse in yet another attempt to curb his drinking.

All this knowledge had turned Pete into a man who didn't comment on much of anything. Frankly, if he heard that aliens had landed in Haddan and were eating the cabbages out of the fields and getting ready for battle, he would simply have told his customers they had better stay at home, doors locked, and take care to spend as much time as they could with those they loved best. All Pete knew was that people deserved privacy; they had a right to meet death as they saw fit and they had a right to live their lives that way, too. He had never discussed a customer or a friend's personal life, at least not until now. He pulled up a chair and sat down; he had a right to be tired. He'd been standing for the best part of forty-five years, and he'd been keeping quiet that long, as well. He sighed and shined his glasses on the white apron he wore. Sometimes a man did the wrong thing for the right reasons, a decision often made on the spot, much like diving into a cold pond on a broiling August day.

"Gus used to come in here every afternoon. He told me the boys he lived with were making his life miserable. One time I suggested some medication, because he couldn't sleep. The worst thing was some kind of initiation he had to go through to be part of the house where he lived. He said they gave him a task they thought no one could complete. They wanted him to turn white roses red."

"That was the initiation?" Abe was confused. "No drinking until he dropped? No blindfolds and nights of terror?"

"They chose an impossible task," Carlin said. "That way he would fail and they could be rid of him."

"But it wasn't impossible." Pete held up the packet of powder. "Aniline crystals. It's an old trick. You sprinkle them on white roses, turn around for a minute, use a mister to add some water, and there you have it. The impossible's done."

Later, as Carlin walked back to school, she stopped at the Lucky Day flower shop. The bell over the door rang as she entered. All the while Ettie Nelson, who lived half a block down from Abe on Station Avenue, waited on her, Carlin thought about the many forms cruelty could take. She had a list too long to remember by the time she had chosen half a dozen white roses, gorgeous, pale blooms, the stalks of which were crisscrossed by black thorns. An expensive choice for a student, which was why Ettie had asked if the bouquet signified a special occasion.

"Oh, no," Carlin told her. "Just a gift for a friend."

Carlin paid and went outside to find that the sky seemed to be falling. The snow was coming down hard; the sky was misty and gray, with endless banks of dense clouds. The roses Carlin had chosen were as white as the drifts that were already piling up on the street corners, but so fragrant that people all over town, even those who fervently hoped for the return of good weather as they shoveled out doorways and cars, stopped what they were doing in order to watch her pass by, a beautiful girl in tears who carried roses through the snow.

ON THE FIRST DAY OF THE NEW YEAR, WHEN midnight was near, the van Harry had rented pulled into the parking lot at Chalk House. Carlin might not have been aware of anything, for both the engine and the lights were cut before the van glided into the icy lot, but her sleep was disrupted when Amy turned the doorknob with a click and a clatter, then stole into their room with what she surely believed was caution. Pie had returned earlier in the day, but she was such a deep sleeper she would never have noticed that Amy carried the scent of deception with her, or that as she stripped off her clothes and hurried to bed it was possible to see love bites on her shoulders and throat.

"Have fun?" Carlin called, in a hoarse, chilly whisper.

She could see Amy startle, then pull the blanket up to her neck. "Sure. Tons."

"I didn't know you could ski. And I thought you hated cold weather."

Carlin had sat up, leaning against the headboard for a better look. Amy's dark eyes shone, wide awake and anxious. She forced a loud yawn, as though she couldn't keep from falling asleep. "There's a lot you don't know about me."

Amy turned her face to the wall, assuming Carlin couldn't perceive betrayal from the back, but such things are infinitely easy to read. Carlin supposed she should be grateful to Amy for making it easier to break up with Harry, but as it turned out she was out of sorts in the morning, the way anyone duped into giving her love away might have been. Harry, on the other hand, acted as if nothing between them had changed. When they met crossing the quad, he grabbed Carlin and hugged her, not noticing her hesitancy.

"You should have come with us." Harry's breath billowed out in the cold. He seemed revitalized and more sure of himself than ever. "The snow was great. We had a blast."

Perhaps Harry planned to have them both. It wouldn't be difficult to go behind Carlin's back and assure Amy he was trying his best to end it with Carlin, then drag their breakup out for months. He could tell Amy he was a gentleman, and as such, never did like to break anyone's heart unless it was absolutely necessary.

"I've got something for you," Carlin told him as she ducked his embrace. "Come to my room later. You'll be surprised."

She left him there, curious and more interested than he was in most things. That's what had intrigued him in the first place, wasn't it? How different she was from the other girls. How difficult to second-guess. He'd have to do some sweet-talking to explain to Amy why he was seeing Carlin, but Carlin had faith that he'd manage to spin a believable tale. A good liar always found excuses, and it seemed clear that for Harry such things came far easier than the truth.

He arrived before supper, throwing himself onto Amy's bed, where, unbeknownst to Carlin, he'd spent quite a lot of time, making sure to keep track of the hours Carlin spent at swim practice while he seduced her roommate, not that the assignment had been a chore. Harry fancied the idea of having had two girls in the same bed and he pulled Carlin toward him. Again, she drew away.

"Oh, no. I told you, I've got something to show you."

Harry groaned. "This better be good," he warned.

He hadn't even noticed the white roses, there on the bureau in a vase borrowed from Miss Davis. He leaned up on his elbows when he spied the flowers.

"Who sent those?"

By now, the roses were limp and imperfect, with the edges of the leaves turning brown; still, in Miss Davis's lovely cut-glass vase the bouquet was impressive, the gift of a rival perhaps.

"I bought them for myself. But now I've changed my mind. You know how it is when you decide you want something new." She took the black coat from a hook in the closet and slipped it on. "I realize I want red roses."

There was a flicker of distrust behind Harry's eyes. He uncoiled himself now, the better to watch Carlin's display. He didn't like being tricked, still he'd been well brought up and the smile he bestowed on Carlin was not without appeal.

"If you want red roses, I'll get them for you."

"Get them for Amy," Carlin suggested.

Harry ran a hand through his hair. "Look, if this is about Amy, I admit it, I made a mistake. I figured she was your friend, I didn't expect anything to happen, but she was all over me, and I didn't say no. If you had gone to Vermont, none of it would have happened. Amy is nothing to me," Harry assured her. "Come on over here and let's forget all about her."

"What about the roses?" Carlin kept her distance. She had been spending so much time in the water that the white moons of her cuticles had turned faintly blue; her complexion was so pale she looked as though she'd never seen sunlight. She turned her back and took the packet of aniline from the inner coat pocket. There was a lump in her throat, but she forced herself to face Harry. There were only enough crystals to cover one flower, but even before she could add water, as Pete Byers had instructed, the single rose began to turn color, one vivid bloom, scarlet amongst the rest.

Harry applauded, slowly. His smile had broadened, although Carlin knew it was not an expression that necessarily revealed what he felt inside.

"Congratulations," Harry said, impressed. "Who would have thought a little bitch like you would have so many tricks up her sleeve?"

Harry had left Amy's bed and was already pulling on his jacket. He'd always known when it was time to leave and when he'd gotten as much as he could out of a situation.

"I learned the trick from Gus," Carlin said. "But of course, you've seen it before."

Harry came close enough for Carlin to feel him, his body heat, his warm breath. "If you're implying I had something to do with what happened to Gus, you're wrong. I wouldn't have wasted my time on him. I just don't think it was that great a loss, and you obviously do, and that's the difference between us."

When he'd gone, Carlin took the roses, wrapped them in newspaper, and threw them in the trash. She felt disgusted with herself for having been with Harry, as though she'd been contaminated somehow. She went up to the bathroom and locked the door, then sat on the rim of the tub, letting the hot water run until the room was steamy. She felt filthy and stupid; all those hours she'd wasted with Harry, time that would have been much better spent with Gus. She couldn't bear it, truly she couldn't, and that was why she reached for one of the razors kept on the bathroom shelf. But how many times would she have to cut herself to feel better? Would twelve strikes be enough, would fourteen, or a hundred? Would she only be happy when the bathroom tiles ran red with blood?

The razor should have been cold in her hands, but it was burning, leaving little hot marks in her skin. She thought about

Annie Howe's roses and how hopeless it was to make a strike against yourself. In the end, she did the next best thing. She chopped off her hair without even bothering to look in the mirror, hacking away until the sink was filled with pale hair and the razor was dull. This act was meant to be a punishment, she'd thought she'd be ugly without her hair, to match the way she felt inside, but instead she felt astonishingly light. That night, she climbed out to her window ledge, and as she perched there, she imagined she might be able to fly. One step off the rooftop, one foot past the gutter, that's all she need do to take off with the north wind that blew down from New Hampshire and Maine, bringing with it the scent of pine trees and new snow.

From then on, she sat out on the ledge every time Harry came calling for Amy. Poor Amy, Carlin pitied her. Amy thought she had won an exceptional prize, but each day she would have to worry that someone prettier and fresher would catch Harry's eye, and she'd bend herself around him, like the willows beside the river must in order to survive along the banks.

"He's mine now," Amy gloated, and when Carlin replied that she was welcome to him, Amy refused to believe that Carlin hadn't been torn apart by their breakup. "You're just jealous," Amy insisted, "so I refuse to feel sorry for you. You never appreciated him in the first place."

"Did you do that to your hair because of Harry?" Pie asked one night as she watched Carlin run a comb through her chopped-up hair.

"I did it on impulse." Carlin shrugged. She did it because she thought she deserved to be torn apart.

"Don't worry," Pie said to Carlin, her voice sweet with concern. "It will grow back."

But some things weren't so easily repaired; at night Carlin lay in bed and listened to the wind and to the sound of her roommates' quiet breathing. She wished that she was still the person she was before she came to Haddan, and that she, too, could sleep through the night. Whenever she did fall asleep, during the gray and freezing dawn, it was Gus Carlin dreamed of. In her dreams, he was asleep underwater, his eyes wide open. When he arose from the water to walk through the grass, he was barefoot and perfectly at ease. He was dead in her dream and he carried with him the knowledge of the dead, that all that matters is love, here and beyond. Everything else will simply fall away. Carlin could tell he was trying to get home; in order to do so he needed to climb a trellis covered with vines, not that this obstacle deterred him. Though the vines were replete with thorns, he did not bleed. Though the night was dark, he found his way. He climbed into his attic room and sat on the edge of his unmade bed, and the vines came in after him, winding along both the ceiling and the floor until there was a hedge of thorns, each one resembling a human thumb, each with a fingerprint of its own.

Was it possible for the soul of a person to linger if it so desired, right at the edge of our commonplace world, substantial enough to move pots of ivy on a windowsill or empty a sugar bowl or catch minnows in the river? *Lie down beside me,* Carlin said in her dream to whatever there was left of him. *Stay here with me,* she begged, calling to him in whatever way she knew how. She could hear the wind outside, rattling against the trellis; she could feel him beside her, his skin cool as water. The hems of her bedsheets grew muddy and damp, but Carlin didn't care. She should have followed him over the black fence, into the woods and along the path. Because she had not, he was with her still, where he would remain until the day she let go.

VERY FEW PEOPLE IN TOWN REMEMBERED AN-nie Howe anymore. Her family's acreage had been sold off in parcels and her brothers had all moved west, to California and New Mexico and Utah. Some of the older residents in the village, George Nichols at the Millstone, or Zeke Harris from the dry cleaner's, or even Charlotte Evans, who hadn't been much more than a child when Annie died, recalled spying her on Main Street, certain that they would never again see a woman as beautiful as Annie, not in this lifetime or in the next.

Only Helen Davis thought about Annie. She thought of her daily, much the way a devout person might utter a prayer, words summoned forth without design. Therefore, she was not in the least surprised to smell roses one cold morning at the very end of January, a day when ice coated every growing thing, lilacs and lilies and pine trees alike. Carlin Leander also noticed the scent, for it overpowered the caramel aroma of the bread pudding she had in the oven, in the hopes that dessert might tempt Miss Davis's appetite. Miss Davis had gone to bed the previous Sunday and simply hadn't gotten up again. She had missed so many classes a substitute had been hired, and the members of the history department grumbled about the extra work they were forced to take on in Miss Davis's absence. Not one of them, including Eric Herman, knew that the woman they'd feared and disliked for so many years now had to be carried to the bathroom, a task that all but defeated Carlin and Betsy Chase working together.

"This is so embarrassing," Miss Davis would say each time they helped her to the bathroom, which was the reason Betsy had not told Eric how dire the situation was. Some things were meant to be kept concealed from public view, and that was why every time Betsy and Carlin stood outside the open bathroom door, they kept their eyes averted, trying their best to offer Helen a bit of privacy. The time for privacy, however, was over and with it the pretense that Miss Davis's health might improve. Yet when Betsy suggested a trip to the hospital or a call to the Visiting Nurses' Association, Miss Davis was outraged. She insisted it was only the flu that had her down, but Carlin knew the real reason she demurred was that Miss Davis would never tolerate being prodded and poked and kept alive past her time. Helen knew what was coming for her, and she was ready, except for one last act of contrition. In hoping for forgiveness, even those who are failing may hold on to the material world, they cling to the edges until their bones are as brittle as wafers and their tears have turned to blood. But at last what Miss Davis had been waiting for had arrived on this cold January afternoon, for it was then that she breathed in the scent of the roses, and the fragrance was so strong it was as if the vines had grown up through her bedroom floor to bloom and offer her absolution for all she had done and all she had failed to do.

Helen looked at the window to see the garden exactly as it had been when she first came to Haddan. She, herself, had always preferred red roses to white, especially those gorgeous Lincolns, which turned a deeper shade with each passing day. She did not panic the way she had feared she might when her time came. Although she was grateful for her life, she had been waiting to be forgiven for such a long time she'd thought she might never experience what she wanted most of all, and now here it was, all in a rush, as if grace and mercy were flowing through her. Things of this world fell into their proper place and appeared to be very far away: her hand on the pillow, the girl coming to sit beside her, the black cat at the foot of her bed, curled up and sleeping, breathing in, breathing out.

Helen felt a sweetness rising within her and a vision so bright she might have been gazing upon a thousand stars. How quickly her life had gone by; one moment she had been a girl taking the train to Haddan and now here she was in her bed watching dusk fall through the window, spreading out across the white walls in pools of shadow. If only she'd known how short her time on earth would be, she would have enjoyed it more. She wished she could let the girl beside her know as much; she wanted to shout, but Carlin had already gone to dial 911. Helen could hear her asking for an ambulance to be brought around to St. Anne's, but she paid little attention to Carlin's distress, for Helen was now walking to school from the train station, suitcase in hand, on a day when all the horse chestnut trees were in blossom and the sky was as blue as the china cups her mother used to set the table for tea. She had come for the job at the age of twenty-four, and all things considered, she had done well. The girl fussing about seemed silly and Helen wished she could say so. The panic in the girl's voice, the sirens outside, the cold January night, the thousands of stars in the sky, the train from Boston, how her heart had felt that day when her whole life was about to begin. Helen signaled to Carlin, who at last came to sit beside the bed.

"You're going to be fine," Carlin whispered. This was not at all true and Miss Davis knew it; still she was touched to see that the girl had turned pale, the way people did when they worried, when they truly cared.

Don't forget to turn off the oven, Helen wanted to tell the girl, but she was watching the roses outside her window, the gorgeous red ones, the Lincolns. There was the lovely sound of drowsy bees, the way there had been every June. Each year at that time, the campus had exploded into bands of red and white, ribbons of peach and pink and gold, all because of Annie Howe. Some people said bees came from all over the Commonwealth, beckoned by the roses at Haddan, and it was well known that local honey was uncommonly sweet. *Don't forget to enjoy this life you're walking through,* Helen wanted to say, but instead she held on to the girl's hand and they waited together for the paramedics to arrive.

This was a volunteer crew, men and women called away from their dinners, and as soon as they walked into the room, they all knew no lives would be saved tonight. Carlin recognized some members of the team: there was the woman who ran the dance studio, and the man who worked at the mini-mart, along with two janitors that Carlin had passed many times but had never paid much attention to. The woman from the dance studio, Rita Eamon, took Helen's pulse and listened to her heart while a canister of oxygen was wheeled in.

"It's pulmonary edema," Rita Eamon told the others before turning to Helen. "Want some oxygen, honey?" she asked Helen.

Helen waved the offer away. There was blue sky above her and all those many roses, the ones that gave off the scent of cloves in the rain and the ones that left a trace of lemon on your fingers, the ones that were the color of blood, and those that were as white as clouds. Cut one rose, and two will grow in its place, gardeners say, and so it had happened. Each one was sweeter than the next and as red as gemstones. Helen Davis tried to say, *Look at these,* but the only sound she could force out led them to believe she was choking.

"She's passing on," said one of the volunteers, a man who'd been doing this job long enough so that he did not flinch when Carlin began to cry. He was one of the janitors, Marie and Billy Bishop's son, Brian, who had worked at Haddan for quite a while and who had in fact fixed Miss Davis's refrigerator some time ago. People said Miss Davis was nasty, but Brian never saw any evidence of that; she'd had him sit at her table when he was through working, which was more than anyone else at the school had ever done. She'd given him a glass of lemonade on that hot day, and now Brian Bishop returned the favor. He took Miss Davis's free hand and sat across from Carlin as if his own dinner wasn't cooling on his table at home, as if he had all the time in the world.

"She's going easy," he told Carlin.

Someone from the rescue crew must have turned the oven off when they went into the kitchen to phone the police station and report a death on campus, because hours later, when Carlin remembered the bread pudding and hurried to retrieve the pan, the pudding was perfectly done, the syrupy topping bubbling and warm. At the president's house they knew something was wrong when the ambulance pulled up. Dr. Jones called Bob Thomas, who went out to the ambulance to ask what was going on and was surprised to find he recognized the fellow at the wheel from somewhere; although Bob Thomas couldn't quite place him, the driver, Ed Campbell, was a member of the grounds crew and had been mowing the lawns and salting the paths at the Haddan School for more than ten years. It was a gloomy evening, and bad news hung in the air.

Bob Thomas waited until the hospital in Hamilton called to notify the school that the death certificate had been signed, then he asked the janitor on duty to ring the chapel bells. When the community gathered in the dining hall, Helen Davis's passing was announced. She had been at school for so long no one could quite imagine it without her, except for Eric Herman, who had been waiting for more years than he'd like to count to take her place as the chair of the department.

"If she was that ill, it's better this way," Eric said when he saw how upset Betsy had become.

But his words weren't any comfort. Betsy felt as if something had been tossed down a well, something precious and irretrievable; the world seemed much smaller without Miss Davis as a part of it. Betsy excused herself and walked back to St. Anne's; the sky was black and starry, as cold as it was deep. A north wind was shaking the trees, but in the arbor behind St. Anne's a pair of cardinals slept in the thicket, one gray as the bark, the other red as the deepest rose.

Carlin was still in the kitchen, cleaning up. She'd tied one of Helen Davis's white aprons around her waist and was arm-deep in soapy water, crying as she scrubbed the pots. She had already consumed three glasses of the Madeira stored in the cabinet under the sink and was extremely tipsy, with a pink cast to her skin and her eyes rimmed red. For the first time the black cat hadn't begged to be let out at dark, rather it perched on the counter and mewed uncertainly. When Betsy came in, she draped her coat over a kitchen chair and examined the half-empty bottle of Madeira.

"You can turn me in if you like." Carlin dried her hands and sat across from Miss Chase at the table. "Of course, I never turned you in for having men in your room."

They stared at each other, dizzy from the scent of roses, their mouths dry with grief. Betsy poured herself a glass of wine and refilled Carlin's empty glass as well.

"It was just one man," Betsy said. "Not that I need to explain myself to you."

"Miss Davis had a crush on him. She invited him to Christmas dinner. It's none of my business, but in my opinion, he's definitely the better man."

The Madeira had a heavy, bitter aftertaste, perfectly suitable, considering the circumstances. A few nights earlier, Betsy had gone to the phone booth at the pharmacy and called Abe, but as soon as he'd answered, she hung up, completely undone by the sound of his voice.

"It's all over now, and I'd just as soon nobody knew about it."

Carlin shrugged. "It's your loss."

"What is that I smell?" Betsy asked, for the scent of roses was everywhere now. Surely, the fragrance was too floral to be wafting over from the bread pudding set out on the table. Betsy was surprised to discover that Carlin was such a good cook; she didn't think anyone made desserts from scratch anymore, not when there were instants for just about everything other than love and marriage. She gazed out the window, and seeing the cardinals perched there she grew confused; for a moment she believed them to be roses.

They let the cat out when it mewed at the door, then locked up, even though there was nothing to steal. In only a few days the maintenance crew would have the place down to bare wood and walls, carting the furniture down to the thrift shop at St. Agatha's and toting boxes of books to the secondhand store in Middletown. By now the odor in the apartment was so strong that Carlin had begun to sneeze and Betsy felt bumps rising on the most tender areas of her skin, the base of her throat, the backs of her knees, her fingers, her thighs, her toes. The scent of roses was seeping into the hallways, winding up the staircases, streaming beneath closed doors. That night, any girl who had something to regret tossed and turned, burning up while she slept. Amy Elliot, with her terrible allergies, broke out in hives and Maureen Brown, who could not abide rose pollen, awoke with black spots on her tongue that the school nurse diagnosed as bee stings, although surely such an affliction was impossible at this time of year.

A funeral mass was said at St. Agatha's early Saturday, the last cold morning of the month, with several townspeople in attendance, including Mike Randall from the bank, and Pete Byers, who'd ordered the flowers from the Lucky Day and who sat in the first pew alongside his nephew and Carlin Leander. Abe came in toward the end of the service, wearing his grandfather's old overcoat, for lack of something of his own that might be appropriate for such an occasion. He stayed in the back row, where he was most comfortable, nodding a greeting to Rita Eamon, who had come to pay her respects, as she did with every 911 patient the rescue team was unfortunate enough to lose. He waved to Carlin Leander, who looked like a pixie from hell with her hair all chopped off and the worn black coat, which was coming apart at the seams.

After the service, Abe waited outside in the raw January air, watching as parishioners left the church. Carlin had wrapped a green woolen scarf around her head, but when she came down the steps, she looked chalky and chilled to the bone. Sean Byers was close beside her; anyone could judge his attachment from the look on his face. To see a wild boy so concerned made people passing by pity him and envy him at the very same time. Pete had to drag the boy back toward the pharmacy to get him away from Carlin, and when at last he had, Carlin went over to Abe. Together, they watched six strong men from the funeral parlor carry out the coffin.

"You're not going to break Sean Byers's heart, are you?" For Abe could still see the love-struck boy looking over his shoulder as he followed his uncle down Main Street.

"People break their own hearts, if you ask me. Not that it's your business."

It was a good day for a funeral, brutal and cold. The burial was at the school cemetery and Carlin and Abe set off in that direction. Carlin didn't mind being with Abe; it was almost like being alone. She didn't have to be polite to him, and he clearly felt the same way. When the scarf on her head slipped back he nodded toward what she'd done with the razor. "Walk into a lawn mower?"

"Something like that. I mutilated myself."

"Good job." Abe couldn't help but laugh. "If Sean Byers wants you when you look like this, he'll take you any way."

"He didn't even notice," Carlin admitted. "I guess he thinks my hair was always this way."

They passed the Evanses' house, and Abe waved to Charlotte, who was peeking out her front window, curious to see who was walking along Main Street on such a dreadful day.

"Why did you wave to her?" Carlin shook her head. "I wouldn't bother."

"She's not as bad as she seems."

"Some people are worse than they seem. Harry McKenna, for instance. I think he's guilty of something. If nothing more, he knows what happened to Gus. It's disgusting how he gets to go on with his life as though nothing happened."

"Maybe." They had cut through Mrs. Jeremy's yard in order to take the fastest route to the far meadow. "Maybe not."

Now they made their way through the tall, brown grass, taking the path where the thornbushes grew. The gravediggers had been at work earlier, for the earth was frozen and it had taken three men quite some time to break ground. A small number of mourners had gathered at the graveside; faculty members who felt it was only civil to pay their respects. A pile of dirt had been deposited outside the fence and icy clods littered the path.

"I've been thinking about leaving Haddan," Carlin told Abe.

Getting out of Haddan seemed like a fine idea to Abe, especially as he was forced to watch Betsy, who was standing between Eric Herman and Bob Thomas. She had on the black dress she'd worn when she'd come to his house and stayed the night, but today she wore sunglasses and her hair was combed back and she looked entirely different than she had on that night. The priest from St. Agatha's, Father Mink, a large man who was known to cry at funerals and weddings alike, had arrived to consecrate the ground, and the circle of mourners stepped back to accommodate his girth.

Abe watched as those in attendance bowed their heads in the pale winter light. "Maybe I should be the one thinking about leaving."

"You?" Carlin shook her head. "You'll never leave here. Born and bred. I wouldn't be surprised if you got special permission to be buried right in this cemetery, just to stick it to the Haddan School."

There was no way Abe was going into that cemetery, not today and not when he was ready for his final resting place. He preferred to meet his maker out in the open, as the woman buried out at Wright's farm had, and he'd pay his respects right out here in the meadow as well. "I bet I'm gone before you are."

"I don't have to make bets," Carlin said. "Miss Davis left me money, enough to cover all of my school expenses."

The instructions in Miss Davis's will were absolutely clear. Her savings, wisely invested by that nice Mike Randall over at the 5&10 Cent Bank, were to be used in a fellowship program for students in need, providing funds each semester that ensured the recipient would not have to work and would also be free to travel during vacations. Miss Davis had stipulated that Carlin Leander was to be the first beneficiary of this award; all of her expenses would be seen to until the last day of her senior year. If she wanted clothing, or books, or a semester in Spain all she must do was write up a request and present it to Mike Randall, who would process the check and forward any cash that she needed.

"I have nothing to worry about financially." Carlin secured the green scarf around her throat. "If I stay."

Last week Carlin had turned fifteen, not that she'd told anyone, or felt she had anything to celebrate. Today, however, she didn't look more than twelve. She had the blank expression of disbelief that often accompanies the first shock of bereavement.

"You'll stay." Abe was looking at the little stone lamb, which had been festooned with a garland of jasmine.

"Miss Davis told me that people bring flowers here for luck," Carlin said when she noticed his gaze. "It's a memorial for Dr. Howe's baby, the one that was never born because his wife died. Every time a child in town is sick, the mother presents one of those garlands to ask for protection."

"I never heard that one, and I thought I'd heard them all."

"Maybe you never had anyone to protect."

When Carlin went on to the cemetery for the service, Abe stayed where he was for a while, then turned and retraced their path through the meadow. Father Mink's voice was harsh and mournful and Abe had decided he would prefer to hear birdsongs in memory of Miss Davis, who, no matter how ill, had always made certain to set out suet and seed.

His ears were ringing with the cold and he still had to get back to the church, where he'd parked his car, but he found himself heading in the opposite direction. It made no sense, he should have stayed away from the school, and yet he kept on through the meadow. It was a long, slow trek and he was freezing when he finally reached the quad. There were starlings perched in the trees, and because of the thin sunlight, the rose trellis outside St. Anne's was filled with birds. Abe couldn't see them, but he could hear them, singing as if it were spring. He recognized the chirrup of cardinals as well, and the black cat also heard the call. It was poised beside the trellis, head tilted, mesmerized by the pair of birds nesting there.

There might be another black cat with one eye in Haddan, but it wouldn't be wearing the reflective collar Abe had sprung for at Petcetera in Middletown Mall last week. Helen Davis's cat and his were definitely one and the same. If it hadn't shown up at his door, Abe would have been happy to be alone, but now things were different. He'd gotten involved, buying collars, worrying. Now, for instance, he found he was actually pleased to see the wretched creature, and he called to it, whistling as he would for a dog. The birds flew away, startled by the tinkling of the bell on the new collar, but the cat didn't glance over at Abe. Instead, it walked in the direction of Chalk House, navigating over ice and cement, not stopping until it crossed the path of a boy on his way to the river where a free-for-all game of ice hockey would soon begin. It was Harry McKenna who gazed down at the cat.

"Move," he said roughly.

Harry had always felt the need to excel. It made perfect sense that he'd surpassed those fools who'd thought themselves so brave, trapping helpless rabbits on the night of their initiation. He had chosen the black cat instead, and therefore had in his possession a souvenir far more original than a rabbit's foot, a memento he kept in a glass tube taken from the biology lab. By now, the yellow eye had turned as milky as the marbles Harry used to play with; when he shook the tube, it rattled like a stone.

On his way to play hockey, Harry knew he was finished with Haddan; he was as sure of it as he was certain whatever team he played on would win. The future was all he was interested in. He'd been granted early admission to Dartmouth, yet he sometimes had nightmares in which his final grades rearranged themselves. On such occasions, Harry awoke sweating and nauseated, and not even black coffee could separate him from his dreams. On these mornings, he grew nervous in ways that surprised him. The slightest thing could set him off. The black cat, for instance, which he came upon every once in a while. Although impossible, the cat seemed to recognize him. It would stop in front of him, as it did on this January afternoon, and simply refuse to move.

Harry would then have to shoo it away, and when that wasn't effective, he'd threaten it with a well-aimed book or a soccer ball. It was a disgusting animal and Harry felt he really hadn't done it much harm. Its owner, that nasty old Helen Davis, had spoiled it more than ever after the incident. The way Harry saw it, the cat should probably be grateful to him for ensuring it be granted a soft life of pity and cream. Now that Miss Davis was gone, the cat would probably follow her lead and good riddance to both of them, in Harry's opinion. The world would be a better place without either one.

The black cat did seem to have a surprisingly long memory; it peered up at the boy through its one narrowed eye, as though it knew him well. From where he stood, Abe could see Harry chase off the cat with a hockey stick, shouting for it to stay the hell away, but the cat didn't go far. Cruelty always gets found out in the end; there's simply no way to run from all that you do. Frail and inadequate although this evidence might be, it was all the proof Abe needed. On this cold afternoon when the starlings had all flown away, he had found the guilty party.

THE
DISAPPEARING BOY

WHAT THEY HAD PLANNED WAS
very different, but plans often go awry.
Look at any house recently built and it will
always be possible to spy dozens of errors,
in spite of the architect's care. Something is
bound to be off kilter: a sink installed on
the wrong wall, a floorboard that squeaks,
walls judged to be plumb that simply do not
meet at the proper angle. Harry McKenna
was the architect of their plan, which,
when it began, consisted of nothing more
than intimidation and fear. Wasn't that the
root of all control, really? Wasn't it the force
that obliged even the most unruly to adhere
to rules and regulations and join in the
ranks?

August Pierce had been a mistake from
the start. They'd seen it before. Boys who

liked to play by their own rules, who'd never been members of any club; individuals who took some convincing before they learned there was not just strength in numbers, but lasting power as well. That was what pledging was all about, learning a lesson and learning it well. Unfortunately, Gus never cared about such matters; when forced to attend meetings, he wore both his black coat and an expression of disdain. There were those who claimed he kept a set of headphones on, hidden by the collar of his coat, and that he spent his time listening to music instead of jotting down the rules the way other freshmen did. And so they set out to teach him his place. Each day they piled on both work and hu-miliation, forcing him to clean toilets and sweep the basement floor. This hazing, meant to initiate him into a code of loyalty, backfired; Gus dug in. If an upperclassman demanded he return trays in the dining room or collect dishes, he simply refused, which even the freshmen at Sharpe Hall and Otto House knew wasn't done. He would not share homework or notes, and when he was told his personal hygiene did not live up to Chalk stan-dards, he decided to show them what filth really meant. From then on, he would not change his clothes, or wash his face, or send his laundry out on Wednesdays. His hygiene suffered fur-ther when several boys thought it would be a good lesson to turn off the water while he was in the shower. The upperclassmen waited for him to tear into the hallway, shampoo burning his eyes; they had their towels twisted for strategic hits on his bare flesh. But Gus never came out of the bathroom. He stood in the shower for a good half hour, freezing, waiting them out, and when they finally gave up, he finished washing at the sink and re-fused to shower from then on.

Despite this harassment, Gus had discovered something

about himself that he hadn't known before: he could take punishment. To think that he of all people had strength was laugh-
out-loud funny, although when it came down to it, he might just
be the strongest man in town, for all he'd survived. The other
freshmen at Chalk wouldn't consider saying no to their elders
and betters. Nathaniel Gibb, who had never had anything to do
with alcohol before, had so much beer poured down his throat
through a tube that farmers on Route 17 used to force-feed geese
and ducks, that he'd never in his life be able to smell beer without vomiting. Dave Linden also refused to complain. He swept
out Harry McKenna's fireplace every morning, even though soot
made him sneeze; he ran two miles each day as the seniors insisted, no matter how dreadful or damp the weather, which was
why he'd developed a rumbling cough that kept him up far into
the night, leaving him to sleep through his classes, so that his
grades fell dramatically.

It was odd that no one had figured out what was going on at
Chalk House. The nurse, Dorothy Jackson, never suspected anything, in spite of the alcohol poisoning she'd seen over the years,
and all the freshmen plagued by insomnia and hives. Duck Johnson seemed easy enough to fool, but Eric Herman was usually
such a stickler, how was it that he hadn't noticed something
amiss? Was he only concerned if his own work was interrupted?
Was silence all he asked for, damn what else happened on the
floors above him?

Gus had expected some measure of assistance from those in
charge, and when Mr. Herman refused to listen he went to speak
to the dean of students, but soon enough he understood he
wouldn't get far. He'd been made to sit waiting in the outer office
for close to an hour, and by the time the dean's secretary, Missy

Green, had ushered him in to see Thomas, Gus's hands were sweating. Bob Thomas was a big man, and he sat impassively in his leather chair as Gus told him about the nasty traditions at Chalk House. Gus sounded pitiful and wheedling even to himself. He found he couldn't bring himself to look Thomas in the eye.

"Are you trying to tell me that someone has assaulted you?" Bob Thomas asked. "Because, the truth is, you look fine to me."

"It's not like being beat up on the street. It's not an all-out attack. It's the little things."

"Little things," Bob Thomas had mused.

"But they're repeated, and they're threatening." To himself he sounded like a spineless tattletale from the playground. *They threw sand in my face. They didn't play fair.* "It's more serious than it sounds."

"Serious enough for me to call a house meeting and have all your fellow students hear your complaints? Is that what you're telling me?"

"I thought this charge would be anonymous." Gus realized that he stank of nicotine and that he had half a joint hidden in his inside coat pocket; in stepping forth to make this accusation, he might be the one who was expelled. Definitely not what his father had in mind when sending him to Haddan.

"'Anonymity most often points to a lack of courage or a flawed moral compass.' That's a quote from Hosteous Moore from the time he was headmaster here and it's a sentiment I second. Do you want me to go to Dr. Jones with this information? Because I could. I could interrupt him, even though he's at an educators' meeting in Boston, and I could bring him back to

Haddan and I could tell him about these little things, if that's what you want me to do."

Gus had been the loser in enough situations to know when a fight was pointless. So he kept his mouth shut; he certainly didn't tell Carlin anything for if he had, she would surely have gone running to Dr. Jones, probably more indignant about all those rabbits killed over the years than anything else. She would have wanted to do his fighting for him, and Gus could not have tolerated that. No, he had a better plan. He'd managed to best the Magicians' Club. He would complete the impossible task Dr. Howe had long ago set forth for his wife.

It was Pete Byers who told him it could be done. Pete knew a bit about roses because his wife, Eileen, was a superior gardener. Even Lois Jeremy phoned every now and then for advice concerning a no-pesticide method to remove Japanese beetles (a spray of water and garlic was best) or a remedy that would remove toads from her perennial beds (welcome them, was the answer, for they'll eat mosquitoes and aphids). In June, blooms of the spectacular Evening Star grew right outside the Byers's bedroom window with a silver color that made it appear the moon had been caught in their backyard.

Pete was merely a helper in the garden, there to spread mulch and plant seedlings. Thumbing through a horticulture magazine only days earlier, trying to figure out the fertilizer situation, he'd been amazed to discover that a piece Eileen had submitted on her favorite topic, white gardens, had been published. That she'd done so without telling him had shocked Pete; he'd never thought of Eileen as having secrets, as he did. He'd read the article carefully and so he remembered how Eileen had noted that

Victorians often filled their gardens with white flowers precisely because they liked to amuse one another with the exact trick the boy had been searching for.

Gus let out a whoop when he heard the transmutation was far from impossible; he leaned over the lunch counter to grab Pete and give him a bear hug. Each day afterward, Gus stopped by to check if his order had arrived, and at last, on the day before Halloween, Pete handed him the aniline crystals.

That night, Gus went to the graveyard to calm his nerves and think about all the magicians he'd seen with his father. What they'd all had in common, the mediocre and the transcendent alike, was confidence. Up in the tall elm, the crow called out its disapproval at Gus's slouching figure. A bird such as that was far better at sleight of hand than Gus would ever be, swift as a thief. Still, Gus knew the most important attributes were always invisible to the naked eye, and he was practicing silence and patience when Carlin Leander, who'd been avoiding him for weeks, came walking along the path.

Gus should have remained silent, but instead he let his pain out in a blast of anger. After they'd argued, and he'd climbed over the iron fence, an odd calm came over him. It was after midnight when he returned to Chalk House, and the others were waiting. It was the hour of tricks and deep resentments, the time of night when people found it difficult to fall asleep even though the village was quiet, except for the sound of the river, which seemed so close by anyone from out of town might have imagined its route followed Main Street.

Gus went to Harry's room on this, his pledge night. The boys formed a circle around him, certain that by morning Gus Pierce would be gone; his initiation a failure, he'd either go of his own

free will or be expelled when the proper authorities found the
marijuana Robbie and Harry had stashed on the top shelf of his
closet. Either way, he'd soon be consigned to the evening train
and Haddan history. But before he left, they had a surprise waiting for him, a going-away present of sorts. They had no idea that
Gus had a surprise of his own. Although Harry's room was overheated, Gus wore his black coat, for the white flowers he'd
bought at the Lucky Day were concealed within. He believed his
father would have been proud of his style, for he had rehearsed
until he was able to pluck the roses from his coat with a flourish
worthy of a professional. The blooms were luminous in the darkened room, and for once those idiots Gus had to live with, those
fools who took so much pleasure in humiliating him, fell silent.

It was a long and beautiful moment, quiet and sharp as glass.
August Pierce spun away from his audience, quickly sprinkled
the aniline over the flowers, then he wheeled back to face his tor-
mentors. There, before their eyes, the roses turned scarlet, a
shade so alarming that many in the room thought immediately of
blood.

No one applauded; not a single word was said. The silence fell
like a hailstorm, and that was when Gus knew he had made an
error, and that success was the last thing he should have tried to
achieve. In the light of Gus's small triumph, something poison-
ous had begun to move through the room. If Duck Johnson really
considered that night, he might recall the quiet in the house; he
would remember there had been no need to announce curfew,
and although that was rather unusual, he was ruminating about
problems with the crew team—lack of leadership, lack of
spirit—and he took no notice. Eric Herman heard them later on,
there were footsteps in the hallway and urgent, hushed voices; if

pressed he would have to admit he felt annoyed, for there never seemed to be peace and quiet at Chalk House, even after midnight, and he had work to do. Eric turned up his stereo as he graded papers, grateful to at last hear nothing but cello and violin.

Two boys held their hands over Gus's mouth, and although he could not shout, he managed to bite down on someone's fingers, hard enough to break the skin. They dragged him down the hall and into the bathroom, no doubt the commotion Eric had heard before he put on his headphones. The boys at Chalk weren't about to allow Gus's success to alter their plans for a send-off. They had all used the toilet in preparation and it was filled and stinking as they lifted Gus up and plunged him into the bowl headfirst. They were all supposed to be silent; it was a vow they had taken, but several of them had to cover their mouths and hold back their nervous laughter. Gus tried to get away at first, but they jammed his head down lower. There was a snicker when he started thrashing his legs around.

"Look at the big shot now," someone said.

Gus's legs were soon jerking weirdly, as if he had no control, and he actually kicked Robbie Shaw in the mouth. Filthy water spilled onto the tiles and when Nathaniel Gibb gasped at the brutality, the sound echoed with a high-pitched metallic ring. Some actions, once begun, have nowhere to go but all the way to the end, like a spring that has been wound up tightly and set. Even those who offered an unspoken prayer could not back down; it was far too late for that. They kept his head in the toilet until he stopped struggling. That was the point, wasn't it? To get him to give up the fight. Once the battle was over, he seemed like a rag doll, all batted cotton and thread. They'd meant to scare him and reduce him to his rightful place, but what they got when they pulled him out was a boy who'd already begun to turn blue, suffocated in their waste and venom, unable to draw a breath.

Some of the older fellows, tough, competent students who played vicious games of soccer and sneered at whoever they considered to be weak, panicked immediately and would have run off had Harry McKenna not told them to shut up and stay where they were. There was a purple bruise on Pierce's forehead where he'd hit his head against the inside of the commode; he'd lost consciousness early on in this game and therefore hadn't fought back as they'd expected him to, at least until the very end when the struggle was involuntary and already impossible to win.

Harry pounded on Gus's back, then turned the body faceup and called Robbie over. Robbie had been a lifeguard for the past two summers, but he could not be persuaded to put his mouth to Gus's, not after Pierce had been soaked in all that excrement. In the end, Nathaniel Gibb frantically tried mouth-to-mouth resuscitation, trying desperately to pump air back into Gus's lungs, but it was too late. There was water and waste all over the floor as moonlight poured through the window illuminating what they'd wrought: a six-foot-tall dead boy, sprawled upon the tiled floor.

Two of the most practical fellows ran to the basement for buckets and mops and did their best to clean and disinfect the bathroom floor. By then, the older boys had carried Gus Pierce out of the house. Dave Linden was instructed to sweep the path behind them to clear their tracks away as they proceeded in silence, out the back door and down the path to the river. They trod along through the woods until they found a spot where the bank sloped gently. The area smelled faintly of the violets that bloomed there in spring, and one of the boys, suddenly reminded of his mother's cologne, began to weep. This was the place where they laid the body down, quietly, slowly, so that several green frogs asleep in the grass were caught unawares and crushed beneath the unexpected weight. Harry McKenna knelt over the corpse and buttoned the black coat. He left the eyes open, as he imagined they would be had someone chosen to walk into the river on a clear, moonlit night with the intent of drowning himself. Then came the end of the journey. Gus was hauled down the bank to the shore that rolled easily into the dark water. The boys maneuvered him past the reeds and the lily pads until they were knee-deep, floating him between them like a black log, and then they let him go, all at once, as though they had planned it. They released him to the current and not one of them stayed to watch where it would take him or how far downstream he would have to travel before he found a place to rest.

THE BOYS FROM CHALK began to fall ill during the first week of February. One by one it happened, and after a while it was possible to predict who the fever would afflict next simply by looking into an individual's eyes. Some who'd been stricken were so lethargic they could not rise from their beds; others could not get a single night of sleep. There were boys whose skins crawled with an unforgiving rash and those who lost their appetites completely, able to digest only crackers and warm ginger ale. Attendance in classes fell to an all-time low, with morale lower still. Aspirin disappeared from the infirmary shelves, ice packs were called for, antacids swallowed. Those most affected were the new boys up in the attic, who suffered in silence, lest they call attention to themselves. Dave Linden, for instance, endured debilitating migraines that kept him from his studies, and Nathaniel Gibb experienced a constant tightening in his chest, and though he never complained, there were times when he had to struggle for breath.

The school nurse admitted that she'd never seen anything like this current scourge; she wondered if perhaps a new strain of Asian flu had befallen these boys. If so, those who'd taken ill had no choice but to wait for their own antibodies to restore them to health, for surely, no medicine that had been doled out had done the least bit of good. In fact, the epidemic had not been triggered by a bacterial infection or a virus. The blame for the outbreak rested squarely with Abel Grey, for in that first week of the month, as the afternoon sunshine encouraged stone flies to bask on warm rocks along the riverside, Abe stationed himself on the Haddan campus. He didn't speak to anyone or approach them, but his presence was felt all around. In the morning, when boys raced down the steps of Chalk House, Abe would already have made himself comfortable on a nearby bench, eating his breakfast and scanning the *Tribune*. He was posted at the door of the dining hall at noon and could be found there again in the evening at supper. Every night, after dark, he parked in the lot beside Chalk House, where he listened to his car radio as he ate a bacon cheeseburger picked up at Selena's, trying his best not to get any grease on Wright's coat. Each time a boy left the house, whether going for a run or hurrying to join friends in a game of hockey, he'd be confronted with the sight of Abel Grey. Before long, even the most self-confident and brashest among them began to have symptoms and fall ill as well.

Guilt was a funny thing, a fellow might not even notice it until it had already crawled inside him and set up shop, working away at his stomach and bowels, and at his conscience, as well. Abe was well acquainted with the need for contrition, and he kept watch for the ways in which it might surface, singling out several residents who seemed more nervous than most, trailing along as they went to class, keeping an eye out for the warning signs of remorse: the flushed complexion, the tremors, the habit of looking over one's shoulder, even when no one was there.

"Do you expect someone to come to you and confess?" Carlin asked when she realized what Abe was doing. "That's never going to happen. You don't know these boys."

But Abe did know what it was like to hear the dead speaking, placing blame on those left behind for all they had or had not done. Even now, when he drove past his family's old house he sometimes heard his brother's voice. That's what he was looking for here at the school: the person who was trying his best to run away from what was inside his own head.

As he kept his vigil at the school, he also had the pleasure of observing Betsy Chase. For her part, Betsy did not seem pleased by Abe's presence on campus; she kept her eyes lowered and if she spied him, she turned on her heel and changed direction, even if that meant she'd be late to class. Abe always felt a combination of turmoil and joy when he saw her, even though it had become clear he was unlucky in love, not that good fortune appeared in his card playing during poker games at the Millstone, although by rights, he should have been dealt all aces, all the time.

One morning, when Abe had been at Haddan for more than a week, Betsy surprised him by veering from her usual route and walking directly toward him. Abe had been keeping watch from a bench outside the library after phoning down to the station to ask that his schedule be changed yet again. He could tell that Doug Lauder, who'd been covering for him, was starting to get annoyed, although Doug hadn't complained enough to prevent Abe from being here at the school, drinking a café au lait he'd picked up at the pharmacy. Although shoots of jonquils had appeared in the perennial beds and snowbells dotted the lawns, the morning was raw and steam rose from Abe's paper cup. Gazing through the haze, he thought he was imagining Betsy when she first began to approach, in her black jacket and jeans, but there she was, standing right in front of him.

"Do you think no one notices that you're here?" Betsy lifted one hand to shield her eyes; she couldn't quite make out Abe's expression in the thin, glittering sunlight. "Everyone's talking about it. Sooner or later they'll figure it out."

"Figure what out?" He stared right at her with those pale eyes. She couldn't stop him from doing that.

"You and me."

"Is that what you think?" Abe grinned. "That I'm here for you?"

The sunlight shifted and Betsy saw how hurt he'd been. She went to sit at the far end of the bench. How was it that whenever she saw him she felt like crying? That couldn't be love, could it? That couldn't be what people went searching for.

"Then why are you here?" She hoped she didn't sound interested, or worse, desperate.

"I figure sooner or later someone will tell me what happened to Gus Pierce." Abe finished his coffee and tossed the cup into a nearby trash can. "I'm just going to wait until they do."

The bark of the weeping beech trees was lightening, green

knobs forming along the sweeping branches. Two swans advanced toward the bench warily, feathers drooping with mud.

"Shoo," Betsy called out. "Go away."

Spending so much time on campus, Abe had become accustomed to the swans and he knew that this particular pair were a couple. "They're in love," he told Betsy.

The swans had stopped beside the trash barrel to bicker over crusts of bread.

"Is that what you call it?" Betsy laughed. "Love?" She had a class to teach and her hands were freezing but she was still sitting on the bench.

"That's exactly what it is," Abe said.

After he left, Betsy vowed to keep away from Abe, but there seemed no way to avoid him. At lunch, there he was again, helping himself to the salad bar.

"I've heard that Bob Thomas is furious that he's hanging around," Lynn Vining told Betsy. "The kids have been complaining to their parents about a police presence on campus. But, God, is he good-looking."

"I thought you were crazy about Jack." Betsy was referring to the married chemistry teacher Lynn had been involved with for several years.

"What about you?" Lynn said, not mentioning that she'd been unhappy for some time, having realized that a man who was willing to betray one woman wouldn't mind betraying another. "You can't take your eyes off him."

As for Abe, he sat at a rear table in the dining hall, eating his salad, watching the boys from Chalk House. All he needed was for one boy to confess an involvement and he hoped the others would fall into place, each one scrambling for immunity and un-

derstanding. He believed he'd found the signs he'd been searching for in Nathaniel Gibb, whom he followed when the boy
dumped his uneaten lunch in the trash. All that afternoon he
trailed Nathaniel, stationed outside his biology lab and his alge-
bra classroom, until at last the beleaguered boy wheeled around
to face him.

"What do you want from me?" Nathaniel Gibb cried.

They were on the path that led along the river, a route many
people avoided due to its proximity to the swans. Nathaniel
Gibb, however, had more to fear than swans. Lately, he had begun to spit up blood. He had taken to carrying a large handkerchief with him, a rag that both shamed him and reminded him of
how fragile a body could be.

Abe saw what he'd been looking for, that line of fear behind
the eyes. "I want to talk to you about Gus, that's all. Maybe what
happened to him was an accident. Maybe you know something
about it."

Nathaniel was the sort of boy who had always done what was
expected of him, but he no longer knew what that meant. "I don't
have anything to say to you."

Abe understood how difficult it was to live with certain transgressions. Own it, and the pain ceases. Say it out loud, and you're
halfway home.

"If you talk to me, no one will hurt you. All you have to do is
tell me what happened that night."

Nathaniel looked up, first at Abe and then, beyond him.
Harry McKenna was horsing around on the steps of the gym
along with some of his buddies. The afternoon was filled with
streaky, yellow light and the chill in the air remained. As soon as
Nathaniel saw Harry he began to cough his horrible cough, and

before Abe could stop him, he turned and ran down the path. For a while Abe jogged after him, but he gave up when Nathaniel disappeared into a crowd of students.

That evening Abe could feel trouble coming, just as he always could when he was a boy. And sure enough, the very next day, as Abe was about to leave his post at the school to run over to Selena's to pick up some lunch, Glen Tiles and Joey Tosh pulled up next to Wright's old cruiser in the parking lot of Chalk House. Abe went over and leaned down to talk to Glen through the window.

"I see you're creating your own schedule these days," Glen said.

"It's just temporary," Abe assured him. "I'll make up any hours I've missed."

Glen insisted on taking Abe out to lunch, even though Abe assured him that it wasn't necessary.

"Yes it is." Glen reached to open the rear door. "Get in."

Joey did the driving, one hand on the wheel. His expression was guarded; he didn't look away from the road, not once. They drove all the way to Hamilton, to the Hunan Kitchen, where they picked up three orders of General Gao's chicken to go, in spite of Glen's restricted diet, then ate in the car, on a street facing the Hamilton Hospital. Such a lunch guaranteed privacy, as well as indigestion.

"Did you know the Haddan School has made a contribution that will let us start construction for a medical center in Haddan?" Glen said. "There's a party to celebrate next weekend, and let me tell you, Sam Arthur and the rest of the councilmen will be pissed as hell if anything goes wrong between now and then. It would save lives, you know, Abe. Not having to come all the way to Hamilton in an emergency alone would make it worth it. It might have been possible to save Frank, if we'd had a decent facility in town that had been prepared to deal with gunshot wounds. Think about that."

Abe deposited his chopsticks into the container of spicy chicken. He felt a tightness, as though a band were being pulled around his chest. He used to feel this way when he couldn't please his father, which, it turned out, had been most of the time.

"So all we have to do to get the medical center is to look the other way when some kid is killed?"

"No. All you have to do is stay the hell away from the Haddan campus. Bob Thomas is a reasonable man and he made a reasonable request. Stop harassing his students. Stay off the grounds."

They drove back along Route 17 in silence. None of the men finished the food they'd traveled so far to obtain. Abe was let off by his car in the lot of Chalk House, where there was a thin scrim of ice over the asphalt. Joey got out of the car, too.

"If you keep bothering the powers that be at the school, we'll all suffer," Joey said. "The way I see it, money coming from the Haddan School is owed to this town. We deserve it."

"Well, I disagree."

"Fine. Then you do it your way and I'll do it my way. We don't have to be fucking identical twins, do we?" Joey was already on his way back to the car when Abe called after him.

"Remember when we jumped off the roof?" Abe had been thinking about that time ever since they passed the turnoff to Wright's house on Route 17.

"Nope."

"Out at my grandfather's place? You dared me and I dared you and we were both stupid enough to go for it."

"No way. Never happened."

But it had, and Abe recalled how blue the sky had been that day. Wright had told them to mow the back fields where the grass was nearly as tall as they were, but instead they'd climbed onto a shed, then made a leap for the roof of the house, clutching onto the gutters and pulling themselves over the asphalt shingles. They'd been twelve, that reckless age when most boys believe they will never get hurt; they can jump through thin air, shouting at the top of their lungs, waking all the blackbirds in the trees, and still land with only the wind knocked out of them and not a single bone broken. Back then, a boy could be as certain of his best friend as he was of the air and of the birds and of the ever-lasting that grew in the fields.

Joey wrenched the door of his car open and shouted over the idling motor, "You're imagining things, buddy. Just like always."

After they'd pulled away, Abe got into his car and drove over to the Millstone. It was still early and the place was empty and maybe this was the reason Abe felt as though he'd entered a town he'd never been to before. For one thing, there was a new bar-tender on duty, someone George Nichols must have hired who didn't know Abe by name and who wasn't familiar with the fact that Abe preferred draft beer to bottled. George Nichols had inherited the place and was already considered ancient when Joey and Abe first tried out their fake IDs. He'd busted them sev-eral times, phoning Abe's grandfather whenever he caught them hanging out in the parking lot, where they would plead with the older guys to buy them drinks. When Abe was living with his grandfather he'd wasted one entire week of summer confined to his room after George Nichols discovered him in the men's room of the Millstone with a contraband whiskey sour. "You're not devious enough to get away with this sort of thing," Wright had told Abe back then. "You're going to get caught each and every time."

But what about the boys who didn't get caught, that's what Abe wanted to know as he fished peanuts from a bowl on the bar. Those boys who were so guilt-ridden they broke out in hives or started spitting blood, but who managed to get away with their wrongdoings, how did they live with themselves?

"Where's George?" Abe asked the new bartender, who hardly looked of age to drink himself. "Out fishing?"

"He's got some physical therapy appointments. His knees are giving up on him," the new bartender said. "Decrepit old bastard."

When Abe got up from the barstool his own knees didn't feel so great. He went out and blinked in the sunlight. He couldn't shake the feeling of being a stranger in town; he made two wrong turns on his way to the mini-mart and couldn't find parking on Main Street when he went to pick up one of Wright's sport coats at the dry cleaner's. Why, he didn't even recognize anyone at the cleaner's, other than Zeke, another old-timer who had a fondness for Abe due to the fact that his grandfather had stopped the town's only armed robbery on record thirty-five years earlier in this very establishment. That there had been only fourteen dollars in the cash register didn't matter; the robber had a gun pointed straight at Zeke when Wright happened to walk through the door, arriving to pick up some woolen blankets. For this reason Abe was given a twenty percent discount to this day, though in fact he rarely had anything to dry-clean.

"Who are all those people?" Abe asked, when the line of customers before him had thinned out and he could pick up Wright's coat.

"Damned if I know. But that's what happens when a town starts growing. You stop knowing everyone by name."

But for now, it was still Abe's town and in his town it was not against the law for a taxpaying citizen to wander across Haddan School grounds. If there had been such a law, local people would have been incited to riot before the ink on the edict had dried. Imagine Mrs. Jeremy's son, AJ, being kicked off the soccer field when he arrived with his golf clubs to work on his short game. Imagine the yoga club, meeting on Thursday mornings for more than ten years, thrown off the quad as if they were common criminals rather than practitioners of an ancient discipline. Abe was pushing his luck, he knew that, but all he needed was a little more time before Nathaniel Gibb broke down. He began to track the boy again.

"Just talk to me," Abe said as he trailed after Gibb.

By now, Nathaniel was panicked. "What are you trying to do to me?" he cried. "Why won't you leave me alone?"

"Because you can tell me the truth."

They were on that same path beside the river where before long fiddlehead ferns would unfold; there really was nowhere for Nathaniel to run.

"Just think about it," Abe went on. "If you meet me here to-morrow and tell me you don't want to talk, then I won't bother you anymore." It was the time of year when those Haddan boys had needed to be rescued by Abe's grandfather, the season when the ice on the river appeared thick to the inexperienced passerby, but upon closer inspection the surface revealed itself to be clear rather than blue, the way river ice is right before it begins to break apart.

"It wasn't me," Nathaniel Gibb said.

Abe did his best not to react; he was not about to scare this boy off, even if his head did feel as if it were about to explode. "I know that. That's why I'm talking to you."

They arranged to meet early the next day, at an hour when the blackbirds were waking and most students at Haddan were still asleep in their beds. The sheen of spring was everywhere, in the yellowing bark of the willows, in the cobalt color of the morning sky. Though the season would soon change, it was brisk enough for Abe to keep his hands in his pockets as he waited. He waited for a long time, there on the path to the river. At eight o'clock, students began to appear, on their way to breakfast or the library, and by nine most classrooms were full. Abe walked over to Chalk House, tinkered with the lock—an easy push-button type any rookie could get past—and let himself in. There was a directory in the hallway. Abe was not surprised to see that Harry McKenna had what appeared to be the best room, nor was he surprised that Gibb's room was up in the attic.

"Hey, there," Eric Herman called when he saw Abe on the stairs. Eric had just finished compiling his exam for the following week's midterm and was rushing off to class, but he took the time to stop and look Abe over. The dean had made an announcement asking to be informed if anyone who didn't belong was found on campus. "I think you're in the wrong place."

"I don't think so." Abe stayed where he was. He'd never before been face-to-face with his rival. What had he imagined? That he'd challenge Herman, that a fight would result, with

punches aimed to inflict the most damage? What he found was
that he merely felt he and Eric Herman had something in common, they were both in love with Betsy. "I'm looking for Nathaniel Gibb."

"You're out of luck. He's in the infirmary."

Abe could tell from the way Eric was glaring at him that he
wouldn't get any more information out of him, but fortunately
Dorothy Jackson was a regular at the Millstone, and much
friendlier when Abe approached her; in spite of the dean's warning not to speak to Abe, the nurse let him visit the infirmary.

"He's had a bad accident at hockey practice. Five minutes,"
she granted Abe. "No more."

Nathaniel Gibb lay on his back on the cot nearest the wall.
Both his arms had been broken. He'd been driven by ambulance
to the hospital in Hamilton where X rays were taken and casts
had been fashioned, and now he was awaiting his parents, who
were on their way from Ohio to bring him home. For months, he
would have to be fed and dressed, as though he were an infant
once again, and it was somehow fitting that he had also lost the
ability to speak. Whether this development had been caused
when he bit down on his tongue, nearly severing it as the group
of boys at hockey practice rammed him into the wall, or whether
the words had simply been scared out of him really didn't matter.
He could not speak to Abe.

"I don't know what you want from this boy," Dorothy Jackson
said when she brought up a glass of ginger ale with a straw. "But
he probably won't be able to talk for a month. Even then he'll
need speech therapy for some time."

Abe waited for the nurse to leave, then went over to
Nathaniel and lifted the glass so that the boy might quench his

thirst. But Nathaniel wouldn't even look at him. He would not drink even though his tongue, stitched together at the emergency room by a resident who had never before performed the procedure, was throbbing.

"I'm sorry." Abe sat down on a nearby cot. He was still holding the glass of ginger ale. The infirmary smelled of iodine and disinfectant. "I was probably wrong to get you involved. I hope you can accept my apologies."

The boy made a guttural sound that might have been a laugh or a snort of contempt. Nathaniel peered over at Abe, hunched on the metal cot across from his own. Sunlight poured in through the windows and the dust motes whirled into the shape of a funnel. In only a few hours Nathaniel Gibb and his belongings would be loaded into his parents' car, ready to drive far from this place. Here was one boy who would never again have to set foot in Massachusetts or go through another of its wicked winters. He would be miles away, safe in his home state, which is why he forced himself to open his mouth and move his tortured tongue, straining to utter an initial, the letter of the alphabet that hurt him most to recite, a clear and single *H*.

By the following morning Abe had been released from duty, the first officer in Haddan ever to be asked for his resignation. Abe wasn't even dressed when Glen Tiles arrived on his front steps to tell him the news. What had he expected, really? A dozen or more of the staff at Haddan had seen him stalking students, helping himself to food in the dining hall, bothering the faculty with questions. And then there'd been Eric, who'd wasted no time in contacting the dean.

"You had to push it," Glen said. "You couldn't take my advice. I had the attorney general's office call me on this, Abe. Somebody over there is an alum."

The two men stood there facing each other in the cold, bright light. They had measured each other against Wright's legacy, and neither believed the other would ever come close to the old man's stature. At least now they wouldn't have to see each other every day. By lunchtime, everyone in town knew what had happened. Lois Jeremy and her friend Charlotte Evans had already mobilized, but when they tried to reach Abe to inform him they had started a petition to have him reinstated, he didn't answer his phone. Over at Selena's, Nikki Humphrey made up the sandwich Abe usually ordered for lunch and had it waiting for him, but he never showed up. He didn't even bother to get dressed until sometime past noon. By then, Doug Lauder had been told that he was being promoted to detective, and truthfully, Doug deserved it; he was a decent guy and he'd do a good job, although the job would never mean as much to him as it had to Abe.

Toward the end of the day, Abe went out for a drive. He still had Wright's old cruiser, and he figured he might as well make use of it in case they came to repossess it. He spotted Mary Beth in the park with her children. Even though the new baby was due in a few weeks, MB still looked great, and both girls on the swings, Lilly and Emily, the eldest, resembled their mother, with dark hair and wide-set hazel eyes. Abe knew nothing about children, but he knew they had big expenses, and that Joey would want to provide them with all that he could and more. It was the more that was the problem. Abe got out of the cruiser and went to greet Mary Beth.

"Hey, stranger," she said, hugging him.

"You look great."

"Liar." MB smiled. "I'm a whale."

A person could really learn to hate February living in this part of the world, although the kids surely weren't bothered by the gloomy weather; they screamed with glee as they went higher and higher on the swings. Abe remembered exactly what that felt like—no fear. No thought of the consequences.

"Not so high," Mary Beth called to her children. "I heard about what happened at work," she said to Abe. "I think it's just crazy."

Joey and MB's son, Jackson, was a maniac on the swings; he went as far into the sky as possible, then came rushing down to earth, breathless and hollering out loud. Joey was crazy about this kid; on the day he was born, Joey had thrown open the doors of the Millstone, inviting everyone to have a drink, charged to his tab.

"I heard about it from Kelly Avon. Joey didn't even tell me. What's happened between you two?" Mary Beth asked.

"You tell me."

Mary Beth laughed at that. "Not possible. He talks to you more than he talks to me."

"Not anymore."

"Maybe he just grew up." Mary Beth put one hand over her eyes in order to keep watch over her children in the dwindling sunlight. "Maybe that's what happens with friendships. I think he sees the kids getting older and he wants to spend more time with them. If this was before, he'd be planning a fishing trip with you over the Easter break, now we're all going to Disney World."

A vacation such as that was an expensive proposition for Joey, who in the past had often needed to borrow from Abe to pay off his monthly mortgage payment. As he thought this over, Abe noticed that Mary Beth's wreck of a car had been replaced by a new minivan.

"Joey surprised me with that," Mary Beth said of the van. "I've been driving around in that old station wagon for so long I thought I'd be buried in it." She took Abe's hand. "I know it's not the same between you, but that won't last."

She'd always been generous about their friendship; she'd never complained about including Abe in their lives or griped about the time Joey spent away from her. She was a good woman who deserved a minivan and a whole lot more, and Abe wished he could be happy for her. Instead, he felt as though they'd both lost Joey.

"I hope you're going to fight to get reinstated," Mary Beth called when he headed back to his car, even though it was clear to them both that it would be pointless for him to do so.

Abe drove to the school out of habit, like a dog who insists on circling the same plot of land, certain there are birds in the grass. Because he stood a good chance of being arrested if caught venturing onto private property, Abe parked down by the river and walked the rest of the way. He could feel his heart lurching around in his chest, the way it used to when he and Joey took this route. They didn't have to talk back then; they knew where they were headed and what they meant to accomplish. He went past the place where the violets grew in spring and along the dirt trail to the rear of Chalk House. He didn't even know what he wanted until he came to a window through which he could see Eric Herman's living quarters. He could feel something fill up his head, blood or lunacy, he wasn't sure which. He was wearing gloves, because of the chill in the air, or maybe a break-in was what he'd intended all along. Either way, he didn't have to protect himself when he put his fist through the window, shattering the glass, then reached in to unhook the latch.

He pulled himself over the ledge; it wasn't as easy as it once was, he was heavier, for one thing, and there was his bad knee to think of. He was breathing hard by the time he was in Eric's living room. He brushed the glass off and began to take a look around. A thief could decipher a great deal from observing a person's lodgings, and Abe could tell that Betsy would never be happy with the man who lived there. He could not imagine her in this tidy room, beneath the sheets of the perfectly made bed. Even the refrigerator revealed how wrong Herman was for Betsy; all he had was mayonnaise, bottled water, half a jar of olives.

Whenever Abe burglarized a house he could always sense where he would find the best loot, he had a natural ability to zero in on treasures, and as it turned out he hadn't lost that knack. There it was, in the living room, the midterm for Eric's senior history seminar, five pages of questions on Hellenic culture. A typed class list had been paper-clipped to the exam. Quickly, Abe looked down the page until he found what he was looking for. Harry's name.

He rolled up the exam and kept it inside the sleeve of his jacket as he went through the door that opened into the hallway of the dormitory. It was the dinner hour and except for a few boys who were ill, no one was around. It was easy enough to walk down the hallway, and easier still to discern which room was Dr. Howe's old office: there was the mantel into which so many lines had been carved, there were the golden oak floors, and the woodwork that was dusted by the hired maid every other week, and the desk, into which Abe deposited exactly what Harry McKenna deserved.

CARLIN WAS ON HER WAY HOME FROM A SWIM meet in New Hampshire when she felt him beside her. She had claimed a double seat on the bus for herself, throwing down the black coat, not wanting to be forced into making polite conversation with any of the other girls on the team. It was just as well that the seat next to her was vacant, for now there was room for what was left of August Pierce to settle in beside her, drop by watery drop.

Although Carlin had performed well at the meet, it had been a generally disappointing evening and the bus was quiet, the way it always was after a defeat. Carlin hadn't even bothered to shower before she dressed; her cropped hair was wet and smelled of chlorine, but the droplets of water that now rolled down the plastic seat weren't from her hair, nor from her soaking bathing suit, stowed away in her gym bag. Carlin glanced to see if a nearby window had been left ajar, for there was a fine drizzle falling outside, but all the windows were shut and there were no leaks in the roof of the bus. The liquid Carlin noticed wasn't rainwater; it was murky and green as it spread out over the seat, a watermark that had both weight and form. Carlin could feel her heart racing, the way it did when she pushed herself to the limit during a race. She looked straight ahead and counted to twenty, but she could still feel him beside her.

"Is that you?" Carlin's voice was so small no one on the bus took notice; not even Ivy Cooper in the seat right behind overheard.

Carlin moved one hand to touch the black coat. The fabric was soaking and so frigid to the touch she immediately began to shiver. She could feel the cold moving up her arm, as if ice water had been added to her veins. The bus had already entered Massachusetts and was headed south on 93, toward the Route 17 exit. Outside, it was so dark and damp everything disappeared into the mist, fences and trees, cars and street signs. Carlin reached her hand into the pocket of the black coat to find it had filled with water. There was silt there, too, in among the seams, the grainy mud from the bottom of the river, along with several of the little black stones so often found when the bellies of silver trout were slit open by fishermen's knives.

Carlin glanced across the aisle to where Christine Percy was dozing. In Christine's hazed-over window, she could see Gus's reflection. Inside the black coat, he was as pale as tea water, so translucent his features evaporated in the glare of oncoming headlights. Carlin closed her eyes and leaned her head against the seat. He had appeared beside her because she had wanted him to. She had called him to her, and was calling him still. Even when she fell asleep, she dreamed of water, as if the world were topsy-turvy and everything she cared about had been lost in the deep. She plunged through the green waves with her eyes wide open, searching for the world as she'd known it, but that world no longer existed; everything that had once been solid was liquid now, and the birds swam alongside the fish.

It was not until the bus pulled into the parking lot at Haddan, gears squealing, engine straining, that Carlin awoke. She came back with a start, arms flailing, the way the girls on the team had been taught a drowning person's might, and a wave of panic moved through the bus. At that point, Carlin was making a gurgling sound in the back of her throat, as though she were already past any rescue, but thankfully, Ivy Cooper had a cool head; she quickly handed Carlin a paper bag, into which Carlin breathed until her color returned.

"You're freezing," Ivy said when their hands touched as Carlin gratefully returned the paper bag. "Maybe you were in the water too long."

Carlin reached for her black coat and her gym bag, ready to rush off, then realized that most of the girls had turned their attention to a car parked on the grass in front of Chalk House. In spite of the drizzle and the late hour, Bob Thomas was out there along with some other man none of the girls recognized.

"What's happening?" Carlin asked.

"Where have you been?" Ivy Cooper stood beside her. "They're kicking Harry McKenna out of school. They found a midterm exam in his room. There was a hearing last night, and he couldn't talk his way out of it. I heard he broke into Mr. Herman's quarters to get the exam. He smashed the window and everything."

Sure enough, the trunk of the parked car was filled with suitcases and a heap of possessions tossed in hurriedly. Everything Harry owned was there, his sweaters, his sneakers, his books, his lamp. Some of the girls from the swim team had begun to file out of the bus and were already running through the rain toward St. Anne's, but Carlin stayed where she was, gazing out the window. At last Harry came out, as though he were in a hurry to get somewhere. He was wearing a sweatshirt with a hood, so that it wasn't possible to see his fair hair, or even to manage a good look at his face.

He flung himself into the passenger seat of his father's car, then slammed the door shut. Carlin got off the bus, the last to leave. She could still see Harry from where she stood in the parking lot, but he didn't look at her. The dean and Harry's father didn't bother to shake hands; this was not a friendly parting. Dartmouth had been informed of Harry's expulsion and his admittance there had been retracted. He would not be attending college in the fall, nor would he graduate from high school this year, as he'd been asked to leave before the end of the semester. Carlin followed along behind Harry's father's car as it slowly traversed the speed bumps in the parking lot, then turned onto Main Street. She walked along through the rain, which was falling harder now, hitting against the roofs of the white houses. The car was a luxury model, black and sleek and so quiet most people in town didn't even notice it on the road. Once it had passed the inn, the car began to pick up speed, splashing through the puddles, leaving a thin trail of exhaust that drifted down the center of town.

It was after curfew when Carlin sneaked into her room, and although the hour was late, Amy Elliot was up in bed, sobbing.

"Now are you happy?" Amy cried. "His life is ruined."

Carlin got into bed, fully dressed. She wasn't happy at all; Harry's departure wouldn't bring Gus back. Gus wouldn't rise from the river in the morning to retrace his steps; he wouldn't wake in his bed, ready for school, eager for his life to go on. When the morning did come, Carlin didn't attend classes. It was the harsh end of the month and torrents of rain were now falling, none of which prevented Carlin from going to the bank to speak to Mike Randall, then taking the bus to a travel agency in Hamilton where she used her funds from Miss Davis to buy a plane ticket. She rode the bus back to Haddan late in the day, going directly to the pharmacy, where she sat down at the counter. By then it was after three and Sean Byers had reported for work. He was at the sink, rinsing out glasses and cups, but when he saw Carlin he dried his hands and came over.

"You're drenched," he said, his voice a mixture of longing and concern.

Puddles of water had collected on the floor around Carlin's stool and her hair was plastered against her head. Sean poured her a hot cup of coffee.

"Do you ever feel like you want to go home?" Carlin asked him.

Although the pharmacy was usually busy at this hour, the heavy rain seemed to be keeping people off the streets and out of the stores. Sam Arthur from the town council was the only other customer in the place; he was going over the plans for the ground-breaking celebration for the new medical center, muttering to himself and enjoying a strawberry milkshake, an item that was definitely not on his diabetic diet plan.

"Is that what you're thinking about doing?" Sean asked. He hadn't seen Carlin much since Christmas vacation, at least not as much as he would have liked. He still sneaked into the pool, late at night, hoping that she'd be there, too, but she never was. It was as if the time they'd had together existed separately from the rest of their lives, like a dream that's in danger of dissolving as soon as the dreamer awakes. "You're running away?"

"No." Carlin was shivering in her wet clothes. "I'm flying." She showed him the one-way ticket.

"Seems like you've already decided."

"They kicked Harry out of school," Carlin told Sean.

"Nah. Guys like that never get kicked out of anything."

"This one did. Late last night. He was expelled for cheating."

Sean was gleeful. He did a little victory dance, which made Carlin explode into giggles.

"You're not pretty when you gloat," she told him; all the same, she laughed.

"You are," Sean said. "I just wish you weren't such a coward."

A group of ravenous Haddan students had braved the rain on a mission for hamburgers and fries and Sean was called to take their order. Carlin watched as he tossed meat patties onto the grill and started the fryer. Even here in the pharmacy, Carlin felt as though she were stuck underwater. The world outside floated by—Mrs. Jeremy with her umbrella, a delivery truck of hibiscus pulling up to the Lucky Day, a gang of kids from the elementary school racing home in rain slickers and boots.

"I'm not a coward," Carlin told Sean when he returned and refilled her cup with steaming black coffee.

"You're letting them chase you off. What do you call it?"

"Wanting to go home."

Because of his extremely dark eyes Sean Byers had the ability to hide most of what he felt inside. He'd always been a good liar; he'd talked himself out of situations that would have landed any-one else in jail, but he wasn't lying now. "This is what you always wanted. Why would you leave if you weren't being chased off?"

Carlin threw down some money to pay for her coffee, then headed for the door. The potatoes in the fryer were sizzling, but Sean followed her anyway. He truly didn't care if the whole place burned to the ground. The rain was falling in such torrents that when it hit against the asphalt it sounded as if guns had been fired or cannons discharged. Before Carlin could plunge onto the sidewalk, Sean pulled her back beneath the pharmacy awning.

He was crazy about her, but that's not what was at stake here. The rain was coming down harder, yet Carlin could hear Sean's heart beneath the fabric of his shirt and the rough white apron he wore. All the world out there was liquid, all of it enough to pull her down, and so, for this brief time she held on tight and did her best not to drown.

A TENT HAD BEEN SET UP IN THE FIELD BEHIND town hall and above it a flag had been raised to wave in the wind so that no one in town would fail to notice the ground-breaking celebration. The Becker construction company had been retained by the town council and Ronny Becker, Doreen and Nikki's father, had already bulldozed a level area that allowed the tent to be set up on flat ground; it certainly wouldn't do for any of the older guests such as Mrs. Evans, who'd recently been in need of a cane, to tumble over the ruts and break a hip or a leg.

The Chazz Dixon band played that afternoon, and two dozen of Mr. Dixon's violin and flute students from the elementary school were allowed to miss their last class in order to attend. Thankfully, even though it was the rainy season, the afternoon was clear and sunny with a brisk, rather enjoyable west wind. Just to be safe, portable heaters had been set up inside the tent, to ensure that those in attendance could enjoy the salmon sandwiches and cream cheese puffs that the staff of the Haddan School cafeteria served on large silver trays. It came as no surprise to anyone that while people from town tended to congregate over by the bar, the staff and faculty of the school gathered around the hors d'oeuvres table, gorging on deviled eggs and clam cakes.

A motion had already been passed by both the board of trustees at the school and the town council to name the health center after Helen Davis and a bronze plaque with her name etched upon it had been set into the cornerstone. The dean had asked Betsy Chase to commemorate the occasion with a photograph, and she was there to preserve the moment when Sam Arthur shook hands with Bob Thomas, each man standing with one foot balanced on the cornerstone. Betsy was then asked to photograph the doctors who'd been wooed away from an HMO in Boston, along with the center's new administrator, Kelly Avon's cousin, Janet Lloyd, who was delighted to be moving back to Haddan after eight years of exile at Mass General.

On the way over, Betsy had noticed the cruiser Abe drove, one of dozens of cars left at the curb along Main Street, where the no-parking signs had been covered with burlap hoods. In spite of herself, Betsy found herself looking for him, but the place was crowded, filled with people Betsy didn't know, and she didn't see Abe until the Chazz Dixon band was playing its final set. He was standing beside the makeshift cloakroom, a direction Betsy needed to go toward anyway, in order to retrieve her coat.

"Hey," she said as she approached. "Remember me?"

"Sure I do." Abe raised his drink to her and said, "Have fun," then quickly moved on. He had decided that he was finished getting hit over the head with rejection, so he made his way to the bar to get himself another beer. In spite of all the initial hoopla, people were managing just fine without Abel Grey on the police force. Mrs. Evans, for instance, had taken to phoning Doug Lauder about the raccoon that came into her yard to eat her birdseed and rattle her trash cans. A new uniformed cop had been hired and in the mornings he could be seen at the crosswalk in front of the elementary school. On days when the garden club met, he was posted outside town hall, directing traffic and gratefully accepting the thermoses of hot chocolate Kelly Avon had taken to delivering. Residents who had invited Abe into the most personal moments of their lives—Sam Arthur, for instance, with whom Abe sat vigil when his wife, Lorriane, was in that head-on collision while visiting their daughter in Virginia, and Mrs. Jeremy, who had wept while Abe talked AJ out of jumping out a second-story window one horrible spring night, a leap that probably wouldn't have done any more than rattle a few of AJ's bones considering how drunk he'd been—now seemed startled when they ran into him, embarrassed by all the secrets he'd once been privy to. Actually, Abe himself didn't feel that comfortable with most people, what with Joey and Mary Beth clearly avoiding him and all those busybodies from Haddan School who'd reported him for harassment keeping an eye on him.

The only reason he'd shown up at the festivities was to pay his respects to Helen Davis. He'd already had two beers in honor of her memory and he figured a third wouldn't hurt. He'd have a couple of drinks and get out, no damage done, but when he turned he saw that Betsy had also come to the bar. She was asking for a glass of white wine, and looking his way.

"There you go, following me again," Abe said, and he was surprised when she didn't deny it. "Give her the good stuff, George," Abe told the bartender, George Nichols from the Millstone.

"The school's footing the bill," George said. "Trust me, there is no good stuff."

"I heard you got fired," Betsy said as she moved aside to let AJ Jeremy get to the bar.

"I prefer to think of it as a permanent vacation." Abe looked past AJ and signaled for George Nichols to add only a small amount of vodka to the double vodka tonic AJ had ordered. "Looks like they roped you into being the inquiring photographer," he said when Betsy stepped back to take a shot of Chazz Dixon, wailing on his saxophone with a fervor that shocked many of his music students. Betsy turned and found Abe in her viewfinder. Most subjects were shy, they tended to look away, but Abe stared back at her with an intensity that flustered her and made her snap his picture before she was ready. It was those blue eyes that were to blame, and had been from the start.

"My turn," Abe said.

"You have no idea how to take a decent picture." Betsy laughed as she handed over the camera.

"Now you'll always remember this day," Abe told her after he'd taken her picture. "Isn't that what they say about a photograph?"

It was a big mistake not to just walk away from each other and they both knew it, but they stood together awhile longer and watched the band.

"Maybe you should hire them to play at your wedding," Abe said of the musicians.

"Very funny." Betsy drank her wine too fast; later in the day she'd have a headache, but right now she didn't care.

"I don't think it's funny at all." He was reaching toward her.

"What are you doing?"

Betsy was so certain that he was about to kiss her, that she found it difficult to breathe. But instead, Abe showed her the quarter he'd pulled from behind her ear. He'd been practicing, and although the trick still needed work, in his many free hours he'd discovered that he had a gift for sleight of hand. Already, he'd finagled close to a hundred bucks out of Teddy Humphrey, who still could not figure out how Abe always discerned which card Teddy picked from the deck.

"You're good at that," Betsy said. "Just the way you're good at breaking into places."

"Is this an official investigation or a personal accusation?"

Betsy swayed to the music. She refused to say more, even though as soon as she'd heard about the robbery at Eric's, her first thought was of Abe. Even now she wondered if the student they'd expelled, Harry McKenna, might have been innocent of that particular crime. "I think it's too bad Helen Davis couldn't be here."

"She would have hated it," Abe said. "Crowds, noise, bad wine."

"They've found someone to take her place." As the new head of the department, Eric had been on the hiring committee. A young historian fresh out of graduate school had been chosen, someone too fresh and insecure to question authority. "They wasted no time replacing her."

"Here's to Helen." Abe raised his beer aloft, then finished it off in a few gulps.

Betsy had a dreamy look on her face; lately she had been especially aware of how a single choice could alter life's course. She wasn't used to drinking wine in the afternoon, and maybe that was why she was being so chummy with Abe. "What do you think Helen would have changed if she could have chosen to live her life differently?"

Abe thought this over, then said, "I think she would have run off with me."

Betsy let out a yelp of laughter.

"You think I'm kidding?" Abe grinned.

"Oh, no. I think you're serious. You definitely would have made an interesting couple."

Now when Abe reached for her he really did kiss her, there in front of the Chazz Dixon band and everyone else. He just went ahead and did it and Betsy didn't even try to stop him. She kissed him right back until she was dizzy and her legs felt as though they might give out. Eric was over by Dr. Jones's table with the rest of the Haddan faculty and might easily have seen them had he looked behind him; Lois Jeremy and Charlotte Evans were walking right past, chattering about the good turnout, and still Betsy went on kissing him. She might have gone on indefinitely if the drummer in the Dixon band hadn't reached for his cymbals and startled her into pulling away.

Some of the crowd had decided to create a dance floor, up beyond the coatroom, and several locals were letting loose before the band packed up. AJ Jeremy, who had managed to get looped despite his mother's watchful eye, was dancing with Doreen Becker. Teddy Humphrey had taken the opportunity to ask his ex-wife to accompany him to the dance floor, and to everyone's surprise Nikki had agreed.

"Well," Betsy said, trying to compose herself after their kiss. Her lips were hot. "What was that for?"

She looked up at Abe but she couldn't see his eyes. So much the better, for if she had she would have known exactly what the kiss was for. At least she was smart enough not to watch when Abe walked away. She told him once there had never been anything between them, now she just had to convince herself of the very same thing. She ordered herself another glass of wine, drank it too quickly, then got her coat and buttoned it against the changing weather. Above the tent, the flags snapped back and forth in the wind, and the late afternoon sky had begun to darken, with clouds turning to black. It was the end of the celebration, and by then Eric had found her.

"What's wrong?" he asked, for her face was flushed and she seemed unsteady. "Not feeling well?"

"No, I'm fine. I just want to go home."

Before they could leave there was the sound of thunder, rolling in from the east, and the sky was darker still.

"Bad timing," Eric said. Through the fabric of the tent they could see a fork of lightning. "We'll just have to wait it out."

But Betsy couldn't wait. She could feel little bits of electricity up and down her skin each time the sky was illuminated, and before Eric could stop her, she dashed out of the tent. As she made her way along Main Street, the sky rumbled, and another line of lightning crossed the horizon. The storm was moving closer, and there were several large oak trees on Main Street and on Lovewell Lane that were particularly susceptible to a strike, but that didn't stop Betsy on her way back to the school. Before long, fat raindrops had begun to fall, and Betsy stood with her face upturned. Even with the rain washing over her, she continued to burn; she hadn't talked herself out of anything.

Bob Thomas had asked her to rush the photographs, so she went directly to the art building. She was happy to be working, hoping she might keep her mind off Abe, and as it turned out, the photographs she'd taken that afternoon were quite good. One or two of the prints would make their way to the front page of the Sunday edition of the *Haddan Tribune*—the one of Sam Arthur and Bob Thomas shaking hands and another of Chazz Dixon wailing away. It was amazing how the lens of a camera could pick up information that was otherwise invisible to the naked eye. The suspicion on Sam Arthur's face, for instance, when he gazed at the dean; the sweat on Chazz Dixon's brow. Betsy had assumed she'd be most rattled by the photograph of Abe, but in fact he had moved and the image was blurry. It did him no justice at all. No, it was the photograph Abe had taken of her that turned out to be the most disturbing. Betsy let that print sit in the developing vat for quite some time, until it was over-developed and streaky, but even then, it was impossible to ignore what this picture revealed. There, for all the world to see, was a woman who'd fallen in love.

THE ARBOR

IN THE PEARLY SKIES OF MARCH
there were countless sorrows in New England. The world had closed down for so
long it seemed as though the ice would
never melt. The very lack of color could
leave a person despondent. After a while
the black bark of trees in a rainstorm
brought on waves of melancholy. A flock of
geese soaring across the pale sky could
cause a person to weep. Soon enough,
there would be a renewal, sap would again
rise in the maples, robins would reappear
on the lawns, but such things were easily
forgotten in the hazy March light. It was
the season of despair and it lasted for four
dismal weeks, during which time more
damage was done in the households of

Haddan than the combined wreckage of every storm that had ever passed through town.

In March, more divorces came before old Judge Aubrey and more love affairs unraveled. Men admitted to addictions that were sure to bring ruin; women were so preoccupied they set fire to their houses accidentally while cooking bacon or ironing tablecloths. The hospital in Hamilton was always filled to capacity during this month, and toothaches were so commonplace both dentists in Hamilton were forced to work overtime. Not many tourists came to Haddan during this season. Most residents insisted that October was the best month to visit the village, with so much marvelous foliage, the golden elms and red oaks aflame in the bright afternoon sunshine. Others said May was best, that sweet green time when lilacs bloomed and gardens along Main Street were filled with sugary pink peonies and Dutch tulips.

Margaret Grey, however, always came back to Haddan in March, despite the unpredictable weather. She arrived on the twentieth of the month, her boy Frank's birthday, taking a morning flight up from Florida and staying overnight with Abe. Abe's father, Ernest, could not be asked to accompany her; Margaret wouldn't have expected her husband to face the cemetery any more than she would have insisted Abe pick her up at the airport in Boston. She took the train up to Haddan, looking out at the landscape she once knew so well; it all seemed terribly unfamiliar, the stone walls and the fields, the flocks of blackbirds, the multitudes of warblers who returned at this time of year, marking Frank's birthday by swooping across the cold, wide sky.

Abe waited for his mother at the Haddan train station, the

way he did every year. But for once he was early and the train was late, held up outside Hamilton by a cow on the tracks.

"You're on time," Margaret commented when Abe came to give her a hug and collect her suitcase, for he was notoriously late on the occasion of these visits, postponing the sorrow that inevitably accompanied the day.

"I'm unemployed now," he reminded his mother. "I've got all the time in the world."

"I recognize this car," Margaret said when Abe led her over to Wright's cruiser. "It wasn't safe to drive twenty years ago."

They stopped at the Lucky Day Florist where Ettie Nelson hugged her old friend and told Margaret how jealous she was of anyone who lived in Florida, where it was already summer when here in Haddan they still had to struggle with dreadful blustery weather. Abe and his mother bought a single bunch of daffodils, as they always did, although Margaret stopped to admire Ettie's garlands.

"Some people swear by them," Margaret said of the garlands. Some were fashioned of boxwood and jasmine, others of pine boughs, or of hydrangeas, twisted together in a strand of heavenly blue. "Lois Jeremy's boy, AJ, nearly died of pneumonia when he was young, and Lois went out to the Haddan cemetery day after day. There were so many wreaths around that lamb's neck you would have thought it was a Christmas tree. But maybe it worked—AJ grew up strong and healthy."

"I don't know about the healthy part," Abe said as he thanked Ettie and paid for the flowers. "He's a bully and a drunk, but maybe you're right. He's definitely alive."

Frank was buried in the new section of the church cemetery.

Each September, Abe put in chrysanthemums at the base of the memorial and in the spring he came to weed around the hedge of azaleas that Margaret had planted that first year when every day hurt, as if sunlight and air and time itself were the instruments of heartache and pain. Today, as he watched his mother place the daffodils at the graveside, Abe was struck by what a short time Frank had had on this earth, only seventeen years. Abe himself might have had a son that age if he'd ever managed to settle down.

"I should have known it was going to happen," Margaret said as they stood together. "All the signs were there. We thought it was a good thing that he locked himself away from other people. He was studying so hard and doing so well."

Abe's parents had always seemed to agree that what happened that day had been an accident; a boy who didn't know any better playing around with a shotgun, a single instant of misfortune. But clearly Margaret had come to believe this hadn't been the case, or maybe she just hadn't the heart to admit her doubts before.

"When you look backwards everything seems like a clue, but that doesn't mean it is," Abe told her. "He had French toast for breakfast, he washed the car, he was wearing a white shirt. Does any of that matter?"

"He'd be thirty-nine today. The same age as AJ Jeremy. Both of them born on the day before spring," Margaret said. "That morning I knew something was wrong because he kissed me, just like that. He put his hands on my shoulders and kissed me. He didn't even like to be hugged when he was a baby. Frank wasn't a people person that way. He was always going off on his own. I should have known then and there, it was so out of the ordinary. Kissing wasn't his way."

Abe bent to kiss his mother's cheek.

"It's your way," she said, and her eyes filled with tears.

There are secrets kept for self-interest and those kept to protect the innocent, but most spring from a combination of the two. For all these years Abe had never told anyone about the favor he did his brother. He kept his promise, just as he had on that hot summer day. It was so rare for Frank to take an interest in Abe or include him in his life, how could Abe have denied him anything he might want?

"I went with him to get the gun." This is what Abe had wanted to tell his mother since that hot afternoon, but the words had stuck in his throat, as if each one had been fashioned from glass, ready to cut at the slightest admission. Even now, Abe couldn't look at Margaret. He couldn't abide the expression of betrayal in her eyes that he'd imagined since Frank had died. "He said it was for target practice. So I did it. I climbed through the window and got it."

Margaret's mouth was set in a thin line when she heard this information. "That was wrong of him."

"Of him? Don't you hear what I'm telling you? I got the gun." He clearly recalled the look on Frank's face when he crouched down so that Abe could climb on his shoulders. Never had Abe seen such certainty. "I helped him do it."

"No." Margaret shook her head. "He tricked you."

Above them in the sky, two hawks glided west, cutting through the canopy of rolling clouds. The weather had turned nasty, the way it often did on Frank's birthday, an unpredictable day in an unpredictable month. Margaret asked if they might go

out to Wright's farm. She had always believed that kindness be-
got kindness but that truth was more complex, and that it
brought to an individual whatever he wished to take. Truth was a
funny thing, difficult to hold on to, difficult to judge. If Margaret
hadn't been the one to be with Wright Grey on the last day of his
life she would never have known that her husband, Ernest, was
not Wright and Florence's natural son.

"Don't be silly, Pop," she had said to Wright when he told her.

She'd been young and nervous around death and she remembered wishing Ernest would hurry up and relieve her. When she
heard his car pull up she was grateful.

"I found him," Wright had insisted. "By the river. Under some
bushes."

Margaret had stared at the window to where Ernest was taking a hospital bed from the trunk of his car, in the hopes of making his father's last days more comfortable. While Ernest set up
the bed in the front parlor, Wright told Margaret how he'd discovered the baby most people in town believed never took a single breath. That child had in fact been born and lived on, left by
his mother in the care of the swans, tucked into the roots of the
willows and kept out of sight until Wright had come searching
for Dr. Howe. Wright had wanted to dole out some measure of
punishment, for all the mistreatment Annie had suffered, but he
never did thrash the headmaster as he'd set out to, even though
he believed Howe deserved it, for he had been distracted by a
trail of tears and blood that led to the willow where the child had
been hidden from his father.

The very next morning, Wright walked all the way into Boston
with the infant tucked inside his coat. He was a man who'd always held himself accountable, even when the accounts weren't

his. He passed through towns he'd never been to before and villages that consisted of nothing more than a post office and a general store. At last he reached the city limits; at an embankment of the Charles River he spied a young woman and because of the kindness that showed in her face he immediately knew she was the one he would marry. Wright approached her slowly, so he would not frighten her away. Annie Howe's baby was warm and safe inside his coat, sucking on a rag dipped in store-bought milk. Wright sat down beside Florence, who was good-natured and plain and who'd never before had a handsome man look at her, let alone pour out his heart to her. They raised the child as if he were their own, because that's what he'd become. They hoped that the boy would never know grief or loss or sorrow, but such things are part of the natural world; they can't be escaped or denied.

Margaret Grey had married a boy most people believed had never been born, so she knew that anything was possible. "Maybe I should have bought those garlands, the way Lois Jeremy did," she said to Abe as they drove out to the farm. "Maybe things would have been different then."

Margaret thought of all that she knew for certain, that day would always follow night and that love was never wasted, nor was it lost. On the morning when it happened, Frank had gone to the market to pick up milk and bread and Margaret had watched him all the way down the road. People always say that anyone who's watched until they disappear out of sight will never be seen again, and that was exactly how it had happened. There wasn't a thing to be done about it, not then and certainly not now. If she had placed a thousand garlands around the lamb's neck, it might not have kept him from harm.

When they reached Wright's house, Abe opened the passenger door and helped his mother out. Some people were lucky with their children and some people were not, and Margaret Grey had turned out to be both. Abe was so tall and strong he surprised her. People said he would come to no good, but Margaret had never believed that, which was the reason she finally told him who his grandparents were. He didn't believe her at first, he laughed and said that there wasn't a person in town who hadn't told him how much he resembled Wright. But of course, it was possible for both things to be true and to belong most of all to those who loved you.

The deed to Wright's house was in Abe's name. He still had a few developers who came sniffing around, including some fellow from Boston who wanted the acreage to build a mall like the one over in Middletown, but Abe never returned their calls. Route 17 was getting so built up that it seemed as if they were pulling into a different time when they turned onto the dirt road that led to Wright's place. There were dozens of robins, returning from wintering in the Carolinas, and they perched in the apple trees that grew near Annie's grave, the one in the meadow, to which Wright used to bring the flowers he picked by the river. Because of the circumstances of her death, Annie had not been allowed a burial at the Haddan School cemetery, where her husband was later put to rest, or in the churchyard. Wright had been the one to retrieve her remains from Hale Brothers Funeral Parlor, and he and Charlie Hale had dug the grave themselves on a windy day when the dust was flying everywhere and there wasn't a cloud in the sky. Love someone and they're yours forever, no matter how much time intervenes, that's what Margaret Grey knew. The sky will always be blue; the wind will always rise up across the meadow and thread its way through the grass.

IN APRIL, PEOPLE HEARD THAT ABEL GREY WAS planning to leave town, not that they believed the rumors. Some people are predictable; they never wander far. Neighbors begin to set their own lives by the clockwork of such individuals and they want to keep it that way. As far as anyone knew, the only times Abe had ever left town were on those occasions when he'd gone fishing with Joey Tosh or when he'd visited his parents in Florida. People believed he'd no more move away from Haddan than he'd dance through the streets naked, and one or two of the boys at the Millstone put money down, with serious odds, betting that Abe would remain in his house on Station Avenue until the day they came from Hale Brothers to carry him to his rest.

And yet facts were facts. A man who's about to leave town always leaves a trail as he finishes up his business, and such was the case with Abe. Kelly Avon reported that he had closed out his bank account at the 5 & 10 Cent Bank, and Teddy Humphrey witnessed him searching through the recycle bin behind the mini-mart for cardboard boxes, always a sign of a move to come. Every morning, people at the pharmacy discussed whether or not Abe would go. Lois Jeremy was of the mind that Abe would never leave the town where his brother was buried, but Charlotte Evans wasn't so sure. A person never could tell what was inside somebody or what they might do. Look at that nice Phil Endicott her daughter was married to, how his personality had changed so completely during the divorce proceedings. Pete Byers, who never gossiped in his life, now looked forward to contemplating the direction Abe's future might take every night at dinner. He'd begun to close the pharmacy early in order to get home and discuss the possibilities with his wife, Eileen, who he'd recently discovered had a great deal to say, having saved up twenty years' worth of talk, so that the two of them were often up all night, whispering to each other in bed.

Betsy Chase heard about Abe when she was at the Haddan Inn meeting with Doreen Becker, going over the final plans for her wedding reception. It was the first day of spring vacation, and Betsy had taken the opportunity to deal with the details of her personal life. She had already let Doreen know that she didn't want to hire the Chazz Dixon band, not that they weren't terrific musicians, when Doreen's sister, Nikki, phoned to inform Doreen that Marie Bishop had told her that she could look out her living room window and see Abe packing up his car, that old cruiser of Wright's no rational man would have bothered to keep.

The inn was overheated, and maybe that was why Betsy felt faint when she heard the news of Abe's leaving. She asked Doreen for a glass of water, which did no good at all. In the hedges outside, a starling sang sweetly, the first strains of its spring song, a trilling that was a lullaby to some ears and a restless call to others. Mrs. Evans's and Mrs. Jeremy's perennial gardens were filled with jonquils and tulips, and the oaks along Main Street had clusters of fresh, green buds. It was a beautiful day, and no one thought anything was amiss when they saw Betsy walking down Main Street later on. By now they were used to her wandering through town, asking directions, and making wrong turns, until at last she found her way.

People who thought they knew her, Lynn Vining and the rest of the art department, for instance, would never have predicted that Betsy would leave the way she did, with a hasty grade sheet drawn up for her classes and a call to a storage company to come for her furniture. Lynn herself was forced to serve as St. Anne's houseparent for the rest of the year, a job that gave her a continuous migraine. No wonder that afterward Lynn told anyone within earshot that she now believed it was impossible ever to divine a person's truest nature. Eric Herman, on the other hand, was not really surprised at Betsy's sudden departure. He had seen the way she'd looked at lightning, and to his closest friends he admitted he was relieved.

The black cat was already pacing on the other side of Abe's door, begging to be let out, when Betsy arrived. As it happened, neither Betsy nor Abe had much to pack. They threw their belongings into the trunk of Wright's old car, then had coffee in the kitchen. It was close to noon by the time they got going, time enough for anyone with doubts to back out. Since Abel Grey was the sort of man who liked to tie up loose ends, he rinsed out his coffeepot before they left, and emptied the containers of milk and orange juice so they wouldn't spoil in the refrigerator. For the first time in his life, he had a clean kitchen, which made it all the easier for him to leave.

He tried his best to get the cat to go with them, but cats are territorial creatures and this one was especially stubborn. It could not be coaxed into the backseat, not even with an opened can of tuna fish. Despite this bribe, the cat gazed back at Abe with such disinterest that Abe had to laugh and give up. When they were set to leave, Abe crouched down on the pavement to pat the cat's head, and in response the cat's one eye narrowed, with disapproval or pleasure, it was impossible to tell. In truth, this cat was the individual in Haddan Abe felt sorriest to leave, and he waited for a while in the idling car with the back door open, but the cat only turned to trot down the street, never once looking back.

They drove out of town, past the new housing developments, past the mini-mart and the gas station and the fields of everlasting. They went on until they reached the road that led to Abe's grandfather's house. The day was so bright Betsy thought about putting on sunglasses, but the sky was too beautiful and too blue to miss. In the woods, the violets were blooming, and hawks swooped above the meadows. They got out when they reached the farm, slamming their doors shut, so that the blackbirds took flight all at once, weaving above them as if cross-stitching themselves onto the sky. Bees were rumbling around the lilacs beside the porch and although the farm was miles from the marshy banks of the river, there was the call of spring peepers. Abe went out to pay his last respects with a bunch of wild irises he'd stopped to pick alongside the river road. Aside from the fence, no one would have any reason to believe this was anyone's final resting place; it was just another stretch of land where the grass grew high and turned yellow in the fall.

Watching him, Betsy ignored the urge to reach for her camera, and instead she stood there and waited for him to come back to her. The grass he walked through was new and a sweet smell clung to his clothes. There was blue dye on his hands from the wild irises. These were the things Betsy would always remember: that he waved to her as he made his way back through the field, that she could feel her own pulse, that the color of the sky was a shade that could never be replicated in any photograph, just as heaven could never be seen from the confines of earth.

For a time they stood looking at the old house, watching as

the shadows of clouds settled onto the fields and the road, then they got back into the car and drove west, toward the turnpike. It was days before anyone realized they were gone, and Carlin Leander was the first to know they'd left town. She knew long before Mike Randall at the 5&10 Cent Bank received a notice to sell Abel's house and wire him the money, before the Haddan School understood it would be necessary to find someone to take over Betsy's classes. She knew before Joey Tosh used his key to check inside Abe's house, where he was surprised to find that the kitchen was tidy and neat, as it never had been before.

Carlin had traveled home for the Easter break, as most students did, the difference being she had no definite plans to return to Haddan. Sean Byers had borrowed his uncle's car to drive her to Logan Airport and he'd noticed that she had more luggage than most people had when they were going away for only a week. She had packed a tote bag of books and brought along the boots she'd bought at Hingram's, even though there'd be no need for such things in Florida. In spite of his fears that she might not return, Sean kept his mouth shut, which wasn't easy for him. His uncle Pete had taken him aside that morning and told him that when he got older he'd understand that patience was an unappreciated virtue, one that a man would do well to cultivate even when he was the one who was being left behind.

And so, instead of going after her, Sean had sat in his uncle's parked car and watched her leave. He was still thinking about her when she walked out into the bright, humid Florida afternoon, instantly dizzy in the heat.

"Are you crazy, girl?" Carlin's mother, Sue, asked, as she greeted Carlin with a huge hug. "You're wearing wool in April. Is that what they taught you up in Massachusetts?"

Sue Leander was polite about Carlin's cropped hair, although she did suggest a visit to the hair salon up on Fifth Street, just to give her daughter's new hairstyle a little oomph with a perm or body wave. As soon as they got home, Carlin stripped off the sweater and skirt she'd bought at the mall in Middletown in favor of shorts and a T-shirt. She went to sit on the back porch, where she drank iced tea and tried to become reacclimated to the heat. She'd been cold for so long she'd gotten used to it somehow, that crisp Massachusetts air that carried the scent of apples and hay. Still, she liked hearing her mother's voice through the open window; she liked seeing the red hawks circle above her in the white-hot sky. When she told her mother she wasn't sure about going back, Sue said that would be just fine, she wouldn't be letting anyone down, but Carlin knew that she and her mother had always seen things differently and that the only one who might be let down by such a decision was Carlin herself.

One afternoon, the postman brought Carlin a package, mailed from the post office in Hamilton. It was a Haddan School T-shirt, the sort they sold in the notions aisle of the pharmacy, along with a Haddan coffee mug and a key ring, all of it sent by Sean Byers. Carlin laughed when she saw the gifts. She wore the Haddan shirt when she went out with her old friend, Johnny Nevens.

"Boola boola," Johnny said when he saw the shirt.

"That's Yale." Carlin laughed. "I'm at a boarding school. Haddan." She pointed to the letters across her chest.

"Same difference." Johnny shrugged. "Little Miss Egghead."

"Oh, shut up."

Carlin slipped on a pair of sandals. For the first time in her life she was worried about the snakes her mother always said came out after dusk, searching for insects and rabbits.

"I don't get it," Johnny said. "All these years you've been telling me how smart you are, and now that I'm finally agreeing with you, you're pissed."

"I don't know what I am." Carlin raised her hands to the sky as though pleading for answers. "I have no idea."

"But I do," Johnny told her. "And so does everybody else in this town, so you can relax, smarty-pants."

They went over to the park on Fifth Street, the only hangout in town other than the McDonald's on Jefferson Avenue. It was a gorgeous night and Carlin sat on the hood of Johnny's car and drank beer and looked at stars. She'd spent the past few months tied up in knots, and now she felt herself get loose again. The cicadas were calling as if it were already summer, and there were white moths in the sky. The moonlight was silvery, like water, pouring over the asphalt and the streets. People were nice to Carlin and several girls she'd known in grade school came over to tell her how great she looked, in spite of the haircut. Lindsay Hull, who had never included Carlin in anything, went so far as to invite her to the movies on Saturday with a group that went to the mall together on a weekly basis.

"I'll call you if I'm still in town," Carlin told Lindsay.

She wasn't certain if she was looking for a way to get out of the invitation or if in fact she had not yet made up her mind whether or not to stay. Later, she and Johnny drove down to the woods, to the place where they had once had the misfortune to confront an alligator. They were just kids and to Johnny's enduring humiliation, he'd been the one to run. Carlin, on the other hand, had hollered like a demon until the alligator turned tail and headed back to a pool of brackish water, moving quicker than anyone would guess a creature that big could manage.

"Man, you stared him right in the eye." Johnny was still proud of Carlin's long-ago encounter. He talked about her at parties, referring to her as the girl who was so willful and mean she could scare a gator back into the swamp.

"I was probably more terrified than you were." The night was darker here than it was in Massachusetts, and much more alive, filled with beetles and moths. "I was just too stupid to run."

"Oh no," Joey assured her. "Not you."

All that week, Carlin sat in front of the TV, addicted to The Weather Channel. The sky in Florida was clear, but in New England a series of spring storms had passed through and Massachusetts had been hit especially hard. Sue Leander appraised her daughter's expression while she took in this news, and Sue knew then and there that Carlin would not be staying. In the end, Carlin went back to school a day early, arriving on the empty campus after the worst of the storm damage had already been done. She had sprung for a taxi from Logan, using money from the travelers' fund Miss Davis had arranged. It was a luxury Carlin hardly enjoyed once they arrived in Haddan and she saw how much devastation there had been in her absence. Streams that had been running high from melting snow had overflowed and the fields were now green with water rather than cabbages and peas. Several silver trout had been stranded on the road, their luminous scales crushed into the blacktop, and anyone traveling this route needed sunglasses, even on the cloudiest of days.

"Spring squalls are the worst," the taxi driver told Carlin. "People are never prepared for them."

They had to bypass Route 17 entirely, for a five-foot-deep puddle had collected beneath a highway bridge. Instead, they drove along the long, loopy road that passed farm stands and several of the new housing developments. There was still a bite in the damp, green air, and Carlin slipped on Gus's overcoat. She'd brought it with her to Florida and kept it in her closet until her mother had complained of water seeping onto the floor. Carlin had thought she'd leave what had happened behind when she left school, but in Florida she had continued to find black stones, on the back porch, in the kitchen sink, beneath her pillow. She felt Gus's presence whenever she stepped out of the sunlight, like a splash of water. Every morning, she had awoken to find that her sheets were damp, the fabric gritty, as if sand had drifted over the cotton. Carlin's mother blamed the humid air for soaking the bedclothes, but Carlin knew that wasn't the cause.

When at last the taxi drove through the village, Carlin took note of the storm damage. Several of the old oaks on Main Street had been split in two and the eagle in front of town hall had been permanently tumbled from its bronzed perch. Some of the big white houses would have to be reroofed, but the Haddan School had been hit with the most severe damage, for the river had risen four feet above its highest level, flooding the buildings, which had fortunately been emptied of residents during spring break. Now, the sopping carpet in the library would have to be torn up and removed, and the parking lot behind the administration building was still being drained with a sump pump belonging to the department of public works. Worst affected had been Chalk House, built so perilously close to the river. The house had tilted and lurched as the river rose; at last whole sections of the foundation were swept away. When Billy Bishop, the town building inspector, was called in, he announced there was nothing to do but take the whole mess down before it fell down. It was an emergency situation, with the real possibility of structural col-

lapse, and the house was razed during vacation. Two afternoons
and some bulldozers did the trick, and people from town not only
gathered to watch, they applauded when the timbers came
crashing down, and several local children swiped bricks to keep
as souvenirs.

Students returning from the holidays came back to a hole in
the ground, and although several boys from Chalk House did not
return after vacation, stricken still with that dreadful flu, those
boys who did come back were sent off to live with local families
for the rest of the year, until a new dormitory could be built.
Some of these boys grumbled about their new circumstances,
and two were so offended by their lodgings they left school, but
the rest settled in, and Billy and Marie Bishop grew so fond of
their boarder, Dave Linden, they invited him to spend the summer with them and in return, he mowed their front lawn and
clipped their hedges for the next three years.

Without Chalk House in the way, Carlin now had a view of
the river. She was up in her room admiring the expanse of water
and willow trees, when the black cat climbed the trellis to her
window ledge. It was the hour when the sky turned indigo and
shadows fell across the grass in dark pools. Carlin could tell from
the way the cat came inside and the proprietary manner in which
it settled on her blankets that it had come to stay. Cats were sensible that way: when one owner left, they made do with whoever
was at hand, and sometimes the situation worked out just fine.

When the cat moved in, Carlin knew that Abe had left town,
and after going downstairs to find there was no answer at Betsy's
door, she was pleased to discover that Miss Chase had changed
her mind. Not long afterward, the photograph Betsy had taken in
Gus's room arrived in the mail. For quite some time, Carlin kept

it in a silver frame beside her bed, until the image began to fade. She still thought about Gus when she swam laps in the pool and once she felt him there beside her, matching her strokes, cutting through the water, but when she stopped to tread water she found she was alone. In time, the weather grew too warm to wear his coat, and nothing surfaced in the pockets anymore, not silver fish or black stones.

In the height of the fine weather, Carlin began swimming in the river, at the hour when the light was pale and green. There were days when she swam all the way to Hamilton and when she made her way back to Haddan, the sky would already be dark. But soon enough dusk held off until seven-thirty, and in June the evenings were light until eight. By then, the fish had grown used to her, and they swam along beside her, all the way home.